More praise for *Someone You*

An NPR, *Washington Post*, Book Riot, *Library Journal* and Audible Best Book of 2024!

A Most-Anticipated Book of 2024 from Amazon, Polygon, io9, Apple Books, Goodreads, Reactor, Book Riot, *Writer's Digest*, and Nerd Daily

"People fall in love with monsters all the time, but few monsters are as lovable as Shesheshen . . ."
—*The Washington Post*

"This unusual queer romance is a heartfelt fable about disability and the possibility of reconciling conflicting needs through love and understanding."
—*The Guardian*

"Surprisingly sweet, unsurprisingly horrific, and entirely humane—only John Wiswell could have written this monster and her book, and I'm so very glad he did."
—Arkady Martine, Hugo Award-winning author of *A Memory Called Empire*

"Wiswell raises the bar on the outcast as protagonist . . . the ultimate monster slayer story, if the monster is just a misunderstood creature searching for love."
—*Library Journal* (starred review)

"A romp that's both bloody and sweet."
—*Bookpage* (starred review)

"*Someone You Can Build a Nest In* is the future of fantasy: a fairy tale with boundaries, an imaginative world created in the shape of collective values rather than the boring old id, a portal to a place you've really never seen before instead of just a princess in a different outfit. This novel is going to change the entire genre."
—Meg Elison, Hugo and Locus award-winning author of *The Book of the Unnamed Midwife*

"This is a fast-paced and gloriously weird novel, full of explosive shenanigans and touching sentiment . . . a remarkably accomplished debut."
—*Locus*

"Wriggly, heartfelt, and carnivorous."

—Max Gladstone, *New York Times*-bestselling co-author of *This is How You Lose the Time War*

"Inventive enough to push the boundaries of romance and dark fantasy . . . A wonderfully weird horror romance." —*Kirkus*

"I love the wonder and the darkly enchanting danger of this story."

—C.L. Polk, bestselling author of *Even Though I Knew the End*

"The wonderful thing about Wiswell's monster, Shesheshen, is her sensible vulnerability. . . . I can guarantee you won't ever forget Shesheshen and Homily, and will be warmed inside forever."

—Julie E. Czerneda, Aurora Award-winning author of the Night's Edge series

"Clever, funny, and oddly gentle. . . . Make sure this is on your TBR if you want those squishy-warm feelings of falling in love . . . and those squishy-in-general feelings of viscera, gore, and other things humans prefer to keep on the inside." —Jodi Meadows, *New York Times*-bestselling coauthor of *My Lady Jane*

"*Someone You Can Build a Nest In* is the best kind of horrifying, beautiful, by turns hilarious and heart-wrenching, and entirely unforgettable: a story about what makes a monster, what makes a person, the scars of trauma, and the transformative (and sometimes traumatic) act of falling in love."

—Vivian Shaw, author of *Strange Practice*

"Charming, horrifying, sweet, and funny—everything I could have wanted from John Wiswell's debut novel and more! With the perfect blend of humor and darkness, it's a wholly fresh take on a monster story." —A.C. Wise, author of *Hooked*

"A beautiful monster story with a heart, Wiswell treats his outcasts as heroes. He is an author the world desperately needs."

—J.R. Dawson, author of *The First Bright Thing*

"Horror blends with heart and whimsy in Wiswell's trope-twisting debut. It's monstrously fun!"

—Beth Cato, author of *A Thousand Recipes For Revenge*

"The coziest, most unexpectedly wholesome love story about a monster who devours humans and wears their bones that I've ever read!"

—Naomi Kritzer, Hugo Award-winning author of *Catfishing on CatNet*

"Besides being a masterful inversion of fantasy monster-slaying tropes, this is a fantastic examination of what it means to be family, and how that trust can be horrifically misused."

—Jenn Lyons, author of the Chorus of Dragons series

"This novel is for anyone who has ever felt like an outcast—or been bewildered by society's absurdities. I fell in love with Shesheshen's wry voice and dark sense of humor."

—Ray Nayler, *Locus* Award-winning author of *The Mountain in the Sea*

"Oozing with—among other things—Wiswell's inimitable charm and tenderness, this is a monstrous love story like nothing I've ever read before."

—Premee Mohamed, Nebula Award-winning author of *Beneath the Rising*

"John Wiswell expertly blends horror, humor, romance, and bloody disembowelments in a story about a monster who will not only swallow your heart, but make it her own."

—Jason Sanford, author of *Plague Birds*

"A good book is a predator, and this one had no problem dragging me off, kicking and hooting, into the tall grasses to make a meal amidst my ribs before finally taking my heart for its own."

—Jordan Shiveley, author of *Hot Singles In Your Area*

Also by John Wiswell

SOMEONE YOU CAN BUILD A NEST IN
WEARING THE LION

SOMEONE YOU CAN BUILD A NEST IN

Cover illustration by James Fenner
Cover design by Katie Anderson
Interior design by Fine Design
Edited by Katie Hoffman

DAW Book Collectors No. 1959

DAW Books
An imprint of Astra Publishing House
dawbooks.com

Printed in the United States of America

Library of Congress Cataloging-in-Publication Data

Names: Wiswell, John, 1981- author.
Title: Someone you can build a nest in / John Wiswell.
Description: First edition. | New York : DAW Books, 2024. |
Series: DAW Book Collectors no. 1959
Identifiers: LCCN 2023051936 (print) | LCCN 2023051937 (ebook) |
ISBN 9780756418854 (hardcover) | ISBN 9780756418861 (ebook)
Subjects: LCGFT: Fantasy fiction. | Romance fiction. | Novels.
Classification: LCC PS3623.I8486 S66 2024 (print) | LCC PS3623.I8486 (ebook) |
DDC 813/.6--dc23/eng/20231109
LC record available at https://lccn.loc.gov/2023051936
LC ebook record available at https://lccn.loc.gov/2023051937

ISBN 9780756419745 (trade paperback)

First paperback edition: 2025
10 9 8 7 6 5 4 3 2

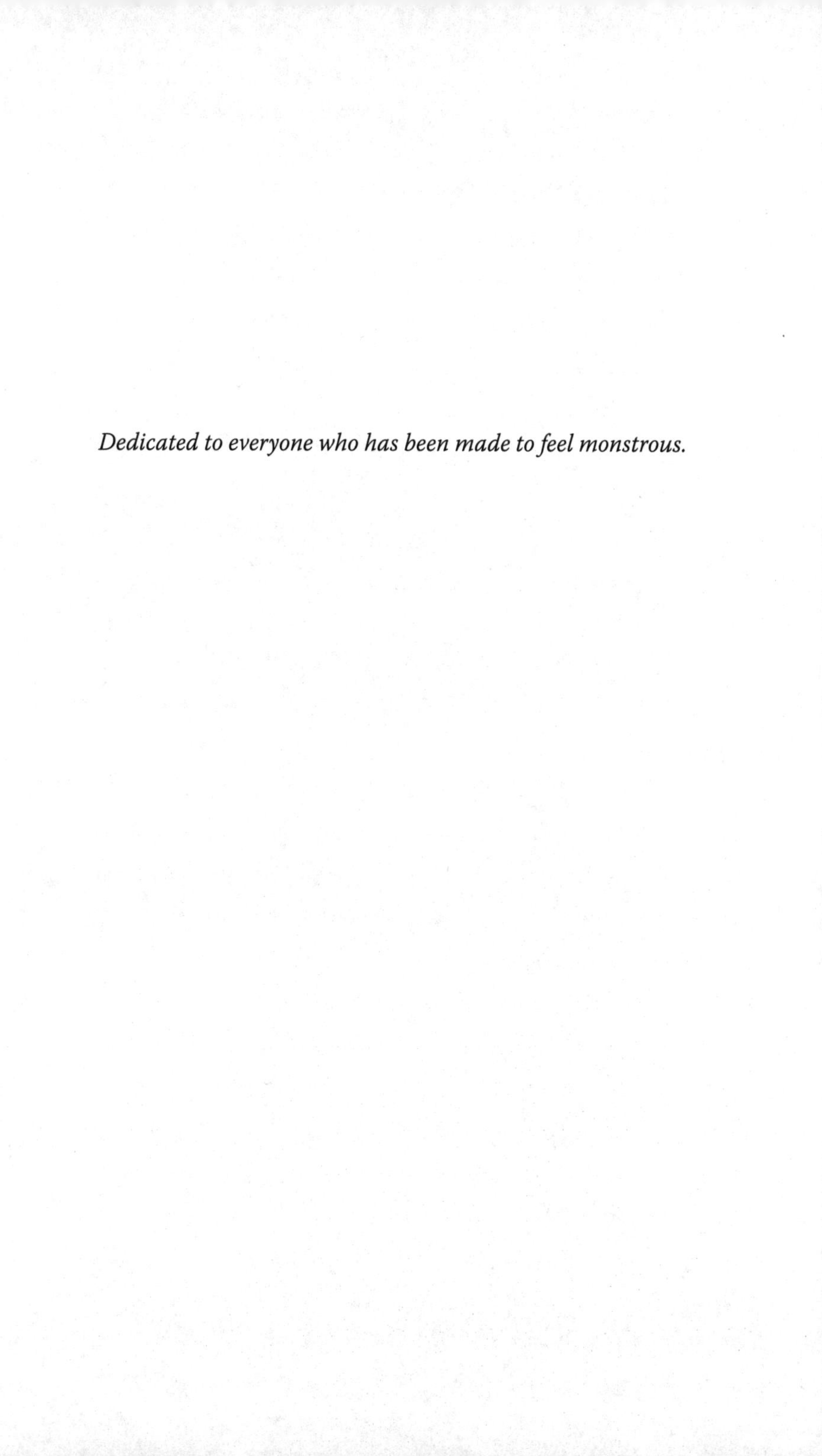

Dedicated to everyone who has been made to feel monstrous.

PART ONE

THE WYRM OF UNDERLOOK

CHAPTER ONE

Each year when Shesheshen hibernated, she dreamed of her childhood nest.

Oh, the warmth of it. A warmth unlike anything in the adult world, soft and pliable heat keeping her and her siblings alive. In that warmth, they were fed raw life. Her father's ribs, rich in marrow, cracking delicately in their mouths, and providing the first feast of their lives. His fat deposits were generous, and his entrails sheltered them from the cruel winter elements. If Shesheshen could have spent her entire life inside the nest of his remains, she would have.

But all childhoods end. Hers ended when one of her sisters bit off Shesheshen's left heel. Her siblings matured too quickly and hungered for more than their father. Shesheshen had to defend herself using jagged fragments of their father's pelvis—his final and most gracious gift. The assault was a gift from her siblings, too, for she spent a week dining on their savory carcasses.

Mourning wasn't natural to her. She missed the succulence of her siblings for some time, and had the errant moment of nostalgia for sharing their body heat. Little of her prey was memorable. Of her mother, she only remembered her wide maw and the artificial steel fangs she'd worn. Still, Shesheshen would always miss the nest that her father had made out of himself. He had been a good parent, and a better setting.

Nothing matched that nest. These ruins were little more than an unloved cave. Where weather had caved in the ceiling, ornery spruce trees grew and plugged up the gaps. Poison ivy and spiderwebs were the few decorations, overgrowing everything architects had once achieved.

Deep beneath the ruins lay an underground hot spring that some aspiring human had connected to a bathing room. Nowadays the chamber was flooded with humid murk, gone brackish and amniotic from

Shesheshen's excretions. It was nearly opaque down in the waters. They were a refreshing place to hibernate through winter seasons.

Yet noises had roused her prematurely. Her lair had unwelcome visitors again. They did not even wipe their shoes.

She heard them before she saw them. The water of the hot spring stretched into so many cracks in the building's foundations. Sounds from all ends of the property traveled through the network of water, alerting Shesheshen when something worse than a bear was coming.

"Good gods, above and below. Rourke? Do you smell that?"

"Yeah. Like death without the sulfur. This is no wyrm."

There were two visitors. Both human men, with two feet each, trampling over the weeds at her threshold. They paused in the foyer, snuffling and fighting with their gorges. Her foyer opened to many hallways, and one would lead them to Shesheshen. It was fortunate they didn't know which one. She had to act before that changed.

The one called Rourke said, "Malik, don't pass out on me. Put your mask on."

"I'm fine," the one called Malik said. "The contract is for a wyrm. Could it be an eastern wyrm? From the Al-Jawi Empire?"

"Those smell like burned bread. This just stinks of infection. I'm telling you, whatever is in this place isn't a wyrm."

The one called Malik spat upon the floor. He didn't clean up after himself. "Then what is it?"

The one called Rourke muffled his coughing, probably behind a fist. "I'm not sure. But we need priests. At least three of them."

Shesheshen liked priests. They tasted righteous.

"Did I hear you two mention priests?"

Shesheshen had thought there were two. She was wrong—distracted and foggy-headed from having her hibernation interrupted. Whoever had yelled was a third voice, matched by the clank of heavy armor heading into her foyer.

She listened carefully around his footfalls; the noise of his gear was cacophonous, but she believed this third man was the last.

The one called Malik said, "Sire Wulfyre, from certain environmental details we have reason to believe we need religious assistance—"

"For the last time," the third man interrupted, "my family is not employing the entire region. You said you were experts. Experts don't need to hire bonus people. That's the point of expertise. You want priests now? Do you two hunt monsters or just pray at them?"

The one called Rourke said, "Sire Wulfyre, you're not going to want to come in here yet. The odor is overpowering."

"Don't tell me what to do. I've slain lords. The Wulfyres have killed off wyrms since—"

His words dissolved into wet choking sounds. The metal plates of his armor clicked musically, as though he was bending over. This third man was definitely retching. She hoped he had a helmet on so it painted the inside. It would serve him right for trespassing.

The name "Wulfyre" was familiar, too—a family who claimed some ownership over her lair and occasionally sent killers after her. She'd never actually met a Wulfyre before. She was in no mood to meet one now.

Rourke said, "We warned you about the odor."

Sire Wulfyre said, "Next time come *outside* and warn me. Give me one of your breathing masks."

Malik said, "This is sensitive equipment."

Sire Wulfyre said, "Equipment my family is paying for. Now find this wyrm and kill it before I go looking for monster hunters who actually hunt."

Listening to all their words was exhausting. They were so noisy for professional killers. Any self-respecting hunters would've used the element of surprise. Why, if Shesheshen had been cold-blooded enough to kill people as a source of income, she would've slipped in here while she slept and poisoned the pool with rosemary and lye so she'd die in her sleep.

But Shesheshen was not a monster hunter.

She was prey.

Three armed visitors, and she was still weak from hibernation. From the weakness in her flesh, she ought not have roused for weeks. Tensing her soft tissues made them tremble as though threatening to liquefy. She didn't have the strength for a great battle today.

She had to do something, and soon. These murderers couldn't be allowed to find her room and corner her. They'd do something awful like set the place on fire or collapse it atop her.

She opened pockets in her flesh and took in her first real breath of the season. The air was stale and frigid, making it feel as though icicles were forming along her innards. She shuddered, using the air to puff out her body, and emerged from her pool. Water streamed from the many lumps of her body, gone loose from weeks of slumber. The water sloshed across the stone floor, until she wholly emerged. All that submersion in water left her flesh sodden. She took a step, and collapsed against the nearest wall.

It was always tricky, getting the hang of being conscious again. Hopefully the monster hunters hadn't heard that. It would be embarrassing to die in this state.

Most bones that she kept inside herself during hibernation digested down to nothing.

Her kind did not naturally have many solid internal structures, just as the hermit crabs on the north beaches naturally lacked shells. They had to scavenge. Her mother had worn prosthetic steel fangs to compensate when she hunted. That one memory of her mother taught Shesheshen the importance of keeping tools around.

Along the floor of the bathing room lay iron rods and dense stones, which she'd left out last season. She rolled across them, letting them cut through external layers of her flesh with a sting that felt like waking up. Her innards squeezed those rods and stones, aligning them into a loose skeletal structure. A steel chain once used to bind her now made an excellent spinal column, flexible without breaking when catapults lobbed debris at her.

Inside her chest, where humans put their lungs, she placed an open bear trap. It was her prized skeletal possession. It did not trap bears anymore. Instead, she kept it as a secret pair of jaws, for when people needed to be bitten.

The harder ends of her makeshift bones tore apart her insides, and her poor tissues had to generate cartilage and tendons to adjust. It was an ache that left her shuddering against the wall. Was this how getting older felt?

Wulfyre was louder now, audible through the limestone walls and down her hallway. He hollered, "I want the wyrm slain before Mother reaches the countryside. Do you know how upsetting it would be for her to encounter that thing? Of course you can't. Now you say you don't even know what it is."

Malik's voice was softer. Shesheshen had to strain to hear him. "The creature has left many markings in the stone that could be claws or teeth, and we haven't found any droppings yet. We're still investigating."

"Father died fighting this thing, so I can promise you my family knows what it is. It's a wyrm."

That was a familiar word. Shesheshen had been called a wyrm many times, often by startled hunters. She'd also heard "wyrm" used to describe drakes, harpies, qilins, kappas, and giraffes. In her experience, it was an epithet for whatever thing greedy humans wanted dead and were too afraid to kill themselves.

"Wyrm or not," Rourke said, "if you really want this thing dead, there is only one way to go about it. To purge it and harm it enough to slay it, you're going to need to burn this lair to the ground."

"Oh, yes. I'll just burn a stone building. Thank goodness I hired professional advice."

"It could be tucked anywhere in here. With enough oil, fire will find it."

"This place is my family's ancestral home. Of course you don't care about the priceless heirlooms being destroyed. But I hired you to bring me the wyrm's blood. One of you two can read, can't you? It's in your contract. Mother wants its heart. We can't exactly bring her a heart that's burned up."

Malik said, "Perhaps we should talk strategy in private."

The Wulfyre kept ranting. "No strategies that include broiling it. If you want to get paid, you're slitting it open over a vase. Mother was very clear: blood, not fire."

Well, this was interesting. The Wulfyre family was going to be disappointed when they learned she didn't have blood. She didn't have one of those pesky mammalian circulatory systems at all.

Rourke said, "You're not paying us enough to die in here."

"Go on, then. Breach the contract. Then you'll be outlaws. Let's see how much business you get with Mother and L'État Bon hunting you."

Malik whispered like a man who didn't know how to whisper. "Rourke. Come on. We have rosemary oil. Locals swear it works."

Then there was the rustle of leather being pulled off of blades. Rourke said, "How much rosemary do we have?"

That made Shesheshen grip the limestone bricks of her wall. These people had rosemary oil?

She cursed out of multiple orifices. These monster hunters had done their research. One of the things she couldn't tolerate was rosemary. Once a local girl had candied it and fooled her into eating it, and Shesheshen pissed bile for a week.

As it was, her flesh struggled to keep her aloft on her makeshift bones. She needed to eat and gather strength. A fight would not go pleasantly. The last thing she wanted to wake up to was dying.

Getting older had given her wiles. While the humans chatted about how best to kill her, she went through some growing pains and formed two relatively passable legs. She hobbled for a while, convincing herself that these knees and ankles mostly worked.

On a rack beside the door was a set of wigs she'd made from the scalps that people hadn't been using anymore. She selected a wig of sooty black hair for her disguise. Then she added a red riding hood; it was a leftover possession of a bygone occupant of the lair, from back when this building had been a castle or brothel or whatever humans enjoyed.

As her innards churned to form an esophageal passage, she wrapped the red garment around herself, pulling the hood low to hide how little of a face she had. It was an old role. By shifting her body mass within the cloak, she gave the illusion of a lithe frame. The belled-out bottom of the cloak gave her plenty of room to hide most of her body mass. She had passed as a human on plenty of excursions when she was at full strength. Doing so depleted from hibernation was a gamble.

Shesheshen pushed downward on the door as she opened it, so that the wooden door scraped along the stone landing. The sound stung her ears, and if it bothered her, it was likely to make these men soil themselves. Part of the plot was announcing herself in advance.

She ran with wet feet slapping the floor, loud as she could be. They would know something was headed in their direction, and they would be ready for a nightmare.

What they got was a girl's harried face poking out from under a red riding hood, gloved hands flailing. She turned as frightened a face as she could on them—it was easy to make, since they made three frightened faces at her.

All three of the murderers she'd eavesdropped upon stood in her foyer. Two of them wore practical leather gear and chain mail, with awkward half-masks over their mouths and noses. One man was much younger, shaped like a barrel that had grown arms, with several jeweled piercings in his ears. The other was a withered old root of a man with tufts of gray hair sticking out of every spot on his uniform, and eyes the green of pine needles.

These two must have been Malik and Rourke, standing in front, each holding polearms with their blades pointed down the hall at her. They protected the third man.

The third man hid behind them, wearing golden plate armor all the way up to his throat. Who wore gold for defense? It wasn't holy, it was terribly heavy, and it was one of the softest metals Shesheshen had ever bitten. His chestplate was molded to have the likeness of nipples and rippling abdominal muscles. Parts of her salivated at the thought of crushing that chestplate. At his hip, he held some kind of crossbow at a bad angle, more likely to hit one of his underlings than her.

Well, it was easy to pick out which one was Wulfyre.

Shesheshen said, "Sires and masters. Thank the good gods, above and below, that you came. The wyrm could wake at any moment. Please, keep your voices quiet or we'll all be skinned alive."

She kept her own voice soft, since a whisper was easier to fake than a full-throated human voice. It took quite some concentration to keep a vocal passage open and functional like this. It would be easier once she consumed one from a person. Perhaps one of the hunters would donate.

The older hunter, Rourke, lowered his polearm. "What are you doing here, lass? The townsfolk said no one has approached this lair in years."

"Sire," Shesheshen said. "The wyrm has kept me in darkness so long that I have no memory of when it kidnapped me. It held me in one of the lower chambers of this place."

The younger hunter, Malik, made a holy sign in front of himself, then asked, "It held you?"

Rourke said, "I thought anyone abducted by this thing would've been consumed before it went to hibernate."

Well, the old hunter was right about that. Shesheshen never left food in the cupboard before hibernation. If you did, the remains spoiled and attracted scavengers. Scavengers were a nuisance when you were trying to regenerate.

She mimicked Malik's holy sign with one hand, then resumed clutching her cloak. For some reason, clutching at clothing was a classic human sign of being pathetic. In her experience, clothing never ran away from you even when a monster literally ate your head.

"Sires, the wyrm spares my life for my songs. It can only slumber when I sing to it the dark songs of distant lands. I know not where these verses come from, and they chill me to my core. Yet if it wakes, it will destroy the village with its ravenous appetite."

"Your squeaky voice?" said the man in gold, definitely Wulfyre. "I guess a hellbound monster would have shitty taste in music."

Both monster hunters shot glares at their employer. Yet those glares were gone before Wulfyre saw them. Hedged sincerity. A classic human trait.

Malik asked, "What is your name, madame?"

Shesheshen pondered. "Roislin."

It was a plausible Engmarese name. Someone she'd eaten had probably had it.

Rourke said, "Roislin. My name is Eoghan Rourke, and this is my partner, Nasser Akkad Malik. Our employer here is Catharsis Wulfyre, son of the Baroness. We have seen so much pain that monsters have created in this world. Nobody should be left alone with a beast so unholy and wretched. Come with us. We've got water and honeycomb in our wagon. Right, Malik?"

"That's right," Malik said, holding out a hand for her. "We'll get you out of here. You'll be in town by tomorrow."

Town was the last place she wanted to go. It was full of wretched humans, precisely the kind that hired monster hunters in the first place. What she needed was rest and isolation.

Adding more squeak to her voice, she said, "Sires, if we flee together, then the wyrm will be on us before we reach the second hill. She knows my scent above all at this point. Instead, I need you to retrieve me a weapon."

Wulfyre was the one to say, "A weapon?"

"Please. On the northernmost island of Engmar, in the west, there grows a flowering plant that the locals call summoner's jaw. It is the only herb the beast fears. It can rend her skin and make her husk wither. A curse from the good gods, above and below. If you can collect it, I can keep her slumbering until you return, and we can be free."

Actually, she was not even mildly allergic to summoner's jaw. Merchants called it a remedy for minor cuts and bruises. However, Engmar was multiple nations away. By the time these would-be murderers finished their trip, she would be fully rested, fed, and ready to deal with them. If she got lucky, they'd spread the rumor of her one weakness so that later hunters would make the same mistake.

Malik said, "I've heard of summoner's jaw. It's used for medicinal purposes. Stands to reason that devils would be weak to medicine."

Rourke lowered his mask, then unstrapped his bowl helmet and held it over his chest. "Roislin, I am also from Engmar. I have traveled the world many years, and seen many cultures. To stay in this cave, singing a monster to sleep, in the hopes we will find its bane? You are the bravest hero I have ever encountered."

"Fuck off." Catharsis Wulfyre barged between the two monster hunters, causing Rourke to drop his helmet. It clanged off the floor, and Wulfyre kicked it so that it skidded out through the entrance of the lair. "I'm not riding around the countryside until my ball hairs turn gray looking for magic weeds. Mother is paying you to kill the thing this week. It cannot be alive when she arrives."

Malik said, "Sire, this herb is the key to slaying your monster."

"You don't hire locksmiths to find a key. You hire them to pick open the lock," Wulfyre said, spinning the cap off a jug as he went. He doused his breastplate and gauntlets in a viscous fluid. It puddled beneath him, on the floor at the end of the hallway. "Tie this girl up. Let's go."

Rourke paused in the pursuit of his helmet. "Tie her up? She's an innocent."

"She's one of those virgins that wyrms love eating so much. On top of that, we know the monster likes her voice. It'll crawl out of its shithole if we have the right bait. That bait isn't a plant. Bait needs to squirm."

Wulfyre bustled along the hall, coming straight for Shesheshen. The oil from the jug dulled the shine of his armor. Malik raced after him, grabbing the man's gold-plated bicep. Malik said, "Wait, wait. There has to be another way."

From the exit, Rourke said, "We're in over our heads here. Unidentifiable monster. Unfamiliar ground. We need whatever advantages we can get to kill it."

Malik said, "Like the summoner's jaw."

Wulfyre held up his gauntleted fingers, oil dripping between them. "We don't need summoner's jaw when we already know rosemary works on the thing. It's not going to eat me with this much of the stuff."

This had to slow down. Shesheshen tried to shrink into the adjacent hallway, while pushing a few of the sharper stones inside her body toward the surface, readying claws. "Sires, your voices. If you rouse the monster, no one will be safe."

Wulfyre batted Malik's hand away. "My family has slain wyrms this way for generations. Leave a useless commoner out where the monster can smell them, and when the monster comes out for a snack, we get the drop on it. Slit this thing's belly, get the blood, and you two can spend the rest of your lives trying to spend all the money you just made."

Malik's feet slowed. He wasn't chasing his employer anymore. "No."

Wulfyre said, "My family is paying. I'm giving the orders, or you're becoming wanted men. Which would you prefer?"

How Shesheshen wanted one of the hunters to stop this. For one of them to stand up for common sense, if not for the rights of a young damsel. A damsel who had offered them a perfectly good reason to get lost for a few weeks.

But humans never stood up for the right thing. They stood around feeling uncomfortable, and later pretended that feeling uncomfortable meant they were virtuous. Now Malik stood to one side, only slightly obstructing Wulfyre's path. Surely he'd feel awful about this tomorrow when he was spending his blood money, before running off with his partner to the next kill.

And they called *her* monstrous.

There was a way to salvage this without fighting them and getting killed. She started, "Sires, perhaps there is summoner's jaw in Underlook Forest, to the south of here. It is where Papa and I first made sight of the monster, and Papa said he thought he saw its peculiar color in the brush. It could be why the monster so seldom hunts there. Less than a day's travel. You could—"

Catharsis Wulfyre's hand felt like winter had abruptly returned and fallen exclusively over Shesheshen's face. His gauntlet dug into her flesh, squeezing her mouth closed.

He said, "That'll shut her up. Get some chains."

Worse than the metal or his strength was the chilling burn. While Shesheshen had no sense of smell, her flesh tasted the rosemary, making her hide bubble up, boils rising everywhere the oil made contact. Her eyes fled deep inside her head to protect from that hideous pain. It was so awful that the urge to vomit overcame her.

She opened up her throat and chest cavity, and vomited the wide-open bear trap at him. It clanged shut, the noise echoing throughout the hallway, cutting off Wulfyre's shriek—as well as his right hand. Her bear trap had been too enthusiastic, biting straight through gold and bone alike, severing his hand between its jaws.

Wulfyre clutched at his mangled forearm. "Fuck! Fucking gods, help me!"

Shesheshen spat the trap and hand away, not wanting another taste of rosemary. Every spot where the rosemary oil had scalded her continued to crack and corrupt. She had to tear the skin off her own face and neck, screeching as she forcibly shed onto the floor. Stray juices poured from the wounds. Pain made her lose coherence, so that the bone-rods in her body jutted out and punctured her hide, knocking bricks from the walls in her flailing. She hoped she beheaded one of these damned self-important mammals.

By the time she could see clearly again, Rourke was gone. He'd fled as fast as a ghost that smelled reason in the air. Malik remained, bobbing around Wulfyre, trying to wrap cloth around the stump of the man's arm as he guided his employer to the exit. It was a gusher of a wound, painting the floor with rich crimson.

Catharsis Wulfyre kicked one boot between Malik's legs, snagged a knee, and tripped him to the floor. Malik went straight down, his skull making a heavy report against the stone floor.

Wulfyre stepped over his fallen henchman and kept going for the sunlight of the exit. He kept his mauled arm elevated, left hand trying to squeeze metal plates and apply some pressure. Gore still streamed out, painting his expensive armor with his own insides.

"Mother will come for you, you fish-drowner! You're going to be a trophy!"

In the middle of his cursing, he stepped on a puddle of rosemary he'd left on the floor when he'd decided to baste himself. One heavy boot landed with a mild *splish* sound. Before he could raise the other leg in stride, he slipped. All several hundred pounds of man and gear veered across the corner of the hall, and he went straight down on his back.

Then there were two unwanted people on Shesheshen's floor.

She let strands of her flesh dangle free of the cloak, the ends dragging on the floor until they found stones. She braced herself with the rods inside them. The stones served as decent feet, but could be repurposed into flails. Her bulk swelled with each step, lumbering over the two intruders.

She was fantasizing about cracking Wulfyre's armor like the shell of a lobster when he reached down with his remaining hand. Before she could leap on him, there was the thunking sound of his crossbow.

The bolt hit her high in the chest, near where the bear trap had been lodged. Now that was all raw tissue, so soft that the bolt pierced deeply through her innards. Its tip pricked the hide of her back.

Wulfyre said, "Right in your heart."

Much as she didn't have blood, she did not have a heart. She looked forward to ingesting this man's soon enough. She grabbed the end of the crossbow bolt, which was unusually thick. A jerk did nothing to free it, and gave her seven smaller stings, where hooks from the bolt must have lodged inside her. She commanded her inner tissues to relax and release it. Instead, they went feverishly rigid. Her meat seized up and refused to obey her.

It was going to be a nuisance digging that thing out of herself. She needed to get her strength up. Fortunately, she had these two humans over for breakfast.

"Not today!"

It was the rusty voice of the elder monster hunter, Rourke. The old man ran into the hall with a torch burning orange in the air. He waved it wildly as he came at her.

"About time," said Wulfyre, trying and failing to roll to his knees. That armor looked disgustingly heavy. He raised his arms at Rourke. "Get me out of here."

Rourke ran to Wulfyre—then past him, and to Malik. He caught the younger man under the armpits, holding the torch in front of both of their bodies as he lugged him to the exit. They were both lucky that she was still getting her footing and fighting this contraption lodged in her chest. They would escape.

While Catharsis Wulfyre bellowed about broken contracts and what he'd do to their testicles, Shesheshen straightened up. If those monster hunters returned with proper weaponry, she needed to be ready. She formed two thick tentacles and wrapped them around the base of the crossbow bolt. Jerking it made her knees weaken, and half her frame quivered from the pain. It hurt like a week of starvation jammed into one instant. What had they poisoned her with?

Wulfyre tried to sit up, and his ornate breastplate stopped him. That was what he got for wearing golden armor in the likeness of abdominals.

Still he sneered up at her. He turned those strong cheekbones and his blond stubble up at her and said, “At least you’re dying with me. The Wulfyres never forget.”

Those were not the words of a worthy father. They were the words of breakfast.

CHAPTER TWO

Surely this wasn't the first time Catharsis Wulfyre had been found wanting. This was simply the last time.

He had the chest of a man who exercised for sport, which made for pleasant chewing. His marrow was unusually sweet, and his bones hard against her orifices. Sturdy bones scratched pleasantly against her insides, and she squeezed them into alignment so she could hold new shapes. Much of his flesh and innards went to her digestion, turning into sustenance for healing against the poison.

Other parts of him, she kept for subtler uses. It felt good to have some kidneys and a pancreas inside her again. After she plugged them into her own innards, they reminded her body how to get its juices flowing.

In hibernation most of her body mass had reverted to impressionable lumps of flesh. They needed instruction. They needed more people's organs, to remind them how to become herself again for the new year.

Minutes later she picked stray scraps of the man from his armor. Her appetite was merely stoked. It was a cold burn throughout her innards, demanding more sustenance.

That crossbow bolt wasn't helping. It felt like a tree trunk was stuck through her chest. The thing tasted of unusual metals. Was it crafted from a fallen star, or blessed by one of those insipid religions that all called her a monster? It scorched her like it thought she was a blasphemer. Several barbs from the shaft broke off and lodged in her raw innards. Still more barbs held fast to the shaft, digging into her, the rosemary oil keeping her wound rigid until its flesh felt as firm as the metal. There was no getting her innards to relax enough to remove the thing right now.

Dizziness addled her senses, and she braced herself against a brick wall. The bolt was a brilliant contraption, poisoning her long after it had pierced her. She dearly hoped she could meet whoever designed this tool.

She wanted to eat that inventor, have the inventor go to some hell, and then descend there herself to eat them again.

In case the monster hunters were planning a return attack while she feasted on their employer, she lumbered to the door of her lair. Midday wind off the isthmus raked at her bare skin. Wind was something she could handle, so long as it wasn't accompanied by arrows or fire bombs.

Instead of arrows, she was greeted by a deep and gut-shaking roar. Her pet must've woken up.

Outside, Rourke and Malik clambered onto a cart and whipped the poor horses into a run. Crates of weaponry jostled as they hit stones and divots in the hillside; it had been years since there was a proper path leading out to the highway from her lair. Shesheshen let the ivy and weeds claim anything they liked. It discouraged visitors. The monster hunters would be lucky if their wagon didn't tip over in the first mile of their escape.

If their wagon overturned, then Shesheshen's pet would make a brunch of them. That pet let loose another roar as it pursued the wagon.

She was a massive bear, some relative of the brown bear that grew nearly twice as large. Her fur was dense, and though streaked with hickory, was mostly the color of dusty lapis lazuli. In clear afternoons like this, the bear looked as blue as a sapphire's dreams. Hence why travelers had named her.

"Leave them, Blueberry," Shesheshen called. She swung a few pounds of stray intestine outdoors, leaking their fecal contents across her weedy stoop. Blueberry loved the runny bits of a victim.

Blueberry relented in her chase, which was for the best. Her joints had declined in recent years. The bear waddled over to Shesheshen, haunches swaying in the air. Shesheshen held the intestines out to her snout, offering her the treat.

The bear sniffed, clearly interested. But first she rubbed the top of her head into Shesheshen's flank, as adoring as a cat. Blueberry's huffing sounds were affectionate. She was more verbal by nature than Shesheshen herself.

Shesheshen gave a sweet whine as she scratched along the bear's scalp, getting behind her ears where she couldn't reach to please herself. They cuddled together, and Blueberry snacked on the remains of the man who'd paid to kill her.

It was some sort of love. Not the kind of love that made you plant your eggs in someone and turn them into a parent, but a kind of love.

Shesheshen manipulated what bones she'd swallowed, creating a pair of proper hand-like limbs. First she flexed the fingers to make sure they worked, and then she gave the bear a better petting. She worked under Blueberry's chin, and down her furry bib, and over the scar where a trap had once broken Blueberry's left front foot. The old girl still ran with a limp.

Getting in close like this eased some of Shesheshen's aches, too. Blueberry ran hot, especially in early spring. Shesheshen leaned into the bear's fur, drinking in some of the heat like humans thought they drank in love. The warmth seeped into her blood. It had been Catharsis Wulfyre's blood until he made the mistake of interrupting her hibernation. Now it was Shesheshen's blood. Her malleable tissues formed vessels and circulated it around the crossbow bolt's shaft, trying to fight the rosemary poison.

Still, she was so cold. It wasn't from the isthmus wind from the south ocean, but that rosemary poison.

Blood circulation wasn't enough. Already she craved to digest the blood directly, into more energy to fight off the poison. That wouldn't be enough either. She needed more meat.

In her younger days she would've burrowed for rodents. In some stretches the isthmus was three miles wide, and back then wooded areas had plentiful deer and smaller morsels scampering around them. However, as though to drive her away, the local village had hunted most of the nearby areas dry, until only the cleverest bucks and skunks remained. How she would've savored a skunk today.

The only animals that the humans permitted to live in the isthmus nowadays were ones the humans wanted to kill and eat later. Kill and eat, or wear. Because wool was growing in demand in their western countries, the townsfolk converted much of their livestock pens to sheep. They could sell the parts of a sheep's body that were fashionable, and eat and excrete the rest. If Shesheshen ever went near those flocks, droves of human guards would descend on her. Meanwhile townsfolk wore the wool while eating those very animals.

And somehow Shesheshen was the monster.

Had she ever worn a human while she ate them?

She thought that over while rubbing her new jaw. Catharsis Wulfyre's jawbone was awkward with that thick chin. She tried to push it into different positions. The better her handle on this mouth, the easier it would be to speak. The next time a human crossed her path, she'd have to do a better job at socializing to throw them off. Talking was so annoying.

For speech practice, she asked Blueberry, "Any leads on breakfast?"

Blueberry had a lovely olfactory system that Shesheshen had never been able to copy. If there was anything out here to eat, she would find it.

Grunting, the bear tilted her ears eastward. She snuffled toward the pinprick orange glows over the hills and through foliage, at the swirls of smoke rising from chimneys. Blueberry knew what Shesheshen needed.

It was very early to be awake, and Shesheshen was very weak for this kind of work. But if she was going to survive this damned poison, then she had to feed. She had to go to town.

CHAPTER THREE

The citizens of Underlook were vultures. All trade routes from east and west had to cross the isthmus—that one little land bridge. With so few wild animals to eat, Shesheshen had to attack caravans that crossed the isthmus, seizing their meat and leaving behind useless lamp oil and pink salts and high-thread-count undergarments. Underlook then descended and divvied up the spoils, such that even the most mediocre of their children wore britches and capes meant for monarchs. People had trouble proposing marriage for all the gemmed rings clogging up their fingers.

And they never once thanked her for it.

In her optimistic youth, Shesheshen had prowled these streets and selected the right person for her meal. Using different bones for each visit to the town meant she never looked identifiable, and was seldom suspected by the locals. If she acted like she had money, vendors went out of their way to normalize her presence. She could spend an afternoon pretending to enjoy ale while she shopped for a loan shark or a cruel sheriff. There was a sophisticated pleasure to terrorizing and devouring someone who thought they were above everyone.

A good predator was also a reminder, she thought.

After their assassination attempt in her own lair, Underlook clearly needed a reminder.

Blueberry helped carry her much of the way to town, until the smell of society grew too strong and threatening for her. The bear dumped Shesheshen off before waddling north, behind the shadows of pines.

Underlook lay at the very center of the isthmus, the only place to shelter on the route between mainlands. Shesheshen circled Underlook to enter from the town's east end, where the poorer classes lived. This entrance to town was always less strictly guarded. The sheriffs mostly serviced the west and north parts of Underlook, where moneyed people lived. It was the older families that clutched most of the wealth, even though it was harvested by the laborers. What the laborers got out of it that kept them from eating the rich, Shesheshen didn't understand. She was a mere monster.

She fixed herself up before entering the town. Leftovers from the gold-plated Catharsis Wulfyre gave her two reasonably solid legs, so people wouldn't be suspicious of her gait. She had a full skull and most of his jaw. She squeezed the bones up, forming a head-like structure, holding the bones in place with all the spare tendons available. The rosemary poison left her epidermis gray, but plenty of humans had ashen complexions, and she covered herself in the red riding hood and cloak. This could work.

In morphing her body, she had to be careful of her chest. The wound was worsening still, and merely jostling the crossbow bolt hurt so badly that her hands spasmed around their bones.

Wounded and undernourished, she needed to concentrate and not let her human guise slip. She didn't need townsfolk getting suspicious. Smoke streamed out of chimneys on the west side, like so many bowls of dust overturned and spilling, except spilling in the wrong direction. Its form was unintentional art. Smoke always struck her as beautiful; it sprawled, resisting form, like she longed to do with her body when a hard day's hunt was over. The chimneys sent swirls through the murky orange of sky's dusk. That was usually a sign that the humans were inside for the night, yet there were relatively few visible through the windows of the squat homes.

Underlook's outskirts were less populated than usual. There wasn't a single person at the entrance to town. She'd expected to be greeted by at least a couple people competing to rent her a room for the night.

The shrines were vacant, too. Every street in Underlook had at least one shrine, gazebo-like structures where traveling priests gave speeches and where locals drew their prayers on the walls. At the bottom of the walls people drew little line segments for the "gods below" who helped humans in their endeavors, while other people drew the same line segments for the "gods above" at the tops of the walls before the ceiling, asking for protection from the endeavors of others. These god marks invoked the myriad nameless gods for aid, drawn in ink, or chalk or charcoal, or whatever paints people got their hands on. Travelers from all countries patronized these shrines.

There were no gods in the shrines she passed, at least not visible ones. Gods never showed themselves to humans even when they dumped miracles on them, which Shesheshen thought was wise. If humans got used to the presence of gods, they'd probably hunt them for profit and glory and other nonsense, just as they did to monsters. Gods were smart to keep a light touch.

But where were all the people? Someone should have been drawing god-mark prayers in a shrine tonight with her out there lurking.

Somewhere in town, someone knocked out rude sounds on a piano. Drums rumbled in next, and voices slurred their way through what sounded like five parts of a three-part harmony.

Shesheshen followed the musical sounds for street after street until locals staggered straight into her path. Two men accidentally tripped each other into the mud. They hooted like bulbous owls, then started laughing and splashing each other with it.

The sounds of human activity were coming from Underlook's town hall, a renovated barn. The massive double doors were left open so people could mill through freely. A bonfire crackled in the center of town, and the town hall's doors looked like hands warming themselves over the glow. Several humans scaled the doors to sit atop them, tooting horns and wailing on bagpipes.

So many people danced that the sheer tonnage of twirling made Shesheshen nauseous. There was so much heaving flesh, so many desperate breaths and spasming arms. Alcohol was everywhere, in the hands of dancers and onlookers alike. Around the bonfire children split pint glasses of bitter and played dice on the cobblestone paths.

She walked toward the barn doors just as a throng of humans thrust their glasses into the air, foam sloshing over the rims and to the ground. What were they celebrating?

All she knew was they were celebrating in the direction of an oblong, gray puppet. It had a dragon's jaws and wolves' paws and several kinds of wings sewn onto it. The ugly toy was carried by several gawky teenage girls, and at the blow of a whistle, they hurled it onto the bonfire. It wilted like so much demonic lint.

Among the logs of the fire, the blackened remains of several more toys burned. It was as if the whole party had been in favor of getting rid of toys they couldn't sell.

Was this a holiday she usually hibernated through? It was miserably noisy for her tastes. She shifted her ear canals to be narrower and blot out some of the sound. One thing she didn't understand about humans was how they could think with so much stimulation around.

Merely trying to concentrate around all of this made her juices trickle out around the crossbow bolt. She groaned and leaned against the town hall for a moment. She was so close. Food was dancing all around her.

The worst thing about this holiday was that everyone was here. No matter where she went in this square, people moved in groups. If she attacked anyone, the entire town would catch her. Then she'd be the next thing tossed onto their bonfire.

Someone asked her, "Pretty sight, isn't it?"

She swallowed, despite not having an entirely formed throat. It was an abrupt reminder to get her vocal passages in order. Internally, she demanded herself to focus.

She asked, "Pardon?"

"I meant you, but the bonfire's not bad either. Drink?"

It was a man of decent proportions, as best she could tell through his wool vest and trousers. He had a pale honey complexion. Jeweled rings were braided into the long blond hair that fell over his eyes, so that they glittered when he nodded. It must have been fashionable. Otherwise, the obstructed view would make it too impractical to bother maintaining. He smiled at her as if he expected gratitude for the view.

He carried two mugs of dark wine, one in each hand. He stretched one out to her, which she declined by sinking further inside her cloak.

She said, "I'm not thirsty."

Did her voice sound human enough?

It did for him, since he took a slurp out of both his mugs at once.

"Don't turn down wine in Underlook. My family brings in the best from every part of the world."

"I'm not an enthusiast for the offspring of grapes."

The man chortled. "Oh, you're something else. What do you like?"

He said it like he was offering. Her innards gurgled, bile and other juices swelling up and seeking more fat and protein to digest. The telltale ache along her spine suggested she was already digesting herself for strength to fight off the rosemary poison.

Still, it was probably inappropriate to ask this man for a hundred pounds of beef.

Trying to sound interested, she asked, "You like to fetch things?"

"Trading and shipping are my family business. We keep things safe from all the bandits."

She knew better than that. There hadn't been bandits in the isthmus in years. "Your family is important to Underlook?"

"If it wasn't for the Baroness and families like mine, Engmar or L'État Bon would've conquered the isthmus long ago. This is technically an unincorporated barony you're standing in. Every nation wants to swallow it. People like my family keep it safe."

So he was a defender of the town. She almost groaned. "Oh. You're private military?"

The man choked on his own wine. "Hardly! Nothing comes through this town without my family's stamp. We are one of the trade houses that keeps commerce moving. L'Étatters want sheepskin shoes made in southern Engmar, and northern Engmars want Al-Jawi Empire steel. Everything flows through us. Everyone's interest in our business keeps us free. I'm doing one contract right now. Do you know how to make a fortune selling whistles?"

Shesheshen said, "I did not think there was much money in whistles."

Whistles had never been much on her mind. She minded the singing crowd, and how she and this man were isolated. He maneuvered around her, like he was trying to get her into the privacy of the alley adjacent to the town hall. That might work out for her.

He said, "From your accent, you're from Boletar?"

"Not quite. I've heard of it."

She had not. It did not matter.

"It's a dot on the map between L'État Bon and the Al-Jawi Empire. Well, the Boletars have never heard of whistles. They think they're the height of music. So our company arranges for all the whistles the Engmar islanders don't want anymore to travel, and we trade them for a killing. Engmar is in the middle of another one of their civil wars. Famine is terrible out there. They'll sell anything we ask for, at whatever price."

A husky brown-skinned woman in poofy yellow pantaloons flew past them, tossing a wooden carving onto the bonfire. The whole town square cheered for her as the flames engulfed the crudely hewn image of a wyrm. Shesheshen's new drinking buddy cheered along with everyone else. Shesheshen clapped slowly, to hide that she didn't have as many fingers as she wanted.

She shied toward the man with the inconvenient hair and asked, "What are they celebrating?"

He set one of his mugs aside and smirked down at her through a thin mustache. "I knew you were from out of town. One of the travelers from the highway? You picked the perfect night to come in. Stick with me. I won't let any of them fleece you. It's going to be an expensive night."

"Why is that?"

Either he didn't hear her, or he didn't care. He said, "What's your name?"

"I'm Roislin."

"It's going to be a pleasure, Madame Roislin from out of town. Call me Laurent."

She was going to have to socialize. Reading what humans wanted from each other was so much easier than when those attentions were directed at her. That's how things had gone wrong with Catharsis Wulfyre and his hired killers. Better to get this man to focus elsewhere and talk about the town.

"Laurent," she said, like a name was an incantation to get annoying people to do what you wanted. She gestured to the drunks spinning around the bonfire. "What is all this?"

"This is the town monster."

"The town monster?"

"Don't get worried. They killed her today. One of Baroness Wulfyre's children and two professional monster hunters."

She moved an arm under her cloak, touching the crossbow bolt still lodged inside her. "And they killed her?"

"That's what everyone is saying. No way a sleeping beast could stand up to three grown killers. The Baroness's son is a wyrm slayer himself. He's killed so many corrupt lords and beasts in L'État Bon. I figured you were one of his starry-eyed admirers and followed him from there."

The drums meant something new. All the chattering, all the excited hoisting of lovers into the air, all the pudgy children playing games outside past bedtime were draped in the same ugly veil of context. If she wasn't slowly succumbing to poison, she would've felt a chill.

She said, "They're celebrating because the hunters killed the monster?"

Laurent cocked a neatly manicured brow. "That's what the party is about, yes. You sound skeptical."

"I guess I am a little skeptical."

"Well, so am I." He lowered his voice, until it required effort to hear over the crowd. "I've got a little secret. It's something few in Underlook know."

Now chills fell over her despite the poison. Did this human man recognize her? Was he going to identify her in public, in front of the embarrassing murder fire?

Her wig nearly slipped off her churning flesh, and she fixed her hood to cover it up. As she did, she looked around for an alley where she could drag this human man. Pretend they were kissing and snap his neck. It was her only way out.

The alcohol on his breath assaulted her eyes as he said, "There's no such thing as the monster."

"There isn't?"

The human Laurent sucked wine from his thumb. "The Wyrm of Underlook is a hoax. After the Baroness left Underlook for better locales, the town elders cooked it up to scare off foreign invaders—and to spook travelers. Then those travelers stay in the well-lit town, and they buy garlic and rosemary and holy symbols. They spend out the nose to protect themselves from their imaginations."

She peered at his throat from under the ends of her hood. It looked soft.

She asked, "People will jump at anything for a profit, won't they?"

The human Laurent fixed his vest, propping his thumbs under the sheepskin collar. "That's what I've always said. I've lived here for half my life and I've never seen one hair from this legendary wyrm's hide. Sometimes someone winds up missing in a town of four thousand heavy drinkers, and they say it must be a monster. It spares the parents to believe a lie, and . . ."

He twirled a pinky. She took it as a possible sign he wanted her to finish his thought for him, so she said, "It helps the economy."

He said, "You're catching on, Madame Roislin."

These were emotions she didn't know how to carry. There was the insult of having her death celebrated when she wasn't even dead. When she was, in fact, amidst them all right now, and only out here because they'd sent killers to fail in her home.

But this? To be dying from the poison of those assassins, and while looking for emergency food to survive the injury, to be told by a drunk rich boy with inconvenient hair that she had never really existed? Now their songs made unkind sense to her. This revelry was a kind of fear, for hatred was the fear people let themselves enjoy.

Never had she imagined such a thing. Humans were so creative in their disappointments.

An uninvited hand found her shoulder. It was Laurent's, firm flesh and gripping her like she was prey. She made sure there were enough bones in her shoulder to keep up the illusion, to fool his hand. His hand was unwanted, but it wouldn't be his hand for very long.

"Sire Laurent, from around here, was it?"

"That's it to the syllable, Madame Roislin from out of town. You'll want to remember my name."

She touched her chin. "Do you have a place around here?"

"It's in a two-story over on the west side. I let the staff off for tonight."

"I somehow guessed you were from the west side."

"Feel like some privacy, Madame Roislin?"

"That I do, Sire Laurent."

He raised a brawny arm—he might have more meat on him than she'd originally believed—and crooked his elbow. It was one of those gestures humans sometimes made as an offer of courtship. She thought she was supposed to hold onto his elbow. It would actually be convenient, given how faint she was feeling. They'd fix that soon.

Dancing waned into erratic commotion from around the bonfire. People hurried to the path on the opposite side of the town square, many of them joining in the nonsense shouting. They shrieked in what Shesheshen assumed was another of the consensual oral horrors that humans called music.

She had no interest in seeing what effigy of herself they burned this time. Instead she looped an arm around Laurent's and knocked herself against his hip. "Lead away."

"What's going on over there?" he asked, rising onto the tips of his polished shoes to see over the flames. Shesheshen wrapped her other arm around his elbow, hoping to weigh him down. They were already late for supper.

"Give me a minute, woman," he said. He raised his voice at someone on the other side of the fire. "Florian, what's the story?"

He pushed her aside, the hairy knuckles of his hand brushing the wound under her cloak. If the pain hadn't surged through her body, she would have bitten his jugular out right then and there. Instead she shrank against the town hall's exterior wall, trying to keep her body from convulsing. Was the tip of the crossbow bolt piercing through her back now? She couldn't tell.

It was lucky the lout hadn't been paying attention or he might have noticed she had no ribcage inside her. He didn't even notice the stab wound he'd bumped. What was so interesting to him, anyway?

Two of the newcomers to the bonfire stood infectiously still in their chain mail. Their stillness spread to the people around them, leaching their cheer and replacing it with concern on their faces. The bonfire was awful to make out facial features by, and the din of the crowd's chatter made it difficult to hear exactly what the newcomers were saying.

Then Shesheshen saw the half-mask hanging from one of the men's necks. It was part armor, part breathing apparatus. She'd seen several monster hunters wear that kind of gear when they came after her. This man had modeled this very mask in her lair this morning.

It was Rourke, with a shoulder helping prop up his young partner Malik. The monster hunters had made their way into town. Shesheshen didn't need to hear what he was muttering to know that the news was about to break.

"Florian!" Laurent yelled near Shesheshen's side. "Florian, what are they saying? Get your deceptively supple ass over here."

Three people bellowed in unison, "It's still alive!"

Someone said, "What?"

Another yelled, "The wyrm is alive and walking around! It could be anywhere."

Perhaps Florian was one of those voices, or one of the many more people who repeated the same news in their own personalized shrieks. Laurent started toward the bonfire. For someone who didn't believe in her existence, he looked abruptly ashen. His skin almost matched hers.

With as much composure as she had left, Shesheshen scratched at his shoulder and said, "Sounds like gossip about that monster we both know isn't real. Come on. Don't you have a house you want to show me?"

Her scratching on his shoulder made him tense up, and he paused. The corner of his mouth suggested a grin. Laurent said, "It's a loft. You'll love the bed."

She asked, "Do you ever eat in bed?"

"You're from out of town. You won't believe what I do in bed."

That was enough to get him walking toward the adjacent alley. Thank his good gods for abandoning him, he was going to lead her home by darkened pathways.

"We thought she was a little girl," went Rourke's voice. It was his crackling accent. "Because she hid most of her body."

"In what?" asked a high-pitched voice. "Horns? Fur? I heard it has quills like a porcupine."

"It was . . . it was . . ."

She recognized that voice and stammer. Without looking to the bonfire, she knew Rourke was processing something. His eyes could've cut holes in the back of her head. At his side, Malik was pointing straight to Shesheshen.

All those gossiping, anxious people had been loud since the moment she set foot in town. Why did they have to go quiet at this one moment?

"A red cloak! It's her! Right there!"

Reflexively she formed a few tentacles from the flesh on her neck to clutch onto her hood, like holding onto it would keep her safe. She despised attention.

Laurent stopped in the middle of the street, and his hand went to her shoulder. "What? You all know the monster's a hoax. She's a beauty. This isn't a beast. Is this the mouth of a beast?"

Shesheshen tried to duck into an alley, but it was too late. The handsy rich man grabbed her hood and yanked, so that it came free in full sight of the murderous locals and their bonfire of effigies. Everybody got a look at the gray tentacles sticking out of her face.

The only solace she had in this night was the sound Laurent made as he soiled himself.

Then it was time to run.

CHAPTER FOUR

It was going badly enough. It might as well go badly on horseback.

She darted through the town, trampling drunks and amorous couples who couldn't wait to get indoors before rutting. No matter whether she survived this one night or a thousand more years, she would never suffer another handsy rich man to live.

Plenty of people were handsy now. Whereas most people ran for their lives at the sight of her allegedly hideous visage, several people jumped up, rang alarms, and loosed their dogs. Humans tore along the alleys and jumped through the windows of shrines, scooping up rakes and burning logs from the bonfire.

"Fire! Fire is the wyrm's one weakness!"

Being burned was a weakness of hers, insofar as it was a weakness of every living thing she'd met. You could roast a sheep or a human on a fire and nobody called that their "weakness." Having fire thrust into their eye sockets was a threat to them. Weaknesses were a human invention. They called it your weakness if they fantasized about murdering you with it.

There was ample fire; one of the fish-drowners set the straw sections of a roof ablaze as she tried to lug an iron torch through too narrow a gap. A pack of feral teenagers raced along rooftops, each of them holding burning lumber as well. One slung his log at her, smacking the back of her skull and scorching her cloak. She stumbled, fighting to keep on her feet and keep moving forward. If Shesheshen couldn't run faster, they were going to roast her.

So she flung herself onto the back of the first horse she saw in the stables. It was a creamy gold creature with a white mane and tail, the sort that had once run wild in bands before Underlook had swollen. This one was freshly brushed, and didn't look twice at Shesheshen as she hopped aboard.

Thankfully she still had legs. She kicked the horse's ribs with her heels, just like human riders did, and it launched out of the stables. She wrapped her arms around its neck and hugged herself into its mane and its body heat.

Of all people, Laurent stepped into their path, yelling, "Not my horse!"

His horse shoulder-checked him aside, sending him ass-first into a watering trough. Bewildered guards took the hint and peeled out of her path. The horse burst into the town outskirts, into the open air of the moonlit plains. Underlook's cobblestones trailed through the weeds and raw dirt of the outlet that led back to the main highway.

Beyond were patches of wild daisies overtaking hills, and the bursts of lilacs, violet petals bleached nearly white by the intense three-quarters moon. Something whined over her head and shredded two lilac bushes, right through their cores. It'd been a few seasons since she'd heard the song of an arrow.

She glanced backward and found wretched civilization was close behind her. There were already five people on horseback, breaking from the mouth of Underlook. One was a slender woman in black, nocking another arrow onto her yew bow. Here Shesheshen could barely stay on top of her horse, and there were people who could loose arrows in full gallop? She needed to eat whatever gave that woman her sense of balance.

Of course they'd tracked her. The horse was following the outlet, and they were nearly to the highway. Humans made roads, so they knew them well. As the archer behind her aimed another arrow, Shesheshen yanked the horse's mane and kicked its ribs again. Her horse broke straight into the lilacs and diagonal hills beyond. This way would take them to the ravine, with its grand and safe caves.

The horse sped along like it knew the highlands better than she did—and at this speed, it did. The wind clawed at her body, stealing her precious heat. All of Catharsis Wulfyre's blood threatened to go cold, and she hugged onto the horse for shreds of body heat. There was nothing worse than being full of cold fluids.

One thing might have been worse: the party of riders was still on her tail. Some riders slowed their horses around where she'd left the road, while three others came into the hills after her. One's silhouette drew a bow on her. The other two wore chain mail and half-masks. The damned monster hunters were coming to finish the job.

There were only three of them, she told herself. She could escape them. The horse was taking her toward the ravine anyway. If they went deep enough into the craggy hills, to spots where the moon cast no light, she could spook her mount into going ahead and misleading them. Then she could split them up, and either hide or pick them off. Shesheshen had survived years as the last of her father's children, in a motherless life. Civilization would not slay her.

She looked away from the hunters and to her horse, too late. In the horse's fright, it had brought them to the ravine too soon. The vast chasm stretched in front of them, like a second nightfall rising out of the earth's carcass. It hungered for her.

Wrapping her limbs around the horse's neck, she tried to strangle it into veering in any other direction. It swung rightward so violently that Shesheshen's hindquarters flew up in the air. Before she could wrap more of herself around it, it neighed and bucked as though to exile its own spine. It tossed her into the ravine's maw, where all she could do was fall, and where only jagged rocks and white rapids awaited her.

PART TWO

SEVERAL KINDS OF FALLING

CHAPTER FIVE

Something should have eaten her by now.

The ravine was rife with bottom-feeders and scavengers that liked to think of themselves as hunters. Rocks and rapids should've torn her up badly after she lost consciousness, but even as she decomposed, there would still be plenty of good meat on her. Surely she smelled like fresh steak to any carnivores out there.

Yet as she roused, she found not one bite had been taken from her hide.

Well, it was their loss.

It was also warmer down here than she would have expected. She'd hit the river with all the elegance of cream pie against a brick wall. The current could have dragged her all the way out to the southern ocean. Why wasn't she freezing? She should have been dying of cold faster than bites from scavengers.

Wherever she was, this was remarkably dry. She shifted, groping internally to see how many of her bones were broken, and the terrain underneath her refused to shift. This was hard, dry land. Maybe those gods were reasonable after all, and had had the good taste to abandon humans for her.

All the warmth emanated from a campfire. Kindling popped and begat orange flames that illuminated the clearing. Thin smoke clotted against an overhang of smooth stone, jutting from the side of the ravine. At firelight's edge the river whispered by, with all of night's chill riding along it. The ravine's wall and this overhang created a pocket in which the fire's heat bathed her. Someone had drawn a few fresh god marks on the stone overhang above, to the gods above.

A miracle, then. Shesheshen might have to look into that religion thing.

She squeezed herself to roll closer to the fire, and found she couldn't move. Something clutched at her body. She had all her limbs, but her arms were trapped to her sides. The bondage did not constrain like silver or steel. This was a queer net.

She tested her bonds for several moments before realizing that she was wrapped in quilts. They were finely woven, with strong stitches and patterns like wildflowers. Who had trapped her in quilts?

"You're awake!"

The voice sent a shock through her worse than any fall. A human voice—likely the bondage artist that had trapped her here. Shesheshen squeezed her body until it was almost a tube of flesh, preparing to squeeze herself out of the head hole of her bonds if she had to fly.

Her captor approached around the left side of the campfire, belly swaying with her motion. She was a stocky human woman, with a strong chin and round cheeks, tatters of girlhood still clinging to a few of her features. Her cheeks glowed deeper than the fire, and her beige skin was pleasantly pockmarked, mostly unadorned except around her eyes, where she had clusters of freckles. It was like a witch had taken a handful of freckles and thrown them into her gaze.

"Lie still," the woman ordered. "You had a terrible fall. I thought you hit the rocks, but you would have crushed your head. Missing them was amazing luck, if you believe in that."

She had a husky, stuffy-sounding voice, like her sinuses were packed. Yet her tone was accustomed and comfortable with itself, so this clearly wasn't allergic irritation. It gave the woman's words a bawdy rasp, which enticed Shesheshen. People who sounded like that had the most delicious-tasting heads.

A faded green quilt hung around the woman's shoulders, over a knitted jerkin of thick tan wool. A verdant green scarf was wrapped around her neck, bunching against the flesh of her under-chin. Her unruly brown hair gave the impression of a bird's nest. She dared come even closer, squatting with her powerful thighs. Either one of this woman's knees could crush the life out of Shesheshen in her weakened state. Her size was equally enticing and threatening.

Shesheshen tried to stiffen her limbs and strike her captor. Yet her body was sore and too weak to break through the covers. One limb couldn't flex at all. It was trapped in a vise of wood and rags, forced to remain rigid. Shesheshen looked at it in confusion, a lump under the quilts.

"I gave it the best splint I could. You have some unruly bone structure. It will heal, though."

Shesheshen kept struggling with her splinted arm. She could re-spool that flesh into her body—there was no way the pulverized stones inside were going to heal like a mammal's bones would. The notion of someone trying to heal her like a person was alien. It couldn't be trusted.

The woman cast her eyes down, which made no sense. There was no tactical advantage to taking her eyes off of Shesheshen. "Uhm. I'm sorry if I offended you somehow. You were badly hurt."

This was too much to process. What was this human woman's game? Was she teasing her about her injuries and her new helplessness? Shesheshen had to get out of here.

Unfortunately her supply of blood was lower than before. In her comatose state she'd digested much of Catharsis Wulfyre's blood, in order to survive. If anything, she was fortunate the rest hadn't gushed out through her crossbow wound, leaving her to die of starvation in unconsciousness. It would've been a pathetic way to go.

She probed at her wound, bracing herself for the pain. She flexed the soft tissues and found minimal ache. Most of the sting was on the surface layers of her tissue, which tingled like medicinal herbs were trying to eat her. She squeezed her innards together without incident.

The bolt wasn't inside her anymore.

This explained the soreness and weakness in her flesh—and explained why she was alive. Where the metal intruder had punctured, now her flesh was packed with a bandage, with all the care a human wound would have needed. Someone had been delicate enough to remove the bolt without killing her, and to clean and suture her skin. In her unconsciousness, her body had gone along with the surgery's attempts to heal her. It probably would've gone far worse if she'd been awake and on guard. It was such an odd sensation, feeling threads that belonged in clothing now inside her. Shesheshen had never been sutured before.

"I stopped the bleeding as best I could," the human woman said, still looking down. Beneath her knees lay a pile of rags that tempted with their odor of spilled gore. That gore had spilled from Shesheshen's own body.

The human woman said, "It looked grim for a while. Are you anemic?"

Shesheshen was not entirely sure how to answer. The woman waited.

Damn it, this woman wanted her to speak. She wrapped more internal tissues around the broken parts of her stolen jawbone. She had to make words if she was going to understand this.

How was she supposed to answer, though?

She tried honesty. "I have some trouble with blood inside me."

"I promise you're patched up now. What you need is fire, food, and sleep. There's a town nearby, called Underlook. I can take you there in the morning and find a real physician."

Shesheshen was not going to be dragged in this humiliating blanket bondage into that town. She'd sooner perish.

The woman said, "My name is Homily, by the way."

Shesheshen needed an alias. A different one from before.

"I'm Shesh . . . She . . . Siobhan."

Homily went on. "Hello, Siobhan. I'm very glad to see you with your eyes open. I have spare clothes you can borrow. I promise I maintained your modesty as best I could while I fixed you up. I-I promise I didn't look at anything."

Then Homily made a sidelong glance that made no sense. Shesheshen stared at her, trying to understand, and something about that made the woman blush. Further staring made the blush worsen.

Thinking about the blush got more confusing with every moment. She thought about it so intensely that all the blood Shesheshen had left inside her ran to her own face, in a mirror reflex of Homily.

Homily saw, and bit her thumb for a moment.

That part Shesheshen understood. She also wished to bite things right now.

Shesheshen's innards squelched, telling her what she already knew: she was dying of hunger. It was not as pressing as dying of poison. There was a serious question, though, of whether she could overpower this large woman. Shesheshen might be tossed into the fire for trying. How was she going to eat in these circumstances?

Homily said, “That sounds like the dinner bell.”

“Did you put bells inside me?”

“Bells inside you? Oh, you’re a funny one. Here, let’s get you fed.”

The woman turned, belly and hips swaying enough to make Shesheshen salivate. On the fire there was an iron kettle—part of a kit that Shesheshen had missed before. There was a handcart in their camp, and a bedroll, and a tin teapot to one side of the fire. Homily stirred her kettle with a crudely carved wooden ladle. She raised the ladle, blowing cool breath against the steam that rose from the contents.

Was it poisoned? Seeing that ladle coming toward her, she couldn’t believe this woman really meant to nourish her. Yet her expression seemed genuine.

“Here,” Homily said. “Have some broth. It’s a rabbit I caught, and some pork, and miscellaneous stock. It will give you strength. You don’t want to fight an infection unarmed.”

Shesheshen tried to maintain the meat illusion that she had a human mouth. She kept her teeth in view, and puckered her lips as the ladle came in. It was eerie to feel that wooden lip against hers, as someone, for the first time in her life, fed her.

The broth was so strong that her entire body shuddered, once, before she captured herself. She strained against the quilts and sipped. It filled her entire head, from chin to purloined skull, with nutritious heat. Immediately her tissues cycled up to the pathetically thin neck that a human form forced them to have. She spread the broth’s minerals thinly, so that every part of her could start to revive. Every part of her could share in the liquid heat.

The monster moaned, a meager sound. Immediately she dreaded it would give her away.

Instead Homily fetched her another ladle full. A small chunk of flesh floated at the top. The prospect of chewing on that morsel made Shesheshen want to weep.

Homily asked, "Is it too much? Can you keep it down? I added some turmeric and ginger."

Shesheshen needed something smooth and social. She needed to sound like one of these chatty humans.

She said, "M-more?"

"I know you don't have much of an appetite after the traumatic thing you've been through."

Trauma. The lasting pain that haunted people. Usually humans called Shesheshen a trauma; at the gentlest, any exposure to her was called a trauma for them. What an odd notion: That she might experience such a thing? That someone would take sympathy with her?

It was enticing. It made her hungrier.

She was desperate for another sip of liquid heat from a woman who had cared for her wounds. But this was not just a someone who helped her. She was a human. She had a handcart in sight nearby, and as Shesheshen awoke further from her near-dead stupor, she saw the glint of blades in that cart. There were traps with iron teeth, and glass jars that could have contained anything.

Armed humans played games with the lives of non-humans. There was no question. Shesheshen had to kill this beautifully round human woman, before she was slain herself. She would not be tossed into a bonfire like a crass effigy.

"One more ladle, Siobhan?" Homily asked. She brought the ladle close to Shesheshen's mouth in offer.

With her free hand, Homily touched Shesheshen's arm through the quilts. Her touch was so warm, different from the fire. Heat made flesh, and offered.

Shesheshen made a sidelong glance, and moved her head for another sip of rabbit broth.

It made no sense to fight now, at her weakest. She would kill this woman tomorrow instead.

CHAPTER SIX

Shesheshen ate until her consciousness dwindled. The world faded out as she held a chunk of flesh in her mouth, humming into it, relishing in the flavor and the sensation of it melting and becoming a part of her. Thread by thread, she would knit her monstrous body back together. Thread by thread. Thread by thread, until sleep was upon her like a sudden night.

For what of the evening she was aware, Homily rested beside her. Humans sometimes did this in camps, to conserve body heat, and to protect themselves if anything preyed on them in the night, the way they preyed on everything else during the day. There was the temptation to prey on her as the woman snored away. Sliding a tendril under the woman's scarf would be easy. Then it would be done, and she would be safe.

But the human woman was warm, and she was very tired. Her awareness kept ebbing, such that she wasn't sure when she'd slept and when she'd blinked. Her tired mind flickered like the flames of the campfire. She was so exhausted that she nearly convinced herself she and the fire were connected, and when its light dipped, she could no longer see anything. No longer hear. No longer perceive time.

Oh yes, she was definitely fighting off rosemary poison.

At some point she opened her eyes and Homily was loading her onto the wagon. The human woman moved boxes of tools up to the driver's bench and made a bed out of the quilts for Shesheshen. She was nestled firmly between one edge of the wagon and a crate of yellowing books.

"I hope these fit," Homily offered her some spare clothes. "They'll have to do until we reach Underlook."

The gray dress was enormous on Shesheshen's withered frame, and she wrapped the sleeves twice around her arms, covering her mostly boneless hands. The dress was nearly as threadbare as herself, patched in many places with rough, red squares of material. It being so flimsy comforted her, in case she needed to tear her body free of it and escape.

"I'll trade you this for that blanket."

Homily handed her a hat so large Shesheshen wondered if this belonged to some species other than humans. It had a tall, pointed top, presiding over a brim so wide that it would shade one's entire torso.

Homily explained, "When I grew up, I always thought witches would wear things like this. But none of the witches I've met wore hats. It was a little disappointing."

Shesheshen was not a witch, so she wore it. It hid how tattered her wig had gotten in the fall, and there was an inexplicable comfort to holding onto the two sides and pulling its brim over her shoulders. It was an article of clothing you could hide in. Why didn't all humans wear witch hats?

Planks in the wagon rattled as the oxen stirred up and began to pull. Homily casually held their reins in her left hand, while leaning her right arm across the seat back of the driver's place.

The wagon bounced and shuddered like it, too, was a dying organism. The violent shaking of the wood planks was oddly soothing. It reminded Shesheshen of being born. It lulled her into short sleeps, none deep enough to dream. It made the terrain more difficult to follow, as they wound up a rocky path and between narrow pairs of boulders.

One particularly hard bump made Shesheshen flinch with her entire body—parts of her still felt like a collection of small cuts. When she unclenched her body, she saw Homily slowing the oxen, to smooth out their ride.

This still didn't make sense. Lying in her nest of quilts, Shesheshen asked, "Why are you helping me?"

The human woman fidgeted with the green scarf around her neck, and said, "If I fell off a cliff, I'd hope somebody would help me."

Of course you hoped that. Nobody actually helped each other. That's why people had religions, hoping gods would provide help where people refused.

Shesheshen did not understand this woman. But she did get the sense that explaining that would not help her cause.

Instead she said, "I am bad at talking to people. I should have thanked you. Sooner than now."

"Don't you worry about it. I was never good at talking to people either."

That didn't make sense either. The woman clearly liked talking at great length. She should, with that stuffy-nosed voice that had so much more character than typical human voices.

As though she heard Shesheshen thinking, Homily turned to her. She reached into the bed of the wagon and held a hand over Shesheshen's quilt-covered feet. She clearly wanted to touch Shesheshen. So why didn't she?

Then she realized the human woman was waiting for consent. Shesheshen sank more under her witch's hat, and extended a foot. Once it was offered, Homily patted one of her meaty hands on Shesheshen's calf. Why was she doing that? And why did it feel pleasant?

As they bounced and jostled and rocked along through the wilderness in search of the highway, Homily asked her, "Where do you live in town?"

The idea of living in Underlook filled her with a dream of burning.

"I am not from town."

"You're a traveler? Me too. I've been in Sour Island, south of Engmar, for months before crossing out here."

Shesheshen did not know that island. She envied islands, things that got to spend their entire existences surrounded in water, untroubled by hunters. Nobody stabbed and poisoned islands. If Shesheshen ever got onto one, she might never leave it.

Those thoughts weren't appropriate for conversation, especially not with someone who could still learn her identity and kill her. She restrained her thoughts down to something more mundane. "You were on a nice island, and traded it for a cold ravine? One with nobody else in it?"

"Well, you were there." Homily smiled, and Shesheshen clutched her hat tighter over her face. Homily said, "It's actually embarrassing."

"I hate being embarrassed."

"You don't know the half of it. See, there was a bear."

Shesheshen's flesh writhed from the surprise. Thankfully this gray dress hid much. "You found a bear?"

"I was down in the ravine a day and a half ago, experimenting with some scent-based lures. I'm testing some claims made in my book collection. And I realized, you know, there's no map of the river basin. I don't think it's been charted. So I got carried away finding key points, until this huge blue bear came at me."

"The bear was blue?"

"There are strange things in this isthmus, aren't there?"

There were. Like women who did surgery on strangers.

Shesheshen said, "I might have seen that bear before. It is large. It likes odors."

"I didn't realize there were bears on the isthmus. I'm sure my scent lures attracted it. I wasn't prepared. Luckily for me, it was spooked off when you fell into the water."

This explained why Blueberry had abandoned Shesheshen in the middle of their hike to town. She'd gone north, in the direction of the ravine. She'd smelled a tasty scent and thought it was supper. And to be fair, Homily did look delicious.

Shesheshen loosened her grip on the sides of the hat. "We are both lucky, then."

Homily leaned back and sang out the words, "Lucky travelers. What are the chances?"

Shesheshen said, "I am not a traveler. I live here." That was not true, and not untrue. Shesheshen tried again. "I live in the isthmus. Outside of town."

"Oh. That's darling. Are you a shepherd?"

"I sometimes work with sheep."

That was kind of true. She stole and ate them when it was possible.

Homily steered them around to a softer path of dirt and moss. "Is your place nearby? I'd hate to run into bandits out here."

"There are no bandits in the isthmus," Shesheshen said, peering over the edge of the wagon, and the next lurch sent her careening into the boxes. She huddled, trying to adjust her eyes to the landscape. The crashing half-hills were hard to discern. They were surely northwest of her lair, but how far away was impossible to tell with all the bouncing and her fatigue.

Around one mossy outcropping of rocks, a black snout protruded.

There were flecks of blue in its fur. There she was, out here and following them. Blueberry peeked around the corner at her, before resuming her hiding place.

So Blueberry knew where she was. She was likely as confused and concerned as Shesheshen was. Perhaps she had heard the story, and wanted to argue about the details.

That brief view of the animal's moist eyes made Shesheshen realize something else. No matter how close they were to her lair, and no matter how many imaginary bandits she feared, there was no way she was taking Homily there. That was a place for eating.

Homily did not necessarily have to be eaten. Not yet.

Why Shesheshen didn't want to eat her, Shesheshen decided not to consider. She was busy.

She said, "It is not nearby. It is a long trip."

"I'll tell you what," Homily said, reclining comfortably against the chest that co-piloted her wagon with her. Her voice was so comfortable in its unusual stuffiness. It reminded Shesheshen of things she didn't remember, like an itch inside her mind. It was awful, despite feeling nice.

"I have a large room at the Red Dragon Inn in Underlook. It's actually too big for me, which is part of why I camped out last night. You can rest there while we find you a physician."

Since "no" was not a viable answer, she tried saying it as, "That seems like a lot of work. For you." Eyeing where her pet bear was hiding, she said, "I could get off here. Lighten your load."

A noise came out of Homily like a nightmare god had decided to birth out of her throat. It was a husky braying sound that made her throw her head back, pointing her mouth at the heavens. She slapped the chest with a hard report, and Shesheshen instantly shuffled to the rear of the wagon.

Was this it? Was this when they fought to the death? It had come out of nowhere. Shesheshen stuck an arm in one of the crates, grabbing a jar to shatter over the woman's head.

Homily kept making the insane sound until she wiped a tear from the corner of her eye. "Yes, I'll just let you crawl home and get eaten by wild bears. You're a funny one, Siobhan."

Laughter. The human woman was laughing. Shesheshen had heard it before, but never caused it, never received it as a reaction. Raw and sincere joy, aimed at her? It made her question every laugh she'd heard humans make at each other. It looked spastic, like an alien presence had seized the woman's body.

"Heh heh," Shesheshen said, trying to approximate polite mirth. She hoped she did it convincingly.

"The highway's coming up," Homily said, pointing between two sharp hills. "We'll have you in civilization before noon."

Shesheshen fisted her fingers in the brim of her witch hat. She tried to pull the hat over her entire head. "Great. Civilization."

CHAPTER SEVEN

The trouble started when they reached the boulders marking town. No sooner could Shesheshen make out the chalk god marks that decorated them than two women with pale patches of vitiligo appeared, wearing matching indigo shawls. They were churning goat butter or whatever humans liked doing in their spare time. Their churning slowed and they leaned to whisper at each other, while watching Shesheshen.

This was all Shesheshen's fault. She should have eaten Homily on the road and used the resultant strength to crawl back to her lair. Exhaustion had been an excuse. Instead she'd let herself pass out for most of the ride, and disguised herself so badly that the humans had seen right through her.

Those women clustered together with a third person, a lanky man in rancher's chaps, all stepping into a shrine as though for divine protection. She didn't need to hear the gossip to know it was dangerous. As the wagon rolled onto the town's muddy road, it only became more obvious they were being watched.

Shesheshen sank until only her eyes and the hat were above the lip of the wagon. There were ample books and jars to toss as projectiles, if it came to that. She needed to be properly armed.

Somehow, Homily hadn't noticed. She faced straight ahead, guiding the oxen to the stables, her jaw stiff and eyes hard. She was awfully fixated on such a simple task. Shesheshen didn't understand how she could be missing the beginnings of a mob.

Shesheshen said, "Excuse me."

Homily said, "It's fine."

Then she let out a hot sigh. That was a kind of breathing that humans meant things by. Exhalations that weren't words but were words. Shesheshen hated that nebulous sub-language stuff.

When they thought Homily wasn't looking, that trio pointed at her. They scarcely spared a glance for Shesheshen and her witch hat.

She reflected on Homily's appearance again. Her humble jerkin and green scarf. Her skin was a color that many humans had when they weren't dead. What was unusual about her? That her weight was superior to most humans'?

Shesheshen asked, "Is it fine?"

"Yes."

"Do you know those people?"

"No. And I don't want to."

A couple of middle-aged humans lugging a sack of grain paused, then crossed the street to avoid the wagon. Soon they joined the gossiping party.

Homily's broad face drew into a scowl, like she might bite something. It was the first time Shesheshen had seen her in such a foul mood. With her wide shoulders hunching, she looked like Blueberry when she was upset over having a fish taken away.

Where it came from, Shesheshen didn't understand. But she drew closer to the human woman as they rode. If the crowds grew, they would have to bite things together.

As they left the wagon, Homily said, "How are your legs feeling?"

"I like them. I should grow some more."

That got another demonic laugh out of the woman. It was probably good laughter, not a predatory sound. Her face smoothed to its typical perky state, smiling for Shesheshen. Homily gathered two crates of the most expensive supplies—most of which looked like books—and slung them all over her shoulder.

She said, "Don't hurt yourself."

Shesheshen still carried a satchel of herbs and tools. With that poisoned bolt gone, and her stomachs full of nourishment, she was ready to face humanity. She even put extra bones in that side of her body to make sure it would be stable against the satchel.

"I'm stronger than I look."

"Especially for a woman who was stabbed in the belly. Your sutures will only be so strong. Be kind to yourself, all right?"

Shesheshen had no idea what you were supposed to say to that. Submit to Homily's intrusion on Shesheshen's autonomy? Or refuse with the kind of contrarian banter that humans mistook for charisma? Homily's niceties were puzzles.

Fortunately some strangers made a distraction. An elderly couple in top hats clutched at each other's elbows at the sight of Homily, and crossed the street. They dodged around two oncoming carriages, all while gawking backward at Homily. Afterward, they loitered under the awning of a kebab shop, still watching Homily and Shesheshen.

Homily did not watch them in return. She set her jaw again, walking with head up and seeking her inn. This time Shesheshen inspected her face for signs of illness, since this treatment of distancing and pointing was something humans usually reserved for plague or poverty. Was she sick?

Homily hesitated before the entrance to the Red Dragon Inn. The entrance was not terribly imposing. The double doors were painted cheap red, color flaking off at the hinges and around the brass handles. It was the most expensive place to rent a bed in Underlook.

On the second floor, they took a right into a totally different lair. Shesheshen had never been inside one of these inns before. There were so few doors that the rooms must have been large. The floorboards were dusted and gleaming with wax. Her own lair was mostly conquered by plant life. This place expunged all life that didn't pay for residence.

Homily's room was everything Shesheshen didn't like about people. A bed larger than any human's surface area, and the sheets were so tight across it that you would have to wrestle to get under them. Mirrors hung on the walls, to trick you into thinking you were company. Dressers and bureaus to encourage people to change clothes more frequently than made sense. Bedrooms were made out of bad habits.

It was certainly a room furnished by humans. By their idiosyncrasies, it could be desirable.

On the floor, right in front of their door, was an envelope. Spying it, Homily sucked air between her teeth and squatted down. Shesheshen had seen few letters, but based on Homily's exhalations as she read it, this was a bad one. They were all bad to her, but that feeling was partially because she was illiterate.

Shesheshen asked, "Is it a curse? From one of the witches you know?"

Because that was a problem they could fix. She was amenable to hunting down any offending witch and devouring them. Especially if it would improve Homily's noises.

"It's from the innkeeper."

"Yes?"

Homily crumpled the paper up like she wanted to strangle it. "He wants us to stay for free."

Her tone was acidic for someone getting free lodging.

Shesheshen asked, "We don't like staying for free? You were letting me stay for free. I thought."

A rattling breath fell out of Homily's mouth, and the woman closed her eyes. Without seeing what she was doing, she uncrumpled the letter. She smoothed it out between her hands, fixing each crease. Somehow, her fastidious fixing of the letter was more violent than the crushing.

She said, "I know why he's doing this. I talked to him already. I insisted on paying."

"Is he evicting you?"

"No. We can stay. You can stay." Homily deposited the letter on top of her belongings and looked into one of the false companionships a mirror afforded. "Not that I want to."

This had to be one of those human customs where the humans all knew what was wrong. They put the pieces of their horrible puzzles together automatically, and outcast anybody who could not. How was one supposed to do that?

Shesheshen forfeited. She was a monster, after all.

She said, "What is wrong?"

"Can we not talk about it right now?"

"Yes. I love not talking."

Homily gave a winsome crack of a smile. There was almost a laugh.

Shesheshen leaned against the bed, testing its give. It was no pool of water, but it was more inviting than hard ground or waxed floors. Another spell of unconsciousness tickled at her mind. Homily should come be unconscious with her, in their free bed. They could figure out how to adequately punish people for making it free later, after Shesheshen figured out why free things were bad.

Homily removed her straps and fixed her belt with both thumbs. She said, "You are a wonder, Siobhan. I don't know who stabbed you with that thing, but I hope they fell into the ravine too and never surfaced."

Shesheshen had thought they weren't talking. She wasn't ready for more talking. All she had was an inadequate stare.

Homily's put a hand to her bunched-up scarf around her neck. "Oh, no. Was that horrible of me?"

This part Shesheshen could fix. The woman felt wrong in some way, so all she had to do was express she was right.

"Yes! So horrible."

The compliment did not work right. People who were complimented did not hide their faces behind their palms. Homily trembled in the still-open doorway, her breathing noisy with meaning again. She worked the heels of her hands into her eyes, as though to dig them out. Before Shesheshen could offer to help extract them, the woman moved to the hallway.

"I need to clear my head. You get some rest. I'll check your sutures when I return."

There was no opportunity to ask what foods Homily wanted. She left too quickly.

It was not the first time Shesheshen had been alone. It was one of the rare times where she suspected that it was her fault.

CHAPTER EIGHT

Shesheshen slept on top of the covers, on top of the bed, like an ornament of flesh. The fireplace roared in the main room on the first floor, and its heat crept up through the floorboards and the bricks of the chimney that passed through one wall. She could burrow under the sheets, but it was not her place. This was Homily's room. It was her right to come ruin the too-tight sheets to her liking when she got back.

That was a story Shesheshen told herself, anyway. The story let her anticipate the human woman returning to her with an explanation for why her compliment had been wrong. Let her anticipate the human woman returning at all.

In that way, she passed out, knowing she was in denial. When she next roused, there was nobody else on the bed. Homily was not here. Behind the root-colored curtains, the sun was on its way out too.

Rest was not doing its job. She did not feel restored like she ought to. Her insides longed for more nutrition, and more than nutrition.

So she wrapped herself in loose trousers, and draped the patched-up gray dress into the trousers for layering. Then she fixed suckers on her scalp to her wig, and the witch's hat over that. The mirror reassured her that she had a suitably humanoid shape, and that little of her graying flesh was showing. She loitered in front of her reflection, waiting for it to expose itself and walk away.

Hunger made her walk away first.

The streets were much emptier than the previous night. People stayed indoors like it was winter, except the weather they feared was a monster. They huddled around stoves and chess tables, like they were safe behind their windows. They didn't know a monster was watching. Shesheshen much preferred all the humans being in their proper buildings, where they could not identify her and make trouble.

A few walls bore drawings done in peculiar colors. They warned of a red triangle with a black face and fangs and claws. It was inaccurate enough to equally offend and amuse. Artless as it was, she appreciated that the folk of Underlook were afraid of her, and warning each other to watch out for something she didn't look like. Perhaps some fisher would come across her riding hood on the end of a hook next week and think he'd slain the beast.

Civilization sounds, including violins and unnecessarily loud chatter, came from the westerly-center part of town. It was best to know what the humans were doing. If she could eavesdrop on any hunting parties they put together, she could get the drop on them.

There was no bonfire tonight. Heaps of ash and unloved structures sank into a pit in the center of town. Underlook had made a mess in their celebration of her death, and then used their fear of her still being alive as an excuse to not clean up after themselves. That lack of accountability was typical to humans.

The violins were muffled by the town hall's doors. The old barn structure had been shut up tight, such that one could only enter through a proper door on the south side. Inside, humans twirled and flirted and lied to each other under the light of candles. A band played for them. For as many people were shut up afraid on the east side of town, here where power lay, there looked to be ample humans ready to congregate and enjoy themselves. All they had to do was shut the doors to pretend they were safe.

Shesheshen shopped through the windows. Neither of those wretched monster hunters were inside. Sheriffs drank at a table together and berated the comelier youths to come join them. There were many ripe humans in tight-fitting garments that distorted their figures, with deliberate pleats and ironed smoothness, and all the colors of birds in search of mates. There were so many smiles, all sharing that baited quality. Shesheshen knew not to trust those kinds of smiles.

In the southeast corner there were two tables with no one sitting at them, which made no sense. It would be easy for any of the couples to take one and talk each other into making mistakes. All around the building, people ate platefuls of food while standing. Didn't humans enjoy sitting?

At first she'd missed the third table, behind those. At it sat Homily, her face buried in a book. Her size and that green scarf were unmistakable. So was the fact that she did such a bad job of pretending she was reading and not following the goings-on of the hall that even Shesheshen recognized it.

Nobody approached that barrier of empty tables, because they feared to go near her. They were treating her like she was monstrous.

She was not monstrous.

This was monstrous.

This was a human party, with so much alcohol that it made Shesheshen's eyes sting, and she was standing outside the building. Humans were supposed to be able to find company. Homily had to have come to a place like this in search of it.

Instead Homily sat with a border of unused tables. A wasteland of furniture.

Homily's chocolate eyes glanced up from her book, giving herself away again as she watched human women her own age dance. Those people, likely none of whom ever had someone cross the street to avoid them, or had fingers and gossip pointed at them, and who had definitely never been chased on horseback off the edge of a cliff.

Then, Shesheshen knew what she was doing tonight.

CHAPTER NINE

Deep in the poorer side of Underlook was a butcher's shop, operating far away from where anyone else sold food. It mostly serviced people who needed loans of food. Its proprietor was Farhan Janabi, descendant of a poor family from the Al-Jawi Empire. His family carved out a living in gravedigging and butchery—handling dead things for money. Farhan had grown successful enough that he had numerous fat babies.

Shesheshen and Farhan did not know each other. She had merely eaten a couple of sheriffs that had tried to extort his family. That was as familiar as she got with humans.

Nowadays he was so successful that he no longer had to sleep in his shop, and so it was undefended. After stalking around the premises for several minutes to make sure Farhan's good fortune had continued, Shesheshen sneaked in. A few rats were the only things that squawked at her entrance. As payment to the proprietor, she ate every rodent on the premises.

No butcher shop kept meat on the premises after hours; otherwise she would've feasted there the other night. Anything he sliced up was gone by the end of the day. Anything with decent marrow was likewise gone.

However, at Farhan's, there were unsold bones. From sheep, and goats, and turkeys, and pigs with their wide haunches. Shesheshen tried on anything that wasn't cracked, sucking it into herself and spitting it back out if the feel was off. She still had Catharsis Wulfyre's skull and most of his arms, but she needed a proper outfit.

It was an inelegant process, pulling a set of ribs inside her flank, and measuring which ones to snap off. Hog scapulas made firm padding along her torso and thighs, as she tailored a humanoid shape that wouldn't collapse under pain or fright. There was a spree trying on turkey bones that could make new fingers, and toes, and joints.

The very last details came at her feet. She slid succulent bone into her soles, and then rounded pieces to get a flexible heel and ball of the foot. Every trial meant re-knitting her flesh into new tendons and connectors.

It was worth the pain. By the end of the hour, she had the feet for dancing.

She was sure nobody else was as dressed up as herself tonight.

She proved it on the other side of town. Sometimes bait was making a leg look shapely in an alley. In this circumstance, it was making her posture look unsure. When she saw him coming, she put her hand to her mouth, like she was chewing her fingernails over whether or not to go to the privileged people's dance.

Laurent approached her with what some human men mistook for swagger, raking a hand through the rings that decorated his gaudy blond hair. Tonight he wore a black vest and striped overcoat, both done with bright white thread to show off that they were tailored. Untailored clothing hid its stitches, whereas this fashion showed it off.

She let him utter two syllables of his come-on before she interrupted. It was like a second chance. She got to drag him into the alley like she should have the previous night, wrapping two tendrils of raw muscle tissue around his face. One bound his head around the upper lip, while the other bound his lower jaw. He could only work his mouth to make noise if she consented.

Leering at him from under the brim of her hat, she said, "Good to see you again, Sire Laurent. Are you still enjoying not believing in things?"

He gave a mousy squeak. That was enough of an affirmative for her.

"You gave the impression you have many people who would do work for you. Many resources. Were you lying?"

"Hn? Hn? Never, no, please let me go, I can give you anything."

"How many people can you have ready to ride on a job on short notice?"

"Uh. Un? Five? Ten. Ten, I swear my life on it."

"Do you like lying?"

"At least . . . five. Maybe three. I can guarantee you three people, just don't eat my—"

She didn't care what parts he was willing to have eaten. She sealed his mouth closed with a generously gentle squeeze of both tendrils. The man whined until she gave him a stare. Then he knew to listen.

Shesheshen said, "One of two things is going to happen tonight. I could eat every piece of you that you don't need to stay alive, until there is nothing but a fleshless bundle of organs and prime bones. Then I will swallow your still-sobbing self inside of my flesh, and keep you alive, and make your mouth my own. I will hunt your family down and work your jaw such that I eat them with your own mouth. Only when there is nothing left of you will I swallow you and let you weep in an oblivion of stomachs.

"Or . . ." She paused. "Do you want to hear the *or* there?"

Slackening her tendrils gave him enough space to nod vigorously, his styled hair swinging around his cheekbones. He was a better listener than she'd expected.

She continued, "Or you will gather a party of your most trusted confidants. Your party will assemble every cleanser they know of that can destroy odors and grime. And you will personally ride with them to my lair. There, you will clean the antechamber and the first three rooms to your right as you enter. Primp them until you yourself would happily spend the night in one."

Laurent's eyes darted in useless directions. He was frantic, but clearly listening. She was surely offering a gentler fate than he anticipated, if his harried breathing was to be believed.

"You will leave right now, and go directly there. Because eventually I will come home, one way or another. And if I do not find those rooms in a state that pleases me, I will find you. And you will not believe what I will make your mouth do."

With that, she slithered the lower tendril away from his jaw. She only needed the one around his head to break his neck or crack his skull against the wall if he tried something foolish.

She asked, "Which of these two events would you like to happen tonight, Laurent of Underlook?"

Laurent put both palms on the wall, like it was the ground now and he was lying on it while standing. He looked up into her face with a gaze that reminded her to blink.

A moment later, he chose wisely.

CHAPTER TEN

The border of Homily's discontent was now four and a half tables wide. She sat on the same wicker chair, shielding herself with the same book. Her free hand worried at one end of her scarf, her thumb working through a hole in the knitting that had doubtless been worn by many other nights of similar emotional displacements.

Now the town hall was less populated, couples trickling off from the dance to more private activities. Two violinists kept circling each other and performing, though, in their own shameless form of musical copulation. That permitted the spriest of the townsfolk to keep gyrating together, arms draped over shoulders, hands adjusting on hips, noses in necks. It really would have been more practical for them to eat each other.

No one offered Homily such pseudo-cannibalistic harmony.

Not until Shesheshen approached her.

Shesheshen tipped her hat up and extended one nicely rendered palm. It was perfect, with a heel specific to the thumb, and the requisite number of fingers. People ought to have been more proud of her immaculate hand forgery.

"May I have this dance?"

Homily looked up from her book like she was suddenly the one who was illiterate. Her pupils dilated, chocolate brown eyes melting in sudden moisture. "W-what? Siobhan, you can't be up now."

"I can be up. I am."

"You're hurt, and you'll risk infection. We have to get you to bed."

Homily dropped her book on the nearest table and reached for Shesheshen, likely to drag her off to the Red Dragon Inn. That free room was not appealing right now. Like in the wagon, Homily did not fully touch her. She reached and waited for consent.

Consensual touch was such a foreign idea. Shesheshen intercepted that warm hand, applying enough weight and strength to demonstrate that she had weight and strength. "I'm healing, thanks to you. Let me thank you."

Hopefully all of Homily's rapid blinking was a good sign. "What do you mean?"

Shesheshen separated their hands so that she could offer her own this time. She put her palm up, fingers extended, like a harmless trap. She was sure this was the right gesture. Other couples had done it all night.

"This is what I mean. You are who I mean it to."

Was that too opaque? Too threatening? The amount of social cues she had to care about bewildered her. Talking was awful when you weren't threatening people.

It was not too threatening, since Homily was on her feet in a moment. She followed Shesheshen between the tables, nudging chairs out of their way with horribly wooden groans. Homily actually giggled—a smoky sound that made Shesheshen lose control of the bones in her legs for a moment.

As the dueling violinists struck up the next song, Homily came in close, like a wolf going for the jugular. It would have been a pleasant bite.

Their bodies eclipsed, Shesheshen's narrower frame sinking against the protective warmth of the human woman's chest and belly. It was better than any bed's embrace. There was an uneasy safety about it, an allure and simultaneous urge to run, as thighs glanced against hips, and their hands fluttered in search of appropriate purchase. All of this intimacy, without any of the expectation of an attack. Dancing always seemed implausible from afar. Now, under its power, Shesheshen was completely lost as to how humans could do this in public.

She leaned in close to Homily's scarf-wrapped neck and whispered, "I have a favor to ask."

Homily positively beamed. "Tonight? Whatever it is, you've got it."

"Do you know how to dance?"

"I've done it once or twice, yes. Why?"

"Great. Can you lead?"

There came a pleasant dimple upon the human woman's cheeks, and hands moved to show Shesheshen where to go.

"Here. We'll go slowly."

Homily fished out one of Shesheshen's hands, lacing their fingers together delicately until they were a wickerwork of flesh. Shesheshen wondered if wicker chairs felt this happy about interlacing. Once more their bodies melded together, and she luxuriated in the woman's generous heat. It was like cozying up to an unusually soft oven.

One foot stepped to her right and Homily's body tilted in that direction. The link of their fingers guided Shesheshen with her, and she followed. The objective seemed to be walking in bad circles, in a partnership. Imitating the steps was not so difficult at this pace. Mirrors did this sort of imitation, so she could too.

Soon Homily took her eyes off the work, choosing to rest her cheek on Shesheshen's shoulder. Shesheshen made sure there was adequate meat padding there for her, and held on tighter. It felt like they were the only ones on the dance floor.

In fact, they were the only ones dancing. The broader their dancing ellipses grew, the more humans fled for the outer tables, or the walls. The faces Shesheshen saw were drawn into concern, and more tentative emotions that she didn't understand—and didn't care about understanding. Were they afraid of Homily? They should've been afraid of Shesheshen herself. It was funny, for once, to be the companion of the intimidating person.

What they feared didn't matter to her anymore. Perhaps these humans had never met someone with actual compassion, and it repelled them, like rosemary repelled her.

She wanted to wrap more of herself around Homily. To grow large enough that this kindly fat woman could be protected inside her. To consume her, without the harm, until all their motions were complementary. Homily held onto her both like she was fragile and like she would slip away into the sea if she released her grip. She wanted to tell her it was all right to hold on. That she was monstrously durable. Anything to keep her near. Their dance was like consensual hatching.

That was when she realized. It felt so obvious now. Why did she feel so strongly for Homily?

Her generosity. Her medical knowledge. She even came with a pair of oxen that their young would love devouring. It all made so much sudden sense. Homily would make a beautiful nest.

Shesheshen's insides churned as she imagined laying eggs in Homily's lungs. Every breath she took would bathe them in oxygen, until they were strong enough to burrow out. They would be born from the love of this generous woman's flesh.

Surely, this was how love felt to everyone. It only seemed odd because it was Shesheshen's first time. Was she blushing?

As the dance wound down, Homily put a hand over her chest and caught her breath. There was such gratitude in that face. Then, Shesheshen was sure she was smitten. She wanted to spend the entire night devouring everyone in this dance hall with Homily.

That would take some explaining. Breaking that she was not a totally normal human would take work.

She started by swallowing, and coming in close as though for another dance. Homily's lips quivered for some reason.

Shesheshen said, "I'm glad I fell off that cliff."

Homily held insistently on to Shesheshen's shoulders, even though they were not dancing to the next tune. This was another action, like dance, except not. Shesheshen held on in turn, and said, "You dislike these people as much as I do. You don't want to stay in this town."

Homily looked askew, at a spot of wall where no one waited. "I . . . I really don't. But what can we do?"

"My home is humble. It does not have fancy beds and lying mirrors. It also does not have people who treat you wrong."

"Isn't that too much?"

"Going there without you would be too much."

Homily fetched her book. In short order they were aboard her wagon, this time sitting side by side, sharing warmth.

CHAPTER ELEVEN

It was much nicer tonight than last night, and not just because Shesheshen wasn't dying of poison this time. The clouds had run away, ceding the sky to the moon's dominance and the tapestries of the cosmos. All those planets and stars twinkled like motes of sapphire dust, casting a sweet blue light over the highway. The fields had never looked so deeply green, not even after the strongest rains. Like piles upon piles of gems, they could have been a wyrm's hoard.

Shesheshen had her gem already. She and Homily huddled together on the wagon, with a blanket draped across their backs as though they were one creature with four shoulders. Soon, they sat close enough that their joint creature only had two. An iron mace jostled between their legs, rusted but hefty, something Homily traveled with in case of bandits. It was quaint. Shesheshen was so excited that she didn't bother arguing about there being no bandits on the isthmus.

It was a hardy blanket, made of something sterner than sheep or alpaca. Shesheshen had never eaten a fiber like it, nor did she eat it now. She merely occasionally licked it, when Homily wasn't looking, to figure out what it was. Definitely some mammal fiber. It kept their body heat circulating, so that the two warmed each other. Was this why humans shared beds so much? Because it reminded them, ever so vaguely, of when they had nested inside their parents?

It had to end. You could not love someone like this—could not make them a nest from which your children would one day burrow out—while deceiving them. That would be truly untoward. A rare person like Homily deserved to be informed before her body was turned into a nest.

How was she supposed to do this? For years she'd fantasized about prying a limb or two into the perfect mate's flank and shapeshifting parts of herself into slimy eggs. But would it work? Would she naturally produce the eggs the way they were supposed to? What if she made them wrong?

She'd never actually created an egg, since she'd never had anyone who felt like a true parent worthy of them. Instantly her abstinence felt like a mistake.

As they rounded the south bank of the highway, and were sheltered from the moonlight by umbrella-shaped stone pines, Shesheshen fiddled words together.

"Do you ever dress up as someone you're not?"

"Like a costume party?" The heat was obvious in Homily's cheeks, despite the emerald hue of the evening light. "I haven't been to one since I was a child. It was tremendous fun. I played a vampire."

"You know vampires aren't the only mythical creature that eats people."

"I have a book about that," Homily said, removing one hand from the reins to grope around in one of her crates. She plopped a thick, illustrated tome into Shesheshen's lap. "There's a theory that all human-eating creatures are descendants of the same single beast. They see a lot of phylogenic differences. But something like a vampire isn't a species unto itself. It's a curse that merely alters an existing creature. It's a disease rather than a genus."

Internally she cursed every god, above and below alike, who had ever helped humans develop language. What a mess this was.

She tried, "What I meant was . . ."

Homily leaned into her side, all the pliable flesh and body heat that made Shesheshen's internal organs malfunction pleasantly. The human woman said, "I can't believe we're doing this. I've never spontaneously fled in the middle of the night before."

"That's not so odd. Night is very similar to day. All the same things are on the ground. Just different things in the sky."

"How are you so funny?" Homily asked, putting up a palm. This time Shesheshen knew what it meant. "I can't believe we're doing this."

Shesheshen put a palm against that one, and they held their hands that way for a longer moment. She said, "It is kind of . . . pleasant."

"What if the wagon breaks? What if we run into highland bandits?"

"There are no bandits in the isthmus. You know, on account of the Wyrm of Underlook. She makes them feel less social. Which . . ."

There was actual concern in Homily's eyes. She gestured to the mace handle resting against her knee. "The monster doesn't scare you? Living all alone?"

Shesheshen pulled her hand away so she could make fists in the blanket, for no good reason. It wasn't like she could punch the oncoming truth. "I feel like, like you don't understand some things. About me. That I should have said."

"No, no," Homily said, swatting at her own chest, like she had done something wrong by letting Shesheshen speak. That was too human a thing for Shesheshen to understand. "I'm the one who should cough it up. I'm sorry, Siobhan."

"We don't have to apologize."

"I do. You fell into the river, and the next thing you knew I was caring for your injuries. You probably think I'm some sort of angel. I'm not."

"I like you better than angels. In most stories, angels are very violent."

"You see? Because we just met, and you're still sick from your wounds. I'm not some sweetheart. And I kind of let that impression get away from us."

"Homily, I'm not that simple. I . . ."

Homily brought both hands up to her scarf, clutching it like it was the only thing that kept her head on her shoulders. "Siobhan, the truth is . . ."

"There's a toll on this road."

The voice came out of nowhere.

Which wasn't true. It came from somewhere, and Shesheshen hadn't been paying attention. Neither had Homily, given how she swung around looking.

Out of the emerald fields emerged three figures. Two were on horseback, their horses' manes like raw brass under the moon, riding near either side of the wagon's bench. They must've ridden out from Underlook Forest far south off of the highway while Shesheshen had been distracted. Now they got close enough that they could reach Homily or Shesheshen.

All three of them dressed alike, wrapped in black cloaks. Black never blended in with night, as Shesheshen had learned from many failed disguise attempts. These figures wore it like they meant to be seen. Each wore an oakenwood mask, with holes carved for the eyes and frowning mouths. They gave the impression of a macabre theater troupe.

The third figure strutted out on foot, walking straight up to the wagon and blocking the road. She stroked one of the oxen's faces, drawing it to stop. The ox snuffled and went still.

That masked woman said, "You two gab birds are out late. It's lucky you came across us and not some criminals. My name is Aristocracy."

Shesheshen said, "My name is—"

They did not care what her name was. Aristocracy talked over her, "These are my workmates, Plutocracy and Kleptocracy. Welcome to the toll station."

The entire wagon creaked as Homily rose halfway to standing. "A toll station? Out here?"

"It keeps things maintained. You can sit back down. It'll go easier that way."

The color in Homily's face defied the emerald romance of the night. "From whom do you have authority to establish a toll station here? The isthmus doesn't belong to any nation."

Through her mask, Aristocracy rolled her eyes. She already sounded bored talking. "This highway and all the towns it connects owe fealty to the Wulfyre family."

"Do you have a writ from the Wulfyres? About your right to establish a toll station here?"

"Of course I do, madame. It's right here."

The human called Aristocracy stepped away from the oxen and used a gloved hand to raise her cloak from her left hip. There was no scroll or notice hanging there. However, there was a very convincing short sword.

Her workmates on horseback put their hands on their own swords. One clicked his blade so that it unsheathed halfway, catching moonlight on the edge.

For her part, Aristocracy merely tapped the hilt of her sword, letting it clank. She said, "If you look close enough, you'll see it's signed. Would you like to look closely?"

Slowly, Homily sat down onto the bench. Her hand lit on the seat's lip, near a lump in the blankets that hid her mace. Her voice was brittle. "That will be all right. There doesn't need to be violence."

"I agree. Plutocracy? Kleptocracy? Let's see what they have to pay the toll."

The two masked goons directed their horses even closer, until hay breath breezed over Shesheshen's skin and the brim of her hat. The goon nearest to her—she guessed that one was Plutocracy—grabbed onto the rim of the wagon and leaned to look inside all the crates aboard. He paid no heed to Shesheshen herself, like they were both shoppers at an open market.

It would've been so easy. He had a long shirt on, with a collar that covered the lump of his throat. If she thrust two bones out through her shoulder and under the man's wooden mask, through that collar, Plutocracy would bleed out before he could define his form of government. From the slopes of his shoulders under his cape, he had the kind of meat on him she needed tonight.

So she was wrong about there being no bandits in the isthmus. But if they all had that much meat on them, then she wouldn't mind being wrong.

But Kleptocracy mounted Homily's side of the wagon too, and he kept a hand on his short sword the whole time. Surviving a stab wound was not Shesheshen's concern. The concern was how to get to each of them without one of them harming Homily.

And if her biting off a bunch of people's heads was how Homily learned her identity, it would probably stifle their relationship. Romance was awful. She couldn't even do something as simple as murdering rude people anymore.

Plutocracy said, "What the hell? It's mostly books."

Aristocracy said, "Flip through them. Not the first people to hollow out books to smuggle things along the highway."

The bench creaked as Homily twisted, watching with concern as the so-called toll workers brutalized her book collection. "They're not hollow. They're for research. It's a collection of histories and biologies."

Kleptocracy dropped a third book onto a loose pile. It toppled off the rear end of the wagon and splashed into the murk of the road. "I don't feel anything in any of these."

Aristocracy clucked her tongue. "Unlikely to have much resell value unless we travel far out of our way. Take anything that looks better than that. They have to have something else."

Glass clinked against glass, and Homily blanched. Both of the toll workers shoved the crates of books over, earning more rattling sounds. Below were a set of different crates, packed with straw, harboring dozens of bottles. Fluids sloshed inside each, under corks and waxed seals.

"Found the liquor cabinet," said Plutocracy, with a tone like he'd drink anything that dripped. "They always hide good shit at the bottom."

There was the threatening *shlick*ing sound of a blade drawing, and Aristocracy climbed up between the oxen. The moonlight obscured her face through the holes in her mask, like she was raw darkness underneath. "You held out on us?"

"It's not liquor," Homily said, one hand trying to reach out to three people at once. She had too few hands. "Please don't open those."

She had too few hands, but one was sneaking toward that mace.

Kleptocracy swirled one bottle up in the moonlight. It was a deep amber color, and thick for a liquid. "Maybe perfume?"

Homily said, "Those are animal urine samples. The tag will tell you if it's from a predator, or from the favorite prey of a predator. I strongly don't recommend opening them unless you want skunks to mate with your neck."

All the wooden masks around them hesitated. Kleptocracy's grip moved to the neck of the bottle, like he was about to swing it and shatter the bottle over Homily's head. "You better have something better than that."

Aristocracy said, "We'll take what bottles look good to us and decide what's piss. But what about what's on you two? Is that scarf valuable? Do you have rings? Show me your hands."

Submission and silence were not working. Shesheshen shifted on her side of the bench, at once trying to form fingers out of her flesh to show these bandits that they were empty, and trying to form them into bony spikes she could stab with. It was difficult to make up her mind.

Her indecision ruined everything. In her shifting, the bestiary book fell out of her lap, thunking off the wagon and landing in the weeds with a cloud of rock dust. In the faint green light, there was visible an illustration of a vivisected snake.

All three wooden masks whipped at her, their shadowy frowns growing into grimaces in the dark.

"What was that?" Aristocracy asked. "What did you drop there? Think you can sneak something by us?"

At least two swords whipped up, long white triangles that pointed at her. She rose in her seat to make herself a better target. Let them all bury their blades in her body, so Homily could get clear.

"Get away from her," Homily said, and swung the mace. It thunked against Aristocracy's mask, and pieces of wood sprayed the oxen below them. The blanket came with it, fluttering between the two women as the mace and the short sword clanged together.

Plutocracy and Kleptocracy sprang to the rear of the bench, flashing their swords. "You b—" one of them said, and neither of them finished, since they were foolish enough to position themselves out of Homily's sight.

This had to be how humans felt when they took off their girdles and brassieres. Shesheshen let her bulk unfurl, tearing her sleeves and forcing every tissue fiber to go rigid, jutting out the bones inside. Before either toll worker could turn, her wrist bones shredded the flesh at the base of their necks and skewered on through. She forced finger bones onward until they severed spinal columns and poked out through the skin. Folds of flesh wrapped around their masked faces, muffling the last sounds they ever made.

Homily howled, falling off her side of the wagon. The last bandit had her by the hair, climbing atop her, her sword hidden between their bodies. The mace thumped to the ground.

Shesheshen leaped over both of them, aiming for the masked woman. Artlessly, she brought both legs down on Aristocracy's neck and jaw. The three of them fell together, their combined weight drilling Aristocracy into the ground. Her face flattened so violently under heel that Shesheshen drooled. This was working up an appetite.

This wasn't a time to eat. Not yet. Shesheshen kicked the covers from her feet, trying to find Homily.

"Are you hurt? You're in here somewhere."

Homily limped up, resting one side against the wagon's front wheel. She held a hand over her shoulder. "Don't worry. I'll be fine."

So that was how she sounded when she lied. The fingers clasping her shoulder were slicked red.

Shesheshen fled to her, putting one of her own clammy hands over the wound. "No . . ."

"It's a flesh wound. It deflected off the shoulder bone. I'll be fine."

Shesheshen could not look away from those fingers. She wanted to lick them clean, and spend the rest of her life protecting that shoulder. This was her fault, for lying wrong. If she'd confessed sooner, secrecy wouldn't have felt necessary. Homily wouldn't be bleeding.

Even with both of them squeezing on the shoulder, the bleeding had not stopped. It was the worst warmth she'd ever felt from Homily. Her stomachs juggled inside her, all threatening to rupture and dissolve her. She had to think.

She said, "We need to get you somewhere."

Homily pushed from the wagon wheel, leaning her nose in against Shesheshen's shoulder. It was like when they'd danced, except much colder.

With a weak smile, the woman said, "Got a ravine for me to fall into?"

Stone pines were still in sight, and the weeds weren't as strong here. Perhaps two miles still lay between them and the safety of her home. The pleasant cover of walls and ceiling that she could trust. On a deep, animal level, she needed that stability. As many problems as it would bring.

She helped Homily toward the wagon again and said, "Hang onto me. We are almost home."

CHAPTER TWELVE

It was the first cleaning the threshold had seen since before Shesheshen had been born, and the first thing Shesheshen did was smear her girlfriend's blood on it. It was unintentional. That made it no less offensive. She'd fought the entire trip here to not lick the blood off her hand. At her distress at smearing it, her body reflexively absorbed some of the blood through her pores. It was a fight to ignore how full-bodied and tangy the love of her life tasted.

She had to think about anything else. Homily was waiting in the wagon, and needed to come inside soon. To be warm. To be safe. To be home.

"Laurent!" Shesheshen bellowed, her esophageal passage collapsing halfway through the name. She didn't have to put up as human a front here. "You better not be laying traps for me, or you're the one who'll die in them."

The foyer was so different she might have stepped into the wrong lair. Purple carpets unfurled down the hallways, covering broken floor tiles. Colors blurred and bobbled in the flickers of candlelight. She owned no candles, yet in the center of the foyer there stood three candelabras made from a burgundy-stained wood. Each was carved to have seven perilously thin candle stems, though not one bowed under the weight of its milky wax candles. The chorus of wick lights accentuated the arches of the ceiling, which were missing most of their cobwebs and moss. She found arches overhead she'd never seen.

"I did everything I could. I wish you'd given me more time," said the man who had once been Laurent. His shirt sleeves were rolled up and still badly dirtied, and his hands were scuffed to misery. He'd used three of the rings in his hair to tie it all into a messy bun.

Shesheshen's throat rattled in threat. This had to be an illusion. Her actual home would be a disaster too unfit and too unclean for the injured Homily. “What did you do?”

“Got four of the best maintenance people I know, and broke off two fingernails,” he said, worrying at his thumb. “Most of this is what we brought with us. These candelabras were in a storage room. I know you said to only do the first three rooms on the right, but I didn’t have anything to work with. You have to give an artist color, you know?”

She did not know. She did not invoke artists often. This might have been her first commissioned art.

The chamber’s orange light gave it a funny feeling. It was warmer than usual in here, perhaps from the latent body heat of all the labor that had happened in the space. It was certainly more welcoming than Shesheshen usually permitted it to be.

She poked at one of the candelabras and asked, “Would you say yes if someone proposed marriage in here?”

“I . . . I don’t know. This is all so sudden. I know I’m well to do, and have an effect on women, but do you feel like . . .”

“I’m not asking you to marry me. I’m asking if this room is suitably romantic.”

“Of course you aren’t.” He sounded off. That was too much. She would figure that out later. “Can my people go home? Everyone is exhausted. And, actually, terrified. I said you’d lay eggs in them if they didn’t comply.”

She twisted her head at him, baring Catharsis Wulfyre’s teeth. “You did?”

“It was the only way to get help that fast.”

“Go into your room with them. Wait until I say you can go.”

“Yes, madame.”

Did he sound a little excited?

No, she didn’t have time to examine his fetishes. She had surgery to perform.

As it was safe, she hurried to bring Homily indoors. They had wadded up the blanket to stop her wound, and it dragged like a gruesome bridal train across the lair’s floor. For someone who was critically injured, she had a winsome smile.

"I love the lighting, and the . . ." Homily swallowed, looking up at the gaping hole in the ceiling. The old tree that had planted its roots through the hole blocked most of the moonlight, branches swaying instead of stars twinkling. "The natural airflow."

Shesheshen had never felt less equipped for talking. She guided the human woman into the first room, and pulled the pillow off the bed so she could sit on the floor. They pulled candles nearer so they could examine how closed the wound was. It took several moments to separate the jerkin from her body, each motion eliciting a hiss. Humans were not built for hissing. That was too evident in each sound.

"Leave this," Homily said, pinching the folds of the scarf closed beneath her chin. She raised her elbows, though, to let her chest be exposed.

"Of course," Shesheshen said. "It is your neck. You make its decisions."

Underneath the jerkin was a corset made with a funny, flat bone the color of old fingernails, although this was much more durable. Freckles spilled from the scarf all the way across Homily's shoulders and to the bulging flesh at the top of that corset. She was slippery with perspiration, and fabric fibers and stray hair clung to the wound. It was not closing. Blood welled immediately upon exposure, sending a red streak down the thick creases of her back and under her corset.

Shesheshen clasped both hands over the wound, leaning more of her weight onto it. Homily's whine made her feel guilty, like she might as well have been holding the short sword herself right now.

Homily asked, "How bad is it?"

She easily could have gotten her fingers more than two knuckles deep inside that thing. She had rent people's limbs with shallower purchase. And worse, Homily's flesh was turning a flavorful pink.

"Siobhan . . . ?"

"I have something for this. Please, hold still for me."

Did she have something for this?

Well, she had one thing. She had an idea.

For decades she had ingested mammals of all sorts. She intuitively turned their skin and muscle and sinew and blood into her own unique flesh, as naturally as violinists turned strings into music. And since before she could walk, she had shapeshifted her flesh into whatever she wanted. Her body was as versatile as her imagination. If she wanted legs, she grew them. If she wanted to look human, she could. With enough study, she often grew useful organs.

Was it so different to turn some of herself into what Homily lacked?

She loosened some of the epidermis in her right palm, thinking of all the times she'd been stabbed. The best memory was the stitches—some still stuck in her chest, even though the wound had closed on its own. Homily had sewn her up, not knowing that Shesheshen was her own stitches.

Feeling the swollen and slick and bleeding wound on Homily's shoulder, she focused on the sensation of the stitches in her own body. On the sensation of not needing them. On filling her own gaps, so that she was woundless.

That way, her hand kissed Homily's wound. The flesh dripped away from her, still pale and gray and hairless, not what most humans fancied. Its edges pinkened. She squeezed it, staring, demanding that she take the shape of healing.

"Oh," Homily moaned, inappropriately. It should have been a pained moan. Instead, it was a moan like she'd tasted unexpectedly nice tea. "What is that? A clove salve?"

"It's a family remedy."

Shesheshen kneaded across it for several moments, and wiped the old blood away. That gift of her flesh succumbed, becoming as pliable as the rest of the human woman's shoulder. Then she tore a strip off her own gray dress and folded it twice over the wound. That would keep it private.

It was a strange feeling, abruptly being unable to feel her flesh. The dollop of herself that closed Homily's wound no longer answered to her. It was Homily's skin now.

Shesheshen leaned forward, resting her forehead against the human woman's bare back. She wondered how much of herself she could give. How her eggs might feel inside this splendid nest of a person. The way Homily's hair tickled at her skin made Shesheshen's insides churn.

Homily touched at the fabric covering her wound. "It doesn't hurt at all. Is there a numbing agent? And without sutures?"

"You won't need to sew. It will encourage your body to suture itself."

There was a shift, and Homily reclined, resting the heavy curves of her back against Shesheshen. "I didn't know you were an actual witch when I gave you that hat."

Shesheshen was new to this, but she caught that Homily's tone was sly. She was being playful. That had to mean she wasn't in danger anymore.

Shesheshen tried being sarcastic back. "I can't promise I'm a good witch."

"Come on," Homily said, reaching behind herself with her good arm. The hand squeezed Shesheshen's knee. "You brought me into your humble home. You probably saved my life tonight with this medicine of yours."

Another shift, and Homily twisted and sat in front of her, the warmth of her body offering to pull all of her inside. Shesheshen thought she might like that. Being dissolved had never been so appealing.

Homily started, "We were going to have a talk in the wagon. Before Aristocracy attacked."

Shesheshen said, "Yes. I wanted to tell you something. I am not a witch."

"I'm sorry I didn't tell you sooner," Homily said, hand going to her throat through the scarf. "I get self-conscious."

"If you weren't conscious of yourself, who would you be conscious of?"

This time when Homily laughed, all the ripples in her large body resonated against Shesheshen. It was better than warmth. It was hypnotic. It was a generosity of skin, like all of Homily was consensually shapeshifting for her, taking the form of shelter. Together, they were like the waves on the seashore.

Homily said, "You are amazing. So I want to tell you."

Shesheshen had to tell Homily about her nature. It was time. But she had to wait her turn. Love, she thought, was about patience.

Homily traced a line over her scarf, like she wanted to draw on herself. "The people in town treated me differently because they're afraid of my mother. Afraid of my entire family, really. They avoided speaking to us, and letting us pay for things, because they think one cross word could ruin them. My name is Homily Wulfyre. My family technically owns the barony of this isthmus."

Parting her lips, Shesheshen tapped a finger against her teeth. They were not really her teeth. "Wulfyre?"

A bashful look sprinted across Homily's face, turning her ten years younger for a moment. "Of course you've heard of us. Everyone in Underlook has. But I promise, I'm not like them. Not like my mother, or my older brother. And the rumors about us are overblown."

"Your oldest brother?"

"Yes. Catharsis Wulfyre. You'd know him if you met him. He never leaves L'État Bon without donning that ridiculous gold armor. He's a lady's man."

Shesheshen sucked her lips closed, wondering how best to hide her teeth. "Yes. I would remember."

Heaving a breath, Homily slumped more weight onto Shesheshen. "Catharsis is around here, somewhere. He left for Underlook a day before I did. He's supposed to be hunting the great monster of the region. The wyrm. But I haven't seen him yet. I bet he's drugged out of his mind and at the bottom of a pile of lovers right now."

This plump, adoring woman was related to the gold-plated fish-drowner? The one who'd stabbed and poisoned her in her own home?

It wasn't possible. Shesheshen's mind threatened to melt and leak out of her orifices. Every thought she tried to begin dug its barbs into her psyche and refused to leave.

Homily said, "We need him to hunt this monster, though. Our whole family does."

Shesheshen retreated several inches. "You do?"

Homily straightened out of her slump, eyes going icily sincere. "This is why I didn't tell you. Why I don't want to get close without you knowing. The entire Wulfyre family shares this curse."

A curse. It must've been a curse that befell Shesheshen, as the whole of her world was resonating. The world was a bell and it was ringing. None of this made sense. It wasn't possible. She refused this curse.

"You said you've lived out here all your life. Any information you have about how this monster actually behaves, well, could save my life. You see, the Wyrm of Underlook cursed the entire Wulfyre line. It said that first our rule and holdings would dwindle, and then all of us would die until our line was erased. Now the Wulfyre family lives off-isthmus, in a small protectorate of L'État Bon near Boletar. My Aunt Agatha died of inexplicable causes. The curse is coming. My mother, myself, and my siblings? We're next."

Shesheshen asked, "You will all die?"

Homily put a hand over the cloth on her shoulder and drew a shuddering breath. "You see, that's why I'm here. I followed my brother, figuring he wouldn't take this seriously enough. I was down in the ravine using scent lures hoping to find the wretched monster. It's already plagued the land for long enough. It's killed so many people—people you've probably known. And if I don't get its heart, one of my siblings will be the next to die. It might be me. So please, I know this is a lot to ask, but perhaps after we've rested, help me find this thing."

PART THREE

A PRIVATE VIOLENCE

CHAPTER THIRTEEN

Shesheshen fled into the part of her lair that wasn't tarnished by civilization. None of it shined or was polished. No soaped carpets or illumination by needlessly ornate lighting fixtures. Rats' nests crumbled underfoot, along with the remains of chairs and unloved halves of skeletons. Her feet kicked through everything until she gave up on having feet at all, and unspooled her lower half into a series of tails.

She writhed and thrust open the door to the hot spring, where mist clogged the air. Laurent hadn't tidied up this end of her life. Scum floated and congealed along the surface of the waters, like a wide scab. Neither her damaged eye nor her undamaged one could see through its murk.

This was what she needed.

She dove into the depths, grabbing onto stones to anchor herself. She grew more limbs to dig at the mud of the bottom, seeking to bury herself underneath the pool. When she couldn't get any deeper, she let herself scream.

She screamed until the air bubbles rushed around her so rapidly it felt like the water was boiling. She screamed until her artificial lungs collapsed, and then she coughed the lung tissue out and spat it into the water. One more breath in the rest of her life would be too much. One more pretense of humanity.

Her lungs weren't enough. She gouged at herself, plunging claws into her skin and ripping out organs. Out went Catharsis Wulfyre's lower jaw, and his cracked skull. Out went the hooves of sheep, and the ribs of pigs. The many fine bones that had once seemed such a good idea to build fingers from? What had she touched with those fingers that she didn't regret now? She threw her own hands away.

Still, all that tearing didn't expel the worst part of her.

Still, in the depths of the pool, Homily's smile haunted her. The human woman's body heat, and the gentle way she wielded her size and her softness. The soup she'd made. The attentiveness.

You could not excrete memories. They could not be surgically removed. It was unjust. She was badly designed. Had her mother been around to raise her, Shesheshen would know how to carve this part out of herself.

Of course Homily was a Wulfyre. It made cruel sense. Homily had bragged about her scent lures, and about reading texts on arcane creatures. She had lured Blueberry into a trap meant for Shesheshen, and then lured Shesheshen herself in with false kindness. This human woman had made unkind bait out of the feeling that Shesheshen shouldn't be alone.

Companionship. That was civilization's trap and snare.

And Shesheshen had stepped right into it.

The people of Underlook didn't avoid Homily because she was monstrous. They avoided her because none wanted to tell her that her brother was as dead as she would soon be. That she was great and mighty and doomed.

She was doomed, and cursed. How exactly was Homily cursed? Shesheshen knew no magic. She'd never cursed anything, much less an entire family line. Although, if she could, she probably would've picked the Wulfyres for sending so many assassins after her. Truly she was the one cursed by that family's persecutions, and their apparent desire for her heart.

Shesheshen did not even own a heart. She ate hearts. The Wulfyres wanted her blood? The only blood that ever coursed through her body was borrowed. She'd hunt the last of them down, so their blood was hers. That would be her curse on them.

Damned ignorant humans thought they knew everything, when all they did was ruin everything.

She knew what she had to do. Her home was unsafe with that human woman in it. Killing Homily would hurt worse than any lance of rosemary. But Shesheshen had hurt before, and survived.

The pains of stitching herself back together were her punishment for being so foolish. She spent so many trembling minutes digging finger bones and vertebrae out of the muck. It was harder to undo the self-dismemberment, all that carnage that she should've subjected the Wulfyres to instead. Legs had never been so hard to grow as this time when she had to swim up and face destiny. As she broke the water, she formed two humanoid hands, and used them to force Catharsis Wulfyre's jaw back into her mouth.

As she fixed the wig and witch's hat on her head, she spied the most important organ. Her old bear trap. It reminded her of her mother's precious steel fangs. Those two pointed fangs made up the one memory she had of her mother. Monster hunters had slain her and taken any other chances at memories away.

She forced the bear trap inside her chest. This would give her lover the right kind of kiss.

She passed through hallways, across where she'd killed Catharsis. The death stains were missing. Laurent had done too good a job. That spot should have remained marked.

Homily's door was ajar, casting candlelight out into the hallway. Shesheshen slowed as she approached the reach of that light, and peered inside. This was the last time she would come upon this woman.

Atop the sheets, atop her bed, the human woman lay on her back. Her feet were up in the air, soles resting against the wall, unshaven legs jutting from her skirts. Lying that way, she peered up at a book that she balanced on her bosom, squinting at whatever the words were telling her. Her eyes narrowed further, and further, in the beginnings of a doze. Light snores started to spill from her, each time ending in a sucking sound, like she was pulling the sounds back inside herself. It was an animal grinding noise. It was a thing Shesheshen could have listened to for a lifetime.

In a different lifetime, she told herself. Not this one. She had to do this.

Shesheshen loomed over the bed, stretching an arm behind herself and forcing a claw bone out through her palm. What was the quickest method? If she moved the scarf aside, she could get at her jugular.

Homily's breathing slowed and her eyes fluttered at Shesheshen. As soon as recognition crossed her face, she sat up and pulled herself closer with a broad-cheeked smile, and hugged around Shesheshen's waist.

She said, "I'm sorry I conked out. We were so focused on my injury that we never even looked at your sutures. You must be exhausted. Please, let me make you something to eat. I have tea leaves in my wagon. Do you like tea? What kind do you like?"

The claw retreated into Shesheshen's palm before she wanted it to. She curled her fingers over it, wrist trembling. She needed resolve.

Homily squeezed her waist again, peering up at her. "What's wrong? Please tell me you're not sick."

"I . . . I am not sick."

"Seriously. You should rest." Homily sprang up and stared down at the blankets like they were made of fire and landslides. "Don't let me take your bed. I'd never forgive myself. I can sleep on the floor. Floors are good for my hips."

More of Shesheshen was trembling. She needed more bones or she was going to tumble. She put a hand to the bedpost and tried not looking at Homily. She failed. She stared at that sweet expression.

Homily tilted her head like Blueberry did whenever she was confused. "Then what's the matter? Tell me how I can help you."

Shesheshen fell into sitting on the bed, unable to escape the pillowy warmth of this human woman. She tried to move her mouth to say other things. What she said was, "I am trying to figure out how we can hunt your monster."

CHAPTER FOURTEEN

Shesheshen had a plan.

Homily made the two of them hide in a ditch a quarter-mile south from the nearest stretch of the highway, quite the trek from her lair in the north. Two shields of dried and flattened straw served as a roof, creating a blind that would distract wildlife. One end of the roof was propped up three inches, giving them a view of the highway passing into the dense oaks of Underlook Forest.

Homily asked, “You’re sure the monster passes through here?”

Shesheshen stared out through the gap in their hiding place. Birds sang their nonsense about hunger and nest safety, and foxes chased morsels on legs. The feathers of three arrows stuck out of the dirt not far from their hiding spot. She was pretty sure she was sitting on a smashed helmet that had been left here a couple years ago, when monster hunters had dug this particular ditch to ambush the Wyrm of Underlook. It had not gone well for them.

“Oh, I’m sure,” Shesheshen said. “The monster is often here.”

“You see the monster often? If it frequents this area, you’re putting yourself in jeopardy. You have to take care of yourself.”

“I am . . . careful.”

“We’ll just get a look at it today. Nothing reckless.”

The flatland was uneventful for the moment. Homily had left some spare meat out to rot, with a sauce of sheep urine extract she swore would attract the monster. Shesheshen would’ve admired her girlfriend’s intelligence, if she wasn’t using that intelligence to kill her.

Shesheshen also had a plan. But that required waiting a little longer. She leaned a little against the human woman’s side. “I have a question.”

“What’s on your mind?”

“Can you tell me more about this curse you’re under?”

Homily took a sip from her waterskin. "I was just a baby when it happened. Father and Mother used to live in this isthmus, until the wyrm attacked them. Father died, and when Mother tried to avenge him, one of the wyrm's offspring survived and cursed our entire family line. Our power in the isthmus was to wane, and we were each to die as it waned. One by one. It's taken my aunt. Soon it'll come for Mother. And my big brother Catharsis. Eventually myself, and my younger sister Epigram. And the littlest, poor little Ode. This younger wyrm is coming for us all, every bit as vile as the old one. We have to stop it."

So many Wulfyres. And still Shesheshen hadn't broken it to her that Catharsis was dead—and technically, by Shesheshen's doing. That hadn't been a curse, though. It had been self-defense. Self-defense was not a curse, was it?

Shesheshen tried to sound sincere. "Does monster blood fix curses where you are from?"

"It's in all the literature."

"The words on the paper say this monster has blood?"

Homily finally looked at her instead of the highway. "A creature of that size? It might have as many as three hearts to deal with its circulatory system. Once, out in L'État Bon, Mother and Catharsis slew a great wyrm that had that many hearts."

Reflexively, Shesheshen squeezed her own insides. There were a few fluids, and none of them were blood. If anything, she could go for the iron flavor of a few pints right now.

That urge wouldn't help here.

She asked, "Does the monster put lots of curses on people? In your books?"

Homily rested a cheek on a fist. "What would that matter?"

"I've lived here a long time," Shesheshen said, shifting until something poked her hindquarters. Yes, she was definitely sitting on the pointy, broken remains of a helmet. "I don't remember anyone ever being cursed. The monster has many enemies. Many people it might curse if it could."

"Wyrms can curse people, Siobhan," Homily said, like she was correcting a child. "They have grim powers. It probably just hasn't done it in a while because it feasts on most of its victims."

Feasting was a decent solution, most of the time. More efficient than cursing people. Shesheshen had never seen a curse in person. They seemed unavailable. It would be useful to have some at her disposal. That would get Underlook in line.

"Mother remembers it clearly," Homily said, with such remorse that the temperature of their ditch plummeted. She squeezed her eyes closed. "I've heard her tell the tale so many times. How haunted she is by the memory of Father's screaming as the wyrm dragged him away to do unspeakable things to him. That day broke her. Everyone says she was never the same."

As carefully as she could, Shesheshen slipped an arm around the human woman's shoulders. It was the right thing; she knew because Homily heaved a sigh and dried an eye on her sleeve.

It was easier to comfort than argue. Arguing was the hardest version of talking. You could have reasonable points and try to show as much empathy as possible, and lose miserably. At this point the prospect of speaking another sentence made Shesheshen want to burrow into the bottom of this ditch and never come out again. If she had the ability to curse people, she'd have plenty to sling right now.

Homily whispered, "Wait."

Her face drew tight, like a skunk recognizing predators. She pushed her face to the gap in their straw roof. Both of her hands laced together, covering her mouth.

"There it is. Between the trees."

A white shape emerged from the shade of Underlook Forest. Errant sunlight reflected off the swords half-buried in its flank, surely left over from previous monster hunters. Much of its body was coated in white wool, although its head and legs were dirty black. Tall horns rose from the crown of its head, forked in many places, as though threatening to gouge the world.

Shesheshen nodded to herself. Her plan would work.

With hands still covering her mouth, Homily watched the creature. Now she was the one who needed to be reminded to blink.

Then she said, "Wait."

"Is it too horrible to face?"

"Is that a sheep with deer horns tied to its head?"

"What?" Shesheshen pushed in to look at the Wyrm of Underlook. The horns sagged to one side, ready to fall off the sheep's head. But she'd dug the swords really nicely into the wool to simulate battle wounds. Any reasonable human should have been intimidated.

The fearsome monster got within a hundred yards of their carrion bait, then stopped to chew the grass. The sheep was the one ruining the plan.

Shesheshen said, "I think it's distracted. Maybe we could steal its heart. While it's not paying attention."

This monster's heart was not enough, it seemed, since Homily heaved backward and fell on her butt. Her hands climbed up into her hair, fingers dragging white lines on her scalp. "Damn it all. I've been here a week and all I've found is livestock in a costume."

"You're sure that's not your monster?"

Homily's fingers went rigid, digging at her temples. She let out a shuddering breath. "You don't know Mother. If we don't have that thing before she gets here, everyone in Underlook will suffer."

CHAPTER FIFTEEN

Shesheshen left Homily to hide in the ditch for as long as she wanted. There was little danger of encountering any other non-human, non-sheep monsters out there. For now, it was important to let Homily feel like she was doing work that mattered—while not exposing Shesheshen to feeling like she had to die to please her girlfriend.

Separating let Shesheshen return to her lair and make sure no monster hunters were lying in wait. The irony that she had to make sure no monster hunters killed Homily, who was off hunting a monster, made Shesheshen question her own existence. When had she become like this? Skeptics should disbelieve in her. She scarcely believed in herself right now.

Fortunately there were no newcomers in the foyer, short of a particularly noisy hawk that was building a nest in the tree above. She wanted to hunt that thing down for its olfactory system later. As the bird shrilled about threats, Shesheshen put her body to the ground, listening for any heavy bodies in motion.

There were five people on the premises, all in one room on the right. A thrill shot through her; ravaging some lousy humans would improve her day. From their footfalls, they didn't seem heavily armed either.

Then the door opened a crack, and Laurent stuck his head out.

Immediately Shesheshen drooped. Of course. Her hired help hadn't gone home yet. They were probably waiting for mercy from her, the terrible monster.

"Shesheshen, the great and terrible," Laurent said, too breathlessly for her taste. "Some of the workers were wondering if they could, you know, return home."

He remained in the doorway, with only his face poking through, as though he thought the door would protect him. Proving him wrong could've been fun, another time. Now, the mood was soured.

She waved for him to come out whenever he found his courage. "Leave. Take some treasure or whatever you people were already planning to steal as payment."

"We weren't—"

"Lie to me and I will eat your lips."

That shut him up. Laurent slipped into the chamber for a moment, relaying that his crew could depart. There came the scraping and whispering sounds of them collecting belongings.

Laurent came out first. His hair was fussed to a fine style again, curls threaded through rings to fall over one eye. How hard it must have been on him, worrying about dying while poorly dressed.

He asked, "Shesheshen, great and terrible, what are you planning?"

Shesheshen rose until she was taller than him, and dragged her claws along the floor, making those noises that always made humans shiver. "What makes you think I have a plan?"

He flinched against the wall. "I . . . I'm sorry that presuming your intelligence offended you. I'm not sure what I'm supposed to say here."

"What do you think I'm planning?"

"Well, the Baroness will be in town in the next day. I figured you had a vendetta against her family, so you were using her daughter to get close and kill her."

That was too much insight. She rasped in a breath and twisted her head until it was entirely upside down, just to feel her flesh strain. "You knew my guest was a Wulfyre?"

The man pressed himself up against the wall, palms lying flat, probably praying for a secret panel. "Is she not?"

"And you didn't tell me?"

Now Laurent was fighting to breathe. "I'm sorry, great and terrible. The scope of your plans are probably outside human understanding."

They were outside her understanding, too. She slithered in close, exhaling fetid breath from her borrowed lungs. She said, "If I had a plan, which included you and your underlings, what do you think it would be?"

"I can't presume!" he said, eyes locked on her teeth. "If we're part of it, and you're letting us go, right before Baroness Wulfyre arrives, it can't be a coincidence. You would have us all go to Underlook and say you don't live here anymore, so you wouldn't be harassed. Since you obviously want privacy here."

She fully exposed Catharsis Wulfyre's teeth. They were unimpressive human teeth, stained and eroded with no special quality. In her mouth, though, they made this human man gasp.

She said, "Why would you have been here, in this story?"

"That part, well. Perhaps I was pompous and conceited and tried to come up here to attack you, uhm, while you were wounded. Finish what Catharsis started. But we found there were no signs of you."

"No signs of me in my own lair?"

He shook his head like he was denying the current circumstances and the future ones. "Like you hadn't lived here in years. When Catharsis got killed here, it must've been a freak coincidence that you were in the area."

"Instead you saw me in Underlook Forest, and the Baroness's thugs should hunt there. If they're braver than you are." She rotated her head around so that her eyes were above her teeth again. She clicked those teeth together, to make Laurent jump. "I am good at planning, aren't I?"

The human man wiped at his flushed cheeks and gave the most disquieting smile. "Great and terrible."

"You should go check on your underlings. Make sure they know what to say."

Laurent's head bobbed so rapidly that his hair lashed the wall. "They'll know."

"Do you need anything else from me to play your part in the plan?"

Fear swirled into anxious energy in the man, as he fidgeted with his gloved fingers and leaned on one foot. "Well, I wondered, if you could . . ."

"What is it? Do you want a reward?"

That smile of his grew even more disquieting. Almost lascivious. Then came his wheezy, needy laugh.

"Nobody talks to me like this," he said. "Do you think you could threaten me a little more?"

This time, she shrank away from him. All the excitement she'd read in him—and why he'd come out to talk to her in the first place—took on grotesque new context. He wasn't afraid for his life. This was the highlight *of* his life.

Or it was both of those things. She did not understand humans. Today, she did not want to.

Oh, she threatened Laurent. Threatened him right through a door, and out of her lair. He left infuriatingly happy.

CHAPTER SIXTEEN

She followed Laurent and his workers to the highway, out of sight and from an appropriate distance. There was no reason to spook them, not until they were at the road. When their wagon left her weedy overgrown path, she emerged from between two hills. She extended her arms to three times the length of her body—a trick done by shrinking her innards down to minimal tissue. The glimpse of a seemingly tall figure with implausibly long limbs, reaching out between the hills toward them, would remind the men to stick to the plan.

She lingered, letting them think their foreboding thoughts. Her intentions weren't sinister today. She just needed to get rid of some bodies.

All three of the bandits were right where she'd left them on the side of the road, near the footpath leading off the highway and down to Underlook Forest. The bandits had become very popular with the local flies. Scavengers had torn good scraps off of them, but there was still plenty of meat left.

There were more spilled fluids now than on the night of the attack. She had to ingest and sift organic materials out of the dirt, so there wouldn't be any traces of dead humans left. Then she lugged the corpses of Aristocracy, Plutocracy, and whatever the third effete "gentleman rogue" had been called all the way back to her lair. It was sweltering work, even in the cold, making her wish she could sweat through pores the way these humans did.

As she went, a drove of flies followed her, buzzing to ask if she was food like the corpses. She answered by letting them land on her, and sucking them inside through her flesh. She'd hoped they would kill her hunger. Instead, they reminded her how desperately hungry she really was.

Deep below the west end of the ruins was a sodden basement. Once it had been a storehouse, although all the grain had long since rotted, and all the rodents that had fed on it were long eaten by Shesheshen herself. She lugged the corpses down into that stone cellar, where Homily wouldn't find them. In the dankness and the darkness, she had her privacy.

The last wood-masked corpse made a ripe thunk against the floor. This much meat would last her weeks if she ate sparingly, and wasn't poisoned again. If the Baroness posed a real threat, she could gorge to increase her mass and strength, and cow the Wulfyres into submission. Although putting on that much body mass would expose her identity to Homily.

This would be easier if she confessed. There had to be a way to explain to Homily that she wasn't a magic-using, curse-making creature, and that she meant the family no harm if they left her alone. She simply had to bide her time and find the right opening. Homily was so caring. She would understand, wouldn't she?

Thinking about Homily brought a cramp into her chest. Her entire left side tensed, and she reached inside herself to soothe the rigid flesh. Whatever was wrong with her, she'd have to investigate herself after she was properly nourished.

There was too much going on. Too many thoughts she wanted to run away from. Was a life with Homily possible? Would the other Wulfyres figure her out and slay her? Would Laurent expose her? How did she get to happiness from where she stood right now?

All those feelings made the pain inside her swell up like an infection. The physical labor of arranging the corpses didn't help, as her doubts refused to be ignored. They haunted her. She wrapped a tendril around one dead rogue's ankle, and it collapsed, oozing flavorful juices. The tissue underneath had lost all its firmness, threatening to slide off the bone in her grip.

Her innards quivered, and then the next thing Shesheshen knew she was diving face-first into the carnage. The feast was on.

Holding steady on that ankle, she bit into a thigh. With a firm pull she dragged the leg between her jaws, scraping off the meat all the way down to the bottom of the shin, where it spilled into the victim's boot. Then she ate the boot, stuffing it into the corner of a mouth and chewing in a daze.

The muscle tissue within was sweetened from decay, and further up the body the skin was sun-dried and seasoned with insect eggs. There was a surprising amount of scar tissue, so rich and chewy. Every pound of flesh she shoved into her maw was another moment she didn't have to think. The rich panoply made her feel alive again.

Stress was making her gorge. It was a bad habit, usually something that came over her after a bad monster-hunter raid. The battles always left her with many injuries that called for new tissue growth. Was love really so traumatic? Apparently, because by the time she caught herself, there was only one head and a quarter of a torso left. The bandits' entire wardrobe sat in her belly, churning as she tried to figure out what of it was digestible.

She forced herself not to digest some of this material. A couple of new lungs fitted her nicely, and a pancreas couldn't hurt. If she was going to meet Homily's mother and fit in with the humans, she needed an olfactory system. Humans loved complaining about the smells of places. By sheer frequency of behavior, it was their second favorite thing, after going in private to defecate.

Excretion was a good idea here. This was simply too much body mass to pass off as her own around Homily. She rapidly cycled the digesting tissues through her body, into a primordial mass that she could turn into anything she wanted. They could become the ligaments for hands, or crude copies of hearts and stomachs.

Through concentration, she kept the material from becoming anything other than raw tissue. It ached like fast atrophy, but she scraped and eased the matter out of herself—until she'd coughed up nearly half of her own body. It was a slimy, gray lump, oozing green fluids on the floor.

Her new nose let her reflect on it. The smell drove her to a tidal wave of salivation. How badly she wanted to eat this leftover part of herself. Its size awed her—she'd never removed a piece of herself so great before. It pulsed without blood, and quivered without feeling. It was like that sliver of herself she'd used to fix Homily's wound, but with so much more potential. She could mold it into anything, if she took it inside herself again.

If the Baroness Wulfyre turned on her, she'd ingest this mess and become something the entire isthmus would truly fear. No one would come after her again. She would—

"Siobhan? Siobhan, are you home?"

That was Homily's voice. It was far too close, coming from the hallway above.

Shesheshen whirled on the cellar floor, strings of fluid still connecting her and the gray lump. She wasn't dressed. Where was her wig? If she was seen like this, it would be over.

"Siobhan? I caught another few rabbits. Would you like me to make that soup again? It pairs well with a tea I guarantee you'll love. It has mint in it."

"One moment!" Shesheshen tried not to bellow, even though that was the only vocal emotion she could summon right now. "I am not dressed."

It wasn't really a lie. Shesheshen rose, and her chest heaved like a burning ball had stuck in there among her new organs. What the hell was wrong with her?

"Oh!" went Homily, who must have flustered herself half to death. "Do you need a hand? Are your stitches bothering you? I could, um, come give them a look."

Imagining the woman blushing made Shesheshen's innards heat up. She sprang to her feet, grabbing every article of clothing that wasn't coated in digestive juices. She dressed as she raced up the stairs, trying to imagine a good excuse for Homily to not go into that cellar after her.

PART FOUR

THE MERITS OF CIVILIZATION

CHAPTER SEVENTEEN

Having a nose made Shesheshen immediately feel more human, because it let her do what humans liked most: complain.

"Who shat this place out?" she asked as they rode past the lichen-conquered boulders that marked Underlook's town limits. She fanned a hand under her nostrils. "I swear, it's worse than usual. Makes me wish my nose would go deaf."

Of course there were humans with deaf noses, who were spared from the ritual of complaining about whatever they smelled. She wondered how often such people acted normal to avoid harm. She wished she'd studied them more, for her survival hinged on passing, and passing meant socializing.

Controlling this borrowed olfactory system was laborious. Underlook offered the smell of steaming vegetables wafting from windows in equal measure to the smell of animal manure. She did not know how to sort those scents from the notes of lemon layer cakes, and wood smoke and stale chamber pots, and the cloying mineral perfumes humans treated their clothes with. How did humans sort what odors to focus on?

"I rather like it." Homily tilted her head back, drawing in a deep breath that swelled her chest. Her loose hair tumbled down the slope of her back. "You can smell the horses, and people working and playing. You can almost taste the food on the smoke. This is what life smells like."

Shesheshen wasn't ready for that. Homily had another way of sidestepping humanity's penchant for complaining: enjoying herself. People could simply choose not to hate things.

Shesheshen wasn't used to them making that choice. Adjusting to it would take work.

She could start, though, by being honest.

She said, "I do not usually have a sense of smell. I was not born with full nasal passages. When I can smell, I might look down on it and make fun of it sometimes to make it feel less special."

"I had a housemate with a similar disability," Homily said. "I'm sorry if I made you self-conscious, too. Thank you for coming all the way out here with me. And helping me fit into this dress."

It wasn't truly a dress. It combined an Engmarese dress jacket with rumpled sleeves alongside a corset and flowing skirt, mostly of solid black fabric with stripes of eggshell white. It was a decent idea that became stunning on Homily. None of its angles hid her size; it celebrated her, and brought the eye to her full shoulders and hips. Whenever she ran fingers through her curls or adjusted her scarf, the sleeves tumbled like attendants at her whim. Shesheshen thought that if she could command black and white like this, then she should never wear color again.

The only thing that broke up the outfit was that green scarf, trailing down her back. The woman never seemed to remove it.

Shesheshen said, "It's no issue. I'm used to tailoring clothing on short notice."

She herself was dressed more conservatively, in an emerald cloak offset by a beige sun hat. The sun hat's brim curled down on the left side, which Homily said was fashionable in some of the island kingdoms off Engmar's shores.

As they finished tying the horses and left their wagon, Homily said, "I just need to make a good impression on Mother."

"I am ready to behave."

"This isn't about you. You're wonderful." Homily started to reach for Shesheshen, then stopped. "I keep choking on this. But I need to tell you about Mother. She is a lot to handle."

"Does she have the normal amount of human hands?"

That got Homily to laugh so abruptly that she lost her balance and tipped over. Shesheshen caught her by the arms, letting her lean as much weight as she liked. It was a pleasant pressure.

Homily said, "Okay, okay. You're invincible."

"I would like to be. I would pick even more fights."

"Mother is a profoundly political person, and she takes everything personally. It's best not to say much around her."

"I love not talking," Shesheshen said, fixing the shoulders of Homily's jacket. "You do not talk with your mother?"

"Conversation is not something she's interested in. She is someone you hear and follow."

"You are not supposed to respond?"

"If she takes offense, she will find ways to hurt everyone around you. She has political connections throughout the border countries, on both sides. Both Engmar and L'État Bon want her to give the isthmus to them. We need to make sure she doesn't bring more pain to the isthmus. We need to hurt as few people as we can. Just the monster."

Just the monster. That comment stung. She was just a monster who had never known a harsh mother. The wilderness raised her.

Homily's eyes trailed over Shesheshen's face with all the comfort of warm fluid trickling out of a wound. For a moment, Shesheshen worried that the hurt she felt had made her warp her body. Were her eyes still in the right places? Had she accidentally gotten rid of her mouth?

Homily was looking past her. She stepped around her, shielding her from the street with the shadow of her body. There was ample traffic out there, with bakers dragging carts of needlessly fragrant pastries and carriages of fine wood and metal. None of it seemed that scary. Shesheshen didn't need to be protected from a tray of tarts.

Someone was looking their way. A human loitered in the doorway of a cafe, her golden breastplate and matching greaves drinking up all the sunlight on the road. She was flanked on either side by feminine young men who stared at her with a mixture of adoration and anxiety. Her red velvet tunic and breeches made it an almost a casual adaptation of military dress. It flattered the short blonde hair that fanned around her delicate cheeks. She looked so familiar.

It was not Catharsis Wulfyre. For one thing, Shesheshen still had Catharsis's jaw in her head. For another, this was almost certainly a woman, and she was far too young. She could've been under twenty winters. She was more like someone dressing up as their childhood hero.

"So you are alive," said the woman in gold and red velvet, dismissing her admirers with a shove to one's chest. She swaggered into the street, sending horses rearing and wheeling as riders forced them to stop. Without a glance at the people she'd dismayed, she addressed Homily. "Who would've thought you'd survive the family curse so long?"

Homily cast her gaze down rather than at the woman. How badly Shesheshen wanted to reach over Homily's shoulder and lift her chin. That chin should never submit, especially not to humans who belonged dead under hooves.

Instead Shesheshen moved behind Homily, close enough for the woman to feel she was there. It was an unspoken offer to lean on her—to invite consensual touch and support. How she wanted to touch that healed shoulder, to remind them of the dark things they'd survived together.

Homily shied from the touch, taking a deep breath and focusing on the woman. She said, "Epigram. I'm glad to see you alive, too."

Shesheshen said, "Epigram?"

Homily gestured to the gilded woman. "This is Epigram Wulfyre. My next youngest sister."

"I'm the one who's going to make this family really famous," Epigram said with an insincere bow. "I'm sure you've heard of me and my older brother. We're the wyrm slayers in the family."

Homily asked, "Did you bring many soldiers with you from L'État Bon?"

At this distance Epigram's armor looked like it had been gilded rather than built out of gold. She pushed around Homily's side, eyeing up Shesheshen like she was prey. "And who's this?"

"I am not interested," Shesheshen said. "That is who I am."

Epigram twitched, jostling her short hair around her eyes. "Excuse me?"

"Your sister asked you a question." It was one Shesheshen wanted answered too; it would be useful to know how big an army was coming after the heart she didn't have.

Epigram wrapped a hand around the knife on her belt, the rubies of its pommel glittering as she came closer. Her steps were light for someone in partial armor as she moved toward Shesheshen. This was not the first impression Shesheshen had wanted to make. She needed to get better at talking.

Homily stepped in the way of their first impression, leading with her injured shoulder. One thick arm wrapped under Epigram's elbows, stopping her. "Siobhan here is recovering from a grave injury. Please don't take offense. Let's go see Mother together."

"You don't touch me!" Epigram shrieked. Her face warped like she was a shapeshifting monster herself, eyes widening until they could've fallen out of her head. "You abandoned our family. You don't touch me."

The way Homily shrank, it was easy to forget that she was the taller sibling. Homily retreated until her back thudded against the wooden wall of a shed. Her cheeks trembled and she clutched at her scarf, as though Epigram was choking her with her eyes.

Epigram said, "You left Ode and me to deal with Mother alone this whole time. Do you know what a mess she is?"

"I came to Underlook hunting the wyrm. I've been out in the ravine and the forest for days, gathering information about the creature. Hearsay and legend aren't going to break the curse for us."

"Mother sent you an order. Were you ignoring family orders? Don't you do enough to piss her off?"

"I said—"

"You and I," Epigram interrupted, grabbing at the scarf around Homily's neck, "we're going to have a conversation. In private. *After* you apologize to Mother."

Shesheshen would've considered an uppercut a polite response. She was willing to turn this little sister into a three-course meal, if Homily would look the other way.

Homily's actual response was a whispered, "Where is Mother now?"

"Where do you think? Look for the center of everything that matters. And don't make us look for you again." Then Epigram was stepping into the street, turning the ire of her gaze on Shesheshen. "Whoever you are, you can do better than my sister. Get clear of her before it's too late."

Shesheshen didn't care what this particular woman did next. She went to Homily's side, offering more touches that the woman didn't accept. She had to help somehow.

"Homily. What do you need right now?"

"I'm fine," Homily said, still too quiet. Her eyes were so narrow it was like she was holding her breath with her entire face. "Let's go see Mother and get this over with."

CHAPTER EIGHTEEN

Whereas the outdoors of Underlook was a mess of distracting odors, the inside of the Red Dragon Inn was concentrated. All of it stank wholly of deliberate smoke—the thing humans called incense. A syrup and cinnamon blend overpowered any other scent profile that dared raise its head. Shesheshen never trusted deliberate smoke. Humans were seldom up to anything good when they burned things on purpose.

Four guards stood before those incense-reeking doors. The lobby was packed, with the left side of the chamber occupied by stacked trunks and leather traveling bags. Those bags were guarded by men in metallic scale mail. Scale was the fashion of the day; there were nearly two dozen men and women wearing it in here, such that merely going to the front desk meant making one's way through multiple ranks of warriors.

So the inn was occupied territory. In a circle of chairs, some of the guards listened to two men who weren't in armor. It was those monster hunters, Rourke and Malik. Malik had a bandage wrapped around his head, stained with some orange chemical. The monster hunters were talking in the hushed tones of self-serious people, gesticulating for the guards about the various sizes of the things they were serious about.

Shesheshen did not need to hear their conversation to know her size was being discussed. She was why the inn was being protected.

The subject of that protection sat on the opposite side of the wall of armed guards. They parted for Homily, and Shesheshen followed her. She wouldn't make Homily face this alone.

On a sofa that was more bed than seat, there rested the Baroness Wulfyre. Annoyance flickered across her face, heavily made up with purple eye-paint, at the bother of having to pay attention to something other than her matching purple fingernails. Those nails were short, belonging to fingers that clearly did active work. How frequently did an attendant have to apply that purple polish to keep it so fine?

Unlike Homily's brown hair, the Baroness had bright blonde, pulled into braids that were woven with lengths of coppery red hair and raven black hair. Like the wealthiest in Underlook, she sewed hair from the finest beauties into her own. She sat up on the sofa, layers of silk and white wolf hide spilling from her broad shoulders. She had some of Homily's wide dimensions, although her exposed arms showed more defined musculature.

She adjusted the doll in her lap. It was over three feet tall, wearing its own layers of silks and white wolf furs, its cheeks rouged and its eyelids painted purple in the same ways. It was an odd fetish for a ruler to travel with and to show in public. It had the most realistic eyes, green with flecks of yellow.

"Homily," the Baroness Wulfyre said, running her purple fingernails through the doll's blonde hair. "Waiting this long to come. It almost would have hurt less for you to not come at all."

They were two of the largest people in this inn, and in that instant they could not have looked less related. Strain ruled Homily's face, and the flesh under her eyes was puffy and unpainted. Where they both had strong cheekbones, the Baroness held them in a damningly neutral expression. Shesheshen had met plenty of carnivores with that expression.

"Mother," came a stringy voice, like an out-of-tune harp. "I don't want her here. Make her go away."

The doll moved, putting its hands on its knees. Its pert nose turned up, and it leaned into the Baroness Wulfyre's chest.

It wasn't a doll. It was a child sharing the seat with the Baroness. That had to be the youngest Wulfyre. Ode Wulfyre. This family had a trend for unsettling mimicry.

The Baroness petted Ode's hair and said, "I'm sure she will leave on her own soon enough. She always does."

Homily should have fought for her dignity there. Instead she bit her lips together, eyes cast down in a way that instantly showed where she had picked up the habit. All the times she had looked at the floor rather than looked out for herself had been a habit learned at this distance from a parent.

If Shesheshen could have ever met her own mother, she would have been nervous like this. However, she wasn't nearly so nervous meeting another poison-tongued human. Having plenty of composure to spare, she dropped to one knee between two of the guards, and removed her hat to hold it over where a human heart would be.

"The actual Baroness Wulfyre," Shesheshen said. "Your Exaltation, it is an honor. It is my fault your daughter was delayed, as she rescued me from grave danger. I owe her a great debt. I come to offer my services in your hunt."

Ode whined, "Mother. We're supposed to have music. Make them go away and bring the musicians. I want to hear a fiddle."

Where Ode was dismissive in her tone, the Baroness was dismissive in her gaze. She continued training the coldness on Homily. "And who is this?"

It was not Shesheshen's place to speak. Bad as she was at talking, she knew when powerful people implied silence. It was one of those violent actions everyone pretended wasn't violent.

Yet when Shesheshen was challenged, Homily came alive. She stood straighter, gesturing to Shesheshen. "Her name is Siobhan. She's a local trapper and apothecary who works miracles. She doesn't live in Underlook—she's spent years in the wilderness and the wyrm has never caught her. No book I've found knows more about this creature than she does."

At Homily's next glance, Shesheshen tried a little speaking. "These soft locals pass off superstitions about the wyrm's fear of rosemary and holy symbols. They know nothing. I will gladly instruct your hunting parties in how to put the wyrm in its place for you."

If she could, she would guide all her hunters into the forest—so she could make sure they never came back.

There was a quirk in the left corner of the Baroness's mouth. That might have been a smile threatening to form. She said, "You think you know better than professional monster hunters, Siobhan?"

"They haven't hunted this monster. I can teach them the signs it leaves in the ravine and Underlook Forest. This land is new to them. It is my home."

"Another local who wants to do me a favor. How thoughtful of you to bring her by, Homily," the Baroness said, reclining on her sofa. Ode followed her, small hands clutching at her mother's robes. The robes parted, and a metallic necklace spilled out.

It was odd jewelry, not only because it was made from steel. It had a crescent curve, like the shape of an upper jaw. Two triangular points jutted down from it, as fangs preparing to bite into her breasts. The solid piece was suspended on a gold chain, starkly contrasting with the steel.

The necklace was quizzically familiar to Shesheshen. It made no sense, as she'd never cared for jewelry; often she didn't even have a neck to hang things on. This item reminded her of looking up into an old mouth.

"Your Exaltation, if I may beg your pardon," she said, hoping it was the appropriate phrase. "What is that item around your neck?"

The Baroness Wulfyre brought a fingertip down to caress one of the triangular points on her necklace. "These? My daughter should've told you. They are all that remains of the last Wyrm of Underlook. It had metal jaws, which it used to pierce and bury its eggs in my late husband. Its young killed him, and so I killed it in kind. When I slew it, I tore this out of its mouth in return. I wear this to remind the world that my family conquers monsters."

The Baroness spat on the floor. The saliva became a shining glob of refracted firelight, quickly losing its shape as it spread apart. Like a body dissolving into nothingness.

Like Shesheshen's mother had, the day she had died.

That was not jewelry. Around the Baroness's neck hung Shesheshen's only memory of her own mother. The steel fangs she'd worn as a prosthetic, to hunt, to fight for her life until it was snuffed out.

Shesheshen kept her head low, trying to hide how many sharp edges were inside her, begging to be loosed. All these years she had grown up in an absence of parentage. Her mother had been a phantom ache, a thing that Shesheshen wanted to outdo someday when she raised her own young.

Her insides tensed up so fiercely that her sternum cracked. She clutched at the shards, imagining fashioning them into the teeth of a second mouth. A mouth that existed solely to tear this woman's throat out.

Baroness Wulfyre said, "My daughter spoke unkindly of me if she neglected to tell you I am the only one who has real experience hunting these wyrms."

Shesheshen had to respond. She had to force words. She had to perform that wretched human custom for the murderer.

"I am awed."

It was all she could say. If she opened her mouth again, she would fling every bone in her body out. With a hundred tongues she would rip her mother's fangs from around the Baroness's neck and then plunge them into her jugular. She would be her mother's final bite, vicarious and venomous, even if these guards killed her afterward.

She didn't get exposed and die in a flurry of vengeance, though. That wasn't what happened.

What happened was Homily came to her rescue.

"Mother, Siobhan is being too modest." Homily stepped to Shesheshen's side. "Not two nights ago I was attacked by bandits on the local roads. I lay bleeding on the ground with no chance of stopping them. They would've killed me if I had been alone. The only reason I am standing today is because Siobhan fought them off."

The Baroness had spent the entire time looking at her daughter, ignoring Shesheshen. And yet now it felt like she was paying attention to Homily for the first time. Why did that change feel so dreadful? Shesheshen didn't understand human faces nearly well enough to understand.

Baroness Wulfyre said, "Is that so?"

"Since then, she's been helping me find more information on the Wyrm of Underlook. She knows the region intimately. She can be an asset to the hunt."

Baroness Wulfyre leaned forward, multicolored braids tumbling down her back. "You spent another year abroad from my court and all you have to show for it is nearly getting yourself killed on the outskirts of a shithole town? This is the selfishness that upsets your sister so badly."

Ode mumbled into a wad of the Baroness's dress, "Can she go now? I want fiddles."

The Baroness said, "How am I to look after this family when you run around jeopardizing us all?"

Homily's hands stuck to her sides, like she was shackling them. "I was researching the wyrm. It doesn't hunt where the locals said it does, so I was testing lures. If Siobhan is right about rosemary being a superstition, we don't even know its weaknesses. I did this for the family."

"Did you go dancing for the family?"

A little jolt went through Homily. Shesheshen wanted to reach for her. But she knew she couldn't.

Baroness Wulfyre said, "You think a dozen sycophants haven't visited me telling tales of how you enjoyed yourself at some barn dance? Of course you went out in the wilderness, having another dalliance with some backwoods girl. Did you indulge yourself? Did you enjoy it while your brother lay dying?"

For the first time, Homily looked dead on at her mother. Her expression made Shesheshen's jaw tighten.

"What do you mean, dying?"

"You know exactly what I mean," the Baroness said, stroking Ode's hair into acute spirals with her short purple fingernails. "While you were allegedly researching, Catharsis was killed."

"No. No, when?"

"Don't lie to this family. Not when Catharsis will never speak again. He came to the isthmus ahead of us all, because he understood actual service and sacrifice. He was going to avenge his father. So please, explain all your *precious research,* and how in pursuing the wyrm you are healthy as ever while my son, your only brother, is dead in a wyrm's belly."

The tears in Homily's eyes were obvious. Her nostrils flared, and veins stood out against the color of her temples. All her strong features crumpled, and her chin sank down against her chest.

It was such a cave-in of emotion that Shesheshen doubted herself. She had never mourned her siblings; they had tried to eat her, so she had eaten them. Watching Homily, for the first time she doubted if she'd been right. Should she have been hurt? Should she have wept when they slid down her gullet? Hers was a pain that made Shesheshen question what being a better person was.

The questions writhed up inside her chest. It stung and did not fade. It was the same tight pain that had haunted her in her own lair. One of her organs had to be malfunctioning out of empathy. It was worse than any rosemary poisoning, and made her clutch at her chest.

Homily opened her mouth, and a hiccup of sobs spilled out. "Not Catharsis. I never . . . never saw him . . ."

"That's right," the Baroness said. "Make this about yourself, like you always do. Pretend you cared about him all the times you left us. He died assuming you'd left this family behind."

Ode lifted her head to cast a cold-eyed stare on Homily. It was raw animal curiosity. The Baroness caught Ode by the hair and dragged her back down, pinning the girl's face to her own chest, refusing to let her look.

"You see?" Baroness Wulfyre said. "Look what you've done to your younger sister. Aren't you cruel enough to me, without hurting her?"

"Catharsis. No. No." Everything else out of Homily's mouth was another sobbing repetition of those three words. Homily shook until she fell to her knees, pain creasing her face. She made fists out of her hands against the floor. "Mother, please. Tell me how I can help kill this monster."

CHAPTER NINETEEN

There was no easy way to ask if Homily wanted her to eat her mother. It would get Shesheshen vengeance, a mother for a mother. At the same time, it would erase the source of so much anxiety and anguish for Homily. Baroness Wulfyre was an obvious abuser. Surely anyone, even humans, could see why Homily ran away from her family so frequently. Slaying the Baroness would solve everything.

How to offer that kind of service was tricky. Killing was simpler than a conversation. Civilization made everything so complicated.

Homily and Shesheshen were allotted the same room in the Red Dragon Inn that they'd abandoned before. Homily brought a bag of clothes, and looked quite composed as she opened it and started sorting things. Two garments in, she keeled over onto the bed. She blubbered, stifling her mouth with a hand as though it wasn't suffocating her to do that.

Shesheshen sat beside her on the bed, not talking, puzzling over what she was allowed to say. With the little tact she possessed, she determined this was the wrong time to offer to eat someone.

In the middle of her sobbing, Homily leaned toward her—except when Shesheshen tentatively reached out, Homily collapsed in the other direction.

Twice more, Homily moved as though she was going to lean on Shesheshen. Those times, too, she stopped herself. She was avoiding taking support that Shesheshen was happy to give her.

Shesheshen had to risk it. Tentatively, she drew a few fingers along Homily's shoulders. A hiccup of sobs popped out between Homily's fingers, but she didn't shrink away far.

So Shesheshen rubbed circles into her back. Gradually, she leaned into Homily's warm bulk, and wrapped her arms as far around her as she could. When she thought Homily wasn't paying attention, she shapeshifted more body length to her arms so they could fit all the way around her. Like smothering a victim, comforting was easier to do with a good grip.

Her weeping had to end eventually. The human body only had so much liquid in it, so she would run out of tears. From how hoarse Homily grew, even behind the muffling of her hand, it was clearly hard work being this upset. She would need a rest from heartbreak.

A diversion was necessary here. What would be comforting to say?

She tried, "You are crying for your brother?"

A man who did not deserve it. That, she did not have to say.

Homily slowed her breathing enough to reply. "He had so much to live up to. The eldest. Yes, I'm crying for him. Why wouldn't I?"

"You would not if you were the person your mother described."

"You don't understand her."

Shesheshen paused the stroking hand on Homily's back. "Do I not?"

"Hers has been a complicated life."

"Does she often take those complications out on you?"

"She means well. Being the head of a stateless state is impossible work. She constantly has to be careful where she rests her feet."

"I'm sure her feet were on the floor. She was mostly sitting."

"Siobhan, stop . . ."

Was that an edge of mirth in Homily's voice?

It was worth the risk.

"It must be very hard for her. Especially with the second head she has growing out of her chest. She calls it Ode?"

Now Homily's hands muffled a guffaw. It sounded even cuter between her fingers, like the mating call of a sad moose with a cold. Her freckles stood out with all the color in her face. Then Homily's eyes went wide, like she was surprised at her own ability to be happy for a second.

Shesheshen responded by wrapping her arms as tightly around the human woman as she could without turning those arms into tentacles.

Resting her cheek atop all of Homily's curly hair, she asked, "Do you like your family?"

Homily dabbed at her eyes with her sleeve. "I owe them everything."

Shesheshen said, “That is not the same as liking someone.”

“Our lives have been hard. Moving from country to country, seeking a foothold where we’d be safe and not have the entire isthmus stolen. So many countries want this land to themselves.”

“Your life has been hard, and you don’t act like this to them.”

“Mother would never stand for me . . . for me . . .” Homily’s lips clamped shut, like she was refusing any other sentiments to escape her. She started to rise and leave Shesheshen’s grip. “I’m sorry. I can’t unburden myself on you.”

“But I want you to. You were there for me.”

“I’m taking advantage of you. Like Mother said.” Homily dropped a fist into her lap. “I’m selfish. I only think about myself.”

“Were you selfish when you fished me out of a river?”

“Philosophers write about this. I only do it to feel pleasure about having done it. It’s not a virtue. I’m not a good person. I need to get out there and break this curse.”

Homily hugged her sides and left the bed entirely, like she was instinctively compensating for making herself cold. Neither of them wanted to be the kind of cold that being alone made you. It was a microcosm of the whole argument. Shesheshen had been so enamored with Homily’s kindness that she’d never thought about where it came from.

Shesheshen now worried, deep in her core, that Homily was giving because it protected her from those who took. Could it be that every quality Shesheshen had fallen in love with was a symptom of pain?

“I need to figure myself out. I need to talk to Epigram, and Mother’s hunters. Find out whether I’ll do the family more good by going to Boletar now or hunting the wyrm. Siobhan, I’m . . . I’m so sorry I dragged you into any of this. I can get you money. Or whatever you need.”

Shesheshen rose more swiftly than she intended, closing the distance between them. Setting a jaw that wasn’t her own, and fighting to keep her hands to herself for the moment, she asked, “What if we fled?”

“Fled?”

“Out to my home. To a deep place under it that no one can find. There’s a hot spring. You might like it.”

"I can't hide here. Siobhan . . ."

Pain rippled through Shesheshen's chest cavity at the mere contemplation of this woman. It wasn't empathy. It was a raw, familiar harm that had hit her in previous times she'd thought of Homily. Now it was sharper, like an entire organ was turning against her. Her body begged her to run from the room and tend to the pain. She refused to give up on Homily so easily, and kept facing her.

"What if we ran further? Ran to a new country? L'État Bon? The Al-Jawi Empire? Someplace north of it all? Or an Engmarese island nobody has put on a map yet. We can weave our clothes out of grass and bother fish for the rest of our lives."

Homily turned away, not that it hid that she was drying her eyes again. "The curse would still kill me. The wyrm's curse found my Aunt Agatha. Now it's taken Catharsis too. It will find me wherever I go."

"I promise you, no monster is going to touch you. In fact . . ."

She ran out of words. There were so many ideas. So many options to expose herself. To end all this.

But Homily had sworn to kill the Wyrm of Underlook. To serve her murderous mother by exterminating Shesheshen's family line.

How did one make words help here?

Then the door to their room swung open. In trotted Epigram Wulfyre, with a thumb tucked in her tanned leather belt and her chest puffed out as though the gilded breastplate wasn't enough advertisement. When her eyes landed on Shesheshen, her lips made the shape of a letter of the alphabet. It was a dirty letter.

"Homily, you indecent thing. You brought her into the bedroom Mother paid for?"

Homily twisted to stand straighter. Suddenly she was standing between Shesheshen and her sister, like a human wall. For the first time, Shesheshen recognized that she wasn't just being kind. She was being of use.

The feeling was worse than anything Epigram could have done to her. Oh, she wanted to eat this entire damned family. She'd show them a curse.

Epigram said, "Let's get going."

Homily said, "I'll be over to your room in a minute. Siobhan and I need to finish talking about—"

"Now," Epigram said, and brought a boot down heavily on the floorboards. "You've run away from the family enough. You're coming with me now."

Epigram reached for her again, and Homily covered her scarf. That sight made it a close thing. Shesheshen didn't need to know why Homily cowered over her scarf to know she was furious. She'd wanted to confess in private, but just as good a confession would be devouring this rude sister in front of Homily's eyes. Once Epigram was dead, they would technically be in private again.

Except Homily gestured for her sister to walk with her into the hall, her eyes cast down.

Briefly Epigram looked at Shesheshen, before stepping out into the hall. "Mother was right about you. How can you screw someone like that hermit?"

She said more, and Shesheshen didn't hear a word of it. Her ear canals closed up in spasms of agonized flesh. All those spasms came from a single source, deep in her chest. It was that malfunctioning organ again, going wild and sending arcs of distress through all of her tissues.

Shesheshen fell to her knees on the floor, and was lucky to keep her knees from melting into goo. She fought to raise her head, and was at least relieved that Homily wasn't seeing this. Then another stab went through her chest, and she clawed at herself.

Odder still was the wetness she felt when she retracted her claws inside her flesh. It was a warm and clingy fluid, a little thicker than broth. When she held the hand in front of her eyes, she found her palm was bleeding.

Bleeding?

That was impossible. She didn't have blood.

CHAPTER TWENTY

This was a new problem. Whose blood was she bleeding? She formed taste buds along several of her internal tissues to test the fluid. It wasn't robust and fatty like human blood. It was overly familiar in a way blood had never been. It tasted like herself.

She sealed up the cut on her hand, then shut the door to the room so she could mull this over. She sat near the chimney, like the heat emanating from its bricks would help her reason this out.

How had the blood gotten inside her? The bandit corpses she'd digested back in the lair had mostly been left there. Most of their fluids that she'd consciously imbibed she had immediately digested. She hadn't kept more than a mouthful of their blood for this trip.

The blood wasn't circulating much, on account of her lack of a circulatory system. Lacking arteries and veins usually felt like a strength. The blood was pumping from somewhere, though.

She stripped away her clothes and put her fingers to her chest, shapeshifting her flesh open as though she were unbuttoning a jacket. Inner organ sacs quivered, all glistening with sticky blood. It leaked from deeper inside her, and she prodded at her organs to find the source. She got up to her elbow inside herself before a sudden pain rocked her so hard she jerked her hand away.

That didn't make sense. What organ would be that tender?

The organ lay within her chest cavity, inside the safety of her borrowed ribcage. The suspicious area ached whenever she tried to touch between her ribs, and it pulsed all on its own. It was like a hand squeezing and releasing on nothing. Had it been doing that for long?

She didn't trust it. It was obviously the same malfunctioning organ that had pained her for the last couple days. The way it pulsed, and generated this unwanted blood, was familiar in untrustworthy ways. She'd ingested hearts before. This was the first time her body had grown one. If her body became dependent on it, life would get so much harder.

She formed new tendons to pull the unwanted heart loose. It was best to recycle and digest it into something useful, like a bowel.

The instant she tugged at the heart, her entire body collapsed to the floor. Half her face melted off, and liquid as it was, it still cringed from the searing pain. She'd never felt anything so severe in her life. She held herself against the bricks of the chimney for support.

What was this physical nonsense? It was her body. She controlled the nerve endings. It shouldn't be allowed to tell her how to feel. A single organ didn't command her.

Examining it more closely, she found the heart wasn't made merely of tissue. There was alien matter wrapped through it. It took several moments to identify the fiber string bound up, like so many knotted and clotted veins. That wasn't live alien matter.

It was the thread Homily had used to suture her. She'd thought she'd expelled the stitches during her fit in the hot springs. She hadn't been paying the closest attention. That gift from Homily had gotten sucked deeper inside herself, and bound itself into her new organ.

She did not feel sentimental about it. The heart had to go.

What she needed was greater strength. Depending on how long Homily was going to be preoccupied with the other Wulfyres, Shesheshen could retreat to her lair and devour her leftovers. Increasing body mass ought to give her enough strength to cut this awful blood-obsessed lump out of herself. It would be nice to be able to think about Homily without it hurting.

Thinking about Homily dealing with her vicious family caused a seizure in the organ. It made sparks of pain rip through her torso, and she shuddered against the chimney. This heart-like abomination's connection to Homily was a problem, too.

Yes, this thing definitely needed to go. The sooner she got to her lair and dealt with it, the better.

A knock resounded off her door. It was actually five knocks—two hard ones, followed by three quick soft ones. Shesheshen wondered if that was the way Homily knocked. It was somewhat cute.

Shesheshen straightened herself up, pushing the parts of her face to where they were supposed to go. Thankfully her clothes hid the disarray of the rest of her torso and legs.

No one entered. She waited a moment.

The five knocks repeated.

Unsure of herself, she said, "Come in?"

The visitor was a beige-skinned human man with some questionable body proportions. His arms and legs were so thin she imagined it would be difficult to balance on them. In contrast, his head was unusually large—including broad ears, it was nearly the width of his shoulders. His graying brown facial hair was in a mustache that stretched all the way to his sideburns.

This big-headed human man looked at her with a worthless expression. It told her nothing.

Shesheshen said, "Hello. Besides the man standing in my door, who are you?"

The man stepped inside, walking in needlessly shiny red leather shoes. Much of his clothes looked the kind of expensive that Shesheshen had never been able to justify.

After he closed the door, he said, "I am Arnau Sernine, of the Sernine lineage in North Framboise, most historic of the provinces in L'État Bon. I serve at the pleasure of the Royal Family of L'État Bon, and their inner court, and by their command, am an attendant to Her Exaltation, the Baroness Wulfyre."

"Oh," Shesheshen said, "I am Siobhan. This is my room."

"Yes, in part it is. On behalf of Her Exaltation, I am to deliver you this gift."

He opened his knee-length jacket. From some inner pocket, he produced a white envelope, sealed closed with a wax-looking stamp the color of brass. This Arnau Sernine man held it out to Shesheshen, perhaps mistaking how interested she was in envelopes.

Shesheshen asked, "What is this?"

Still holding it out, Arnau said, "The contents are ten thousand in Engmarese silvers. The bank notes are small, so you can spend them more freely. They are honored in Engmar and most of its surrounding nations in the west. I'm sure you've seen them traded in Underlook."

"What would I spend them on?"

"Travel. Lodging. Starting a new life. Finding a new woman, or whatever sort of person you are attracted to."

The stringy lump in Shesheshen's chest squeezed tighter. It was an angry pain. She agreed with its sentiments.

She said, "Those things are not my hobbies."

"This is a generous gift. I recommend you do not refuse it."

Shesheshen turned up her chin at the envelope, pondering the brass-colored stamp. It was supposed to contain Engmarese currency. That didn't make full sense to her.

She asked, "Why Engmarese silvers? I thought your Baroness sheltered in L'État Bon. Would she not keep L'État Bon's currency?"

"Her Exaltation has overflowing stores of L'État Bon notes. Those belong to her, and her sanctuary trust through the Royal Family of L'État Bon. You will not be going anywhere eastward, where L'État Bon money is spent."

"Engmar. The opposite direction of L'État Bon?"

"The opposite direction of many locations. You may take any two horses from our company you desire. Her Exaltation wishes you out of the town limits before nightfall. She has an important supper engagement planned."

Shesheshen decided to come closer to the human man. She still had her olfactory passages, and his perfume was quite strong. His potent body odors were painted over by a perfume of sugary berry scents. It was quite a choice he'd made, to smell like food today.

She asked, "Does Homily know about this gift?"

"It is a gift to you. The gentlest deportation. You will not see any of the Wulfyre children again."

"Do you do this often?"

This Arnau Sernine man scratched his mustache with the nail of one thumb. "You are not the first undesirable suitor of Lady Homily's that Her Exaltation has required to see dispatched."

Shesheshen smirked, showing enough teeth that he might recognize the Wulfyre in her smile. She hoped he did. They were in private, after all, behind a closed door.

And she was hungry.

And she had a bear trap hidden in her belly.

Although there was one thing that Shesheshen desired more than food.

"No," she said. "I am not the first undesirable suitor you have gotten rid of. In fact, I am not one of them at all."

Arnau asked, "What do you mean?"

She plucked the envelope from his hand, and reached inside his jacket. She found his inner pocket and stuffed the envelope into it for him.

"I mean you will see me at supper."

CHAPTER TWENTY-ONE

Penetrating this supper party was not so hard. It took a few words.

"You will get me access to the building. If you do not, I will pick an orifice of yours. You will discover which one I pick when you feel me climbing into you. Eventually, you will be less of a person and more of a suit of clothes. You will not believe the things I will do while I wear you."

By the end of her proposal, Laurent was flushed, breathing heavily, and eager to help.

It was not difficult to find the supper party. The town hall had transformed one more time, this time sporting many tables piled high with imported fruits and poultries. The place stank of spice rubs and deliberate smoke.

Around the town hall stood several dozen armored guards, each with a bluish green feather in their helmet. They were armed with halberds and sheathed shorter blades, all likely treated with rosemary extracts. They had the sort of fluted armor that was always harder to crumple in your jaws than Shesheshen expected. There was no way a monster was getting past them and to the guests.

Shesheshen bowed her head to them as they parted for her and Laurent. Yes, she felt quite safe, especially when the guards were behind her. Laurent escorted her inside, and they parted shortly thereafter. His business was gabbing with landed gentry from L'État Bon.

Shesheshen's business was in the rear chambers. All of the Wulfyres entered through the rear chambers, where they wouldn't be bothered. Already the Baroness and most of her living offspring had entered. One was late. The important one.

Nobody caught Shesheshen. She was used to staying out of sight, and squeezing herself into inordinately small spaces. She nestled behind a bookshelf of dusty, unloved tomes and a couple of landscape paintings of some place with more sand than grass.

It was no surprise that Homily arrived alone. Her black and white raiment was gone, in favor of a flowing dress with thick shoulder pads meant for a woman who didn't already have shoulders like hers. The garment was pleated in some foreign fashion, in colors of cream and champagne, that she did not look one ounce comfortable in. It was easy to imagine the Baroness sending it to her quarters with an order.

Homily paused in the doorway to fix her scarf. It was a new scarf, this one a deep red with brown tones. In the candlelight, that scarf made her chocolate brown eyes glow like coal embers in a fire.

Shesheshen was about to reveal herself by complimenting the scarf when she saw underneath it. As Homily tied two ends of loose fabric, her throat was bared. Her skin was the bright pink of an infected cut.

Shesheshen wondered if the Wulfyre curse was real after all. Did the scarf hide what was killing her? Did other Wulfyres have wounds like that? What kind of monster left a curse mark like that?

This was all more than she deserved to know without Homily's consent. It was accidental spying, and she had to stop it. Shesheshen stepped out from her hiding place with deliberately loud clacks of the wooden soles of her shoes.

Homily bolted up, eyes too wide. Her lips contorted like they couldn't decide what expression to make.

"Siobhan? You're here?"

Shesheshen closed the distance, coming to within two steps of the human woman. "Where else would I be?"

"No one's ever . . ." Abruptly, Homily shook her head, brown curls bouncing. "After my family finds someone I get along with, I'm used to not seeing them again."

Shesheshen pointed to the floor under their feet. "Well, there is nowhere I would rather be."

"Why?"

"Because you're here."

"That's sweet," Homily said, peering around Shesheshen's side. They were alone, for the moment. "But are you planning on attending the supper? Does Mother know?"

This was the difficult part. Waiting had not made it easier.

Shesheshen folded her hands in front of herself, like Homily did when she was nervous. Shesheshen said, "I am here to offer to leave."

Homily twisted a hand in her red scarf. "What? You came here to leave?"

"Your family is hard for you. This supper is going to be the start of something. There may be suitors. There may be monster hunters. Do you want to do this? Everything that comes ahead? Alone?"

There went Homily's eyes, down to her pointed shoes. "I . . . I don't know."

"Are you sure you do not know?"

"I should know, shouldn't I? But the moment I saw Epigram in the street, it was like I suddenly tried to stop thinking. My thoughts wouldn't move. Like everything was avoidance."

Shesheshen couldn't help herself. She came a little closer. "Are you afraid of me?"

"No!" That was louder than Homily intended it. Shesheshen could tell because she looked so embarrassed, and then she started flustering. "I worry what will happen to you, that's all. Mother is exacting. I'm not trying to be difficult. I'm sorry. My family makes me feel like I'm not myself."

"You are not trying. You are hurting and confused."

"Sometimes those feel the same."

"You avoid help from me because you are allergic to taking. If I had to face my family, and was distressed, you would want to help me. Would you not?"

Homily rested a hip against the bookshelf. "Do you have family?"

Shesheshen thought of prosthetic steel fangs that some human woman had turned into a necklace. She tried to hide how her hands clenched.

She said, "None still alive."

"I'm sorry. I wasn't thinking."

"Thinking can be hard. Almost as hard as talking. But tell me. Do you want me next to you? Tonight?"

Of course Homily looked down. But before that, ever so briefly, she looked right into Shesheshen's borrowed eyes. After a moment, she whispered, "Thanks for being you."

Out of nowhere, that damned heart-like abomination in her chest blazed. It felt like hands wrung it out, like a dish towel full of blood. Her entire body started to feel wrung out, and she had to seal up various orifices to make sure she wasn't squeezed dry. Was the Wulfyre family even cursed, or was their real curse that their Baroness had somehow bewitched Shesheshen and made this disobedient organ take over her flesh?

It was a struggle to not shudder in front of her girlfriend.

Homily asked, "Are you all right?"

Shesheshen said, "If you like me being me . . . then I will try to keep it up. So long as you keep being you."

One of them reached for the other's hand. Whoever it was didn't matter. They clasped hands, and basked in quiet warmth for a moment, until Shesheshen's world steadied. Then they walked together toward the music.

CHAPTER TWENTY-TWO

Four shorter tables stood in parallel rows, where people dressed too well sat for food that kept trying to drip onto their clothing. Dressing up so that you could eat never made sense to Shesheshen; the food was typically dead and surely unimpressed with its audience.

A fifth and longer table with a crisp violet cloth stood on an elevated stage, perpendicular to the others. It had the fewest chairs, and the best view of everyone assembled. That was where the Wulfyres sat, picking at spiced pheasant and boiled sheep's brains. Ode had cushions stacked on her chair and still didn't reach chin height with her mother. The small girl commanded an orchestra of local musicians in a peculiar game. It seemed like they had to keep a song going, but only the musicians she pointed at were allowed to play.

"No! I pointed at that fiddler!" Ode screeched, clearly pointing at the old man who was already playing. The young enby behind him tensed their wrist on the neck of their fiddle. "Play or Mother will burn your houses down."

Both fiddlers struck up together, and in two seconds were on rhythm. Ode immediately threw her finger to the other side of the company.

"Drums, not fiddles! Gonna burn your houses with your B-A-B-I-E-S inside them!"

Through the serenade of threats, Baroness Wulfyre watched Homily approach, one hand on her stolen steel-fanged necklace. Epigram hid behind a glass of wine, while their mother sat up straighter, tendons in her neck taut as if threatening to tear through her skin. As though by family magic, that same tension rose through Homily's shoulders. With Shesheshen at her side, Homily held her mother's gaze and climbed up onto the stage.

Two spare chairs waited, of gold-painted spruce. Homily drew one out in offer for Shesheshen.

"Tonight, Homily?" the Baroness Wulfyre said. "You care so little for your family as to do this?"

Homily brushed a hand across the red-cushioned backs of the two empty chairs. "Are none of us permitted to bring guests, or just myself? Because I see two spare chairs here, and they still reek of the type of perfume Epigram's lovers would wear."

Shesheshen had to work on her olfactory passages. She didn't notice perfume, but Epigram certainly twitched like the implication was right.

Baroness Wulfyre shoved the steel-fanged necklace under her dress, as though they didn't deserve to see the proof of her murdering Shesheshen's mother. "Well. You brought a temper along with your entitlement. Is this what you want our first meal together after Catharsis's passing to be like? Hasn't this family lost enough?"

That one landed. Homily's eyes lowered briefly as she said, "He was my brother, too, and . . ."

There was nothing on the other side of that "and." She was not built for games of cruelty. This was Shesheshen's turn to help.

Shesheshen said, "And, Your Exaltation, I don't come to take from you. I come to serve. Did you receive my gift?"

Baroness Wulfyre continued watching her daughter, although her eyelids twitched like she wasn't expecting that. "Your gift?"

"I delivered it to your underling. His name was Arnau or something. I hope he gave you the money, rather than keeping it for himself. I assumed you could use the money more than I."

With that, Shesheshen bowed and took the seat beside her girlfriend. It was best that every predator declare herself. She'd never known her mother, but she bet she'd be proud of her.

Baroness Wulfyre was wrathfully neutral. "How thoughtful of you."

"I owe your family much." Shesheshen smiled with as many teeth as she could show. "You raised such a sterling daughter."

Glasses clinked as Epigram reached for a bottle of burgundy wine. She didn't seem to care what she spilled. "Okay, this is enough pretending to be nice until I'm much drunker. Yes, you can come die in the hunting party. We're leaving at dawn. Say goodbye to my sister before you go, because she'll never see you again."

Epigram's comment must have excited Ode, because the girl climbed to standing on the armrests of her chair. She announced to her orchestra, "Everybody drink up!"

"Yes," Baroness Wulfyre said. "Both of you. Have a drink."

The Baroness poured them each half a glass from a dark green bottle that cast a gloomy shadow over the tablecloth. The drink smelled untrustworthy in a way Shesheshen couldn't place. She wasn't used to having a nose. Still, she lifted it.

Homily asked, "You'd test me?"

Baroness Wulfyre said, "Everyone in attendance here has proved themselves so far. Or are you above showing loyalty?"

"Mother. Please."

If it would go more easily, then Shesheshen would pitch in. She took her first sip from the glass, head needlessly high to show off her compliance. Then she paused with it still in her mouth, feeling the room-temperature liquid burn her innards. Her tongue swelled with blisters on contact. Why was it so spiced? Was the Baroness poisoning everybody who came to eat tonight?

Baroness Wulfyre said, "Rosemary wine. We know this harms the Wyrm of Underlook, so if it is in our midst tonight, it will drop dead in its chair."

Homily asked, "You really think this will work? If it's going to kill us, it's not going to sit next to you and chat."

Spitting this out would ruin the evening—ruin it worse than a gut full of lesions. Wrapping additional tendrils around her elbow and torso, Shesheshen steadied her body. She could not so much as perspire over this. As coarsely as it burned her, as layers of her insides melted from the contact of the stuff, she kept poised.

With her elbow up, she gave the impression of taking a long drink from the glass. Inside her, she grabbed one of those lungs humans liked so much and held the opening of it to the back of her mouth. All the unwanted rosemary poison went straight into the lung, a temporary bladder that, being human-grown, would not wilt from the poison. The poison still tried to burn and osmose its way through the lung's membranes, and she forced the lung lower in her body, through one leg, until the entire organ was discreetly shitted into her boot.

Baroness Wulfyre asked, "Enjoying yourself?"

Shesheshen tried to smack her lips. She felt the burn of stray rosemary wine still in her body. It was something she had to conceal. "I like my wine a little bitterer."

"Drums!" Ode screamed, teetering her chair near the brink. "All the drums!"

Epigram leaned across the table, poking at Shesheshen with the mouth of a wine bottle. "Everyone who goes into the woods better take this seriously. We need actual monster slayers, and whatever you know about this fish-drowner, you clearly never killed it either. You know what an impossible fuck my brother was? He chewed up dragons and spit out . . . kittens, or something."

Shesheshen blinked rapidly, trying to focus through the feverish feelings of the rosemary poisoning. "Are we hunting in the woods?"

"That's where the locals most recently spotted this thing. Apparently it ate some virgins or bandits or whatever right where the highway crosses through."

Baroness Wulfyre said, "Worthless Underlook management offered us paltry resources. I want twice the number of conscripts tomorrow, even if you have to drag their children out of bed and shackle them to the carriages. They're only pretending to mourn Catharsis. I'll show them mourning."

"Mother," Homily started. "Are you sure you haven't drunk too much tonight? Are you sleeping? You know how you are without rest."

"If that wyrm isn't sleeping, then how can I? Only when it never opens its eyes again. This curse is walking among us. It's not real to you, is it?"

Setting her wine glass aside, Shesheshen put her freed hand near Homily's under the table. It was an unseen wish, their pinky fingers crossing. It was the support she could offer right now, as she tried to rip iotas of rosemary out of her system.

It was enough. Homily adjusted her scarf, stroking her neck wound as though to soothe it. "It is. We're all working to break the curse."

That gesture made Shesheshen wonder where the other Wulfyres' wounds were. Where did the Baroness bleed? Epigram was partially armored, so hers might be under her breastplate.

Epigram shut her eyes and rubbed her nose, a gesture that was oddly like something Catharsis would have done. Shesheshen wasn't sure the man hadn't done it while he'd been in her lair. Watching the short-haired woman, she wondered just how close she and Catharsis had been. Or perhaps the rosemary had addled her senses.

Epigram said, "I've got a lead. I thought this was a dragon or one of those giant squid things with all the arms. But more than anything, the locals talk about a blue bear."

Homily scratched her cheek. "A bear?"

Epigram slouched into her chair and nodded with feline satisfaction. "The thing's been around for at least as long as the legend of the wyrm. It's far bigger than any bear they've ever seen. And if that doesn't sound supernatural enough, it's blue as a fresh bruise."

Shesheshen hunched over. She was not ready for this family of maniacs to go chasing after Blueberry. That bear had never cursed anyone. If she could, she would've used it on trout.

And if Blueberry got killed on Shesheshen's account, Shesheshen would have to deal with guilt for once. That wasn't happening.

Shesheshen asked, "Are you sure?"

"I met it already," Homily said. "In the ravine."

Epigram said, "You did? Why didn't you bring it up?"

"Well, in part because it isn't a demon." Homily shifted, her weight causing her chair to squeak and acknowledge her formidability. "It followed one of my scent lures to my camp. If it was the wyrm in the guise of a bear, it wouldn't have run away. It would have climbed up the boulders and killed me."

Shesheshen had an opening here. She said, "It ran away? Yes? That doesn't sound like a curse to me."

Epigram scrunched up her nose. "Well, how large was it? I've heard this blue bear is gigantic."

Setting down her spoon, Homily said, "Well, it was bigger than any species I've seen."

"No." That single word sounded like ice cracking underfoot. It was the Baroness, her gaze acidic across all of them. "However much it scared Homily, that thing is not what murdered my son. One of those couldn't have."

Homily asked, "One of those? You think there are more?"

"There used to be. Colorful bears of unusual size didn't used to be so unusual, until the Engmars expanded their kingdom forty or so years ago, right before the war. Then trappers drove the bears to extinction. The testicles on the Engmarese war banner are actually from such a bear. It was the snack of choice of their warriors. Your father and I used to eat with them." The Baroness blotted her lips with a napkin. "An overrated foodstuff."

That actually hurt Shesheshen. Her doting monstrous bear wasn't a freak like herself. She was a dwindling species driven from her home.

Homily said, "The last of her kind? It's quite awful."

There was sympathy in the woman's tone, too. Despite having had an actual encounter with Blueberry, Homily showed her compassion. It sent another of those infuriating pains through the organ in Shesheshen's chest.

Despite the pain, she was moved to agree with her. The poor bear deserved defense. "It has seldom attacked anyone unless starving. I have heard it can be . . . friendly. To some."

Epigram gagged and coughed on her wine. "Friendly? To who?"

Shesheshen didn't know what words to pick. She couldn't say it was to herself. "Perhaps the Wyrm of Underlook?"

Homily asked, "The bear is a servant of the wyrm?"

"Or a good neighbor?" Shesheshen offered. "It has to be polite for the wyrm to never eat that bear."

Epigram sat up, fussing with the velvet collar of her shirt under her gilded breastplate. "So the wyrm fucks the bear? I didn't realize it was a kinky monster. Maybe it does take a bear shape sometimes, to have fun."

Homily said, "Epigram. That thing killed our brother. Could you be more—"

The entire table juddered as Baroness Wulfyre brought her fists down on either side of her plate, sending unwanted bones spinning across the tablecloth. "You will both stop it. Show Catharsis respect."

Ode twirled around on her chair and punched the table, turning a smaller and no less manic version of the Baroness's glare on Homily. "Respect!"

Homily said, "Mother, I didn't—?"

She didn't get to finish defending herself. Baroness Wulfyre shot to her feet, sending her chair toppling behind her. "In front of your sisters? You speak to me like this?"

"Mother, how am I supposed to please you? Tell me and I'll do it."

Fists hammered the table a second time. "Not one more word!"

The pain on Homily's face was too much. There were worse things than tears in her eyes, and Shesheshen hadn't prevented them. Her entire reason for being here—that had distracted her from getting details on how to avoid being hunted to death tomorrow—had been to protect Homily. And she'd failed.

Shesheshen had one option left, and it was more desperate than it was reasonable.

"Your Exaltation," she said, trying to force the conversation in any other direction. "We will avenge your son. We will bring you all the organs and blood from this thing as you like. But how do you want us to find this wyrm? You are the one with the most experience."

Her words wobbled some at the end, but she thought her delivery was decent. If those good gods that humans liked so much decided they liked her, maybe the Baroness would turn her ire fully on Shesheshen and leave Homily alone.

"You want to know how you hunt the sort of thing that killed my husband?"

The hall went as quiet as a rabbit the instant it realized it was too late to escape. Four tables' worth of wealthy scum paused with forks at their lips, and wine overflowing cups, and flirtations dying on their tongues.

"You want to know how you avenge a son, and a spouse, and a curse upon a family? You start by selling your life to whatever country will shelter you. Tell powerful people what they want to hear. Carve up everything that was your birthright and give it to kings with a curtsy. You build yourself into something bigger than a person, and you march that thing down the highways of the world until you come to what should be your home."

Under the secrecy of the tablecloth, Homily gripped Shesheshen's hand. Shesheshen hoped that meant she'd done well.

"So this thing is hiding in my forest. You're going to hunt it for me? Then know what it is." Baroness Wulfyre twisted to yell at the tables of locals below the stage. "This is not some creature with a soul. It is an ancient, blood-feasting wretch. It survives only by eating living flesh. Its kind is so filthy that after a certain age, they can only survive by eating their own. Once hatched, they devour the living person they're planted in. And they only want to reproduce so they can have something else to extend their unholy lifespan.

"I will not live in fear of it. I will lead the hunt myself. You'll all follow me into that forest and bring me this thing's broken corpse. In every hole, in every hollow tree, you stab. No matter how many of you it takes, you bring it down. You drive it out of the forest and pierce it with so many hooks that it can't stop you as you drag it across the landscape. And if you can't find it, you burn the forest down so it has nowhere to hide."

There was a tentative squeeze at Shesheshen's hand. It was a call for strength, and so she returned it with something firmer.

That was the courage Homily needed. "What if none of us can find it, even then? What if we burn an entire wilderness down for nothing because we're too lost in our own pain?"

"Then we burn Underlook to the ground. We raze every building, and into every cellar we roll a bomb. Until there is nowhere it can hide and no one it can pretend to be. That's how you protect a family."

Homily's hand was slack in Shesheshen's. Further squeezes couldn't revive it. Homily was too preoccupied with her horror.

Baroness Wulfyre picked up her fork, seemingly just to toss it onto her plate. The metallic clatter was the loudest protest she got.

"No more disagreements? No more pretending you know how to run a family and a country? Good. The lot of you." She lifted an arm, and Ode climbed onto the table and scampered across it to hop onto her mother. Idly, the Baroness petted the girl's hair with her short purple fingernails as she looked from Epigram to Homily. "Maybe I failed in raising you all so badly that you don't care if your entire family dies. But my story will not end in this stain of an isthmus. We are going hunting."

No one argued with her. Epigram was too drunk, and Homily too browbeaten into acquiescence. As for the assembled crowd? This was what humanity's beloved civilization begat. Dozens of rich and landed people in attendance pretended they didn't know what to say. They all knew what needed to be said. Some of the cowards actually applauded Baroness Wulfyre, not that she gave them a glance for their forced affirmations.

Only one person in the town hall had the conviction, and it was Shesheshen herself. She focused on the lump under the Baroness's top, where the necklace of her mother's steel fangs rested. She would retrieve those soon enough, and show the Baroness how they were used.

She was going to eat her mother-in-law for the common good.

PART FIVE

THE HUNT

CHAPTER TWENTY-THREE

The wind was in a mood. A cumulative whine ran across the isthmus and into the sprucelands all morning, so loud that the riders could barely hear each other's calls. Not a solitary skunk was visible. The trees bent and twisted until their canopies dug ruts in the earth. Long branches snapped and fell onto the train of carriages as the Baroness's hunters rode along.

No tree trunk could pierce those carriages, though. They were a unique sort from eastern L'État Bon design. They were rounded, nearly keg-shaped, their thick wood reinforced with cast iron ribbing. The iron ribs went around the circumference of each carriage, and at multiple angles so that each rib almost supported another.

Shesheshen had never been large enough to crush something like that. No bear could break its way into that. Why, all the Baroness had to do to keep her out was not invite her in.

"You go ahead for me," Homily said, holding Shesheshen tightly. "I have something to take care of with Epigram. We'll follow Mother's guards to camp in less than a day."

"You're sure you don't want me at your side?"

"I'll be all right. I'll pretend I'm you and stand up for myself."

Suppressing the urge to turn her arms into tentacles, Shesheshen squeezed Homily. "That's a start."

She loaded into the carriages until, when nobody was looking, she stole a ride in the third carriage, which was unattended. As the wind shrilled until the sky itself grew hoarse, she pinched the shafts of arrows so they cracked, and snapped the barbs off of traps. There were several cases of foul-smelling poisons, too. There was rosemary in them, along with mint and holy tar, and venoms she had never tasted before. She bet those would give a dragon bowel problems. For those brews, she loosened their corks and stored them upside down.

There were so many guards, soldiers, and mercenaries in their carriage train that they would never prove who had been aboard. It was difficult to tell guards from soldiers, so similar was their armor. Many were encased in metal ribbing and metal plates pulled tight with hide traps and metal buckles. If they ever called Shesheshen deceptive, they ought to reflect on these quivering sacks of meat in metal shells.

Avoiding the armored masses, she shapeshifted herself thin and snaked through the windows of the carriages and into one where all the occupants were sleeping. When the carriage train slowed, Shesheshen stuck her head out through the door and gave a theatrical yawn. They were deep in the woods south of her lair, far off from the road. Wilderness chirped around them.

In the middle of the train was one carriage the cast iron bars of which were gilded. Its garish windows dripped with chains of purple lilies and rosaries. Commoners had drawn god marks all over the bottom and top of the carriage, as though praying the gods would keep the Baroness at peace.

Shesheshen beat all those pesky humans to the Baroness's carriage. Before even the guards inside could open up, Shesheshen dislodged the wooden steps and set them up. When Baroness Wulfyre emerged, the helpful Siobhan was there in scale mail, her black wig tucked under a helm, hand extended to help her down.

The winds were so high that it was a fight to open the carriage's door all the way. The Baroness's multicolored braided hair whipped around like spooked serpents.

Shesheshen said, "Great weather to stalk humans who rely on hearing."

Baroness Wulfyre yelled, "What did you say?"

"Your Exaltation! I said I know your pain."

For someone yelling so loudly, Baroness Wulfyre sounded awfully bored. "Do you?"

"I had family murdered, too," Shesheshen said, eyeing the steel fangs that the Baroness still wore as a necklace. "It leaves a terrible vacancy. I will help you fill it."

Baroness Wulfyre held Shesheshen's hand as she descended, but curled her lip. "Common ground between us? Such an original sentiment."

That necklace swung over the Baroness's steel breastplate. It would have been a prime moment to attack her, if not for the eight armed guards who poured out of the carriage behind her. Vengeance required a little more tact than that.

This moment had to be about gaining some confidence. Shesheshen said, "Perhaps you would like to rest as the camp is set up. I offer myself for the first watch while you sleep."

The Baroness rolled her eyes in the direction of the guards on her right. "I have L'État Bon's military to do that. When I want something from you, you will know."

Shesheshen stepped in close to brace her as her heels touched down on the ground. The Baroness wore a little rosemary in her perfume. It wasn't enough.

Oh, how she would've liked to attack right then and there. She'd morph her jaws and ingest those two steel fangs, feeling the mouth of her mother before she used it to bite off hunks of the Baroness. Every bone her jaws crushed would be an adulation. Then she'd suck her inside, devouring her through a handshake.

She said, "Please do not hesitate to call me, Your Exaltation. For anything."

Baroness Wulfyre cupped an ear in her direction against the wind. "What did you say?"

CHAPTER TWENTY-FOUR

Everyone wanted to pitch camp because that meant they didn't have to go scouting. Brave mercenaries who came armed to the teeth threw dice to see who had to go out first. It would've been funny to lead a party deep into that woods in search of her own footprints. Shesheshen could lead them on for hours, until they were far outside earshot of the main camp. There were some fine spots in the west where she could betray them, and thereby thin out the hunting pack a little.

That would be pushing it, though. She didn't understand humans well enough to lead a group of strangers. Giving orders and directly managing people was another level of socializing than she had, and she wasn't risking exposing herself around a bunch of trained killers.

It was easier to clear away brush and drive tent stakes. Tedious work let her identify the group leaders, and how L'État Bon's soldiers factioned off from the locals and mercenaries. Only L'Étatters got assigned to protect Baroness Wulfyre's tent. They were recognizable by the blue feather each had on their armor. There were twelve guards on duty at the leanest time, going around in groups no smaller than three. It was tight and smart; no easy way to drag one of them into the wilderness and replace them. A catapult was stationed directly behind the Baroness's tent, not that it would be any use for lobbing bombs in the woodland. Any tree trunk could bounce the bomb right back into the Baroness's lap. Soldiers would have to lob bombs using slings—and if Shesheshen got lucky, she might still sling one at the Baroness. The idea brought Shesheshen a little warmth.

Shesheshen fantasized about eating the woman's heart, or her brain, or whatever organ was supposed to retain memories. It didn't work for her; no number of purloined hearts gave Shesheshen the memories of a victim. Even after consuming the Baroness, for the rest of her life, she would have no new memories of her mother, all because of this human.

And she'd told such terrible lies about Shesheshen's father. That he hadn't been her father at all, but was a brief victim? No. He had been a generous, giving man. Her mother hadn't kidnapped him and forced her eggs inside him. That couldn't be true. He had been a splendid nest, giving all his kindness and flesh to his young. He must have wanted it. Otherwise she would have to face things about herself that she couldn't.

Whenever there was a crack in the Baroness's guard detail—whenever Ode annoyed people into looking the wrong way—Shesheshen would find her way in.

L'État Bon soldiers had their tents all around the Baroness's own, while the mercenaries' tents popped up in clusters wherever there was space near a fire. Mercenaries had picked the thickest oak in the area as a temporary shrine, and used their knives to scratch god marks into the bark, a few at the roots for the gods below, but mostly high up in its branches for the protection of the gods above. They scratched their prayers into the tree and then sheltered at fires.

At the nearest fire, an old man whose beard was bisected by the chinstrap of his helmet tossed extra wood onto the campfire. It sent more smoldering pine sap smell into the air, mixing with the toxic smell of rosemary. A gang of humans in full plate armor tipped flasks of oil onto each other, rubbing the stuff in smudges over their gear.

That was likely the next hunting party, hoping rosemary oil would keep them safe from a predator that didn't want to hurt any of them. If they'd all agree to go home and let her eat one miserable woman, she'd let them go. They weren't going to leave without cutting out her heart first, though.

Shesheshen was in the mood to tell some lies of her own today.

She shuffled up to the fire, elbowing between two of the largest armored hunters. She pretended to warm her hands over the flames, and sized up the company of seven. Up close the stink of rosemary was enough to make her want to vomit raw acid on them. That might come later.

One of the hunters brought the flask of rosemary oil to his lips. He was the tallest of them, broad-hipped, with dark brown skin and the thinnest plucked eyebrows. His throat clicked as he drank.

Shesheshen tried to sound bemused as she asked, “Why are you drinking that junk now? If they dispatched you out here, they probably believe you’re a human.”

The man rubbed his lips with the back of a gauntlet, leaving another oily smudge. “Everybody’s supposed to drink some. The idea is it might ward off the wyrm. It won’t attack you if it can’t eat you.”

He actually offered the flask to her. The irony of the gesture was cute. The drink was supposed to make her safe from herself.

“You are not from here,” she said. “That junk does not work on the wyrm. I have lived in the isthmus for longer than most of these trees. One time I saw it tear through a pilgrim’s cart that was carrying only rosemary. Everyone was coated in the stuff, and she still maimed them.”

That much was true. Those pilgrims had been trying to sow the wretched plants around her territory to drive her away. They’d deserved their maiming, even if she hadn’t eaten them on account of their rosemary seasoning.

“I told you,” said a tanned enby in boiled leather armor, elbowing the first man’s side. “This dreck is useless. The wyrm’s afraid of spearmint or something.”

A third mercenary, this one a pale-skinned woman almost as narrow as the knives on her belt, said, “Peppermint. Some apothecaries in town sold me three pounds of it cheap.” She raised an arm to show the green leaves stuffed into the armpit of her rusty breastplate. “The wyrm can’t digest peppermint. It won’t go near you.”

This was a great start. Shesheshen fanned them on a little more, saying, “Most kinds of mint ward it off. I do not go anywhere without some in my boots.”

Shesheshen stamped a heel for the visual effect, letting the hunters imagine how much peppermint she had stuffed in there. Half of them looked at their feet, likely wondering how long it would take to get their armor off and apply herbs in their hose and socks.

“No true wyrm has ever been afraid of mint.”

It was a voice so dry it could’ve come from the fire. The speaker was a shriveled bag of a man. Around the licking flames there leaned the weather-beaten face of the monster hunter Rourke, with his breathing mask hanging loose around his neck.

"The point of rosemary oil is not to make you invincible. This wyrm will still kill you, no matter what protection you have. The point is that if it eats one of us, it will digest the rosemary and then be hindered. If one of us dies, we die bringing the monster to heel. We make it easier for our friends to survive."

All the humans around the fire swallowed and looked anew at the bottles. Even Shesheshen would agree: that was grim.

It was also annoyingly practical. She would have to be careful with who she devoured, and definitely avoid ingesting their stomachs. This man needed pushback before he convinced anyone to be selfless enough to hinder her.

Trying to emulate how the Wulfyres sounded when they talked to helpers, she sniffed derisively. "You're one of the monster hunter duo that Catharsis Wulfyre hired, aren't you?"

"Yes. Name's Eoghan Rourke. I've been on the ground here for two weeks preparing. I've seen one of its lairs in the manor. If you all get out of this alive, it'll be because of myself and my apprentice Malik."

Talking was usually such a labor. For once, she was able to channel her frustrations with it into her voice. She merely had to channel it into sounding as irritated as the Baroness always did. "I heard your story already. You say the eldest Wulfyre got killed fighting this wyrm. Did any of you use rosemary-treated weapons on it?"

"Catharsis got it in the belly with his crossbow." Rourke stuck out an index finger like it was a crossbow bolt. "The bolt was full of the stuff."

The scrawny woman and wide-hipped man traded a murmur.

Shesheshen said, "That is a problem."

The wide-hipped man said, "That is? How?"

Shesheshen made a gesture between herself and these hunters, physically excluding Rourke from the gesture. "Because we use rosemary. You say you filled its innards with rosemary and it is still alive."

"Oh, shit," the scrawny woman said. "It came into town that very night hunting. So how exactly is rosemary supposed to be a poison to it?"

Shesheshen said, "Exactly. You make this alleged poison sound more like flavoring."

The wide-hipped man wiped a streak of the rosemary oil off his armor and looked at his gloved fingers. "I've never heard of a wyrm that had a weakness to rosemary. If the locals are selling us mint, why put stock in this?"

This was a great plan. Shesheshen could undercut their expert sources, and then attack with her own supposed sources. By acting angry, she made them feel they should be angry. If she didn't have a mission of vengeance at hand, she could do this all day for fun.

Rourke said, "You didn't see how it reacted to being stuck with the bolt. It feared it."

Shesheshen spat back, "Feared it enough to eat the man who hired you while coated in the stuff. And you tracked it to a place that other townsfolk swear was not even its lair. I have lived here all my life. It has never laid a finger on me, and I do not use rosemary."

Rourke grumbled and turned away. After a moment, the crowd awkwardly started a conversation about other tricks they had learned about to fight their wyrm. They started arguing about metals, and whose armor was iron or steel or had silver amalgamated in. That insecurity was something she would stoke later. She loved being hunted with silver and gold and other soft metals.

Trees swayed upward, swishing as the winds relented some. The whistling sound dwindled. People stuck their heads outside of tents and strayed from the fire, looking up in search of some sunlight. A sharp whistle pierced the air, and a couple finches took the chance to dart from the trees and head east.

Was this one of those divine signs of good fortune? She really would enjoy believing in gods that favored her.

Following the whistle came hoofbeats and grinding wheels. Those were not divine noises. The noises ran along the road until they came around the bend, sixteen white horses drawing a huge wagon, with two carts carrying something restrained under chains and burlap in tow.

More horses and wagons rode behind them, many ridden by haggard humans that cast wary glances at the wagon's covered cargo.

When the lead carriage slowed enough, its door sprang open. Epigram stuck her head out, cheek-length hair bright in the sunshine. She called, "Mother! You're going to want to see this."

She hopped out of the carriage, showing that her gilded greaves were speckled with gray rock-dust and mud. She trotted down the line, waving her riders to bring the cart with the burlap cover nearer to the royal tent.

Baroness Wulfyre emerged from her tent eventually, with Ode clinging to her left hip. "What is this business? I had just gotten your sister to sleep and you bring every horse in the isthmus tromping through here?"

Epigram put up an index finger. "More than horses. Call this an early birthday present."

Mercenaries bumped into Shesheshen as they left the fire, starting a crowd around the carts. As though roused by the crowds, Homily leaned out of the same carriage that Epigram had ridden in, a fist clamped around her scarf. Her legs swayed and her feet scraped clumsily at the dirt as she dismounted. She gave a cursory glance in the direction of the "birthday present" before staggering through the crowd.

Shesheshen pushed at the mercenaries, trying to get to Homily. "Are you all right?"

Although Shesheshen got close, Homily didn't hear her. The woman skirted around the periphery of the crowd, hugging her coat around herself. She was gone for one of the tents long before Shesheshen could get free.

The crowd grunted collectively as Epigram drew her jeweled knife. She twirled it overhand, clearly basking in the attention she'd won. Shesheshen pushed around the bulky mercenaries and climbed on top of a supply carton, simultaneously trying to see where Homily had gone and what this birthday present was.

Baroness Wulfyre said, "You didn't kill the wyrm already. You weren't even in the forest. I thought you were out carousing again."

"I hunt smart, Mother. That's why you're so proud of me."

Epigram dug the knife into a burlap cover, then ripped it down the side with the sound like the last air being driven from a lung. She tossed the ruined cover aside to expose the thing beneath.

It was a mountain of gray fur, taller than any of the horses in the company. Given the size, it would be easy to think it was just fur, since so few animals grew to that size. Several metallic skewers were embedded in its bulk, stained with scabbing red blood. Whatever the creature was, several chains lashed it to the cart, digging half a foot or deeper into its hide. The grooves those chains dug against its attempts at breathing looked awfully painful.

Upon closer inspection, the creature wasn't gray. That color was from the same rock dust that coated Epigram's shins and the armor of her underlings. Closer to its legs, the rock dust faded and exposed the bear's natural color.

Shesheshen's mouth sealed shut, then disappeared entirely. She got rid of it so she wouldn't scream.

They'd gotten Blueberry.

Epigram leaned on the bear's bound side and fixed her hair. "It wasn't that hard once Homily coughed up the lures that attracted it in the first place. We went to its territory and left some drugged meat around. The thing basically hunted itself."

Baroness Wulfyre said, "That's not the wyrm in an unusual shape. We went over this last night. This is nothing."

"Oh, it's something," Epigram said. "This carrion-chomping piece of shit is the wyrm's friend. What did the locals call it? Its pet? If there's anything the wyrm has an attachment to, it's this. You can send as many morons into the wilderness as you want looking for wyrm droppings and footprints. Me? I'm a Wulfyre. I make monsters come to me. This is my bait."

CHAPTER TWENTY-FIVE

They put Blueberry on display in the middle of a clearing. An iron collar bound her neck, chained to a stake driven deep into the ground, so she couldn't raise her head more than a few inches. More iron manacles were bound around her limbs, each one chained to a nearby tree. The old girl might have been able to uproot one spruce, but not four. Soldiers fastened the chains so tight that Blueberry had to lie with her limbs spread. Her whimpering was the first sign that she'd woken.

Wet black eyes stared into the dirt, and her breathing was labored, like something enormous was lying on her chest. As Shesheshen watched, Blueberry threw up sticky offal onto the grass. Because of her bonds, when the fatigue was too much to stand, she had to lay her head in the mess.

The clearing was adjacent to the main camp. That way two campfires' worth of armored bastards were watching the whimpering bear at all times, ready to mobilize at the first sight of her savior. They marched around in their steel boots, toes as pointed as rats' snouts, squeaking with their proud footfalls.

There were three other breaks in the spruces where someone could approach Blueberry's resting place. There were archers mounted in the boughs above all three of those spots. Every half hour, a patrol came around to check the iron-jawed traps, and to stab the shrubbery in case Shesheshen was lurking in there.

She wasn't lurking in the shrubbery. She wasn't that good a friend. Instead, she was lurking among cooks and mercenaries. She stood thirty yards away from Blueberry, and there was no way she could get to her.

If logs and provisions needed moving? She lugged them across camp.

If fires needed stoking? Water needed dispensing?

Anything that let her stay in sight of Blueberry. She was so close, trapped in a helpless distance.

Could she get onto a patrol detail? It was possible. But if she did, what could she do from within a group? They'd notice if she tried to sabotage the traps. There was no way to undo one of those chains without being caught, and Blueberry would never make it out with the rest of her manacles on.

Shesheshen could pretend she'd seen "the monster" out in the wilderness and lure a party away from camp. But that would still draw people to guard Blueberry. Security would heighten and make this harder.

There had to be a way.

"Why doesn't it roar?"

Ode was louder than any of the adult humans around their campfires, whose chatter was weary and low. Where they were nervous, the girl sounded irritated.

Normally human children were put to bed this close to night. Under the uneven, milky orange sky and rising moon, the girl wove through the camp. Her white dress was stained at the bottom with grass, and a cloak of wolf fur around her dragged and snagged on branches. She kicked equipment and helmets out of her path as she made for the bound bear.

Behind her followed a company of six tall guards in fluted armor, steel from toe to scalp. Each had three feathers sticking from the right side of their helmet, which probably signified they were elite. Most L'Étatters only had one feather. Each hesitated to be the one to actually grab the child.

Ode said, "Dragons and lions and bears go 'roar.' It should roar. Why is it making dumb sad noises?"

She came right up to Blueberry's rear haunches. Out of the folds of her cloak she brought a long piece of wood. It was a practice short sword, although looking quite long in Ode's hands. She jabbed its tip next to Blueberry's tail.

"Show me a roar."

Somewhere shallow in Blueberry's throat, she gave a hiccup of a grunt. Literal skewers still stuck out of her back, the wounds untreated. A poke with a wooden sword wasn't enough to get her feisty. Blueberry tried to turn her body to see her diminutive attacker. The manacles clanked, keeping her immobile.

Ode tensed from her ankles on up, thrusting her hands down to her sides. She screamed with a loudness humans normally didn't allow themselves to acknowledge they could hit. It was a wild sound, harsh around the end. It was the roar of someone who'd never had to be afraid.

When Blueberry didn't reciprocate, Ode walked around her side, jabbing her in the ribs with the wooden sword. Eventually the tip hit one of those skewers that were dug into Blueberry's skin. Ode perked up at the contact. She smacked a skewer, and Blueberry gave a higher-pitched grunt. The bear's entire body shuddered—that skewer was in her muscle tissue.

Enough of the sunset lit up Ode's face that her glee was obvious. No human had ever been happier. She wrapped both hands around her sword and reared back, looking down at the bound bear's muzzle.

"Come on. Make the monster show up so I can go listen to music. Roar!"

Shesheshen couldn't watch. If she stayed another moment, she'd shed her clothes and devour this damned child in front of all her civilized guards and witnesses. As it was, too many humans were watching. Grown humans wouldn't interfere—in fact several of them tipped back drinks as they watched the display. This was a fun distraction for them as they waited for Shesheshen to reveal herself and die.

Shesheshen couldn't stop this. Only another Wulfyre could.

Across the campgrounds, Homily peered out for a moment from the yellow flap of her tent. She had a book open in her hand as though she was preoccupied with reading something, but she was looking in Blueberry's direction as clearly as any of the hunters. She had to know this was partially her fault, having used her scents and lures to capture Blueberry.

Unlike the rest of her family, the sounds had made her show up in concern. That was why she wasn't like the rest of these humans. That empathy was Blueberry's best chance.

Shesheshen whisked around the campfires and came upon the yellow tent. As she got near, Homily disappeared back inside, the flap falling to cover her escape. Shesheshen caught the flap before it could fully fall, and then held it open. It was an invitation for Homily to come back out.

She wanted to be gentle. The gentlest she could make her words was, "Can you stop her?"

Behind her, Blueberry yowled in an obvious call for help.

Inside the tent, Homily faced away, pointing herself at a small table with three legs. More white cloths lay on it, there, and some bandages. The place had the stinging reek of iodine and alcohol. Homily muttered, "I didn't want to do it. I didn't want them to hurt the bear."

"Of course you did not want it. You are better than these people. So can you come help stop it?"

"I tried to stop them from going at all. I thought I could dissuade Epigram." Homily dropped a cloth onto the table. There were dribbles of red on it, like worm holes in wet earth. "I didn't want this."

Shesheshen couldn't tell if Homily was trying to show her something, or failing to hide it. The difference was too subtle. She came inside, and Homily scooped up the cloths, hiding them against her body. More of them had those bloody marks.

Shesheshen asked, "What happened?"

As Homily threw the cloths into a basket, her sleeve rolled up for a moment, revealing deep purple color around her forearm. The bruises stretched up to the end of her sleeve, and wrapped around her limb like she'd been grabbed.

There was no gentle way for Shesheshen to say that she knew a bear hadn't done that. That was the kind of bruising that humans did to each other.

Another animal whine sprang up from the clearing outside. Homily's face burned pink, and her mouth and eyes widened together for a moment, before she went to cover up her arm. A hand went to her scarf, wrapping it around her neck.

Shesheshen had seen enough terrified animals in her life to recognize raw panic. She didn't approach or retreat. She stayed near enough and made her voice as calm as she could muster.

"What is your family doing to you?"

"It's my fault," Homily said, falling sideways and landing on her cot. The frame squealed and the end of the blanket bounced up against her lap. "Please don't leave. What do you want me to do?"

"What happened?"

"I'll help," Homily said in half a sob, before choking off her own voice. As soon as she breathed again, she repeated, "I'll help."

As many times as Homily said she would help, she made no motion to rise. Her gaze was nailed to the ground at her feet, and her breathing went as erratic as the wind outside. It wasn't a genuine offer. It was a panicked mantra—a last plea to be seen as useful. All of Homily's generosity, from fishing Shesheshen out of the river all the way to inviting her to supper last night, was echoed in this. She wasn't kind because of some angelic virtue. It was insecurity. It was an adaptation to cruelty.

Shesheshen wrapped her arms around Homily and held her to her chest for a moment, mourning the realization that she'd fallen in love with someone's pain.

Squeezing her in that embrace got little response. Homily nosed at her shoulder for a moment and murmured, "I'll help."

She couldn't help, not as she was hiding bloody laundry and fighting her own thoughts just to make sentences. She was trapped in the manacles that her family had made out of her own mind.

Outside the tent, Ode's squeaky voice trilled out in laughter. There was another clang of wood on metal, and Blueberry's guttural voice rose up in a helpless growl, which faded into pained whines.

Gradually, Shesheshen released Homily's sides, letting the human woman sink back into her bed. She wanted to stay and comfort and understand what Homily had been through, but there wasn't time. She had to do something to save Blueberry before this got worse.

Shesheshen was on her own.

CHAPTER TWENTY-SIX

Her one advantage was the horrific night. Clouds veiled the moon so that it cast the thinnest gray light over the spruces. High winds raked at the tents and gusted so that people had to shout at each other from feet away. Camp guards jumped as snare traps snapped around falling branches, or otherwise from the sheer force of wind.

As the midnight patrol gathered for their rounds, the wind kicked up so many pine needles that they could barely make out Blueberry's enormous bulk in the middle of the clearing. No swarm of insects had ever been so thick. Visibility got even worse when they had to extinguish most of the campfires to keep the winds from setting the woods ablaze.

Shesheshen joined the four other volunteers for patrol, hiding her smile behind her hand. It was a great night for hunters to go missing.

They were led by Rourke and Malik themselves. Malik said, "The Baroness insists on a patrol. We'll keep it formal. Keep each other in sight and we can get through this."

"Take the rope, and don't let go if you want to come back tonight," Rourke ordered, thrusting a braided hemp rope into their hands. "It isn't optional. We can't see shit. This keeps us together."

One of the volunteers was Gilles-René, the broad-hipped mercenary she'd met earlier. He asked, "What if we spot the wyrm?"

Malik said, "Then you stick even closer together. The people who run on nights like these die alone."

Rourke nodded. His and Malik's voices were muffled by the breathing masks they had on. "So hold onto the rope like it's your lover's hand."

They did. The mercenaries each took a length of that hemp line, wrapping it around an elbow or carrying it in a hand. None wanted to be too far apart. Shesheshen took up the rear of the line, right behind Gilles-René.

They handed around a cup of rosemary wine, and were so confused and nervous that none of them noticed that Shesheshen didn't swallow.

As she handed it off, Isabeau, another of the mercenaries, said, "You know that stuff doesn't work. The wyrm's only afraid of peppermint and garlic." Isabeau tapped the cloves on the wreath of garlic she had around her neck, over her mail hauberk. "It has to be fresh garlic. I'm going to shove this down its throat and watch it choke."

The links of her chain mail were thick with garlic sheddings and pine needles. The garlic didn't frighten Shesheshen. In fact, what remained of her olfactory passages reported that Isabeau smelled appetizing.

Gilles-René hooted. "When we're done, we can use the leftover garlic to cook that bear."

Isabeau cocked her head at him and yelled, "What?"

These were the seasoned killers that Baroness Wulfyre had assembled to ferret Shesheshen out and cut out the heart she didn't have. Shesheshen almost felt bad for them. Almost.

With his breathing mask secured, Rourke put a steel bucket helmet over his head and eyed up the party. "Let's march, people. And don't let go of this rope."

Rourke shook the rope at them before turning, with Malik at his back. Both of the professional monster hunters carried torches that smelled of sulfur, with metal shafts and claws around the flame. They could be swung like maces, and they'd burn you as well as cut you up, until they went out. The men held them low, shielding their flames with their bodies, trying to see through the whirlwinds of pine needles.

And the mercenaries followed, one after the other, stepping carefully to avoid traps around the periphery of the camp. A rusty bear trap had once been covered in thin spruce limbs, and was now half bare. It was an old model, large enough to snap off a large human's knee. Gilles-René stepped so close to it.

It would've been easy to push Gilles-René into it. But they were mere yards from camp, so the noise had more chance of carrying. And if she struck, she needed to incapacitate Rourke and Malik first. They were the ones who posed the greatest threat. With them down, the others would panic and throw garlic at her.

Malik pointed his flaming mace hard west from the clearing, to where several snares swung like limp branches from the trees. "We've lost all our traps on that side. We need to check those."

Rourke said, "And watch for the bear traps. You'll lose a leg in them."

Everyone clung to the rope as though it tied them to the earth. The wind raked at their legs, blowing every loose piece of fabric to get stuck in joints of armor. One of the mercenaries near the front held up a kite shield and it got caught in a gust. He reached for it as it sailed up into the treetops.

Isabeau and Malik commented simultaneously about the lost shield—from their tone, both were snarky. They fought to be heard.

Gilles-René asked, "Can the wyrm mimic voices?"

Nobody heard Shesheshen say, "Sometimes."

At fifty yards out, all the camp's fires were obscured behind tree cover. A sudden pang of hunger wormed up inside Shesheshen's organs, and she realized she hadn't eaten in almost a day. These six humans would more than fill her up. Any two of them would give her all the strength she needed to free Blueberry.

"Look here," Rourke called. "Claw marks."

Their party moved around one of the slack snares. Bark was stripped from the base of the tree in straight patches, like someone had gouged it with a broad-tipped spear.

The man who'd lost his kite shield pointed at the stripped bark. "Could animals have done this? Like boar? More giant bears?"

Malik said, "The marks are too deliberate. Rourke?"

Rourke yelled something that Shesheshen couldn't hear, and raised his flaming mace. Its fire flickered weakly, threatening to go out entirely. He ignored the threat and held its light behind the line of tripped snares.

Isabeau asked, "What is it?"

Rourke pulled the rope to get them all to come closer. "Something moved out there."

Plenty of things were moving out there. The wind whipped every branch it could touch, and trees swayed in music that human ears couldn't hear. The moonlight itself looked like it was moving, because of how erratically the trees swung.

Malik yelled a question, and it was utterly inaudible. If he repeated himself, Shesheshen couldn't hear it. Everyone was fixated on Rourke's torchlight and the monster that wasn't there.

They didn't realize what was behind them. Should Shesheshen have felt bad about this?

In answer, memories of Rourke and Malik violating her lair to kill her rushed in. The gentlest of these humans sat back and listened to a bear be tortured by a spoiled child. How badly did she feel like feeling for them?

Shesheshen crept up behind Gilles-René, extending both of her hands. The flesh between her fingers split open, and she slid out a few tools she'd stolen this evening: six steel daggers. They were long enough to make exceptional claws. She wound her tissues around their handles so she could manipulate them like they were part of herself.

There was an inviting spot at the base of Gilles-René's neck, where his pauldrons parted from the base of his helmet. It was several inches of perfectly good flesh. She could sever his spinal column and the next person in line wouldn't hear a thing. Every man in the line was focused on holding onto the rope and listening to whatever Rourke was lecturing about.

She neared, lifting her dagger claws to be level with Gilles-René's neck. The collar of his chestplate swelled as he took in a deep breath, chin lifting as he prepared to yell something. Shesheshen jerked her knives at the proper angle, preparing to silence him.

Except in the middle of her swing, Gilles-René stumbled backward into her. The entire group pivoted backward, away from the thick spruces and the snare. They shoved against Shesheshen and she hopped away, wondering if this was a ruse. Had the two veteran monster hunters drawn her out to exactly where they wanted her?

Pain clamped around her left shin, shattering the bones she kept inside. Her entire body heaved and she pitched to one side, groping at whatever had bitten her. Sticking out from a mound of pine needles were the glistening metal jaws of a bear trap.

The lousy humans had caught her. From the way the wound fizzled and boiled, she knew the trap was glistening with rosemary oil. Who had oiled this thing? She squirmed low, daggers in both hands, ready to swipe at whatever hunter got closest.

Gilles-René still faced away, a hand waving behind himself for balance, the other clutching to the rope. Others dropped the rope entirely and fell to the left. Rourke and Malik swung and hurled their flaming maces into the dark woods ahead, screaming orders that were barely whispers in the wind.

One of the fiery maces bounced off of a large body. The firelight illuminated several long branches that were driven into the ground like stakes, except the shortest of them was three feet long. At their tops they were consumed into an enormous wad of gray flesh, coated in a pale slime that dripped over the bark like living sap. The body was gray, with oblong blotches of black along its quivering surface.

The branches twisted and lifted from the ground, stamping into new position like artificial limbs. They kicked the flaming mace aside, and stabbed one pointed end of a branch through the face of the nearest mercenary. He spasmed and went slack as a puppet.

The thing's flesh rippled inward, exposing yellow and decaying bone. Snouts pushed out through the quivering gray tissue, until three deer skulls came to the surface, their jaws wrapped in strings of meat and sinew. More strips of that same stuff looped through their vacant eye sockets, as though binding the deer skulls in place. As one, those deer skulls opened their jaws and wailed.

Amid the crying wind and incoherent screaming of the party, two words were audible. "The monster!"

CHAPTER TWENTY-SEVEN

"Monster!"

"Monster!"

"Monster!"

As though yelling names would help. The thing wasn't dissuaded by talking, and drowned out the shouts of orders with its own bleating and honking. Its voices sounded like the calls of adult bucks, while the skulls that protruded from its mass all came from female deer. It was like an entire herd had crashed together into one grotesque being.

It had more than deer parts, stamping closer on its thick branch legs, kicking holes in the hard-packed earth. The opening at its front quivered like a snout, smelling the entire party. All three of its deer skulls clacked their jaws in unison in Shesheshen's direction, and it snorted her air again. The creature dragged one branch-leg along the ground like a bull about to charge and lowered its flank at her.

Did it recognize her by scent? What the hell was this thing?

The rosemary poison on the trap was too strong for her to yank her limb free. Pain disoriented her leg, refusing to let it shapeshift. Shesheshen pried her daggers between the teeth of the wretched bear trap, working them to get any slack. Her shin bones were crushed and the pain scissored through her soft tissues, telling her there would be no limping on that ruined limb.

As the creature ran at her, Shesheshen sliced the daggers into her own limb to cut it off. It was the only way.

The rope line jerked away from her lap, reminding her that some of the mercenaries kept their heads. Malik slashed at the creature's underside with a broadsword that glistened with oil. Rourke came up behind his partner, aiming a crossbow over the man's shoulder. It loosed a familiar-looking bolt, striking the creature at the seam where one of its branch-legs entered its gray flesh.

The creature wailed again and kicked with its hind legs, knocking both monster hunters to the ground in a shower of pine needles. It kicked until the crossbow bolt and the adjacent stick leg both came loose, thudding to the ground. Deer jaws chattered, and the creature bolted.

"The camp!" Malik yelled, pointing. The creature was headed straight for the clearing, where Blueberry was still bound and helpless.

Malik and Rourke sprinted together, with the spare mercenaries behind them. They didn't cast another look at Shesheshen as she tried to cut her own leg off.

It was better that way. She was too bewildered to put on a show for frightened humans. Her facial features melted away, eyes sinking into her head as she finished sawing off her knee. It took a force of will to pull her face back together, and to clench her wound shut. All that blood her worthless new heart-like organ had made came spilling out, leaching her body heat with it.

There wasn't time to cry over lost fluids. Blueberry needed her.

Tentatively, she picked up the fallen crossbow bolt. It smelled of agony and poison; she had to hold it by the far end, not wanting to get a drop of its extracts onto her. A thing with rosemary-poisoned chambers near the tip had nearly killed her once. It also spooked this new creature, and so she might need it. It was assurance in object form.

She formed a lumpy wad of flesh where her foot had been and lurched on it. Without humans to impress, she moved easier. The clearing was near now.

All the torches were out. What screaming was audible over the wind came from further into the camp; the creature had missed Blueberry thanks to all the soldiers making a distraction of themselves. Shesheshen crossed the clearing and Blueberry snuffled up at her with that moist, black nose wiggling. Busy as the odors were tonight, her old friend still recognized her scent.

Humans apologized with words. Shesheshen apologized by running a long limb over Blueberry's muzzle, up across her forehead, and down between her ears. She held the bear to her side for a moment, partially for help in standing up, and partially out of pity. As they lingered together, she untied the noose, letting it fall atop the stake beneath Blueberry's body.

In response, Blueberry gave a low keening sound. It was more pathetic than all her whines of pain earlier. The skewers still stuck out of her hide, freezing to the touch from the chill of night.

Shesheshen would pull them loose, and heal the wounds with extracts from her own flesh. Any flesh she lost tonight, humans would repay.

Brilliant orange lights flew across the campgrounds. Archers aimed at the rampaging creature, and sent flaming arrows into the wind to harm it. Thanks to the wind, they set more tents ablaze than they hit flesh. Other arrows splintered on the bowstrings as though sabotaged. Soldiers cried that their weapons were defective. Somewhere amidst them, Epigram in her gilded breastplate screamed orders that no one seemed to follow.

There wasn't any more time for sentimentality. Someone would check on Blueberry eventually, and try to use her to distract the creature. They wouldn't get the chance.

Clinging to one of the chains, Shesheshen hopped against the wind, with her wig blowing into her face, until she reached the shackles at the first tree. She loosened the flesh of her fingers inside the lock, fiddling with fine bones. Metal clicked and submitted. She sucked the first lock into her body; it was heavy and would make a decent fist.

Chain after chain, she limped and picked locks, stealing the metal. From the light of the flaming arrows whisking through the air, she could tell the branch-legged creature was getting closer. It battered armored humans to the ground like toys. The deer skulls jutted from its maw and cut a grisly silhouette, before they tilted at Shesheshen.

Was it smelling her again? Was this some freak coming in from the seas? A god answering all of Underlook's prayers and now stalking the apex predator of the isthmus?

Once a couple chains were down, Shesheshen hurried to Blueberry's side. The old bear strained against her remaining bonds, trying to pad away. It made it harder for Shesheshen to sink her limbs into the cuffs, her bones continually getting stuck between cast iron and a furry limb. She strained to focus, the chill of metal chewing her limbs raw.

Somewhere behind her, a heavy weight thudded closer on multiple limbs. More than the wind was wailing around the clearing.

The last shackle clicked open, and Blueberry lurched forward so hard she drove her nose into the ground. New blood seeped from the skewers embedded in her back. Snot and saliva ran in streams from the edge of her muzzle as she worked her hindquarters. The poor beast lumbered away from the sounds of the creatures and the humans.

Turning, Shesheshen saw the ugly three-skulled maw, now dripping with various fluids that the night was too dark to color. Deer teeth chattered up inside its bulk, and it was dragged in the front by three branches. Its rear was propped up by several armored legs—human legs, attached to human torsos. The creature had half-swallowed humans into itself, using their legs to help it advance on Shesheshen.

There was no running for her. Her lumpy temporary foot kept crumpling—she needed new tissue and bones to patch that up. This clearing was all she had. She was alone against this creature. But she had been alone for most of her life.

Shesheshen twisted one of the chains into her left arm, meshing cold metal with bone and muscle fibers. This chain was still anchored to a far spruce, thick and immovable. If she got swallowed by this creature, she would pull her remains out of its guts and drag its intestines behind her.

"Leave her alone!"

She'd heard so much vitriol in her life that she thought the feminine voice was defending the deer-skull creature. How, when she was about to face death, was the one sentiment she heard in all that howling wind someone insulting her?

Around one of the trees raced Homily, skirts whipping around the thickness of her thighs, hair whirling like a halo. There was something off about the way she ran. She lugged a heavy urn with her.

Then the smell hit Shesheshen—the last thing she smelled before her olfactory passages entirely collapsed. For all the onslaught of forest and human odors out here, its stench of rosemary sliced through the night. It hurt to breathe.

The deer-skull creature reared up on several pairs of armored legs, flailing its branch-legs in Homily's direction like a spooked horse. Homily refused to yield, standing in front of Shesheshen. She stuck a hand into the urn, then smeared rosemary oil down her face.

Shesheshen tried to warn her that this wasn't that monster. "Do not!"

But Homily slapped another palmful of the oil across the scale mail of Shesheshen's top. Its vapors stung her eyes, and she tried to shield them with a hand.

The deer-skull creature wasn't so demure. It slammed two branch-legs down into the earth and heaved itself forward, emitting a ghastly wail from inside its maw, from that maw it hid behind the deer skulls. The skulls chattered their jaws, reaching to bite Homily.

Shesheshen looped her arms around Homily's neck, the closest part of the woman she could get. She heaved against her, trying to pull her away from her foolish bravery. The heart-shaped abomination in her ribs burned like a personal sunrise, threatening to melt all of her innards. She'd let it happen if it saved Homily.

Homily splattered another palmful of rosemary oil, this one against the deer skulls and into the maw that waited behind them. The wailing choked off, and the deer-skull creature fell back a step. All that fleshy matter puckered up and spat.

Homily followed the creature over the ruts its limbs had dug in the ground. She took her urn by both of its handles, intimating that she'd toss the whole mess of rosemary oil in the next moment.

The wind lowered, and the deer-skull creature skittered to the left, trying to circle around Homily and her urn of rosemary oil. Those deer skulls were still trained on Shesheshen, like all the creature wanted was to reach her.

Homily reared back, adjusting and ready to throw the urn in that direction.

For a moment, the deer-skull creature sniffed at them both. It lifted its torso until it was half the height of the neighboring trees. So many dead human limbs dangled from its flesh.

Then it ran in a different direction, armored human legs kicking in the air, sword belts jangling and jabbing at its undersides. It lowered its maw and drove between two bonfires, swinging branch-limbs at a squad of guards in fluted armor. Shesheshen didn't understand why it would pick a different fight. Clearly it still hungered.

"This way," Homily said, hugging one arm around Shesheshen's side. "It's over here."

She said more—probably a lot more. Shesheshen couldn't hear her over all the battle. Together each of them took a handle of the urn, and they half limped and half ran around the east side of the tents, as far from the deer-skull creature as they could get. Shesheshen was thankful she still had human facial features for Homily to trust. She had to lean more weight on her than she liked, still fleshing out the second new leg and foot so she could keep up.

They ducked inside a purple tent with gold embroidery. Its internal cage door was ajar, and they slammed it shut behind themselves. The floor was strewn with garlic and mint, and someone had drawn little god marks at the bottom and top of every flap and all along the ceiling. The tent's posts were solid metal, and inside it had a ribbing, more like a cage than a home.

A squeaky voice asked, "Did they kill it? I want to see its heart."

It was Ode Wulfyre, sitting half-sunken into a cushioned chair meant for someone several times her size. She was sulking with her bottom lip out, a silver saber in a jeweled sheath resting across her lap. She was alone inside this cage of a home.

Homily spun around the tent as though expecting some vast company instead of her sister. "Where did the guards go?"

"I don't know," Ode said, theatrically crossing her arms over her chest. "Epigram stole them all to go kill the wyrm. Am I missing it? I want to see its heart."

Homily re-tied the upper tent flaps, then tested the cage door to ensure it was firmly sealed. It was. She put an oil-slickened finger across her lips and trudged across the garlic-and-leaf mess of the floor. A single candle was lit in here, so they were reduced to fainter silhouettes than they had been in the clearing.

At least all the dark and the garlic hid Shesheshen's bleeding. She stripped off her scale mail, trying to get the taint of rosemary away from herself. Underneath her skirt, she had something vaguely resembling a leg, still badly in need of bones. She groped around for any rods or unused chair legs.

Sitting between Shesheshen and Ode, Homily asked, "Where is Mother? She was supposed to meet us here."

"She's fine," Ode said as though safety was a nuisance. "She's in her tent, where I should be. Those stinky butt-eating guards shoved me in here when the monster showed up because it was 'urgent' and I 'needed to be protected.' I hate it here. I want to go to Mother's. Did they kill the stupid monster yet?"

Without thinking, Shesheshen asked, "What was that thing?"

"The Wyrm of Underlook," Homily said. "You've seen it before, haven't you?"

"It looks . . . different."

"What else could it be?"

Shesheshen didn't have a good answer to that. It wasn't like anything she'd ever encountered before. The way to prove it wasn't the wyrm was to give away her own identity. It was suffocating to think she couldn't tell this brilliant woman who'd just saved her life who she actually was.

"Thank you," she said, gingerly offering her hand to Homily. "For coming for me."

Homily adjusted, wrapping both of her hands around one of Shesheshen's elbows. "When I didn't find you in any of the tents, I thought the worst. Why did you go out on patrol? Why did you risk yourself?"

It was in those questions that Shesheshen started to hurt. It was in her chest again, in that awful organ that she needed to carve out of herself soon. Homily was asking why she'd risked her life. But Shesheshen had to ask, "Why did you go out there? No armor. No guards. You could have been hurt."

The wild look in Homily's eyes wasn't so different from Blueberry's when she'd been tied to the ground. "You. You could have been killed."

Shesheshen took Homily's arm in return. "My life is not the only one that matters. And you were . . . hurting. You can give too much."

"I'm sorry," Homily said. "So often, I don't know what else to do other than give. It's like I won't exist if I don't do something."

"I feel that. Sometimes."

Specifically, she felt it for Homily. Was she going to turn into the same kind of wreck? How did one avoid that?

All the sounds outside their tent were dwarfed in a sudden explosion. It was like a thunderstrike they couldn't see, without the flash of lightning. The metal caging of their tent rattled and all the canvas went tight in one direction.

Shesheshen shot up to get in front of Homily, and instead ran square into her side—because Homily was in the middle of rising to shield her. They clawed at each other's arms, faces maniacal in need. Both wanted to protect the other from a sound neither of them understood.

They had to talk about this streak of self-sacrificing, and the secrets they'd kept. They couldn't become good parents to a brood if they lived like maniacs.

Ode pushed toward the tent wall, listening for more battle sounds. "Mother's brought the bombs out? We're missing bombs. You two are boring. Let's go."

The little girl punched at their knees as she waded across the tent to the entrance flap. Silk swished around her knees as she moved, carrying her saber like she'd draw it at any moment.

"Wait," said Homily, reaching for Ode's skirts. "It's not safe out there. Especially not if she's got L'État Bon setting off bombs."

Ode snickered. "Bombs make it safe by killing the monster. It's probably dead. I want to see its heart."

"It could be wounded," Shesheshen said. "You want to be careful with a wounded animal."

"You're so boring!"

There were no more explosions. It was perilously quiet out there now. Beyond the drone of wind, which was lower than before, and the idle flapping of loose tents near theirs, nobody was screaming orders or crying for help from gods.

The swishing of tree boughs was louder than any people. There were a few footfalls, heavy and rhythmic. Shesheshen cupped the sides of her head, honing the fluids that balanced within her inner ears, trying to make sure she hadn't gone deaf again. It had happened a couple seasons ago. Hearing was an irksomely fragile sense.

"Ode, sit down," said Homily, squatting to pursue her sister. "We need to wait."

"You left. You left for a girl." Ode swung her sheathed sword at Homily, missing so badly she fell over. She landed beside the exit to the tent. "I want to see them kill the monster. I bet Mother and Epigram killed it off while you were doing nothing here."

With resolve that Shesheshen would never understand, Homily opened her arms and lowered her voice. "Please come here."

"You're not even really my sister. I want to see Mother cut out the monster's heart!"

An explosion rocked the tent, knocking over the chairs and sending both Homily and Shesheshen keeling to the floor. Her leg was still weak, so Shesheshen threw herself under Homily, trying to cushion her fall. The human woman squirmed, reaching for the exit to catch her sister.

Ode swung the inner gate of their tent open. The bottom of the flap wasn't fastened into place, so her short, pudgy limbs squeezed through it, legs swinging to propel her from behind. Homily crawled after her, reaching for those kicking feet.

"Ode!"

Shesheshen followed, ripping open the flap so Homily could reach for her sibling. She started to yell for them to be quick about it. Ode was already outside the tent.

The little girl stood in the middle of the row of tents, beside a helmet the same height as her knees. She stared up as though she'd never seen the moon before. No moonlight fell on her face. Instead, saliva and thicker fluids dripped from above, spattering on her silk clothes.

Three deer skulls loomed over Ode, jutting from an abyss of gray flesh. What looked like a tent pole was actually a monster's wooden leg, and that enormous gray body came down, now studded with arrows and scorch marks. It lunged for the opening of the tent.

Homily screamed. Homily screamed, and throaty men screamed and their armor clanked as they ran for the tents with poisoned spears aloft, and the wind picked up so that its pitch deafened all, raking at Ode's hair. The wind's touch was likely the last thing she ever felt, before the deer-skull creature swallowed her.

As Homily grabbed for her sister, Shesheshen wrapped her in every limb she had and hauled her away, until they were inside the tent again. She slammed the cage door closed and wrapped her malformed leg around two bars to keep it closed. That didn't stop Homily from wrestling to return outside.

Her sister was dragged into the air and sucked halfway inside the deer-skull creature. The girl's thin legs kicked fruitlessly for two shakes, before there was a resounding crunch. Then her legs went slack. They still dangled from the creature's maw as it ran into the night.

CHAPTER TWENTY-EIGHT

Eventually the wind strangled itself until the trees stood still and it was a mere murmur from an unknown throat. The campgrounds were a mess of fallen boughs and timbers so profound that captains were unsure if missing people had deserted or lay dead under the coverage. Birds had the audacity to return their twittering and singing to the trees.

Birdsong was louder than human chatter, as the camp had thinned out. Patrols went on in the daylight, in groups no smaller than twenty; each carried with them a chest containing a powder bomb, to blow both as a chance to kill the thing if they found it and to signal the other forces to come to them. Rourke and Malik split up to lead two parties in search of traces of where the deer-skull creature had gone. They wouldn't find any.

These hunts were excuses to avoid the Baroness Wulfyre.

"Ode, get over here this instant or there will not be a note of music for the next month!"

Sometime around twilight Baroness Wulfyre had left her fortified tent and begun circling the compound, demanding that Ode appear. She'd known about her daughter's demise almost as soon anyone, but expletive-laden denial seemed to suit her more. Hour after hour, she tromped around the fires and between the tents using a spear like a walking stick, calling for a child who would never return.

"Ode! You were supposed to continue my legacy! All those years grooming that Royal Family's prince for you, and for what? How do you show gratitude to me like this? How am I supposed to continue this family . . . ?"

Shesheshen noted Epigram keeping her distance. She labored in the clearing where they'd bound Blueberry as bait, pretending to look for traces of what had happened. It was an obvious ruse. She didn't have the guts to face her mother, who was the source of all her privilege; nor did she had the courage to go hunting the creature with everyone else.

This was Shesheshen's best chance to get Homily out of here and to

Underlook. She had to be hidden in the heart of awful civilization, where she'd be safe if the deer-skull creature marauded again. And, more importantly, it would get her away from her mother.

"You'll come with me, won't you?" Homily asked, holding onto Shesheshen's sleeve. The two of them crept between the tents, listening for the next outburst to guide them which way not to go. "It's not safe here."

"I have some business to attend to."

Specifically, she wanted to return to her lair and build her strength in case she encountered that creature again.

Homily said, "I won't be able to rest if you're in jeopardy, too. Not after what I did to—"

Shesheshen interrupted. "You helped. That is what you did."

"Mother might need me."

"I'll see to your mother. You are too hurting, inside. Too confused."

"Mother is very complicated."

Baroness Wulfyre didn't seem that complicated to Shesheshen. The Baroness was quite simple, with her simplicities attached to power that meant those simplicities could hurt people easily. People so feared her retribution that they mistook the tension from their constant vigilance for depth and mystique in the individual. That didn't impress Shesheshen. Perhaps it was because she was a monster.

Shesheshen said, "I will manage."

"Alone? You should have help."

"You have helped me in every way," she said, touching Homily's firm chin for reasons she didn't understand. "I will come for you as soon as I can."

"Come tonight. Please."

"I will try to be there by tonight."

"I could have a supper ready for us. Have you ever had egg cakes?"

Behind the next tent, someone threw a piss bucket hard enough that it took out a tent post on impact. This tent was the last between them and the horses and carriages. From the yelling, it was obvious who waited in their path out of here.

"Ode!"

For a moment, Shesheshen wondered if she could convincingly shapeshift into Homily's guise and take her place for this conflict. It wouldn't work, for a baker's dozen reasons: no replacing the gentleness of her countenance, the deceptive size of her shoulders; no convincing Homily that she wasn't herself—except from the expression on Homily's face, she surely wished she was anyone else. Oh, Shesheshen wished she could do this for her.

Homily nudged into her side, resting against her and listening.

"Arnau," Baroness Wulfyre said. "Where are the guards?"

"The ten assigned to your daughter? Most of them died serving Epigram in—"

"Most of them?"

Arnau cleared his throat. "Yes. I believe seven of the ten."

"Find the three survivors and have them arrested and hanged. Find their families, and do the same."

"Very good, Your Exaltation."

"Have the hunting parties retrieved my daughter yet?"

Closer to Homily and Shesheshen's crouched hiding spot, Arnau answered, "We have dispatched as many crews as possible along every conceivable path the wyrm could have taken. Your will is to be done."

"I see people lying around camp."

Together, Shesheshen and Homily poked around the circular tent to see. Three rows of L'Étatters in fluted armor served as a mortal barricade around the Baroness. It was difficult to find her at first, because she had descended into a hole in the ground. It was one of the charred craters her bombs had made in the earth. Inside its well, she curled up, her multicolored hair braids splaying in the dirt, black soot sticking to the oils on her armor. The steel fang necklace clinked against her breastplate.

"Well?" she said. "What have you got to say for these layabouts?"

Arnau said, "Only the injured remain behind."

"Injuries. They always pretend to be injured when they don't want to work. And what is delaying these crews?"

"I'll have runners fetch updates immediately."

"They're clearly taking too long. Have all the supposedly injured mercenaries in camp arrested. If no one comes back with the wyrm's carcass, have all the hunters arrested as well. We'll hang them one by one until we know who is who."

"Madame . . . Your Exaltation. What if that doesn't reveal the wyrm, and we become short on forces?"

"You're a smart man. What do you think I'll do to you then?"

Arnau flinched away, coming into their view for the first time. His mustache and left sideburn were singed and his cheek was blackened. He'd gotten too near one of last night's bomb blasts.

In the middle of his flinch, he turned in the wrong direction. From the ugly relief in his face, he saw Shesheshen and Homily hiding.

"Your Exaltation, your eldest daughter has emerged. She profoundly hopes to speak with you."

That was all it took. Even as a monster, Shesheshen knew they couldn't continue hiding or run away now. The human man wouldn't cover for them; they were his cover. A very civilized solution to his problem.

Homily came trotting out, hands twisting in front of her, eyes down. That typical way of averting eye contact failed her today, since her mother was lying in a crater.

Digging the heel of her spear into the soot and dirt, the Baroness pulled herself up to sit. Despite sitting in a depression, she stared up at Homily as though looking down on her.

All Shesheshen could do was walk with Homily, and be at her back. The Baroness had an army, so her daughter deserved a monster.

The Baroness said, "You."

"Mother, Ode loved you so much that I know—"

"Don't you speak of her. Keep her name from your tongue. What are you thinking?"

"Please get out of that hole. You should sleep before you get sick. Let some of us get you to bed."

Baroness Wulfyre hoisted her spear like she would aim it at her daughter. "Think of the foul lords that Catharsis rode through lightning storms to slay. Think of the suitors that flocked to see a glimpse of the woman Ode would one day become. Then there's you."

In the middle of that rant, Shesheshen reached from behind Homily and touched her shoulder, in that spot a lifetime ago when she'd been stabbed. It felt so long ago when she'd mended the woman's flesh with her own. Now she wanted to remind her not to let herself be wounded again.

At Shesheshen's faint touch, Homily leaned into her. Resting against Shesheshen's hidden touch, she steadied. "Mother, I loved them too. They were my family."

"You. Think of yourself and the scraps you've accomplished. Who would want to be you?"

"What can I do to please you?"

"Tell me. What are you going to make of yourself? Now that our family is a gaping hole. What's going to be worthwhile about you?"

"I tried to save Ode. I had her in my hands, and we had no guards, and nothing—"

"I said don't speak her name! What do I want from you? For you to get out of my sight. This family gave you everything. And I gave this family everything it has. Ode would have grown up to live an amazing life anyone would envy. Who would want to be you?"

One of Homily's hands twitched, in the direction of the piss bucket. Brown water trickled out from the spot where it had damaged the tent. Shesheshen willed Homily to pick up the bucket and put it to good use.

Homily's jaw remained firm, as though wanting to say something that wouldn't come out. It was as if the fight might actually begin.

Except that was a hoax of the eyes. Shesheshen wanted her to say something and was projecting that onto her while Homily suffocated. This was the same mistake so many humans made: believing someone would leap over trauma when it hurt them badly enough.

That wasn't how it worked, and the monster knew it. All Shesheshen could do for Homily was be patient with her, and make space for her, and eventually, one day behind her back, eat her mother.

For now, she looped an arm under Homily's and guided her to a carriage before she fell.

CHAPTER TWENTY-NINE

It turned out that egg cakes were neither cakes nor were they made with much egg. They were small, oblate biscuits treated with cardamom and a sweetened butter. They were light enough that they were inoffensive to pretend she was eating, while actually stuffing them into an isolated stomach that she would later discard. Meanwhile Homily found egg cakes exceedingly digestible, and so they bought half a basket of them. Following her worst encounters with monster hunters, Shesheshen had often disemboweled a young buck to calm herself. Comfort food was not alien to her.

Homily actually smiled at her once as they settled into their room at the Red Dragon Inn, finding a change of clothes and licking crumbs from their fingers. It wasn't the dark mood Shesheshen had anticipated. Was this how psychological breakdowns worked in humans? Another part of them she didn't understand?

Then Homily leaned in, so that the biscuit-tinged warmth of her breath tickled Shesheshen's face. She feared that Homily was going to bite her—this was a distinct biting range. Upon a far too forgiving mattress, sitting atop blankets that felt like dry cat tongues, Homily kissed her for the first time.

In all the mess of recent days, she had forgotten that human people kissed. This was not how she'd imagined their first kiss. She'd overheard enough allosexual virgins gab about the lightning strike at the touch of lips, and the fever rush of blood that reminded them how much of themselves were alive.

This was not like those descriptions. It was another moist orifice pressing into her. A sort of mutually failed cannibalism. She fought the urge to bite into Homily's sumptuous flesh, and Homily suckled on her for a moment without ingesting much. The human tasted like humans always tasted: like permeable skin, and thin juices, and the promise of meat.

Her heart-shaped abomination rippled upward. More than aching, it physically pulled itself against her other organs to get at her throat canal. She pushed herself away from Homily, neck swelling up like she'd vomit the organ. Things inside it that had lain dormant now prickled, bony spurs tearing through its membrane and slicing into her other flesh. She'd never felt such pressure inside her before.

Hearts weren't supposed to do that. They mostly bullied blood around a mammal's body. What was this thing doing? It was malfunctioning worse than before, trying to leave her for Homily. The urge was embarrassing, and blood rushed into her face. How did she explain this to Homily when she'd told her so little already?

This deception had to end. She had to tell her now.

"Thank you," Homily said before Shesheshen could formulate the words. "For looking after me."

"I did not. I would have liked to. But I could not think of anything that would not make your mother worse. You deserved . . . less worse."

"You pulled me into the tent when that monster was rampaging. I would've been eaten too, if not for you. And with Mother? No one has ever come to take me away when she was furious at me like that. Not once in my life."

"Maybe we should introduce your mother to the monster."

Homily ran the backs of two fingers along Shesheshen's cheek. "You don't have to be funny all the time, you know?"

Before she could stop herself, she tilted her cheek into that touch. "Is being funny a thing you do on purpose, or is it a thing people decide you did?"

Still bridged by that touch, Homily asked, "How do you feel about kisses?"

Shesheshen stiffened. "I did not mean to be ungrateful."

"You don't like them, either?"

Either? That was impossible. Someone with Homily's ability to connect to others surely loved all sorts of physical intimacy. It was so many humans' favorite thing. It was unfathomable that this woman was like her, and in this way of all ways.

Shesheshen let herself be honest, for a sentence. "I think I despise them."

"I never had a partner with whom I didn't feel obliged to perform that. Thank you, Siobhan."

"You're welcome. For me. Being myself."

She hated talking. She was not being herself, especially not through words. Why hadn't she corrected Homily on her name? Said that she was not Siobhan at all? She was Shesheshen, the Wyrm of Underlook. The words had to come. She had to tell her now. This damned anxiety was worse than kissing.

Homily deposited the basket on the floor so that nothing was between the two of them. She scooted into that space, the plumpness of her leg warming against the narrowness of Shesheshen's, and she crooked two fingers into her scarf, just above the knot holding it together. At that angle, it looked like she would peel her throat open.

Again the heart in Shesheshen's chest ached, threatening to rupture. It wanted to do something in her throat, and she refused.

Homily said, "You have suffered so much with my family already. You deserve some context of why we are the way we are."

"You do not owe me anything." It was an attempt. If Homily backed off for a moment, then Shesheshen could try to explain.

"Siobhan," Homily said with a kind of finality that chilled the room. "I need to be honest with you."

Shesheshen succumbed. Conversation was too damned hard. She would have to confess at the next opening.

Homily left a hip resting against Shesheshen's, and rested an arm against the headboard. "I was young when Mother moved myself and Catharsis to L'État Bon. We were often separated. There was no sense of family, really, until Epigram was born. It started with her."

Shesheshen asked, "She is much younger, is she?"

"About eight years. I was old enough to remember most of Mother's third courtship. It was the most fraught, as she was trying to leverage her tenuous claim on the isthmus in order to find the safest place to stay. Our family still moved frequently, especially when the civil war began in L'État Bon. Catharsis was seldom with us. He was much older, and was very close with Mother. Often the two of them departed to wage campaigns in support of L'État Bon. So for much of my childhood, I was alone with Epigram. Whenever we had to flee, it was my charge to make sure she was kept safe. Sometimes she called me her aunt."

Homily's eyes followed something across the floor that wasn't there. It took her words with it. Perhaps she was watching a memory.

Shesheshen said, "She doesn't treat you like an elder."

Homily kept watching that memory traveling across the floor, her brow creasing like it hurt to remember. Her fingers sank deeper into her scarf. "My sister was a wrathful child. There were rumors about who her actual father was, and children can be cruel. Early on she realized she could stop children from hurting her by hurting them first. I . . . like I said, children can be cruel."

That was partially true. Shesheshen added, "Adults can stay cruel."

"If you thought Ode was feral, you can't imagine a young Epigram. She attacked her nurses. She tripped maids when they were on the stairs. One time, she pushed . . ." Homily suddenly put her palm over her eyes, like something had hit her. Her voice went clinical. "Like, I said, she was wrathful."

"Did she hurt you?"

"I was old enough to look after her, and prevent her from hurting others. I was helping my family. We played together. We played games. It started as nothing too serious. The games quelled her for a while. When she was at her worst, sometimes we would go alone in a room, and she would play make-believe."

Homily smoothed out one of the pillows, stroking it like it was crying. She didn't hide the hitches in her own breathing. Shesheshen gave her the patience she needed.

"Sometimes, she would pretend that I was the monster that cursed our family."

Shesheshen did her best not to bolt up. "What?"

"She was small, and the world was too big. She wanted to be like our brother Catharsis. Gallant. Worldly. She wanted to break the family curse. Which means she wanted to slay the monster."

"So she hurt you?"

Shesheshen wanted to leave the room right now, rush out into the wilderness and find Epigram. She'd drag her away and show her what a real monster looked like.

Homily's voice stirred like she was about to get angry in her sister's defense. "I let her. And it worked. She would poke me with a knitting needle, or a knife she stole from the supper table. I'd pretend to die, and she'd feel better. Except sometimes, a poke wasn't enough."

Two fingers dug into the knot on her scarf. She pulled that knot undone. She unwrapped the fabric, and let it fall like a snake's unwanted skin into her lap. Homily drew a long breath. She lifted her chin, baring her neck.

Amid her many freckles, there was the wound Shesheshen had spotted the previous night. It was stained orange with healing poultices and the like, and was beginning to heal. A few crude stitches pinched it together.

It was not the only mark on her neck.

Faded pink scars decorated the right side of her neck, starting around the tendon. They were flushed brighter with Homily's breathing. One scar kept traveling, all the way across her throat and to the left side of her neck. It was thicker as well, like it had gone terribly deep.

Homily gestured to the old scar that crossed her throat. "The first time that Mother tried to arrange a marriage for me, Epigram got the most upset I'd ever seen her. She was a goblin in human shape. I wasn't even looking. I didn't even say yes before she grabbed my hair and did this."

Shesheshen fought herself not to lean in and hold Homily's neck for the rest of her life. "How did you survive that?"

"If the suitor's father hadn't been a doctor, I would've died. It caused such a ruckus that they canceled the marriage."

This was a time for words. She couldn't look away from that newest wound and its black stitches, thinking of when Epigram had demanded Homily come to her quarters in private. Homily deserved better than this.

She said, "I glimpsed those cuts by accident a few nights ago. I thought they were your curse."

"I'm afraid they are something else that runs in my family."

"Your sister did that one," Shesheshen said, pointing for as long as she could to the new wound with the rough stitches. "She still hurts you. She has not changed."

"I tried to do what was best for her back then," Homily said, shaking her head at herself. "I was wrong."

"She was wrong. Your family was wrong. What did your mother do?"

Homily laughed so bitterly that Shesheshen tasted it on her tongue. "Mother was wrathful that I brought it to her attention at all. She wanted to focus on court politics and said I was spoiling things for attention."

"How did you blame yourself for any of this?"

"I left," Homily said, sitting up like she might leave again, right now. "That was the first time I decided to take myself out of the home. Get away from the whole family. I wanted to see other parts of the world. Maybe find a way to help someone . . . in a way that worked."

Shesheshen gathered up Homily's hands and kissed every knuckle of them she could find. These were different kisses—the best affection she had. Her malfunctioning heart protested, sending spines of pain through her chest.

She refused to give in. Her kisses were for Homily's hands. The heart would stay where she wanted no matter how badly it ached.

"You deserve better," Shesheshen said. "I listened. All right? I listened. You deserved to be heard."

Homily let out a choked version of, "Thank you."

"What I heard is your family raised you to think being hurt by them was the only valuable thing, and eventually you realized it was a lie and ran as far as you could. And one more thing."

"One more thing? That I'm broken and a sycophant to my mother?"

Shesheshen shook her head so strenuously that her wig nearly came loose. "No. My one more thing is that I am glad you ran."

Damn it. Her one more thing should've been confessing that she was the monster, and that there was no curse she could see, and that this whole family was a curse as it was. She was ruining everything.

Homily twined the digits of their fingers together, into a ball of hands. She murmured, "Can we not kiss for a while?"

"Yes."

It wasn't the literal request Shesheshen expected. The woman wrapped her arms around Shesheshen's shoulders and held onto her like butter held onto bread. Homily's face rested dangerously close to Shesheshen's own neck, where that heart-shaped abomination still was trying to climb.

Restraining this horrible thing in her chest was going to be agony. She wanted to tell Homily that she was the demon that Epigram grew up fearing. That her own hatching had killed Homily's father and left her stranded with the lone parent who saw cruelty as instruction. That Shesheshen was, in a way, the fault of their lives.

Between the pain of suppressing this malfunctioning organ, and the awkwardness of admitting lies that had gone too far? Talking seemed impossible. If only there was a better way.

CHAPTER THIRTY

There were many possibilities, all of them ugly.

The deer-skull creature could be the physical manifestation of the Wulfyre curse, tracking them down after the Baroness marched her army here.

Or it could be some foreign predator that the Baroness Wulfyre had imported to hunt Shesheshen without alerting the guards.

Or it could have imported itself, as some invasive species that got here on its own and sought her out specifically to replace the apex predator.

Or it could have been one of those gods the humans liked so much, answering a violent prayer. Some human had drawn a little god mark somewhere and gotten lucky. There were seemingly infinite nameless gods. This could be any of them.

Whatever it was, Shesheshen was going to defend herself and Homily against it. The Wulfyres and their resources couldn't be trusted. She was going to be ready. That meant she needed to bulk up and produce the spare tissues and organs necessary for a foul fight.

So under cover of dusk, she crept out of the town for the ravine. Halfway to it, she found Blueberry hunched and waiting, licking at one of her wounds. They trudged along home together, and Shesheshen pulled loose the skewers from Blueberry's hide. Each skewer was nearly an inch thick. She kept them, since they made fine leg bones and would make even better surprise attacks.

Parts of her that had been tense all night relaxed upon crossing the threshold of her home. The watery and fungal vapors of her lair welcomed her, filling up her being. Even that awful heart in her chest sagged, beating slower in the dimness. All Laurent's cleaning merely held the place's nature at bay for a little while. Now the wilderness air was returning.

First, she needed to eat. In order to gain the mass necessary to fend off another monster, she had to become a greater monster. It had been wise of her to pre-digest all those bandit corpses and stash them in her basement. They would be the start she needed to fight in the final battle.

The door to the basement was ajar. She'd forgotten to lock it shut. It was fortunate Homily hadn't stumbled down there in a spare moment and ruined everything.

As her boots dragged along the rough granite steps, she pondered again how to talk to Homily about what she really was. Should she have revealed herself last night? Homily was so scattered and vulnerable that adding any more honesty felt selfish.

If not last night, then when? After Shesheshen wiped out the remains of her cruel family? Over the dead body of this new monster? Doing it now felt the riskiest, but it was also the fairest. Lying further wasn't proof of love. What if this new monster killed Homily and she died never knowing that Shesheshen was—

Her own thoughts turned to foam as she clawed at her chest, feeling the deep ache of her heart. This organ was going to kill her. What had it been doing during her talk with Homily? It had tried to extract itself, like it wanted to burrow inside of Homily instead. Homily's body didn't need more hearts.

This was not how a heart was supposed to behave, whether or not it was entwined with sentimental suture threads.

In fact, only one organ behaved like that. Shesheshen had never had such an organ, but instinctively, she knew what part of her would one day be laid in a rightful person. A rightful parent.

She dug her fingers deeper into her chest, carefully pushing aside her bladders and stomachs in her search. She tensed her form to hold the self-made wound open, organs aching and quivering as she tensed them, trying to keep them spread so she could get a look at what she'd thought was a heart. It was a rumpled gourd-shape of thin layered membranes that pulsed, all pink and bloated with blood until it was larger than both her hands. The blood gushed hot around her palms, and the wretched organ stung her when she tried to touch it. Several bony spurs protruded from its membrane, each attached to smaller, hyper-sensitive wads of meat and shell hidden inside the organ. It kept them warm with this fresh cycling blood. The thing that had grown inside her wasn't a heart.

It was an egg sac.

For all the years that her nature had made her expectant, she hadn't been ready for this thing. Why had it shown up now? Was she the right age?

Or had she finally met the right parent?

The mere thought of Homily as the ideal parent made her legs weaken, tendons liquefying and dropping her to the cold floor. She had to lean against the wall or else she'd fall. That yearning, that resonant pain she felt whenever she thought of Homily, wasn't the sentimentality of a malfunctioning heart. It was the resonant demand of her eggs. They demanded their parent.

There had to be another way. A way to suppress the eggs, at least until Homily knew the whole story and could have an opinion on parenthood. She didn't even like kissing. This could not be sprung on her.

If Shesheshen was going to resist and suppress the influence of her eggs, then she needed nourishment. Enough meat to strengthen the rest of her against their impulses. Fortunately, there was a feast waiting in her basement. That would give her the strength to deal with this.

There was something wrong in that basement. A certain vacancy in the air. Crouching for a glimpse of things down there, she didn't see her gray meat sacs waiting for her on the floor. She checked the corners of the room. The meat hadn't slid from the center of the room to any spot. It wasn't there.

There was a thin, viscous slime in the center of the room, just a splotch, streaking toward the stairway. When she brought her boot down on the last step, that slime slicked her heel. It was like something had dragged her meal upstairs.

Some scavengers had dared pillage her domain while she'd been out hunting to help the damned humans. The gall of whatever meat-eaters. She'd have them for finger foods. Had the deer-skull creature done this? Had it robbed her?

She turned around and climbed the stairs hastily, feeling for more of the slime. It dried up outside the door, the last remains pointing toward the lobby and the exit to her lair. She'd walked across streaks of the stuff on her way in without a thought.

She turned around and headed back to investigate. On the inside of the basement door, the wood was stained with slime. She extended a tentacle out of her body, resting it against the door. The remaining slime was cold; no heat remained of the passage. It was stale and dried out to almost nothing. It hadn't been recent.

And the door had been pushed open from the inside, as though by the dripping meat itself.

For the first time, she put the onerous puzzle pieces together. The deer-skull creature walked on borrowed limbs—from trees, and later from humans. It absorbed those things into its gray flesh. It was afraid of rosemary, like only one other creature in her known world: herself.

Shesheshen parted her skirts and stared at her own flank. The flesh there had lost its shapeshifted color, no longer trying to pass as human. She could go as gray as the deer-skull creature if she put no thought into it.

She put a hand over her mouth, which was made up of a skull and jaw stolen from Catharsis Wulfyre's head, and thought about the deer-skull creature.

Had that creature stolen her meal?

Or *was* that creature her meal?

She'd processed it through the organs of her body to be the most malleable flesh possible. It had felt like it would digest and adapt so quickly. She'd never done that before. There were no precedents for it. Had she grown up under the guidance of her mother, would she have been warned about leaving too much of herself lying around, until that part of herself got up and went out?

It was wrong. She was supposed to reproduce by laying eggs in suitable parents, from this horrible egg sac that kept piercing her innards. Reproducing another way was preposterous.

And in a way that didn't harm someone like Homily. It was more knowledge that would have been passed down to her, if the Baroness hadn't robbed her of parentage. There were so many questions.

Why would this queer offspring go anywhere? What would it want to do? It was getting in the way of killing off the Wulfyres. She had to get rid of it. Except . . .

Except what had it done when a mob was out hunting it? What had it done other than track her down to that clearing? Trying to devour her before she could devour it. And in similar time, it had tried to devour the other Wulfyres, attempting to finish what Shesheshen had wanted to do. It had eaten Ode before being driven off by an army. This offspring might be better at being Shesheshen than she was herself.

Now that delectable lump of bad intentions was in hiding, somewhere in Underlook Forest. It could come for her again. Or it could go for the Wulfyres.

The thoughts were too many and too fervent for Shesheshen. Her egg sac swelled, new bony spurs puncturing through innards and sending forth fresh spurts of blood until she felt like a living soup. Her eggs throbbed, making her chest and limbs twitch with their demand. They wanted their nest.

Under that consistent twitching, Shesheshen lay on the basement floor and melted into a pool of loose flesh, with clothing and chipped bones drifting amid her stomachs. She pooled along the slime, and drank it up into herself. It tasted like herself.

Any gods, above or below, they were surely laughing at how badly love had undone her.

PART SIX

THIS IS THE LAST TIME

CHAPTER THIRTY-ONE

She didn't have time to hunt, or even to drag some guard into an alley. Every fear dragged her back to Homily: fear of being suspected if she was gone for too long, and fear that the wyrm-thing would hunt her down, and fear of what the other Wulfyres would do to her. Exhausted and famished and feeling like a failure, Shesheshen dragged herself back to the woman she loved, hoping it wasn't a mistake to be near her when her eggs were so furious.

The top floor of the Red Dragon was a suite of four chambers, typically kept unoccupied due to an exorbitant rate in order to maintain its prestige. The entire floor was currently reserved for Baroness Wulfyre. Shesheshen was relieved her nose had gone dead again so she was spared the perfumes this place was doused in.

As she and Homily climbed the stairs to the suite, they heard Epigram's voice. "That's a shit plan. And why should I be taking ideas from you two? You got my brother killed."

Epigram half-reclined across a sofa that was more pillow than furniture. She was still in her gilded breastplate and greaves, like she might get into a military campaign over breakfast. From the look of her, she hadn't slept, and had spent all night instead on her makeup. Her lips were painted shiny black. Shesheshen had never seen eyeshadow that shade of indigo. She wondered how those eyelids would taste.

On the opposite side of the room stood two annoyingly familiar people: the monster hunters Rourke and Malik. They had exchanged their gear for slacks and doublets of coarse material that couldn't have been much more comfortable than steel. The wound on Malik's temple glistened with a salve, and he held a map of Underlook Forest.

Malik said, "We have been working without additional compensation this entire time, and we were the ones who spotted the wyrm outside your camp. You would not have known it was coming at all without us."

Epigram said, "A lot of good that did us. My sister died that night."

"I'm sympathetic for your losses. I lost my family to a wyrm, and that's why I came to study under Sire Rourke. But he and I have done nothing but work to end this curse."

Halfway through his words, Epigram examined her fingertips. "If I hear right, you're the one who got a bump on his head and left my brother in that lair."

Rourke took a step toward Epigram, pointing a thickly callused finger at her. "That's the last time you throw that in our faces. We were dragged into an unsafe spelunk by your brother, and we did everything to keep him safe until he pushed it too far. Malik was injured while literally carrying your brother out of there."

A sound that typically only came out of sick birds escaped Epigram's throat. She lolled her head back as though rolling her eyes were not enough condemnation. In her theatrical movement, she caught sight of Homily and Shesheshen on the stairs. Her thin eyebrows arched.

"About time you showed up. Are you finished fucking yet?"

It was a good sign that Homily walked by her sister without responding. Shesheshen followed her past the racks of dresses and weapons alike. None of the beds were occupied. She didn't see the Baroness anywhere. The whole suite looked empty except for the monster hunters and the sister in gold.

After poking her head into a side room, Homily asked, "Where is Mother?"

Epigram made a noise like a bowel movement had come out of the wrong end. "She's at an undisclosed location. One she won't even disclose to me. Do you believe that? She doesn't trust anyone to not 'taint her grieving,' as she puts it."

Malik set his map of the forest aside and turned to Homily. "Which, as we were trying to explain to Sire Sernine earlier, is utterly unsafe. A fortified location is the best chance at repelling a wyrm. If the thing tracks her by their curse, or by smell, hiding with a few guards is worse than being out in the open with many."

"Thanks," Epigram said, flipping her cheek-length blonde hair. "I'll be sure to tell her that as soon as I know where the hell she is."

Homily sat down on a broad couch framed by the longer window in the suite and gestured for Shesheshen to join her. The egg sac in Shesheshen's chest pulsed, with more pricking and punctures from the bony spurs of the eggs inside. They demanded she cave to the natural order of things and give them a parent. But she didn't want to be natural. She wanted to be herself, and to let Homily be.

So she sat on a slender chair on the opposite side of an end table from Homily. There was disappointment in Homily's eyes. She'd yet to say anything, but it was obvious she noticed Shesheshen was distancing herself.

Not being able to trust herself was new for Shesheshen. She didn't care for it.

Since so many of them were looking at her, she said, "You have been talking about how to stop this monster?"

Rourke rolled a shoulder like it was stuck. "We have been trying to explain that this monster could be anywhere."

Epigram said, "It's a fat gray lump of shit the size of a bull covered in flaming arrows. We'd see it coming."

Homily leaned forward. "It can take other forms. The locals say it can look like people."

The eggs in Shesheshen's chest threw a riot and dug at her other organs. She clenched her throat against them, slicing slender bones through the inner tissues of her neck to cage the egg sac in. She tried to suppress the grunt, and failed.

When the humans glanced at her because of her noise, she said, "Then we are not safe here? If it wanted to get in, it would."

That was so on the nose she expected the monster hunters would spear her to death right there and then. Rourke gave her a long, sour look before shaking a hand. "Exactly. You can't hide from its hunger."

Epigram's black-painted lips parted to show her teeth. "The point of having guards in groups of four and six and eight is that one monster can't get anywhere alone. Do you see me being eaten? No curse is sneaking in here."

Malik looked down at his left boot, which had a single white scratch on the instep of the sole, like a freshly drawn god mark. Shesheshen had never seen someone draw a god mark on their person before, yet Malik looked at the scratch as though he was asking some god below for strength. "If it knows you are here, then nowhere is safe. The thing we fought would've crushed any three soldiers. It serves evil forces."

Rourke said, "We're lucky if it's mindless. If it's intelligent, then the thing is pure evil."

"Great," Epigram said, teeth disappearing behind a new frown. "So it's either dumb and I'm dead, or it's smart and I'm dead. I can't imagine why Mother doesn't want you people around for morale."

Staying quiet was harder than talking for Shesheshen at this point. She rubbed under her eyes, trying to calm herself against the nuisance of being gossiped about right in front of herself. It would serve them right to be reminded that humans killed more living things—including other humans—than anything else did.

Homily blew out a slow breath that made Shesheshen want to touch and support her. But she couldn't risk getting herself agitated. She tried to make a soft expression in Homily's direction. "What are you thinking?"

Homily said, "We need to find this thing. Not wait for it."

Rourke looked to Malik. "Getting that thing into the open again will be difficult. It knows what we can do."

Epigram scoffed. "You want me to drug another bear? Good luck."

"The bear is the wrong bait," said Rourke. "I've hunted a few cursed things in my time that were tethered to a family or a bloodline. They don't come to rescue their furry friends. That thing was hunting Wulfyres that night. A Wulfyre is what it will come for."

The seat crinkled under Epigram as she sat up, short blonde hair fanning around her eyes. "So, what? You want to shackle one of us to a tree this time? I'm out of little sisters to feed to it. How many troops would surround us this time? All of L'État Bon?"

"You aren't going to like this," Rourke said. He looked at Malik again, and they shared a somber nod.

Malik looked down. "It's a risk. You could lose . . . much."

Epigram looked ready to spit at the man, but Homily interjected. "This isn't easy on any of us. But what is your idea?"

Rourke said, "This is something I've done for a few cursed families before. This time, you can't be surrounded by a camp of troops. We'd have to make it seem like there was nothing but you Wulfyres in the way. One of you might be enough to draw it into the open. Let the wyrm think it can pick one of you off."

Epigram said, "Then I get eaten while you try to catch the thing? Great plan."

Malik jumped in. "Of course, it's a ruse. He . . . he used this to save my life, once."

Shesheshen almost agreed with Epigram. Besides the benefit of Epigram getting eaten alive, if this queer offspring was bent on devouring Wulfyres, then making one of them seem vulnerable was the best way to trick it. It could've worked on herself.

"You could hit it with something," Shesheshen said. "Some rosemary or peppermint or silver charm that wounds it while it tries to flee. Use one of Homily's scent lures. Something trackers can follow."

Of course, she'd plan to follow it too. If she caught up to it first, she could consume it, and that problem would be out of the way. It could be enough raw material necessary to quell her egg sac and gain control of these damnable urges.

Malik said, "We'd only stake out Underlook Forest during daylight hours, when we have full visibility on what's happening."

Rourke picked up, "And we'd set pit traps. Have animals that can follow the scent and attack. We'd be on this thing before it could get to any of you."

There was a dry second, following by Epigram's hacking laughter. She stuck a hand into her hair, raking it from her bleary eyes. Those eyes cast an accusatory glance at Homily. "Good fucking luck with that plan. Who in our family is going to risk their lives like that?"

CHAPTER THIRTY-TWO

Homily's voice was so composed that it was obvious she didn't believe herself. "This will be safer than if I stayed in town. It will take less than a week, and then the curse will be broken. Then we can live."

"If it does not kill you. Homily, please."

Shesheshen followed her from the inn to the storehouse, where L'Étatsters with waxed mustaches cared for inventory and signed out item after item. The Baroness's authorities seemed to have seized every storehouse in town to support the campaign. Between all the townsfolk and the guards on every corner, it was too public for the confession that had to happen.

The liquid samples desirable to make lures were rare, taking Homily several minutes to go through inventory and cross-reference with her notes. For the entire time, Shesheshen paced around her, like any good protector would around its nest. Her egg sac convulsed in a roiling heat, sending blood coursing through her body and more warmth to anywhere than was healthy. All that blood hurried her thoughts faster than she could follow.

"I fended that thing off from you with a pot of rosemary oil," Homily said. "I can take care of myself."

"It is a wild animal, if not worse. We do not know what it is capable of."

"My youngest sister and oldest brother are dead. I'm not going to let another one go. This curse has to end."

"You have saved Epigram many times. You told me how."

Homily lowered a bottle from her eyes, and then drew in so close that it was like she'd kiss Shesheshen again.

Homily whispered, "After what I told you, how couldn't I do this? I ruined her when she was young."

"She was not your fault. And she is not your fault."

"Epigram thinks no one in this world loves her—she wasn't even close to Ode, and Mother mourns Ode like neither Epigram nor I exist. She wanted to be like Catharsis, and now he's gone too. This can be the proof that she needs. Proof that she matters to someone. That it's safe to finally leave what she was in childhood behind. I'm going to save her."

Homily hefted the largest box of supplies, glass jars of transparent substances clinking under her chin. She carried them away from Shesheshen, off to the same cart she'd once used to save Shesheshen's life. The woman had no idea the irony that was raining all around her.

So Shesheshen hoisted the next sack. It was a rough parcel of the Wulfyre family's special bombs. Bombs that could well be turned around and used to end her existence tomorrow. It was worth contemplating.

The bombs were less appalling than the truth. Whoever Shesheshen coupled with would perish, devoured by their young. Homily didn't even know it, and yet, she would agree to it. She would find a way to contort her soul into consenting. It was the same emotion that made her kind, and made her risk her life for a mother and a sister who would never change. Homily would die for a family with Shesheshen because a lifetime of slowly dying for her own family had fooled her into thinking this was right.

Shesheshen looked at the green scarf trailing from Homily's neck. The thought of one of their young eating the scars from that flesh was too much—Shesheshen nearly threw up two of her stomachs and tottered forward trying not to drop the bag of bombs on her own feet.

When she looked up, Homily held out her hands to take the bombs. "I'll load those, thank you."

Shesheshen let her get a hand on the bag, but refused to let it go. She said, "Why is this sacrifice for your family different? What will make it different?"

Homily's expression went tense before she managed to look down. She exposed something fraught in herself. How Shesheshen wanted to hold her in that moment.

"Because," she said, "this is the last time. This is for them, and for Ode, and for Catharsis, and for Father and Aunt Agatha, and for the whole isthmus. I'll help them with this, and then no more."

"You will not let them hurt you anymore?"

"It's the last time, Siobhan. I promise."

Believing her was so desirable. If only she could. Shesheshen dreaded that "the last time" had never been the last time for anything like this.

She said, "I cannot stop you from going. No matter how much it would destroy me to lose you, you will go?"

It was equal parts statement and question.

Homily said, "I have to. It's my last gift to the family. If this isn't enough, then . . . then that's it. But I am going."

"All right," Shesheshen said, pulling her hood tight around her head. "Then I am going as well. Let us hunt your family curse."

CHAPTER THIRTY-THREE

The return to the woods went too quickly. This time the mercenaries were smart, setting camp in a tight circle of tents that had fewer points of ingress. Supplies were watched by rotating groups of four. No one dug a pit trap without several others watching over them. Shesheshen had no time to sabotage. Not with how concerned she was over Homily.

Shesheshen watched as Homily approached Epigram, who was working on a crossbow. Homily began raising her arms, offering an embrace if the partial gesture was reciprocated, and the younger woman turned her body away from her for more polish, as unavailable as a closed door. Epigram heaved dismissive breaths. Once, as Homily said something too delicate to hear over the breeze, Epigram reached to her belt for a jeweled knife that she'd certainly used in the same company just days ago.

Homily's voice rose. "Think about it? Please?"

Then the world came apart. It sounded like the landscape clearing its throat, rumbling through the ground and tearing through the air loud enough to make thunder timid. White smoke billowed from beyond the east side of the camp, immediately springing higher than the canopy, and unfurling like the wings of a waking god. Within the whiteness of the smoke lingered brownish yellow tones like spoiled egg yolks. Clumps of earth spattered the tents.

Two women ran into camp from that direction, howling pure nonsense and shielding their heads with their arms. Shesheshen had never seen humans run while cowering before. It was like if they weren't fast enough, the smoke would drag them in and consume them. Was this another form her offspring could take? It was unlike anything she'd ever seen.

Through the haze came trees, three dark trunks falling and splitting the smoke and landing with additional thundercracks. Half of each tree was charred black, as was all the ground visible through the smoke. It smelled horrid—not so much like heat as like the death of cold. It filled up Shesheshen's lungs and made her seal her breathing passages against the feel of air scraping her innards.

"Impressed? This is the might my family gave L'État Bon."

Shesheshen turned to find Baroness Wulfyre behind her, slouching in a wicker chair. She wore steel fluted armor, from her shins up to her collar. Something about the sharp ribbing of her breastplate gave the image of a wide mouthful of metal teeth. The literal steel teeth of Shesheshen's mother dangled from a chain over the Baroness's breastplate.

Shesheshen said, "Your Exaltation. I did not know you were here."

Baroness Wulfyre scoffed. "The wyrm won't die without me there."

"I heard you were in hiding."

"I don't hide. I arm myself."

The camp grew dense with people. A swarm of armored goons amassed within yards of the Baroness's seat, distracted by the explosion, but hardly distracted enough. Additional guards bolted across the camp for the Baroness's location, and she waved them to cease.

Shesheshen watched the smoky light refract off the steel fangs of that necklace. This wasn't nearly private enough to do what she needed to.

She asked, "Was that a trap out there?"

"A test of one. Someone always has to lose an arm before the team takes it seriously." Baroness Wulfyre gestured to the still-expanding mass of smoke. "This is the strength of my family line. The last time L'État Bon warred with the Engmars, it lasted twenty years and got neither of them anywhere. If L'État Bon treats my family appropriately, then the next time they war with Engmar, it will not last so long."

Shesheshen thought of the holes in the ceiling of her lair. She'd always suspected they were the work of humans. "The Wulfyre family bombs?"

"Stronger than what we used to kill the previous wyrm," Baroness Wulfyre said, fixing her braided hair into a ball and securing it to her scalp in a teal kerchief embroidered with a gold spruce tree. "Catharsis discovered a different kind of explosive using black powder when he was on excursions that improved the family recipe for bombs. It quelled enough so-called revolutionaries to earn him a legacy. Now, his legacy will kill the thing that took him from me."

Out on the periphery of the camp, a couple of guards in thick armor guided Homily inward. She kept trying to approach the guards who had been near the blast, trying to give them tin cups of water. It was reassuring to see she was surrounded by guards. Epigram was gone from her side, visibly complaining to the camp cook about something while filling her plate.

Shesheshen asked the Baroness, "Are you sure you want to use something like that near your daughters?"

Understating threats was difficult for her. She knew that she had to understate reality with powerful people. How to do it required more social experience than she had, or wanted.

Clearly she hadn't understated enough, as Baroness Wulfyre screwed up her face. "Who are you to question me?"

"My apologies, Your Exaltation."

Baroness Wulfyre grabbed the handle of her tall spear, made of oak and steel, and so unusually thick that most humans wouldn't be able to get a hand around it. At the base of the blade was a tuft of red animal hair, like the weapon had grown a lion's mane. Likely that hair was a trophy from a previous hunt. She took it by that mane, stroking the hair as she moved to the edge of her seat. "Like I would risk the last two children I have left if I didn't know what I was doing? It is all measured. You'll never understand what it takes to run a family. Why are you even here?"

Shesheshen couldn't help looking at her mother's steel fangs again. "I owe your family quite a deal."

"You don't fool me. I know your kind."

Staring was not the correct answer. Shesheshen knew that much. Her first instinct was to lie.

She said, "I . . . am not trying to fool you."

"People like you made my daughter grow into a disappointment. I will have a word with you soon. In private, with no eavesdropping guards, and none of my children for you to hide behind."

She didn't breathe. Staring was unavoidable. Shesheshen said, "I look forward to that."

There was a sharpness as Baroness Wulfyre said, "You look forward to it?"

Shesheshen guessed how to please her. "I look forward to it, Your Exaltation."

"There's an obedient girl."

"Mother," Epigram yelled from across the camp. "Who told them to serve goose here? Goose, of all birds?"

Like that, Baroness Wulfyre left Shesheshen to argue the flavors and merits of various birds. The cook shrank behind his kettles, not speaking up for his choice of meats. More armored guards swarmed around them by the sentence.

Shesheshen lingered by the empty chair of a ruler, watching the argument, and watching the thinning of the smoke in the heavens above the canopy. When that one bomb had gone off, the entire camp had lost their civilization. The terror of its violence was greater than a monster or a baroness.

For a moment, Shesheshen wished she was a bomb. An explosion was the closest something could come to godhood. To become the power to erase everything that threatened her.

Amid the thinning smoke, Homily walked beyond the periphery of camp. Mud stained her skirt from where she'd assisted the rattled guards. She tromped along like she didn't mind, and might even get down in the pit for more blasted mud. She hunkered over one of the charred trees and scraped specimens from their bark. Where there was awe for others, there was curiosity for her.

In an hour, she would wander out as bait for a monster with only her mother's fleeting concern to spare her from the next explosion. Shesheshen couldn't shield her from that. And if the offspring was wily enough, it would pick her off before the bombs could give her mercy. It was after the Wulfyres. What else did it want? Except the Wulfyres, and Shesheshen herself?

Slowly, she opened her breathing passages, to take in two lungfuls of the acrid air. She couldn't shield Homily from an explosion. But she could turn one into a distraction.

CHAPTER THIRTY-FOUR

Before she went out to face death, Homily handed out refreshments. She carried a tray of piping hot tea and egg cakes, which she dispensed with the same geniality that had won Shesheshen's love. Watching her now with a helmet buckled over her curly brown hair and sweet-talking the people who were likely to watch her blown limb from limb was hard to bear. This was more of that civilization Shesheshen detested. It should not have been easier for this human woman to harm herself with a smile than tell her family "No."

Then Homily went on her route. She wore a cloak of sheep's wool, a gift from the townsfolk of Underlook, dyed a shade of blue that made it appear that she had wrapped herself in a slice of midday sky. She wore it on her first attempt through the path they'd designed for her, and the engineers stood behind walls of rock with teeth clenched, drawing god marks at the base of their protective walls while they whispered prayers.

"Good gods, above and below. Good gods, above and below."

As Homily turned away from the onlookers, she seemed to gain height and poise. She stepped lightly for her size, with the posture of a tightrope walker, leading with her toe into the east. The midday-sky cloak ruffled around her bulky thighs. Toe after toe, she followed the path she'd memorized across the pine needles. If she forgot where to step, she would be forgotten in a white cloud of smoke.

Seventeen separate pit traps waited out there, some of which Shesheshen had dug herself until she couldn't stand the work anymore. The slightest of them was six feet deep, and at the bottom waited trigger mechanisms and multiple bombs. Shesheshen could not see how, if the offspring did scamper across and fall into one, Homily wouldn't be consumed by the blast, especially if it set off any of the bombs in the neighboring pit traps.

Nor could she see where the pit traps were, despite having helped dig them. Rourke and Malik were skilled at deception, using burlap and fiber nets to mimic the shape of terrain, and giving them a convincing coat of dirt and pine needles. If Shesheshen had been told to go fetch her, she'd certainly topple to her death. How funny it would be for the Wulfyres to get their wish and exterminate her, without ever knowing it.

This was the great plan all human ingenuity had concocted: to make Homily walk an invisible maze until the offspring was lured to its death.

A monster could make a better plan. And she did.

The offspring wanted Homily's blood. But more than Homily, and probably more than any Wulfyre, it would want to devour Shesheshen herself, to become whole and powerful. It was the same longing Shesheshen felt. Thus the best bait to spare Homily was Shesheshen herself.

All Shesheshen had to do was blow a small bomb on one side of camp, to distract the pernicious humans and take the pressure off Homily. While they were gathered in the wrong spot, Shesheshen would be on the other side of camp, alone, irresistible to the monster she'd accidentally created.

She told herself this was a good idea. Some part of her believed it.

Shapeshifting to look like one of the guards was the easiest part. While a couple soldiers sneaked off to fight irritable bowel movements from some allergy to goose, Shesheshen slipped inside their tents and went fluid. She dripped her body inside a suit of armor with a single blue feather on one shoulder. With her gauntleted hands, she plumped out her facial features to look more like Catharsis; she had all the bone structure she needed for it.

When her egg sac swelled and sent more blood to rush and disturb her thoughts, she calmed herself by insisting the rest of the plan was simple. It was about distraction.

She crossed the camp in the cumbersome fluted armor like a professional soldier: swaggering, pretending to scratch herself, and when somebody complained about the goose, she gave her most convincing effort at a fart. Why had she ever doubted her ability to pass? She made a great human.

"Hey!"

Someone yelled in her direction, with the entitled tone that humans associated with authority. That was no good. She forced herself not to look in that direction, and instead walked quicker for the armory tent. It was unguarded, since everyone was on duty to be ready to drop on the offspring if it appeared.

"You. One-feather guard. Get over here."

It was that entitled voice again, and definitely aimed at her. She had to turn and stoop to enter the threshold of the armory tent, and on her way in she saw who was following her. It was Epigram, nostrils flared and fists clenched.

"I want more guards on my detail. My fucking sister isn't the only one who needs protection. Gather a detail for me immediately."

When Shesheshen didn't immediately give in, Epigram came marching in her direction. A crossbow bobbed in her hands, with a peculiar kind of bolt that Shesheshen knew all too well. Of course she had the same poison weaponry as her brother.

This would be bad. Shesheshen had to be quick.

She pushed along racks of halberds and crossbows, searching for the sacks. It was damnably dark in here. Fire was probably forbidden, given its untoward relationship with black powder. She had to grope around, bending over in the thick armor. It was almost impossible to move freely in this stuff.

"Want to spend the rest of your life in prison?"

Epigram's voice was right outside the tent. She'd be in here any moment. There was the temptation to drag her in, but she wasn't the sort to be devoured discreetly. The whole camp would hear them.

The metal toes of Shesheshen's left boot kicked something firm and hollow. She fondled at it, and found it was round. It was one of the orb shells they used for their bombs.

Quickly she tore through the sacks, looking for the smallest bomb they had. There had to be another size. Something she could throw.

There it was. The hard-shell container filled her right hand, less than half the size of the circular ones. She took two of these smaller bombs.

The flap to the tent whipped open, casting sunlight across all the shade and blades within.

But as Epigram entered the tent, she'd find an empty suit of armor sitting cross-legged atop two bags of her family's bombs. Maybe she'd assign the armor to guard detail.

Shesheshen slithered out below the tent, through a gap only rodents could dream of enjoying. No one was guarding the backside of these tents, and the nearest camp border guards were several yards away. She crouched behind a crate of onions and pulled a robe around herself as she reassembled her body. Behind her and inside the tent, Epigram swore at some god or another.

Shesheshen peeked around the tents, just far enough to see where Homily was on her route. She had actually finished the first loop through her route and was taking a brief break, surrounded by a group of panting and relieved guards. The younger monster hunter with all the jeweled earrings, Malik, extended her a cup of tea, and she looked like she was trying to get him to drink it instead.

A shame that tea was going to be spilled. Next to Shesheshen's crate was a sconce with its lit torch. That was terrible safety practice, given the bombs on the other side of the tent. She'd have to tell someone. Later.

For now, she used it to light the fuse. It hissed like a child making fun of snakes. She stepped quickly, spinning around as though to throw a discus. Her ligaments stretched, tendons swelled, and she flung it so far into the north of the forest that it could've been a spooked bird. In another moment, Epigram would be swearing about something much worse than empty armor.

She hid the second bomb against herself and wound her way south around the tents, staying out of sight. There were too many guards along the south side, like they'd been cunning enough to guess what she'd do. More likely, they were guarding the Baroness's location.

As that godlike roar covered them all, and a shower of dirt and smoke attacked the north side, it became much easier to go south. Guards broke from their posts, calling for the glory of the Royal Family of L'État Bon in taking down the beast. It was almost charming.

Shesheshen reached the bare edge of camp and found she was on her own. Opening her breathing passages felt like a mistake, what with the awful tang of black-powder smoke in the air. She choked at first, working through it and exhaling as hard as she could. For whatever the offspring could smell, if it picked up anything beneath the bomb smoke, she wanted it to smell her. To know its apex prey was available.

She climbed over the waist-high bag wall at the edge of camp and set foot into the open wilderness. No traps here. No defenses, except this second bomb of hers.

A hundred voices yelled in fear of what was going on in the north, and who saw the beast, and which way it had gone. One voice stood out. Her ear couldn't avoid seeking it.

"Where is Siobhan? Sire Rourke, have you seen her? Which tent is she in? She has to be here. Please, have you seen her?"

The excuses weren't worth listening to, and Homily's follow-up pleas were too hard to take. Shesheshen had to let her be afraid. It was her role. Bait wasn't allowed to be sorry.

CHAPTER THIRTY-FIVE

Shesheshen stepped outside the camp's boundaries with all that loud human confusion behind her, and from it, all she took was a torch and her second bomb. Ample sunlight prodded through the canopy above, giving her line of sight into much of the woodland. Drainage patterns carved several trenches, some of them multiple feet deep and running far into the south.

It would be light out for hours. The torch was not for illumination.

It was for the bomb in her pocket.

Beneath her robe, she relaxed her organs and pulled parts of herself to the surface. There was a bear trap ready to fly from her abdomen, and three metal skewers surrounding her shin bone that she could force out and puncture with. She'd wrestled plenty of ravenous things in her time. If the offspring was too mighty, the bomb would bring it to heel.

This offspring was slow to fight. Nowhere among the trees did she spot a single stilt leg; no tree trunks or branches scampering like insect limbs.

No monsters came stampeding around the left side of the camp wall, either. She arched up, to make sure it wasn't sneaking between the tents behind her. The offspring had to be on its way from somewhere.

From somewhere in the camp, Homily called, "Siobhan! Siobhan!"

Her egg sac revolted like it was going to tear free of every membrane holding it in place. New bony spikes stabbed her from within. Shesheshen shuddered, muttering apologies to Homily. This wasn't meant to torture her. She was helping.

She just wanted the offspring to come and attack her. It was made of her. It ought to be bolder than this.

Except she was a crafty monster. It's why the entire region feared her. She didn't often kick down doors and ravage people in their beds, unless she was desperate. Typically, she was subtler. She was pickier about her violence than legends let on.

If she were to hunt someone, wouldn't she creep up on them? Collecting herself against the stabbing pains, she turned her gaze to the dips in the earth around her. They were flecked with fallen pine needles and jutting bits of shale.

In the darker bits of those draining paths and trenches, something moved. She held out the torch and spotted slick flesh the colors of earth and fallen pine needles. The offspring was shifting the color of its epidermis to match its surroundings, and it wasn't coming on tall legs of timber. It crawled toward her, with a series of holes opening in its flank as though to breathe—to taste the air, and the scents out there.

From the look of it, the offspring had brought no weaponry. Its body dripped across a trench, nearly flattened, showing few hard substances inside. It had abandoned the deer skulls and branches of its skeleton. Without all its internal matter, it revealed itself to not be terribly large. Its skeleton had given it a greater impression of size the other night. Had that been by design?

Shesheshen put her spare hand into her pocket, ready to draw the bomb if the offspring sprang at her. She wasn't going to be smothered or silenced. When it made its move, she'd catch it.

The blob of gray and black flesh settled at the bank, at the end of the trench, just two yards from her. Shesheshen easily could have made that jump. She'd captured meals in longer leaps than that.

So why wasn't it attacking her? The other night, it had loomed over her, ready to engulf her in its abyssal maw. Now it loitered, flesh swirling like it was a living stew set to simmer.

Gradually she recognized its scent, because it smelled like herself. It had her own exhaustion. It smelled precisely as tired as she did.

She crouched, not drawing closer, and not releasing the bomb in her pocket. She set the torch to one side, so there was nothing in the air between them.

The lump of living flesh bobbled there, without a face, and without fear. It was as though this lump of herself had tracked her down and was offering itself to her. Despite herself, Shesheshen salivated. So many glands got to working, craving that part of herself that could now be a meal. She could be the predator again.

If it was baiting a trap for her, it was working. She'd never been so hungry as when she looked at this missing piece of herself. She regretted the lack of a fight—she wanted to wrestle it to the ground and pierce it with fangs she hadn't yet grown.

The pool of flesh rolled out of the trench and toward her, staying low to the ground. It was like a submitting dog, giving obeisance to a master. Like it wanted to be reunited.

She wanted to ask this thing if it had intended to just reunite with her the other night. If that had all been a mistake. And if it had a mind—if it had other things it yearned for. Things more important than submission and sacrifice.

It oozed toward her, stretching out a round bit of flesh from its smooth body. Was it offering her a taste? Or communion?

She dropped the bomb in her pocket. Splaying her fingers, she reached for this thing that had once been part of herself. Warmth greeted her touch. She caressed over its skin, which promptly squished flat. There were no bones hidden inside. No traps.

A few more holes opened in the lump-thing's back, exhaling air that neither of them needed. It was a heavy sound. A sound she associated with Homily. It was like a sigh before sleep.

There were so many questions she didn't know how to ask. This beautiful, horrible, familiar and still different thing. She could've spent an eternity crouching with it. She wanted to and, stranger still, felt this thing wanted to.

"Out of the way!"

Words tore through their stillness and Shesheshen was forced to the ground. Heavy boots thudded around the earth, and a blade that might as well have been as long as a sunset swung through her vision. It sliced through that extended lump of flesh, sending the blade dead to the ground.

The offspring reared back into the trench, air hissing out of various holes in its hide.

The Baroness Wulfyre pursued it into the trench, swinging her red-maned spear overhead, rosemary oil glistening on both the blade and the red hair that decorated its neck. The spearhead smashed down, metal splintering shale and cleaving the dirt as the offspring wove around. It threw several tendrils from its body, latching onto the wide hilt of her spear. When the Baroness pulled her spear free of the earth, the offspring slung itself up, stabbing another tendril into her neck. The wet tearing sound resonated through Shesheshen's entire body.

She wanted to tackle the Baroness from behind and tear off the rest of her neck, but more people ran around her. Malik and Rourke whirled around her right side, both of them swinging torches at the offspring. Soldiers followed them, their feathers swinging in the breeze, swinging maces and aiming rosemary-poisoned crossbows.

The offspring sprang from the Baroness's face, landing in the deepest trench and scurrying away. With every step, it grew more limbs, so that it was running on dozens before Malik could set a single foot behind it. Malik turned with Rourke, both of them checking Baroness Wulfyre's neck.

"After it, you bastards," the Baroness said, spitting in the dirt. She brought her hand away from her neck, which was clean. Apparently the offspring hadn't managed to break her skin, even as deep as it had looked like it had skewered her. "If that thing isn't dead tonight, I'll have all your families strung up. Get the horses!"

CHAPTER THIRTY-SIX

They were on horseback before Shesheshen could start running. She snagged a horse of her own so that the leaders never got too far ahead of her, not that she knew how to stop them from killing the young blob. Arguments wouldn't work. Fighting an entire regiment of soldiers and professional monster hunters seemed even less wise.

They split up a tenth of a mile in. Her clever little blob-thing kept diving into hollow tree trunks and between ditches, making hunters spread out. If it was lucky, it'd find an underground cave, but those were rarer than legends made them sound.

"I saw it on this side!" called a mercenary up on the north cusp of their sweep. "I see movement."

Rourke waved a torch to dismiss him, then pointed to a smear across some of the shale in a trench. "It bled here. Or pissed. It can't have been up on that side."

Talk like that thinned the groups, so that they moved in packs of four or six. Nobody had the boldness to ride alone, except the Baroness. She kept getting ahead of Rourke and Malik, who stuck near her like shadows. Every few moments she stabbed at another pile of pine cones like it harbored her quarry.

Baroness Wulfyre snarled back at Shesheshen, "Why didn't you kill it when you had the chance?"

"I was going to," she lied. "Someone knocked me over."

From the way the Baroness squinted and then looked away, it had probably been her. At least it shut her up. The necklace clinked against her armor, the steel fangs glowing orange in torchlight.

The light grayed and thinned like an aging widow's hair as they got deeper into the woods. Roots thickened and wove together, troubling the horses for every step they wanted outside of a trench, and riders feared descending into those trenches for what might wait in them. A woman in the nearest group over drew a religious sign on her forehead in rosemary.

Rourke said, “Daylight will only last us so long. If we don't find it soon, we should return to camp and lure the thing out using our original plan.”

“It's too close,” Baroness Wulfyre said, wiping at her bottom lip. “I'm not letting it slip through my fingers.”

This was an opportunity. Shesheshen rode up alongside the Baroness. “I will stay with you. Homily would want it.”

“So you're less afraid of the dark than these big, strong monster hunters I'm paying?” Baroness Wulfyre asked it while looking straight at Rourke and Malik.

“I do not scare easily, Your Exaltation.”

Malik said, “It's not about fear. It's practicality.”

“What's that?” Rourke asked, shielding his eyes and looking around a thick grove of white firs. “Did you all hear that?”

Malik shook his head, nonetheless following Rourke's lead. Rourke asked the Baroness, “Can you hang back for a minute? I need to make sure I didn't just hear it breathing.”

“Go,” Baroness Wulfyre said. “Bring me its heart tonight. Believe me. I'm not as forgiving as my son was.”

Shesheshen cast a smile after the monster hunters as they rode beyond thorny brush and down a dim slope. As they descended from view, her smile grew. Suddenly she was alone with her girlfriend's mother. Did humans get this excited at such opportunities?

Within a minute, Baroness Wulfyre dismounted and had her red-maned spear again. She doused the blade and mane in pungent oil. She held it in both hands, jabbing its tip into innocent bushes. Around her left arm she wound the reins, keeping the horse close like a living shield. She was wary of every direction, except Shesheshen's.

Shesheshen asked, “Baroness?”

Baroness Wulfyre hesitated, then ground the toe of a boot into the earth. “Do you hear a damned thing? One breath of that flesh-eating shit?”

Shesheshen tilted her head back and shapeshifted her ear canals, molding them to what she recollected of the heads of screech owls. Did she hear a damned thing? Not a slither or a scamper of the offspring's movement. If she had to guess, it was long gone to somewhere with actual hiding places. There were squirrels in nests somewhere, a couple skunks in a squabble that was liable to soon grow fragrant. More audible was the distant babble of L'État Bon soldiers, whose thick accents and dialects couldn't hide that they all wanted to go home.

She lied. "It could be close."

"Bring the torch over here."

Shesheshen dismounted, carrying her torch and fiddling a hand over the bomb in her pocket. It would be fitting to blow this woman apart, the same way she'd done to Shesheshen's own mother.

Wherever the woman pointed, there Shesheshen held the torch. It wasn't dark enough yet to be terribly useful. It brought out the orange and red notes in all the dead needles.

Shesheshen said, "Baroness? I wondered if I could ask you something."

"I wondered when you'd come out with it. You people always want something. What is it?"

"All those years ago, in your keep. What was the hunt like? When you slew the previous wyrm?"

Baroness Wulfyre's entire cheek curled up in her smirk. "Ah. You want a ghost story? You want to know what it was like when the horrible wyrm ravaged my husband? That way you'll fool me into thinking we're getting familiar?"

Shesheshen kept trying to imagine her mother, and all she could do was imagine herself in that same fortress, less dirty, with fewer dead bodies. No memory echoed back when she called into her soul. So when she imagined this woman hunting it down, all she had was the image of herself being pursued.

Standing behind the Baroness as she stabbed brush, Shesheshen asked, "What was the monster like?"

"It was like this one, if grander. Like slime made out of skin. It fit into any hole, which is why you'd better watch your footing. Don't become supper and leave me alone to kill this thing by myself."

Despite herself, the flesh of Shesheshen's hands shifted from beige to slate gray. The torch couldn't hide that. "It had gray skin? With streaks?"

"You shouldn't think of it like that. It could make itself look like anything. That's why it took so long to hunt. It was the most conniving thing my family ever crossed paths with."

"Conniving. Yes," Shesheshen said as she adjusted her bones, pulling the steel skewers out of her leg. She sucked them into her left arm, until their tips tickled the flesh of her palm. From there, they could spring out like claws. "And it cursed you?"

"Huh?" The Baroness clicked her teeth together. "Yes. Of course it did."

In that moment, Shesheshen was certain there was no curse. There might not be any such thing as a curse on any corner of the map they called the world. There surely was no such thing hanging over this woman's head—not one chilling her as she kept stomping through the wilderness, far from the camp and the highway, like a monster wasn't right behind her.

Shesheshen asked, "Did it have a voice? Did it say anything, before you pulled its teeth out?"

The Baroness titled her head, an ear aimed at the sky. For all her human features and indigo makeup, in that moment she looked like a curious bird. "Did you hear something?"

Yes, she did hear something. The delicate snipping of flesh as metal tips sprang from her palm, and the rending of soft tissues that propelled them, and the gripping tension of muscle fibers. Baroness Wulfyre didn't have the opportunity to turn further and see the source of the sounds before three metal points drove through the flesh at the top of her neck, and up under her skull. Two points drove through soft matter and struck bone they couldn't crack. A lucky third skewer drove out through the cartilage of her nose.

The sigh wasn't unlike the ones her offspring had made, except this was the last noise the Baroness would ever make. Her lungs seized up, then quit the job. Her whole heavy body dropped, dragged by armored plates, so that she was on her knees by the time her bowels gave way.

Shesheshen kept her grip fast, refusing to drop her any further. She forced the dead woman's eyes to stare out at the forest that she didn't own anymore. By human standards, this woman was warm. Her heat seeped in fluids down the skewers and across Shesheshen's palm as she held her aloft. A curse hadn't killed her. Not unless justice was a curse.

Would Homily call this justice? If she carried the Baroness's body back to camp, even if she was convincing in false panic, the best she could expect was Epigram and Homily hunting her offspring down for misplaced revenge. Talking Homily into accepting that her mother's death was deserved was beyond her reach. Had she ruined everything out of anger?

No, Homily knew enough. Deep down, Homily recognized her mother was going too far. That she had to be stopped, if not for the sake of monsters and wildlife, then for the humans who allegedly had value. How many families was a Baroness allowed to string up or immolate before she lost royal privilege? Royalty was a lie of civilization.

She twisted, feeling the blood from her egg sac course faster and hotter. Calling things "lies" wouldn't save Shesheshen. Not after all the genuine deceptions she'd dumped on Homily for days. Their entire little love story was built out of things that Shesheshen had to take back. How did words explain something like this?

She listened for the monster hunters over on their fruitless pursuit. Their horses breathed so heavily that she could've heard them a quarter mile away. One was turning, hooves clacking against flat stones. It could've been coming this way. Rourke and Malik could be on her in moments.

If they saw her, she had to pretend that they'd been attacked. She had to cover for herself, for now. Taking one proper bite out of the Baroness's head would suffice to convince them a monster had been here. They didn't need to know one still was here.

She started by fingering the chain around the Baroness's neck. The metal was cold under her touch. She wound it around a tendril until she found a flat steel piece, old and smooth, curving into two prosthetic fangs. This was the closest she'd ever been to her mother's touch.

She nearly said hello to the fangs. To a lifetime of knowing a parent.

These teeth belonged to her now. No matter what her creator had done, these fangs were the heirloom of a proper monster. They were steel heritage.

One tug didn't snap the chain. The Baroness had built her necklace from something sterner than typical jewelry. Another tug and links in the chain started to give, while others sank into the soft flesh of the corpse's neck.

The Baroness's corpse twitched to one side. Her shoulder brushed Shesheshen's chest and made the monster hesitate.

Mammals did spasm after death. It was normal. She needed to hurry.

The Baroness's chest plate rose up and outward, with the soft whistle of an inhale. Spasms were one thing. Breathing after death was much rarer in mammals. This was an oddity that she needed to be done with, especially before Rourke and Malik got back.

Shesheshen clamped her free hand onto the woman's armored shoulder so she could snap the chain and be done with this. Listening for the monster hunters, she tensed her wrist and prepared to break the damned chain and free her mother's fangs.

That's when Baroness Wulfyre's hand caught her by the face. At once it felt like it couldn't be Baroness Wulfyre, since her fingers were too lengthy, engulfing Shesheshen's skull like the roots of a tree, fingertips digging into her scalp. Squawking at the grip, Shesheshen grabbed for the hand, only to be dragged up into the air. Her feet kicked for earth they couldn't find, and she went hurtling across the clearing.

Pain erupted in her ribs as a tree branch impaled through her organs. Two livers popped, and at least one stomach leaked black fluids down through her scale mail. She hissed at the bright hot pain. Her feet didn't reach the ground here, leaving the heels of her boots to scuff along the thickest of the tree's roots.

She fought against the branch, willing her flesh to peel away from the impalement and get free. Before she could move, metal slammed into her head, driving it back against the tree trunk. Her skull cracked inside her head. Her eyes came loose. When she tried to see what had hit her, her vision kept coming apart. Focus became an enemy.

Her attacker lumbered toward her, keeping at least two arms on Shesheshen's body at all times. It wore the Baroness Wulfyre's grand armor, various joints splitting so that the creature's limbs could extend beyond human shape. Each of its fingers was over a foot long, with countless gnarled knuckles.

Gray knuckles. Gray as the flesh on its face. Its face was streaked with black blotches, like it was the offspring that had eaten Ode. This thing kept the shape of the Baroness Wulfyre, two braids of blonde woven with ginger-red hair falling over her gray face. It had her eyes, which at this proximity struck Shesheshen as too small for such a head. It was like she'd stolen them from someone who hadn't deserved them.

"Twins?" the Baroness-shaped thing said. "When the stories started, I knew there was one of you left alive out here in the isthmus. I never guessed there were two. Were you meeting it at the edge of camp on purpose? Conspiring together? Wretched little things."

The Baroness-shaped thing had a Baroness-shaped voice. She sounded like she'd never been murdered. But there were holes in her throat where the skewers had gone through. Two of the skewers still protruded from her flesh.

With a low, moist sound, like something being sucked from between her teeth, the metal skewers extended out of her neck. One fell and tinked to the ground with an inappropriately gentle noise.

The Baroness-shaped thing caught the other skewer in the middle of the air. She pushed it against the scale mail at Shesheshen's left side until it punctured her.

"You're both old enough," the Baroness-shaped thing said. "Old enough to have your egg sacs. Where do you keep yours?"

The lump in Shesheshen's throat might have been monstrous eggs, or it might have been anxiety. After the impact against the tree, she wasn't sure she still had a throat anymore. When she tried to speak, the runny mess of her vocal passages managed a wet croak.

Whereas the Baroness-shaped thing's voice was now husky, resembling Baroness Wulfyre's condescending tone. "Did you know it was me? Do you have a way to sense our kind? I tried, but for the life of me, I couldn't smell you. I thought your eggs would make you smell gravid. When I didn't find you, I feared I'd come too soon. That you weren't ripe yet. So tell me. When did you figure out what I was?"

The skewer slid out of Shesheshen's flank, dragging up her body and over her chin, drawing a line of stray fluids over her face. The tip of the skewer found the crack in her skull and scratched at her, teasing like at any moment it would drive into her head.

Shesheshen formed her words carefully. "What? Are? You?"

"Come on," Baroness Wulfyre's voice said, out of the thing's mouth. "You knew. This is why you pretended to love my idiot daughter. You wanted to get me first."

It hurt to think, like the rest of her skull would crumble away if she remembered anything too suddenly. Had she stalked Baroness Wulfyre? How was this thing waiting in her place?

Once again, she asked, "What? Are? You?"

This gray mimic blinked owlishly at her. "You're serious? You wretched, ignorant speck of a thing. I created you. Years ago, I planted you in that shit-heel Baron. An ignorant person would call me your mother."

Impossible. It was a cruel lie by someone after her eggs, trying to disturb her until she exposed where they were. Shesheshen's split-headed gaze fell to the steel fangs hanging around this monster's neck. The relic that belonged to her real parent.

She said, "No. You are Homily's mother."

The Baroness-shaped creature touched her own neck, as though to fetch the steel fangs. Instead she plucked at the neckline of her armor, tugging on it like the lapel of a tailored suit. "Humans are clothing. Baroness Wulfyre is an exceptional mask. Don't pretend you haven't posed as human before, 'Siobhan.' Does Homily know?"

The Baroness creature lowered the skewer, then punctured Shesheshen's left breast, sinking three cold inches deep. It struck a cracked rib, and the Baroness-shaped thing scraped it against the marrow. Shesheshen held herself as still as she could, not letting on that the skewer was a finger twitch away from her egg sac.

Whatever noise escaped Shesheshen, it made the Baroness creature laugh at her.

"I didn't think so. Hiding it from her makes you feel superior. You get to make her decisions for her."

It wasn't like that. It couldn't be that. She squeezed the pieces of her skull together, trying to capture her thoughts.

The Baroness creature fiddled with the far end of her skewer. "Come on. Tell me your lies. Lying always makes the body expose where the egg sac is hiding."

Was that true?

She had no way of being certain. She was new to having eggs.

One thing she did know: her eggs felt colder, retracting inside their sac and into her rib cage. They achingly pressed up against the tree limb that impaled her in place, as though to hide. They had not desired less to leave her since she'd grown them.

She had to change the subject before she was found out.

She asked, "You disliked my father? You did not choose my father because he was noble? Generous?"

That question made the Baroness creature's face freeze up, and she stopped working with the skewer. It had to be something that bothered her.

"He wasn't your father. He was available meat," the Baroness creature said. "I chose him because I was full from devouring his wife and my eggs weren't going to wait another minute. I would've kept him a secret in the cellar if the maids hadn't walked in on us. It became a hell of a game, hunting down anyone who was suspicious, while pretending to hunt myself. You should've heard the things the Baron called me as I ate his wife and planted my brood inside him. I had to bomb the fuck out of the keep just to cover up what happened."

Another puncture made Shesheshen snarl, as her only pancreas and the last of her livers were simultaneously lanced. All that unwanted blood was rushing through her now, heating her up and pumping out of the holes in her hide. Never had blood smelled filthy to her before. Never before now.

The Baroness creature said, "Tell me where your egg sac is, and I'll let you go. It's that simple."

It was the first time Shesheshen had recognized a lie during its telling. The tone was so stiff, so performative. It was utterly human, even though she realized this thing wasn't human. The Baroness-shaped thing had merely taught herself to be as human as she wanted.

There was too much blood rushing through her, addling her thoughts. She couldn't think of another topic. The morbid fascination was too deep. She had to ask, "Why do you want mine? Why not use your own?"

"Do you know why our kind is so rare?"

Shesheshen shook her head, feeling the left half of her skull slide a little further ajar. She tensed, trying to hold the pieces of her head together.

The Baroness creature said, "Each of us develops one egg sac, with one clutch of eggs, in our lifespan. It doesn't matter how long you live. You don't get more."

"You used yours. To make me?"

"It's prudent to plant those eggs early and in a remote location. That way you know where your young will be. Where they'll grow up. So you can come for their eggs."

"Why?"

The Baroness creature put the tip of the skewer to her bottom teeth with a click. "If I didn't plant those eggs and make you, my life span would be less than a hundred years. The nutrients in them are more useful to our adaptable bodies than to new life. So some digest their own eggs. A survivor, though, lets their children grow to offer new eggs."

It was that moment when Shesheshen became excruciatingly aware of the bomb in her pocket. Its hard shell weighed against her right hip. With her limp arm, she lowered her hand to the bomb. It was cold. It was better to fixate on than her eggs.

"It's not much to ask," the Baroness creature said. "I gave you life. Your reign of terror on the isthmus. Are you so selfish as to deny me my old age?"

Shesheshen knew enough not to be honest in that answer. She looked down, the way Homily had so many times when she was shamed, trying to look like she was equally ashamed. It was something this Baroness-shaped thing was used to seeing as submission.

When actually, she was searching for her torch. Where was it? She couldn't light the bomb without it.

Its heat at her right calf, where her boot ended. The torch still burned, its head stuck between two roots of the tree she was pinned to. She could possibly unspool enough of her body and lower her arm down to it, if this Baroness-shaped thing didn't catch her first.

To keep the Baroness creature from noticing, she asked, "Why don't you make more of yourself? Make a blob-thing of your digested materials until it wakes up? Don't those things have eggs too?"

"We're not slime. We can't split ourselves into multiples."

"We can't?"

Now it was Shesheshen's turn to be confused. Her hand was almost to her pocket when she lost track of it. Didn't this Baroness-shaped thing know how to make blobs like Shesheshen's own accidental offspring?

If their kind was that rare, she might not. She might not have done it herself. The Baroness-shaped thing might lack almost as much knowledge as Shesheshen. It was knowledge Shesheshen wasn't sharing.

The Baroness-shaped thing screwed up her face, baring more of her upper teeth. They were so flat. So even. She'd doubtless gathered them from various victims, to make a bouquet of pearly teeth for herself.

"Did you lay your eggs already?" the Baroness-thing demanded. "Are they inside Homily? Tell me before they hatch."

Shesheshen was too preoccupied with what her offspring was, and whether she knew more about their kind than her own creator, to hide anything else. Her face shifted. Without knowing how, she gave herself away.

Saliva was thick on the Baroness-shaped thing's tongue, spattering Shesheshen with her words. "No, you haven't done it yet. They're inside you somewhere."

The Baroness-shaped thing jerked the skewer out of Shesheshen, and ran its bile-laden tip down the scale mail. She was searching for the next place to puncture.

Shesheshen asked, "You didn't birth Homily. Or Catharsis. Why keep them?"

The Baroness-thing licked at her flat upper teeth, like she missed having fangs in her mouth. "They're more clothing. Eventually Baroness Wulfyre will be expected to age and expire. I don't want to be fingered as a witch. My children have to take over."

Shesheshen had never considered playing the role of a human for so long as that. A lifetime. It made her flesh more uncomfortable than all the skewer punctures.

She said, "You replace them?"

"A new generation of the family. Catharsis and Ode were going to be masterpieces, until you pieces of shit killed them. I would have cherished my life as either of them. Do you know how heartbreaking it is to see your future destroyed in front of you?"

Suddenly, the Baroness-thing dug the skewer deep into Shesheshen's right hip. Its shaft clacked against the bomb in her pocket, and Shesheshen whined and shuddered theatrically to distract from it. Pain streamed out of her mouth in an unexpected noise, as all the feelings of this torture caught up with her. She couldn't hold them off. A delirium clouded her senses. With all she had, she fought to focus on the bomb.

The Baroness-thing said, "My Ode was going to rule all of L'État Bon. The Royal Family's brat was half-ready to propose to her. Now I'll be stuck playing Epigram, or Homily. I'll cook you and your twin slowly for that."

"You will be Homily?"

"Once I drive her to a public nervous breakdown, she could make a decent mask. Any behavior I have will be 'a result' of her anguish, and her reverence for her great mother. She would've given anything to please her. In time, I'll make her into someone worth being."

Turning Homily into a nest already seemed too cruel, tearing up all her kindness and trauma to make new life. Wearing her as a blue robe was unfathomably worse. Taking everything she was and discarding it, for the fun of playing another abusive ruler in a line of abusive rulers. All of history would know Homily as worse than any monster, not knowing she secretly was one.

The awe of the moment dulled Shesheshen's senses, so that she barely noticed the human sounds nearby. Thick soles trudged from ditch to ditch, swishing across cold earth and pine needles.

Rourke's bucket helmet came into view first, and then he pulled down his breathing mask. He called, "Madame Wulfyre. Malik's head wound is ailing him again. He's still on the hunt, but needs rest. We're not going to find that thing out here. It's best we all return to camp and regroup before it gets any—"

The Baroness-thing whipped an arm at him, and it stretched all the way across the clearing. Before he ever saw that she was the wrong shape for a human, she drove the metal skewer into his neck. It tore his old skin like wrapping paper. What it unwrapped was wet, and an uneven sound spilled out of the remains of his throat. He clutched at his neck and gurgled, trying to remain standing.

The Baroness-shaped thing glowered at him, sucking saliva from her perfect teeth. Her body half-faced away from Shesheshen, listening for the sounds of any other humans nearby.

This was Shesheshen's one chance. She yanked the bomb out of her pocket and put as much of her body into her arm as she could. Elbows sprouted every couple of feet, jamming her hand down to the base of the tree and the cold bark of the roots. When her knuckles burned, she knew she'd found the torch. The fuse ignited with a desperate shushing sound.

The Baroness-shaped thing twitched at her, and then down at the source of the noise. Shesheshen tossed the hissing bomb between the Baroness-shaped thing's legs, letting it bounce a few feet along the ground.

With what strength she had left, she latched her fingers onto the Baroness-shaped thing's breastplate, burying her head against the metal. The two points of those steel fangs pricked the top of her head, as if the discarded idea of her mother had woken to bite her. The Baroness-shaped thing beat at her with her fists, but Shesheshen would not let go. She held her in place against the tree like a good shield.

The explosion rocked their tree, sending the nearest shrubs flying in burning pieces. The Baroness-thing was thrown forward, smashing into Shesheshen's body, and much of her form splattering against the tree. Then the Baroness-thing fell backward, down to the charred earth, her plate mail crumpled and torn, jagged pieces stabbing into her, dark fluids dripping out from within.

The branch impaling Shesheshen snapped and she fell with a wet thud. The branch came with her, still embedded with her flesh, tearing more of her innards. She hissed through the pain and wrapped tendrils around the branch, waddling along with it like a walking stick that stabbed her with every limp. Her whole body felt like a fleshy echo of the explosion. She wanted to liquefy down to nothing.

Still, she made herself limp forward. Their horses had spooked and run, leaving only Rourke's behind. The old monster hunter sagged limp against the edge of his ditch, a chestnut horse snorting and waiting at his side. The reins dangled loose around its neck.

Behind her, the Baroness-thing's armor clattered as she pulled her well-fed body together inside her armor. The bomb blast had hit her worse than Shesheshen, but she was older and stronger. Shesheshen could not wait a moment while that thing regained her bearings, as a woodland full of her underlings ran to the sound of the explosion to save her.

Shesheshen grabbed the horse's reins and took off. She had to find Homily.

CHAPTER THIRTY-SEVEN

All the wounds the Baroness-shaped thing had left on her kept oozing out her better fluids, leaving her dizzy and nearly falling from the saddle. She couldn't shapeshift one wound closed without finding two more. Her epidermis was being unusually unhelpful. It might have to do with her rampant emotional state.

Far before reaching camp, she abandoned the horse so it could mill around the wilderness. Then she tried on the most humanoid shape she could still muster, and crept toward the sounds of civilization. The sounds of an oncoming conversation she didn't know how to have. How was she supposed to talk to Homily about this?

It wouldn't go well if she burst into her tent with warnings that really her mother had been the monster all along and that Homily was a costume she intended to wear. The Baroness-shaped thing had raised her daughter to be so emotionally subservient that she would have difficulty facing evidence. Worse, all of Shesheshen's evidence was secondhand.

To prove that the Baroness-thing was dangerous, she'd have to explain how she knew. If Shesheshen and the Baroness-thing started pointing fingers at each other, the Baroness-thing was clearly the superior manipulator. Shesheshen couldn't win a duel of accusations.

And how did she know that the Baroness-shaped thing wasn't human?

Homily deserved to know everything. She had given so much, to virtually every party involved in this affair. Shesheshen had been no better than the Baroness in how she duped Homily and let her misunderstand. Without lies between them, Shesheshen could explain how she knew what Baroness Wulfyre really was, and could arm Homily before her mother arrived. Shesheshen prayed that the Baroness-thing wasn't here already.

There were only six guards on the northeasterly side of camp, all of them squatting in the dirt together, whittling and staring into bomb chasms. Homily was gone from the maze of traps. While Shesheshen had been away, they must've blown several of their traps. Clearly they hadn't been that successful, given there was no offspring strung up or impaled on display anywhere.

The rest of the camp was equally anemic, with a trio of guards in feather-marked armor guarding the entrance to some sleeping quarters. Many were resting before tonight, when they expected their human Baroness to order them to go out hunting in the pitch black. If only they knew.

Homily could turn this around. If she listened. If she still trusted Shesheshen after this.

As though in answer to her own guilt, the blue of a midday sky appeared through the camp's dusk. In the opening of one tent, Homily huddled in the blue robe the people of Underlook had gifted her. The hood was pulled up over her head, and she rubbed vigorously at her arms.

It wasn't that cold. Shesheshen couldn't help blaming herself for the chills the human woman was imagining.

After Homily vanished behind the flap of her tent, Shesheshen waited for guards. None came. None were on detail in this part of the circle of tents at all.

She took the chance, slithering on her belly up to the mouth of the tent. Inside, Homily sat on a solitary bed, wrapped in that blue robe and the gloom of the unlit space. The place had the stink of rosemary. Perhaps she'd anointed herself for protection. Through the hood, her breathing was heavy and sore.

"Homily? Homily, it's Siobhan."

Already she was lying. Her name wasn't Siobhan. Telling this truth was going to be uncomfortable, like carving a path through brambles and poisonous brush.

In answer, Homily stirred from under the cover of the robe. She remained facing away, still half-hunched against the chill. Her body language under the robe was closed off.

It was time to make amends. Time to tell the whole story.

What was the whole story? Now, standing behind Homily, she wasn't sure what her first deception had been. When had Homily's mistakes become Shesheshen's lies of omission?

When had a ruse over a gullible human turned into a fear of having a chance at love taken away?

There was one early lie. She clung to it, and offered it up. She entered the tent.

"Homily. My name is not Siobhan. I was not born with a name. I came by one when travelers needed something to curse. I have gone by Roislin, and Rosamund. Chisimdi. Stefan. This was actually the first time I ever called myself Siobhan. I never felt that attached to names."

That wasn't the whole truth.

"I never felt that attached to human names."

That was better. That was how she'd empty out her truths.

"It is true that, at first, I only saw you as an outlet for hunger. I meant to hurt you. I want to lie about this, and that means I must not. Not now. At first, when you mistook me for a human person, I let you have the mistake. It was convenient. Comfortable. Things became complicated before I knew it. Time moved differently when I was around you."

She rubbed at her mouth. Her lips were so chapped that several layers of skin flaked off from her touch. All of her surfaces felt so hot and exposed. Blood was coursing through the worst places.

"You were lonely, and so worthy of company. I . . . liked being that company. I do not like being near anyone most of the time. Because of the harm they can do. Whereas you were worth being harmed for. Does that make sense?"

If that made sense, Homily didn't say. The human woman shifted away from her on the bed, as though reaching for something under her robe. How Shesheshen wanted to ask what she needed. But it wasn't time for that yet.

"For years I thought it was a great love to plant my eggs in someone. To make them a nest for our children. With your generosity, with everything you are, I thought you were the perfect nest. The perfect feast. It was an ugly mistake. My ideas were wrong. I was wrong. I almost made that choice without you."

Her egg sac disagreed, pulsing in the upper regions of her chest. The cloying heat of its constant sucking and spurting of blood made her dizzy.

The edges of two cracked ribs snagged against the sac's soft tissue, and bone spurs punctured outward. Wads of membrane tried to swarm her throat.

She refused to yield to the pressure. She stiffened her chest tissues and dared the eggs to stab her in reprisal. She would not yield tonight.

"I will never do that to you. I fear you might actually let me. Because you give too much of yourself. I don't want to take from you."

She crept closer to the bed, putting one hand on the frame. The smell of rosemary in the air stung her eyes. That blue robe was so close. How she wanted to touch it, and to sink under it with Homily.

Leaving her hand on the bed frame, she faced that blue-swaddled woman. She approached no closer than that, inviting Homily to control what happened next in their space. Instead of getting any closer, she did what she should have done sooner: she said it all.

"I want to be with you. I know some of your kindness comes from pain. Scabs mistaken for flesh. I want to live long enough to see you heal. You are more than your pain. You are made of resolve. You deserve more than your family gives you. You deserve more than my deceptions. If you want, I will leave. If you don't want to share a bed. If you don't trust my companionship. I will leave. To never return. But you need to know about your family, first. About your mother. And we do not have much time."

She put both of her hands to her face, squeezing at the crack in her skull. At least her head hadn't fallen in half as she confessed to being a monster.

This was the most talking she'd ever done. Her mind felt dried up, like the husk of an insect drained of all its juices and meat by the beating sun. How she was going to get through explaining how much jeopardy Homily was in might just kill her.

If she could get Homily to listen to her after what she'd already said.

The blue robe rustled as Homily rose from the bed, with less sound of weight than usual. Her hood slipped free, revealing cheek-length blonde hair. It was trimmed around her sharply angled cheeks. She was too slender, too rigid to be right.

Too slowly, Shesheshen realized this wasn't Homily.

From the other side of the bed, Epigram brushed one sleeve of the blue robe aside, revealing a crossbow. At the center it held a familiar-looking bolt, with so many compartments for barbs and chambers. That was where the stink of rosemary in the tent was coming from.

Shesheshen darted backward for the tent flap, too slow. Quicker than an explosion, the crossbow bolt flew through the air and dug between her cracked ribs. Dozens of small streams of poison carved through her tissues, the egg sac sucking the poison deeper in its thirst for pumping blood. This was going too fast. She had to react.

She expelled all her breath and tried to compartmentalize her innards, and still she fell to the cold ground. She raked her fingers at it, baring her teeth up at Epigram. She kept them bared until she lost the strength to remain conscious.

CHAPTER THIRTY-EIGHT

So much of her melted that time melted with her. The shock of rosemary infusion made pain the sole definition of the passage of time. Her limbs dripping out of their sleeves and puddling with her legs on the floor seemed to take a few seconds, and took all the time Epigram needed to leave the tent twice, and to brew herself tea, and to send for someone.

Who Epigram summoned was beyond Shesheshen, since she was too dazed to focus on sounds. Shesheshen's humanoid form softened until she felt like a collapsing cave of flesh. She was too weak, too poisoned, and too late. The bolt was truly stuck, tissues as rigid as a clutched fist around it from the inflammation, even as the rosemary poisoned her to death. Commanding a new arm to form yielded a brief lump in her shoulder, and the tip of a bone to puncture her thin skin. For half an eternity, she fixated on the cooling sensation her own bleeding made along her skin.

She managed to keep at least one eye open most of the time, binding the folds of the lid to its own sides. That way she watched her captor, as she tossed off the blue robe and kicked dirt into Shesheshen's face. Epigram wasn't nearly the size of her sister. It was shameful she'd ever mistaken one for the other.

If she mistook Epigram for anyone, it should have been her older brother. The way she swaggered when there was no one else around to see her preening, and that fetish for gold clothing. She had eagerly stepped into the role of a dead man. She was like those unused wheels that wagon trains kept aboard in case something broke, so the wagoners could continue on to civilization. She was a second identical blouse in case of a stain. She was a replacement abuser.

As Epigram fingered the ruby pommel of the knife on her belt, it was apparent she enjoyed being that replacement. She paced with such zeal as she awaited her guest. Where did this human draw all that energy?

"Your fucking girlfriend was the wyrm this entire time. She came into my tent and tried to flirt with me because I was napping in your robe. If I hadn't been wearing it, it would've eaten me."

"This . . . this is Siobhan?"

Shesheshen had both eyes open, drying out from the lack of blinking, and was forcing herself to remain conscious. All that and she still hadn't noticed Homily entering. She lolled over on one side to see her.

At the head of the tent, with her backside against the flap, Homily stood. Her face was flushed with bright pink blotches, making her dark freckles stand out. Both of her hands covered her mouth, one over the other, like her words were too dangerous to trust against one palm.

Epigram said, "Instead it professed its fucking love. Do you believe that? It outed itself while I armed the crossbow. I don't see why it took so long to catch such a dumb monster."

"You stopped her from hurting you? The guards didn't help?"

"I stopped her on my own." Epigram held out another of those despicable crossbow bolts, with the head and shaft designed to expand into barbs and dribble their poisonous contents inside the victim. "With one of these."

Homily fixated on the crossbow bolt like it was a hornet trapped in their tent with them. With one trembling hand, she reached for it. She took it by the shaft with the same delicate care she might use for a creature that threatened to sting.

Her other hand remained over her mouth, and still the realization was obvious on her face. She was putting together this weapon's appearance with a thing she'd once surgeried out of Shesheshen.

Returning the bolt to her sister, she took one step toward Shesheshen. She brushed the hand away from her lips, which still had her pink chew marks on them.

She asked, "Siobhan?"

How badly Shesheshen wanted to explain it all. She'd failed to explain it in too many words earlier and ruined all of this, and now poison closed up her insides and squeezed them. She worked her lips, and each parting of her lips tore another membrane inside her. It wouldn't be long before speech was impossible.

In her place, Epigram snickered. "That's not even its name. It cried about how it made 'Siobhan' up to fuck you, but then you made it feel like a real woman or something. Can you believe that? A crying monster."

"Siobhan," Homily said, terser this time, like her emphasis on a name would force more of the past to stay still. "Why did you toy with me this entire time? Why didn't you just fulfill the curse and kill me?"

"Curse?" Shesheshen managed to repeat that one syllable, almost matching Homily's tone. A burning chill ripped through the hollow passages inside her. She held onto those passages as rigidly as she could, trying to get more words out. "There. Is. No. Curse."

"Yeah," Epigram said, slotting the bolt into her crossbow and reaching for the winding mechanism at its butt. "This shit pudding wants us to believe we were never cursed. It must've just liked killing us anyway."

Homily's brow went stiff without moving up or down. "Is it true?"

Epigram said, "I don't know. I never fucking believed in the curse. I always figured it was a scheme Mother used to manipulate politicians."

"Wait," Homily said, resting a hand on the crossbow's front. "You . . . you never believed in the curse?"

"It's a fish-drowning story we tell to get sympathy and push people around. It works. It gets things done. Mother has always been good at moving the pawns. Like you haven't used the story of the curse to loosen people up before?"

There was another question on Homily's lips. It never came out.

"Get on with it," Epigram said. "I was the one who had to capture the bear. I put up with Mother while you went on constant vacations. It's time for you to do your part for the family for once. It's what we talked about before you made me do that to you."

Epigram plucked at Homily's neck through her scarf, right over where the flesh cut was hidden. It made her older sister flinch away. Epigram followed her, pushing the crossbow into her hands. Homily gawked at the crossbow, refusing to coil her fingers around it.

"Hey," Epigram barked. "You know what you did to this family. You gave it access to our family. Clean up your mess."

"But you said yourself. There's no curse to lift by killing it."

"Who cares? This will get Mother to calm down. We'll carve out its heart, bring it to her on a shiny plate, and shut her up for a while until she marries you off."

Shesheshen tried to protest. "No. Mother."

These two still believed Shesheshen had a heart. Of course, her egg sac pumped as much blood as any mammal heart. That had to be why the Baroness had spread the superstition of her heart in the first place. That way people wouldn't question it. Homily would never question it as she carried those bleeding eggs to the Baroness for supper.

Epigram jerked her head at Shesheshen. "You're just as responsible for Ode and Catharsis dying as the wyrm. Do it."

Epigram pushed the crossbow forward until the front billowed into Homily's breasts, like she'd send that bolt into her heart.

Shesheshen tried to say, "Please—"

Epigram spoke over her. "You have to make it right."

Something was wrong with Homily's eyes. She looked around like her eyes were closed, unfocused, seeing sleep where there were shapes. Healthy animals never had that look. Her head started to fall, to gaze at the ground like she always did, but stopped at the crossbow. Her jaw tightened, head falling no lower.

She muttered, "I have to make it right."

Epigram leaned her head back as though basking in her own personal sunshine, hair spilling away from her cheeks. There was a smugness beyond reason. An entertainment to have pushed her sister into finally hurting people like she did.

"Yeah. And remember to carve its heart out, too."

The smallest noise escaped Homily, like a seed pod had been trapped in her lungs for years, drying out until now, when it had finally been crushed. That faint wisp of air that was louder than the world.

Homily reached toward her sister's offered arm. Her right hand went past the crossbow and down to Epigram's belt. She took the jeweled handle of her knife. It rattled as she pulled it free.

Epigram said, "You carve the heart out last, you stupid—"

Then Homily slit her sister's throat.

Her arm moved so easily that it looked like a shallow cut, too effortless to harm. It didn't bleed, not at first. It was a pink yawn where a mouth didn't belong, showing off softer tissues inside. Homily held Epigram's hair in her other hand, keeping her upright. As Epigram twitched, the slit in her throat made a genial gurgle.

The woman's head continued sliding backward as she shuddered, and then the blood poured out. Her hands rose, fingers curling at random knuckles like they weren't sure how to hold this feeling. She pawed at her own neck, and at Homily's shoulders and scarf.

Still with a handhold on Epigram's hair, Homily pulled her in and held her. She let her sister bleed to her heart's content. Carefully Homily lowered her to the floor, as though putting a child to bed for the last time.

It would have been vicious, would have filled Shesheshen with a dark admiration for Homily, if not for the look on her face. With her cheeks smudged by finger streaks of her sister's blood, her eyes had woken up. They were frantic as a moth on fire, jumping around the tent, to the knife, to the flap out of the tent, and to Shesheshen. It was the look of a frightened animal, destined to run or strike again.

Homily kept holding that knife. She stepped over Epigram's twitching legs, avoiding the gilded greaves. When she was three steps away, Homily's knees wobbled. Then all the folds of her skirt betrayed her, and she crumpled like her limbs were made of the same pleated fabric.

Homily took in a staggering breath that tripped her words. "There is no curse? There never was one? We hurt you for nothing?"

Hearing that tone hurt, worse poison than the rosemary. Shesheshen wrapped intestines around her egg sac, binding it and pulling it down from her best air passage. No amount of pain would make her give up on answering this woman.

"No. I never. Cursed. Anyone. But."

"What is it?"

"But. I. Am. Sorry."

Homily rested her palms on the ground, with her weight on her arms. Their faces grew close together, such that the warmth of Homily's breath licked at her.

She said, "There is a curse. A real curse in this isthmus."

"No?"

"My family put it on your life. Everyone. From Mother and Catharsis, down to the whole family, to everyone they sent after you. That we sent after you. I didn't want to hurt you, and I looked away when they did. I was part of this."

Homily raised her sister's knife, and Shesheshen used all the energy left in her to catch her hand. She couldn't wrestle her. She gave a meager tug, a physical suggestion of twining limbs and tendrils. Homily hesitated, then agreed.

They drove the blade down, down forever. They dug it into the earth until half its blade shone no longer. Then more. They forced that cutting into the ground until it was nothing but an expensive handle.

PART SEVEN

YOU WILL ANSWER TO MOTHER

CHAPTER THIRTY-NINE

Homily professed her love by digging a second crossbow bolt out of Shesheshen's body. It was so much clearer a declaration of affection than any of those speeches spun by poets and playwrights, and stuffed into the mouths of actors who pretended to be enamored. One could only pretend to love in language. True love was a woman sinking up to her elbows in her viscera, delicately removing hooks from her rigid tissues. For all the words humans spoke about seeing into one another, Homily truly saw into Shesheshen. There was no inch of her abdominal cavity that she missed.

It was like how they'd met. Homily swaddled her in a net of fabrics, keeping her organs tightly packed together. She had to feed Shesheshen with a long spoon, which she held halfway down the handle, making sure not to spill a drop of broth. No nugget of meat was enough. Time and time again, Homily had to leave the tent to retrieve another bowl. The camp's cooks would think she was malnourished, or with child.

She didn't mean to do what she did, not at first. Except after the third bowl of that thin soup, her hunger was worse than when her stomachs had been empty. You could not heal so many ruptures with a stomach full of liquid. It sloshed around as she rolled off the mattress and oozed to the floor, toward the savory bounty of Epigram's carcass.

Stray blood warmed the earth enough to seep through it, beginning to congeal. It would be more difficult to hide the murder scene if there were stains on the ground. So Shesheshen drank it into herself, letting the dirt clot inside her. She nuzzled at the wound under Epigram's chin, making sure no more leaked out through the hole.

Before she could stop herself, she swallowed the carcass's entire head. The brain was so runny, melting under her digestive fluids. It was grand to have a new skull that wasn't cracked in half and didn't need to be clenched together all the time. She pushed her maw into the stump of Epigram's neck, and was chewing her esophagus free when Homily returned to the tent.

Shesheshen froze, with teeth clamped into the cleft between two vertebrae. She didn't have the words to start a conversation about this.

"Oh. Oh." Homily turned away as though she'd walked in on lovers. "I didn't. Well. What?"

"I am sorry," Shesheshen said, licking Homily's sister's blood off of her upper lip. "You were not using her body for anything. I . . . I am starving. I should have waited. Are you angry with me?"

"Angry about you defiling the corpse of the sister that I . . . that I murdered?" Homily raked her fingers across her scalp so hard one nail snapped off and clung to a nest of curls. She clutched that fingertip into a fist. "No. I guess I'm not allowed to be angry about that."

"You can be whatever you are. If you are mad, I want to know."

"You want to know if I'm mad that the woman, or the monster . . . or . . . or, the person that I like is eating my sister's remains?" Her words were rushed, like bigger ones were stuck behind it and shoving them out of her mouth. "Have you been eating people behind my back this whole time?"

Shesheshen said, "Not many. I ate the bandits that attacked us. I think we both agree we did not like them."

Homily blotted at her forehead with the back of her injured hand. "I wasn't terribly fond of them, no. This is still, well, significant information to take in."

She stuck the fingertip into her mouth for a moment, then pulled it out. She looked from the trickle of blood at her cuticle to Shesheshen beside the corpse of her sister. Her face welled up with so much color that her freckles sank like stones into a mire. "So you eat like this. I took you to supper, didn't I? With my whole family, everyone who was out to kill you. And you drank rosemary wine. Doesn't rosemary kill you?"

"It is highly poisonous. I let it poison me."

"Why?"

Despite herself, Shesheshen looked down. "I wanted to impress you."

Homily came closer, rubbing her face with both hands. "Good gods, above and below. We make a pair, don't we? Homily Wulfyre and, well, you. Should I still call you Siobhan?"

Shesheshen said, "I do not like names."

"That's not really an answer."

It wasn't? Damn it. Shesheshen had been honest. What was she supposed to say when an honest answer wasn't an answer?

"I would like you to call me something. My oldest name is Shesheshen."

"Do you want me to call you that?"

She tried, "I mean, I do not feel the attachment to words. Internally. Personally. Except one time."

"What time do you mean?"

"I like when you call me something."

"You want me to name you, and you don't care what? The puddle of my girlfriend's parts doesn't care so long as I talk to her?"

Homily's lips kept pursing together and blustering apart, like an upset horse. She clutched at the thickness of her belly and shivered, before the ugliest laughter spilled out of her. She bellowed through the tent, and any nearby guards were likely to run. Strings of snot dangled from her nostrils as she shook her head in wide swings. If she kept it up, she would be the one to melt into a puddle on the ground.

The mirth perplexed Shesheshen worse than talking. She climbed off of Epigram's remains, making sure to lap up any spilled fluids so there would be less mess later. Epigram was delicious, far better company as food than she'd ever been as a person. Still, Shesheshen had to quit ingesting her parts. She didn't want to give Homily apoplexy.

"You really *are* you," Homily said, tears and mucus mixing into a viscous stew on her face. There was relief under that stew. "You're still so funny."

Shesheshen pushed herself up from the floor on her arms, arching. Her legs weren't entirely obeying her yet. "You do not dislike being in love with a puddle?"

Catching her breath, Homily reached for Shesheshen. An offer of consensual touch again.

"I've been a puddle on the floor too many times myself."

Shesheshen let herself slump into Homily's hand, forming her shoulder to match however this woman wanted her to feel. "I do not horrify you? You do not want me slain?"

With her face still a nightmare of fluids, Homily squatted, coming closer to Shesheshen's face. "No young woman of means has gone through her entire life without at least once surveying her opportunities and wishing for a dragon instead."

"I am not a dragon."

Homily almost keeled over from laughter. "You see? You're still so funny."

Shesheshen did not see how she was funny. Perhaps this human woman was just deranged from grief.

Homily said, "If your oldest name is Shesheshen, I should get used to that. I want to know what you are."

Shesheshen tried to sit up, but she lacked all the appropriate bones, and half of the strength. Making two legs out of her lower half, she mostly spooled them, so that she sat up like a tamed cobra. It was as human a posture she could take for now.

Homily said, "I didn't believe them when they said it was you. Mother is telling everyone you're the monster and to attack you on sight. It didn't seem possible when I heard it. I don't understand how you can be the monster, though. What did I rescue you from that night in the camp? What was that thing with a mouth full of deer skulls?"

"I think that was my fault."

"That's not true. You were a victim."

"I made that thing. It is my offspring."

"You planted your eggs?" Homily looked aside for a moment, at where her sister's face would be, had it not been eaten. She shivered again, threatening to fall. "Before I got to the tent, Epigram said something about planting your eggs. She said that you had wanted to . . . do that to me."

Before Shesheshen's mind could respond, her egg sac did. Blood spurted into sundry organs as it propelled itself upward, squeezing between ribs, sending searing pains through her chest. Those spines dug into her flesh, trying to surge up to her neck where it could tear its way out of her and get to this humble human woman. It loved Homily in a way Shesheshen could not abide.

The rosemary poison had weakened her egg sac enough that it couldn't scale her rib cage with the ease it had previously possessed. If the bolt had struck her in that egg sac, the cursed organ might've died on the spot. With her returning strength, Shesheshen wrapped her arms around her upper torso, then extended them further at the joints, into tendrils of flesh and sinew. She made herself into her own bondage, refusing her eggs any exit. How was she ever going to live with Homily with these things stalking her?

As she coiled upon herself, she told Homily, "I will not do anything to you. You are not a nest. You are more."

Homily made the poor decision of coming closer, hands up as though to touch and soothe. She didn't understand her jeopardy here. "It looks painful to hold them back. Is it?"

"Quite."

Homily's smile was the happiest kind of sadness. "Thank you for sparing me."

"You shouldn't have to thank me."

"Did you plant some of your eggs in something else? A sheep? A deer? That monster was part tree."

"We have no trees or deer as our parents. We take parts of other life to build our bodies. Like a human uses crutches, and eye glasses, and back braces."

Homily took the body language cues finally and slinked away a few steps. As she moved, she asked, "Like hermit crabs? Finding new shells to wear?"

"Like humans, finding tools. Making tools. Making houses. Making new cultural shells for themselves out of what they can take."

"I hope I live long enough to understand that," Homily said. "So this offspring isn't the product of your eggs. Do you know where it is from?"

Shesheshen mulled over how to make honesty make sense. The two did not seem friendly concepts right now. "There is another way to make more of me. I . . . accidentally made another of me. The thing out there? I made it. From my body. Without anyone else."

"Asexual reproduction? I didn't know wyrms could . . ." Homily stopped herself. More resolutely, she said, "I didn't know you could do that."

"I did not know, either. I did it when I was full of meat, and thinking about you."

Homily tilted her head and squinted skeptically. "Were you trying to be sweet just then?"

An assault of thoughts hit Shesheshen. All the abuses that the creature calling herself Baroness Wulfyre put Homily through. All those abuses she had subjected Shesheshen herself to in years of sending hunters. That her own host parent had surely not wanted to bear her.

Shesheshen had to be something different. That offspring wandering the wilderness to avoid soldiers and mercenaries deserved a better parent.

Shesheshen said, "I do not know what I was trying to do when I created it. I want to help it, if I can."

"So that's the thing Mother is burning down Underlook to find."

Shesheshen rose from her coil of limbs. "She is pursuing it?"

"Mother is convinced your offspring was driven into Underlook. There's a perimeter of soldiers around it, preventing anyone or thing from getting out. With every possible suspect trapped inside, she's started . . . bombing."

She thought of the holes in the ceiling of her lair. "Again with bombs."

"It's her idea of revenge, for Ode."

"No," Shesheshen said, too quickly. "That is not why your mother is after my offspring."

Homily slowed the stroking touch on Shesheshen's shoulder. "Why else would she kill so many people to get it? You said the curse isn't real."

Shesheshen hesitated out of fear this was the last touch she'd get. This was the hardest thing. She couldn't do this without Homily, and if Homily rejected her here, she'd fall to pieces. Her organs might literally tumble out of her skin if Homily didn't help hold her together.

She said, “Your mother is after my offspring for its eggs.”

Homily gave a quick shake of her head. “Mother made up the curse to get your heart, not eggs.”

Shesheshen guided the human woman’s hand over her rib cage, to where the egg sac pulsed in a prison of bone. Hot blood called to her. “We do not have hearts, unless we consume one and keep it. We have egg sacs. They make much blood, so a mammal like you would think it was a heart. Your mother called it a heart so people would bring the egg sac to her without questioning.”

Slowly, Homily pressed her palm to Shesheshen’s sternum, fingers tapping like she was sending a coded message to her imprisoned false heart. “Why does Mother want your eggs?”

Her blood slowed with a chilling ache. How did humans handle having a pulse that rebelled against them so frequently?

“Homily. I need you to believe me.”

“I do.”

“I deceived you. I do not deserve your trust. I also cannot tell you this if you will call me a liar.”

“You’re not the first person to deceive me. I was fed lies until I thought they were food, and you’ve spent your entire life being lied about.” Homily kept her palm on Shesheshen’s chest and leaned in closer, raising her chin. Her scarf spilled open, as though inviting Shesheshen to strike at her throat, or at her scars. There was such trust in that body language. “Let me hear you. Let me judge what’s true for myself.”

They didn’t have time to wait longer. Her offspring was in jeopardy. Scared, newly born, alone in the horror of civilization.

“That thing that looks like the Baroness is not your birth mother. She is a wyrm like me.”

“Mother? She can’t be.”

Convincing someone was one of the worst forms of talking. Shesheshen felt her thoughts jamming together on their way to her tongue. “Have you ever been suspicious of her? Have monster hunters ever searched for a prey on your family’s grounds, and your mother refused them access to her quarters?”

"She has a temper. She would never abide them near her room."

Shesheshen's own hunger inspired the next question. "Is she ever wrathfully hungry? Has she eaten unusual amounts of meat? Have her servants ever gone missing?"

Homily went still, and licked the insides of her lips. From her face, she was recalling specific people in particular. "I am unsure. There might have been a time. Aunt Agatha said some things . . ."

Shesheshen pushed. "Today, she was gouged in the neck by my offspring. A moment later there was no wound. No blood on her armor. Has she had other injuries that mysteriously went away?"

"Mother has seen many battles. She's a terror with that spear."

"In these battles. Were there ones she should not have survived?"

Homily leaned a few inches away, eyes peering into thin air, into the recesses of her own memory. Her voice had the tremor of a musical instrument about to break. "There was a time, when she was fighting in east L'État Bon. Catharsis came home with her, telling this tall tale that she'd gotten ahead of everyone else, surrounded by marauders. By Al-Jawi mercenaries working for the separatists. And Catharsis swore that, as he tried to get to her, he'd seen Mother have her head lopped clean off. He had such a bragging tone that I thought it was a story to mythologize her. To make her seem more frightening."

Shesheshen grunted. "They were lying about lying."

"I wonder if Catharsis knew. He was . . . he was so engaged with her."

Shesheshen imagined going to war herself. Going to all those front lines and carving through human people, or sitting at the tail side and loitering through the piles of dead afterward, like she was shopping for groceries. "She might have gone to war so she could feed freely."

Homily came closer to her again. "Those skirmishes were where she grew her political connections and power. It was calculated. She said she was playing the whole world against itself. But she's always talked like that."

Shesheshen said, "She revealed herself to me in a clearing today, when no one else could see us. She tried to take my eggs, and to use me to get at my offspring. I used a bomb to separate us. She slew the old monster hunter when he caught her."

Homily's eyes cleared in an abrupt concern. "She was the one who killed Sire Rourke? Not you?"

"Yes."

"She said you did it. That you stole a horse and fled. She's imprisoned the other one, Sire Malik, for failing to apprehend you."

Lies were better when they swallowed parts of truth. They weren't so different than monsters like herself. Shesheshen had to learn that trick. Later.

Now, she said, "I did take the horse. I needed to find you, before she did."

Homily's fingers were in front of her lips again. "Why did you come for me?"

Shesheshen squeezed her chest harder than she needed to. With the distance between them, the egg sac had subsided for the moment. Yet the blood was hot under her skin, like it was trying to boil her innards. It was difficult to think with all that blood jostling her other juices.

Homily said, "You should've gotten to safety. You nearly died. Epigram was going to kill you."

"I panicked." That was honest. It was not enough of an answer, though. "I panicked and had to get to safety."

"This camp wasn't safe."

"If something got to you, or told you before I did, or hurt you, I would have been no better than dead myself. I needed to save it."

Homily wetted her upper lip. "Save what?"

Here came her worthless words. "I do not know what you call it. The thing that is not flesh or bone or organs. In the panic, I needed to make sure the greater thing was safe. The demonic laughs you make at things that are not jokes. The way you ask to touch me without words. The pleasure I get from riding next to you. The talking that I mind less than talking to others. The willingness to be harmed myself before letting you be harmed. You feeding me soup by the spoonful because I cannot raise a hand. What do you call that thing that I had to save? I had to save it. I had to save us. You are my safety."

Homily retrieved her hand from Shesheshen's sternum, and brought her palms together for a moment. Her hands wrestled with each other, like they were molding an idea. Wordlessly, she lifted both hands, coated with the grime of their day, one fingernail still cracked and seeping. She held up both meaty arms, opening her warmth to Shesheshen.

It was an invitation.

Not as a victim. Not as a nest.

It was safety that she had molded in her hands, and Shesheshen let herself sink into the grip. She relaxed against the cushion of Homily's chest, closing her eyes so firmly they started to dissolve. They were a wordless, unspeaking lump of good intentions. Together they became a comfort she never wanted to leave.

CHAPTER FORTY

Halfway through talking out their plan, Homily had to retch. She ran outside, as though she didn't want Shesheshen to see her like that. Or perhaps she didn't want her dead sister to see how much hold she still had over her.

As much as Shesheshen wanted to follow her out and comfort her, she had no guise to do it in yet. And it was gentler to spend the time alone doing what they needed done. How could she claim to love Homily, and then carve her sister to pieces in front of her? That felt cruel even before she heard Homily's whimpering.

Through the tent's fabric, those hiccupping noises kept coming. Years of pain and guilt that Shesheshen couldn't help her with. If she could, she would've grabbed all those memories by the hair and slit its throat. Violence had fewer uses than she wanted.

Instead she got to work. She burrowed her snout inside Epigram's breastplate, seeking out fatty deposits. More skin was easy to make. The bone structure was the most important feature here, both in how it would support her as she grew her new limbs, and to tell her how best to mimic the woman's appearance.

Fully fed, she dressed herself. Those gilded greaves were heavy—something denser than gold underneath their coating. The breastplate was snug, and she worked additional bones under it, so that it caged her egg sac. It would be safer inside there, and she would be safe from it trying to escape. The thing pulsed with every pained hiccup of Homily's from outside the tent. It wanted to go to her almost as badly as the rest of Shesheshen did.

She rinsed her new hair as best she could in a bucket of water and lilac perfume. If some gore strains remained, it could be useful. Anyone who looked at her wrong would be an invitation for Epigram's style of verbal abuse, which would convince them that she was who she really wasn't.

As she opened the tent flap, Homily returned. The woman quaked on her heels, eyes widening at the sight of Shesheshen. Except it wasn't the sight of Shesheshen that was bothering her.

Homily fanned a few fingers over her mouth, eyes landing on Shesheshen's neck. The flesh was all newly grown and fine. There were no slash marks. No signs of a crime.

With so much composure that she had to be faking, Homily said, "You look very convincing."

This was Shesheshen's first test of the voice. She hadn't had a complete throat to work with. Molding the insides of her neck, Shesheshen tried to imitate Epigram's voice. "Do I sound the part?"

Homily coiled her fingers in her scarf. "Yes. Quite so."

"I have the wearied tone? The lack of empathy?"

"I said yes. It's convincing."

"Good. Then I have to say something."

Homily looked down into her false face, into the literal eyes of her abuser. Shesheshen kept those lips placid, unwilling to put on Epigram's caustic expressions here. Homily deserved better.

She deserved what Shesheshen had to say.

In the voice of her sister, Shesheshen said, "I am sorry for what I did to you."

Homily fell into Shesheshen's right shoulder, torso bucking with pained hiccup-breaths. Her fists rested against Shesheshen's sides as she said so many nothings. Those touches were cold, like Homily's blood wasn't working right under her skin. There was no simple cure for that cold touch. There was only patience.

CHAPTER FORTY-ONE

It only became uncomfortable when Homily stopped looking at her like a monster. When she could look at the face of her abuser and see only Shesheshen behind it, it was like a psychic membrane between them dissolved. The safety of being disguised, and of not being wholly known, melted away as though by the heat of her blood. There was no reclaiming the safety of anonymity. What she yearned for was unity.

There was no deception to keep her safe from whatever Homily thought of her. If she wanted to be in love, then she had to grow used to it.

They walked together around the south end of the tents, for wherever the guards were clustering. They'd need them in order to get back to town safely. Each additional person who accepted their ruse made it that much more believable to the next person. Armored dolts wearing L'État Bon feathers would work the best.

Shesheshen thought that together, out in the open, they would stay in their mutual deception, and not talk much. Chatter would draw attention.

Yet as they went, Homily spoke to her in a measured voice. "Tell me something."

In Epigram's voice, Shesheshen said, "Yes?"

"Mother didn't raise me to be part of her hunting pack."

Shesheshen said, "No. I do not think she did."

Homily's steps straightened out, feet louder on the ground. She could have been daring someone to hear her. "Catharsis. Epigram. When I think of them . . . and then myself. I think about what she drew us to be. She raised us on a diet of suffocation."

"I am sorry."

"And I'm the weak one. The disappointment."

"Not to me."

"To Mother. Surely to her. She doesn't want to keep me, does she?"

Shesheshen followed Homily, measuring her steps, trying to keep Epigram's sour face up. "She has another plan."

"This whole time she pretended to be someone. She could be anyone. It colors all the times she called me a disappointment. When she said I wasn't good enough. That someone else should be me."

"Should we talk about this here . . . ?"

"Mother could take any form she wanted?"

Homily tripped over her words, speaking faster and slower at once. Was it because her suspicions were being confirmed? Or because she was hearing it from Epigram's voice? Shesheshen couldn't drop the voice act. It would be bad enough if someone heard them accuse their Baroness of being a monster.

"So many nights when she said she wouldn't live forever and that I had to amount to more. That she had to do everything for me, like she wanted to step in and live for me. I thought it was mere scorn. Except her plan is actually to replace me, isn't it?"

"To take one of your lives. Depending on who she liked best."

Homily worried her thumb over her lost fingernail. "She was softening me up, like clay."

"She does not get to make you change anymore. Not one more day."

Shesheshen had known Homily would see through things, once she'd poked holes in a few lies. Like bird eggs, one crack was enough for the young to break through. Homily was too keen not to put this plot together. If there were other mysteries, Homily would figure them out. The venom in her voice would've brought down a bull.

Shesheshen said, "You understand it all. Maybe clearer than I do."

"I'll tell you what I understand."

"What is it?"

Homily loosened her scarf, letting it hang open just enough that the air could kiss her scars. "She isn't eating your child. Not so long as I walk this earth."

Homily strode into the center of camp, in front of Shesheshen, like a shield on legs. Her posture dared the world to volley arrows at Shesheshen. She'd catch them with her gritted teeth.

The sight of them together made the guards stir and straighten up. Most of them were camped out near the bomb craters, some with their legs dangling into the pits. A pair of them were face to face, juggling several small burlap bags. From the money clutched in the hands of the rest, they were gambling on who could go longer.

Shesheshen sucked air between her teeth, one of those petty human sounds. Her sound was all it took for both jugglers to drop their bags.

From their well-armored and better-relaxed crowd came Arnau Sernine, with his unusually large head. He looked like a toy on those spindly limbs, with exaggerated facial features trying to smile through Homily and over to the person he thought was Epigram. It was nice that being in the Epigram character meant Shesheshen didn't have to bother returning the smile.

"You are both safe. This will please Her Exaltation," said Sernine, hands clasping over his black velvet vest. "As it does all who serve in this camp. We have been standing watch to ensure you were safe while you enjoyed your privacy."

Shesheshen sucked between Epigram's teeth again. "Yes. You seemed highly armed."

It was better that they'd all done a terrible job, none coming close enough to overhear the murder earlier. But they weren't getting credit for that.

Sernine said, "We've been astute. That blue bear was nosing around the nearby wilderness. Some of us expected it was serving the wyrm, trying to get at the two of you. Never worry, though. I led some soldiers in driving it off."

Naturally Blueberry would be worried. If they'd so much as nicked her, Shesheshen would have Epigram flay this entire crew. She pulled the lips from her teeth, preparing to vent scorn at them.

Homily spoke first. "Did Mother station you here?"

"She requested the presence of you both," he said, while looking almost exclusively at the woman he thought was Epigram, "at your earliest convenience. Earlier than that if possible, as is her wont."

Homily looked along the lines of armored goons and said, "So you took a hundred people who should be at Underlook, and had a little vacation waiting for us to come out?"

"I assumed you and your sister were engaged in serious business. And if that wretched wyrm is genuinely trapped in Underlook, then perhaps you two would feel safer staying in this outpost. The cooks are excited about the prospect of the next meal. We've caught fresh venison."

The previous Epigram would have jumped on the opportunity.

This Epigram wanted to thrust a bone through her own hide and gouge this toady's eyes out. He was the sort of person who lived richly on the suffering of people like Shesheshen. One of the organs in the beast that was civilization. Out of sight, out of mind, never out of liquor. All of these assembled guards were merely truant killers.

Homily glanced to Shesheshen, then said, "Sire Sernine, assemble all the guards and the remaining carriages. You are to escort us to Underlook. Take us directly to Mother's lodgings."

"You want to go . . . ?" Sernine asked at Epigram.

It was the wrong move, for Homily wasn't getting forgotten today. She said, "The full company, Sire Sernine. I want absolute safety from the Wyrm of Underlook. You may all return here after we are delivered, and no sooner. I want no strangers approaching our carriage train. Even if it looks like my mother, disarm it and strike it down. Let me bear the blame. I'm used to it."

Shesheshen stepped to Homily's side, nodding curtly at the stunned lieutenants around Sernine. Surely they were waiting for her to change the orders. She gave them something else.

"What?" she barked. "You heard my sister. Let's go."

CHAPTER FORTY-TWO

They heard the bombs before they saw them. Owls that should have been deep asleep flew from their hollow trees at the first distant crack. Stray pine needles blew upward from the forest floor. The sound thundered through the highway and the forest alike, as though a storm had fallen to earth and raged against the land in its pain.

As they rounded the last leg of the highway and Underlook came into view, a three-story tower leaned like an arm to wave at them. Then it sank, retreating into the unknown, disappearing behind the town's walls and in a plume of dust and debris. That explosion was so harsh that Shesheshen sealed up her ear canals and put her hands over them.

Fires fanned about behind Underlook's town border, where butcher shops and residences were reduced to ruins. Charred chasms splayed open in woodwork, and around them fires spread, like mad eyes glancing about in every window.

The walls had been meant to keep things like Shesheshen out. Now they forced the citizens of Underlook to remain in, trapped with monsters and politicians. Beyond those point-tipped walls, stray firelight reflected orange off of plate armor. There were too many humans standing out there, with the spears and bows of yew. No fewer than a hundred stood in view from the highway, forming two rows of defense around the town.

Just shy of the entrance to town, an old man lay on the side of the street, holding a wad of his shirt against his collarbone. Red spilled between his fingers, and the same color stained the tip of the spear of one of the guards in the road. They were a living testament to how difficult it was to pass Underlook's borders without Baroness Wulfyre's permission.

How difficult it was to leave Underlook, anyway. Homily and Shesheshen came right in. No one had issue with more bodies strolling *into* the fire.

The heat beckoned them, draping over them like the ghosts of so many forgotten dead. It dragged underneath Shesheshen's scalp, prickling at where she held onto Epigram's hair. Her flesh sweltered and she struggled to keep open pores. This was no environment for a decent monster.

Homily leaned closer to her and whispered, "Are you all right?"

Shesheshen wiped at her feverish brow. "We need to get my offspring out of this town immediately."

"We'll get you both out of here as soon as we can."

Homily squeezed her hand. Her fingers were melting from the intensity of the heat. All that blood inside her wasn't helping cool her down any. Why anyone wanted blood escaped her.

Finding the Baroness-shaped thing wasn't difficult. One simply had to see the explosions and collapsing buildings, and go to the place with the best view of the devastation.

The sound of her berating people was unmistakable, even over the dusty gasp of another building imploding. L'État Bon soldiers carried tower shields on the ends of poles, lifting and angling them as artificial barriers against the smoke and debris. As it billowed, they lowered the shields to the road, blocking any human traffic. Nothing was allowed to disturb the Baroness, not even the remains of the lives she burned.

There the Baroness-shaped creature stood in the road, a good throw away from the rich district, in front of the jailhouse. There wasn't much of a prison system in Underlook. The population was low enough that the one jailhouse mostly oversaw dispute mediations or executions, in a binary idea of justice that mostly served the landed. Thus the building was a modest two-story place of wood with old treaties hanging on the walls as proof someone had agreed to something. The cells were in the basement, with tiny barred windows so the truants could look up at the rest of society, because truants were something humans planted underground, like seeds or coffins.

The Baroness-shaped creature stood in plate armor, hiding so much of her body that her audience would never suspect what lay underneath. She held her red-maned spear as though she might stab any of them and pitch them into a jail cell. Several armored guards with their soot-plastered breastplates and fluttering blue feathers surrounded her, and even more plain-clothed people from the town followed her.

These fools shuffled around the shields, with dust sticking in the oils of their treated hair. Some wore silken night clothes and slippers. Others had thrown on jackets and pantaloons in clear haste, and everyone's attire was obscured under layers of dust and soot. Underlook had woken up in the middle of the night to confront its master.

Laurent came into the light, his ring-decorated hair now heavy with perspiration and ash. He sounded like he'd found a version of fear he didn't find so arousing. "I'm begging you, Your Exaltation. We've gone through the storehouses already. There's no sign of the wyrm in there. You're going to destroy entire livelihoods if you take that building."

The Baroness-shaped creature spun her spear until the tip pointed at the ground between the man's feet, and stabbed down to skewer the road. "To the left, Yvette. You'll want to roll two into that cellar."

A pair of gray stallions dragged a small catapult with baskets of bombs hooked onto the rear, attended by a pair of armored women. The women were inspecting where to breach the next building. It was a tall one, and would surely blanket half the town in ash if it went up. A building that broad had to be one of Underlook's few private warehouses.

Laurent tried to circle in front of the stallions, as though to slow the devastation, while still facing the Baroness-shaped creature. Few of his townsfolk followed him. He said, "Your Exaltation, that's generations of the town's livelihood that'll go up in smoke. This is food, and documents, and everything most of our families have."

"Yvette." The Baroness-shaped creature gestured through Laurent, to one of her bomb crew. "Two. No fewer than two bombs."

Laurent's voice rose in pitch. "Do you want me to renegotiate our contracts? I'll have an office open immediately. I'll have them bring me the paper and we'll ink the contract in this very street. Tell us what you need."

The armored women stopped their cart, and the broader-shouldered of them who was likely Yvette eyed up both Laurent and the Baroness. She exchanged a look with her partner as though they'd like to roll a bomb into the middle of the arguing parties.

"Getting slow in your old age, Yvette. Do you want to wait in a jail cell too?"

Laurent stirred two fingers in the air in a harried gesture to the moneyed people trailing behind him. "I represent everyone present. Livestock companies. Holding companies. Do you want to raise the tax? Do you want a full half? Nobody here is going to turn you down taking half. All we're asking is you let us inspect these warehouses and see if the wyrm is actually inside."

The Baroness-shaped creature walked around her company of guards until she was close to Laurent, making him shrink away. She said, "I live in an estate that wouldn't wipe its boots on this town. What makes you think I need half of anything you own?"

One of the other moneyed people, an elderly enby whose eyelids were puffed nearly to the size of their cheeks, said, "Please, then send Malik, Your Exaltation. He knows the most about finding these things."

Laurent said, "That's right. My laborers and I pooled our private money to pay Malik extra so we can get the job done safely. Your soldiers can go with him to make sure the wyrm isn't on the storehouse's grounds."

In his flurry of words, he swept a hand at the basement windows of the jailhouse. In the nearest cell knelt Malik. He drew little god-mark prayers at the base of the cell wall, while his eyes glared up at the Baroness-shaped creature, as though he was aiming his gods at her.

"This traitor?" the Baroness-shaped creature said. "I'm lenient to not have him executed before morning."

"If anyone can catch the monster, it's going to be that man. Let him investigate the warehouses. Then we can discuss his sentence."

"He didn't protect my daughter or myself from wyrm attacks. He belongs down there. If he's set loose, it will be when I need live bait." She swept her spear at Laurent. "Do you want to serve as bait first?"

Listening to her wield civilization like this made Shesheshen shudder. She wasn't a mere impostor, playing at being the law. She was not a mere Baroness-shaped creature. The Baroness was a role she'd shaped for herself for decades. She was not Baroness-shaped. She *was* the Baroness. The barony itself was the monster.

That monster didn't scare off Homily. She got close enough to the guards to grab onto two of their shields. The guards braced against her, not throwing her away, looking at each other with conflict in their eyes since they weren't allowed to let people in, and were even less allowed to toss the Baroness's children around. With them braced against her, Homily slung a foot up, careless how her skirt flipped over her knee, and tried to climb over the guards. All the while, she made furious eye contact with the Baroness.

"Mother, you can't be out here. We have to get you out of the town immediately."

The spear whirled before the woman. The Baroness Wulfyre turned, raising her weapon from the ground, tilting her chin back at her daughter. "What insults are these? You don't speak to me in public like that."

"We're lucky we found you," Homily continued, barging her way between nervous guards. With both hands she reached up and clasped her mother's pauldrons. "You're exposed. Who knows what could happen to you in the open?"

Shesheshen did her part, trotting up behind Homily like it was a chore. At least it wasn't hard sounding annoyed with everyone in her vicinity. In her Epigram voice she said, "She is right, Mother. This dung-heap town is not worth it. Let us go hide somewhere worthwhile."

"I am hunting what you were hiding from!"

"We're not hiding, Mother," Homily said in too calm of a voice. That calmness was bait. "We're here. We came as soon as we got word. We're worried about you. You look tired. When is the last time you slept?"

In her Epigram voice, Shesheshen agreed, "Go get some sleep. Leave the hunting to us."

"I am not tired."

Homily pressed, "It's been so much. You've carried so much. Do you need Epigram to take you to safety?"

Shesheshen spoke louder, so that Laurent and his whole crowd would hear. "I have got a quiet place we can go. With none of these onlookers."

"Come," Homily said, tugging at the Baroness's chestplate. "Let's get clear of the carnage and talk."

Standing up taller, the Baroness said, "I have survived a dozen actual military campaigns. I don't need to talk. Someone needs to break our family's curse."

"Of course," Homily said, nodding so attentively that she almost fooled Shesheshen. "The thing responsible for all our family's suffering is prowling through this town looking for victims. It might want me next. So let's get distance."

Their petty undermining was working. Not on the Baroness, but that wasn't exclusively who it was for. More of the guards eyed their liege, like they couldn't wait to be off duty. All those moneyed people whose faith held up her barony of the isthmus wiped their bottom lips and murmured among each other. The crowd was loosening like soil under a hoe.

With a bob of Epigram's short haircut, Shesheshen looked to Laurent and his fellow socialites. "Has Mother been behaving strangely? I'm sure she doesn't mean it."

Laurent tilted his head, and an obvious thought flickered in his face. There was some cunning in him. "I wouldn't presume to know the depths of Her Exaltation. Naturally, she has endured some stress."

Homily looked imploringly up at her mother. "You'll calm down now, won't you? Now that the family is together?"

"I am calm!" Baroness shoved at Homily's chest. "Stop your sentimentality."

Homily staggered into a guard, who afforded her an arm to steady herself. Homily put a hand to the scarf around her throat. "Mother. Why are you behaving so oddly? Is it that not all these guards have been tested with rosemary?"

Shesheshen looked from the supportive guard to Laurent. "You better not be letting untested guards near my mother."

"Of course," Laurent said, gesturing to a nearby stack of kegs. "We've tested everyone every half hour. I've got a cellar full of the stuff one street over. Even my piss reeks of it."

Shesheshen said, "Then you can calm down, Mother. The guards are legitimate. We can make them all drink rosemary wine right now if that is what it takes."

Extricating herself from the guard's help, Homily straightened the shoulders of her dress. "Is that the problem, Mother? Do you need them tested again? Because if you don't trust the guards, that's another reason to get clear of Underlook."

All that armor hid the Baroness's form. From her squirming, Shesheshen bet the old monster was losing her shape under the plates, in a rage that her quietest daughter was pricking at her so much. The Baroness shouted, "While you've been frolicking with local women, this thing has been creeping away. You're letting it escape!"

"There's a perimeter around the entirety of Underlook." Homily gestured with a slow sweep of an arm past the smoke of a ruined house to the town walls and the unseen soldiers beyond them. "And everyone in that perimeter has been tested. Nothing is getting anywhere. Who do you think the wyrm is disguised as?"

With that question, Homily nodded over at Shesheshen. This was her cue.

Shesheshen put a gloved hand over her mouth, then asked Laurent and the guards, "When is the last time Mother had some wine?"

There was a lot more than a flicker in Laurent's face this time. His tone became too proper, badly hiding that he was playing along. "She couldn't be drunk. I haven't seen Her Exaltation drink a drop since she returned to town."

Shesheshen asked, "Not one sip of rosemary wine?"

Laurent turned to his fellow townsfolk, asking, "Have any of you drunk the wine with Her Exaltation? Florian? Mansour? Nassos? Has anyone?"

In a pointed tone, Shesheshen asked, "Has no one?"

With that, the Baroness wheeled around as though to impale Laurent. Before anyone could do any quality stabbing, Shesheshen said, "I cannot remember the last time she was thirsty. Mother, you have been tested, yes?"

Homily batted the air in Shesheshen's direction. "No, Mother can't be that thing. Mother, ignore her. I'm sure you drink in front of everyone every day." And as the guards began their skeptical looks, Homily went on, "Not that you would reject drinking a flagon of rosemary now."

Now Laurent wasn't in danger of being impaled. The Baroness held her spear so deathly still, now pointed toward Homily, as she said, "I don't have to prove anything to you. To any of you. I keep this family alive. All you ever do is—"

"I know. You do so much," Homily said, as she took a wooden flagon from Laurent. She filled it to the brim from the wine tap, until it sloshed over her and dripped down her knuckles. She licked the rosemary wine from her skin, slow enough so the crowd could see. "So come share this with me. We'll do it together. And when everyone is pacified, then Epigram, and you, and I can figure out what to do with this wyrm together. After all. We're all the family we have left."

For a moment, the Baroness's face was something else. It looked like so many eels trying to escape through her jaws, and worse, from behind her eyes. It could've given her away on the spot, if enough people saw it. Shesheshen poised herself to leap in and shield Homily from being torn into.

Except it didn't last. The Baroness's face tightened straight, like it was held on by laces and underwire, and pulled into a civilized expression. Eyes narrowed down at Homily, and she spun her spear until it nestled in her armpit, ready to be swung out again in any direction.

"You want to test me? I spend days combing through this strip of land for the thing that will save us from the curse. I lose children on this ground. And you want to talk to me about tests?"

"Share it with me, Mother. I'll go first."

Homily brought the rim to her lips, too late. The spear swung out like the tail of a beast, cracking the wooden flagon into pieces and sending it scattering down the jailhouse walls. Stray wine spattered on Malik's cheeks, and he paused his prayer to glare up as the Baroness advanced on her daughter.

This was escalating too quickly. Shesheshen hastened along behind the Baroness, unsure if she could take her down without exposing herself to all these armed guards. All these guards who didn't want to make a wrong move in front of people who controlled their employment and fates.

Using Epigram's voice, Shesheshen said, "Mother. Come on."

The Baroness didn't come anywhere, other than straight after Homily.

"You think you can tell me what to do? That I know less than the family that needs me for everything? Who would want to be you?"

Against those thudding footfalls, Homily retreated against the jail, one of her heels striking the barred window of the underground cell. Old fear crept into Homily's tensing face. She looked up, and up, and up at her mother, without any pageantry. A lifetime of dread shadowed her features. This wasn't the act they'd intended.

When the Baroness raised her spear, nobody came to intervene. Plenty of bystanders looked conflicted, like they disapproved. Nobody was willing to do something about their disapproval.

"I gave you my life." The Baroness's voice crackled. "If this wyrm slays me tonight, it will be because of you. If I succumb to the curse, I hope then you will see what you should've been."

Moonlight painted the spear tip the white of fresh lilies, lustrous and horrid. It directed down at Homily's throat, in the promise of the next family tragedy.

Shesheshen sprinted forward, nearly losing the firmness of her legs in the strides, her knee joints aching with every bound. She reached with both hands to grab the rear side of the spear, so the Baroness wouldn't be able to plunge it forward.

Not fast enough. She wasn't close to fast enough, no matter how she stretched her limbs.

A sound like wind rattled the walls above the jail cells, and the shutters of an upstairs office bowed outward. The wood splintered into the road, and out flew a mound of gray flesh, snarling and unfurling like a living net. It had no humanoid traits, as wild and nebulous as a bucket of water loosed into a maelstrom, splashing onto the Baroness's face. That gray flesh molded itself into limbs, punching with meaty thwacks and stabbing with shards of wood.

It was the offspring. Shesheshen's unfortunate creation, the lump of meat that had only wanted to help her, had answered her need greater than her own life. It had lost much mass in tonight's battles, such that it was scarcely the size of an adult man's torso.

The Baroness hollered and slashed the spear at her own face, slicing the offspring open. Black juices seeped from its wounds, and it fell to the ground. Guards brought their shields up at the wrong time, and it slithered away as quick as a breeze beneath them, snaking out and around the warehouse's south side. There wasn't much more than town wall and burning homes in that direction. The offspring would be trapped if it didn't find a hiding spot.

It would be trapped if nobody helped it in turn.

As the Baroness righted herself, Shesheshen grabbed her by a pauldron. "It went that way. Let's go, Mother. You and me together. Let's finish this."

CHAPTER FORTY-THREE

Baroness Wulfyre moved unlike any animal in Shesheshen's world. Her entire body faced the direction the offspring had fled, as though watching with eyes in every joint of her form. And yet, facing away from Homily, she still swayed in her direction, like her attention could swing at any moment to pounce on her daughter. It was a conflicted hunger.

"You're coming with me," Baroness Wulfyre said to Homily. "You can't be out of my sight with that thing out there. I'll keep you safe until this is over."

"Mother, I'm not equipped to go hunting. Give me a moment."

"We don't have time. You and I are going to find that thing, together."

Watching the Baroness creep closer, Shesheshen imagined all that would follow. The Baroness would drag Homily through the town until they were alone. That's when she would get her supposedly fatal wound, away from the observation of witnesses. Homily would return to society shaken, with a story of how the wyrm had slain her mother. Ever after, Homily would be a bitterer creature, more demanding, aimed straight for a marriage with L'État Bon royalty. Nobody save Shesheshen would notice the different eyes that looked out from her face.

That wasn't happening. Not tonight. Not when monsters hunted monsters.

Homily shied toward a group of shield-wielding guards. "Mother, I'm not a hunter."

"You need to become one. The family needs you to rise up tonight."

"I'm . . ."

It was Shesheshen who picked up the trail, using a put-upon Epigram voice. "Mother, she is not worth it. If you want somebody to get dirty work done in this family, you want me. Let us get out there before the wyrm escapes."

When the Baroness looked at her younger daughter's face, Shesheshen made sure that she up-nodded, cocky and willful. Epigram Wulfyre was a much more desirable role for an abuser to steal.

Shesheshen said, "Show it the fangs of the Wulfyres. Maybe afterward you and I can talk about all the suitors I have earned."

A dark excitement passed over the Baroness's face. That bait had worked. "You finally want to discuss suitors?"

"Someone has to carry on the family lineage. You cannot do all the work forever."

Then Shesheshen punched the pair of women lugging the bomb cart in their shoulders, and gestured around the south side of the warehouse. From the lack of screaming out there, nobody else had caught the offspring yet. With an arm around the Baroness's shoulder, she led them into a chase.

"Yes," the Baroness said, eyeing Shesheshen's Epigram. "It ends tonight."

For her part, Homily did an admirable job entrenching herself among the guards. She spun two captains and Laurent into a huddle near Malik's cell window to talk. Homily waved still more people over to the jailhouse, peeling them off of the group that would follow the Baroness. "I'll organize the hunting party, Mother. We won't disappoint you. We'll get justice for our family."

Shesheshen hid her smile as they ran. Between the skepticism that had shaken up the guards, and the outright cowardice of the locals, a mere five guards followed behind her and the Baroness. This was excellent. The more alone they were, the better.

She made sure to get ahead of the others, which was thankfully easy given how each of the guards struggled to maneuver their shields and form a protective semicircle around the Baroness. That got harder the further they went, with the erratic directions the Baroness ran in.

Coming around the side of the warehouse, Shesheshen checked for any signs of her offspring. All civilians had been evacuated. A row of stout houses stood untended, with oaken storm doors leading to their cellars. The cyclones that came off the sea sometimes meant humans had to squat down in those for days. Storm defenses hadn't defended them against bombs, though. Several roofs smoked from bygone explosions.

The second-nearest cellar door hung open, with two open jugs of rosemary wine sitting at the head of the stairs. That home must have been converted to a weaponry station for monster hunting. The home above was split ajar, coated in the cinders and char. Whose brilliant plan had it been to bomb their own base in their hunt?

Some motion stirred near the open cellar door. The offspring darted around the rosemary jugs, two gray tails swishing as it fled down the stairs. It was taking the first opening it could find into hiding. Hopefully no guards were still down there. If anyone spied it, the Baroness would have them bomb this entire section of Underlook into one wide scorch mark. And down in a cellar like that, there was nowhere for the offspring to run.

So Shesheshen led the charge in the wrong direction. She pointed to the northmost of the homes, at the narrow alley between the home and the town's outer wall. It gave the hunters a fine tour of bombed and burning homes.

"There! I saw the wyrm go around there!" she said, stabbing at the air for emphasis. "Mother? Did you see it?"

Baroness Wulfyre didn't need to see it. She rushed by, smacking the shield of one of her guards to hurry him up. "Don't let it get away! Get its heart!"

When the Baroness and all of the guards got ahead, Shesheshen pivoted and started in the opposite direction. She kept facing her so-called mother as they chased after the rumor of the wyrm. "I'll go around the other side of the homes. We'll catch it between us."

"Go faster!" Baroness Wulfyre squawked at her guards, beating on their shields as she went out of sight.

Without anyone else watching, Shesheshen ceased her pursuit. She went for the cellar door of that guard station. What a place for monsters to hide.

To her relief, no soldiers awaited in the cellar. Jugs of rosemary wine sat against the right and left walls of the cellar, blocking off sheep shears, old chairs, and an upside-down portrait of a dour-looking family. Traces of the people who had lived here before the army took it as a base.

The northeast corner of the ceiling sagged downward, dust spilling in a stream along split floorboards. Bombing had nearly caved in the house above, and it groaned like it might sink into its own cellar at any time, like one more injured monster seeking to hibernate away its woes. The air was so dry that it sucked the moisture from her skin, and the char in the air was thick enough that Shesheshen tasted it. How miserable it would've smelled had she a functioning nose.

She opened her auditory passages, listening for her offspring. Little was louder than the spilling of dust and the distant noises of frightened people. At least Baroness Wulfyre and her ilk weren't near enough to be audible.

The crack in the ceiling had no sign of something climbing through it. No telltale motion, and no scuffs in all the splinters at the breaks in the boards. There could have been scraps from where it tore itself wriggling around.

So then the thing she'd created had to be somewhere in this cellar with her. Somewhere, hiding from the thing that was, in a way, its own mother. The thought was like having a mind made of struck tuning forks. It rang in her psyche until she took a knee. She had to prove herself to it.

She combed through Epigram's short blonde hair, as though cupping a hat and lifting it from her head. Instead of clothing, she removed an identity. Her cheeks grayed out, and she exhaled gutturally, an impolite noise that civilized people disdained. The odor of her spent breath was likely beastly. For all her time in town, she'd been holding air in half of her lungs, like it needed to hide too.

The wall to her left and behind her clacked, like the stones supporting it were judging her. Canting her head to that side, she saw the clay holding the stones together shift. It went as gray as she was. Her clever offspring had disguised itself as mortar.

More of it peeled away from the stones, slithering to the dirt floor by her side. It really had lost much of its mass in the hunt, although it expanded in many tendrils, like an ashy jellyfish.

Its tendrils squirmed toward her. Perhaps the offspring was smelling her. It had no mouth. It might be less verbal than herself.

She extended both of her humanoid hands halfway to those many pale tendrils. The offspring flopped toward her, artlessly rolling, like it was trying to walk using a ball for a body.

When the first flaps of its flesh smacked her palms, Shesheshen cupped them. She stroked her thumbs across the flank of its body. The offspring was warm and clammy, like a freshly plucked liver. She had the abrupt urge to hunt something and share a liver with this little thing.

It nestled into her, less against the touch of her hands than against the width of her legs. Several tendrils opened orifices to suck at her riding trousers, like it wanted to dissolve the human custom of clothing and bond with her. Its flank squeezed narrower, until it had a shape like one of her bent legs. Like her offspring was trying to fit in with the rest of her body.

Like it wanted to come home to her. It would've been easy to subdue and ingest this thing. So fragile, and so submissive. It was more of a meal than a child. In no time it would be part of her again, restored to the will that it missed.

But it wasn't a part of her anymore. It didn't belong to her.

She stroked across the front of its flank, where a head would have been, if the offspring had wanted a head. Using that grip, she pushed it away, far enough to look down at it properly in the gloom of that bombed-out cellar.

One of the offspring's densest tendrils wrapped around her calf. It was clinging, for reasons she didn't understand, yet those reasons filled up her entire being. They lit her up, such that her blood had never felt so hot. The egg sac in her chest was pumping blood furiously, insisting she abandon the offspring and plant her future in Homily.

From up the cellar stairs, at the edge of the street, a voice called, "Epigram? Is that you down there? Damned fool guards lost the wyrm. Get out here before it gets away entirely."

Shesheshen squeezed both hands on those tendrils at her calf, hard enough that it would likely hurt. They went slack, and her offspring scooted backward on the floor. Its flank tensed up like it was confused. She fully extricated herself from it, and quickly shooed it toward its patch of wall, where it had previously wedged itself.

"Mother," Shesheshen called in Epigram's voice. "How many guards are with you?"

Almost reluctantly, the offspring went. It squeezed and burrowed its body between the stones, releasing soft whinnying sounds. Shesheshen hoped those sounds didn't give them away.

"None," came the Baroness's voice. "They insist there are no traces of it. Cowards. We'll have them all jailed. Come, before your sister convinces more of them to run away."

"Good news, Mother," Shesheshen said, making sure her face shifted to the right color. "The monster's down here."

"What? You found it?"

Shesheshen grabbed a chair and gouged one leg of it as deeply into the far wall as she could. After two seconds of working it between the rocks, there was a decent hole, coated in the mystery of shadow. For a finishing touch she bled between the stones, so that the fluids oozed out of the hole.

"I have it cornered, Mother. Come quickly. I think I pierced its heart. There is blood everywhere."

Baroness Wulfyre scuffled down the stairs so fast she tripped, landing with a staggering step that kicked over a bottle of rosemary wine. The bottle cracked, and as it rolled across the floor, it drooled its evil contents. Shesheshen deliberately avoided the path of the bottle.

Baroness Wulfyre hastily kicked the bottle aside and wiped her boots on the floor, further proving how strong that rosemary wine was. Shesheshen could've tackled her there. But she needed the element of surprise against her elder.

"Where?" barked the Baroness. "Where is it?"

Shesheshen pointed at the far wall, toward the divot she'd dug. She moved toward it, selling how interesting the hole was.

It was convincing enough, since the Baroness shoved her aside and groped for the wall. Her neck lengthened, as though begging Shesheshen to behead her. She said, "This is where it's been hiding?"

"I pursued the wyrm here myself."

As she chattered, she picked up two jugs of the wine. The wine sloshed up to the necks of the containers, suggesting they were quite full. Holding them gave Shesheshen's fingers a faint burning sensation. It was a promising burn, if the mere residue did that.

Baroness Wulfyre jammed two gauntleted fingers into the hole, working them for a purchase on the upper stone. "You saw it climb in here? Is anything on the other side?"

"It might be tunneling. We could bomb it."

"Bomb it? Yes," the Baroness said through a sonorous laugh, as she yanked the first stone free of the wall. She dropped it, letting it crush the chair at her side. "Do you remember that time in Moselle? In the tower, with all those miniature cakes?"

Shesheshen hid the two jugs behind her body, poising so that when she got close enough she could spin and hit her in the face with both. Getting the poison inside her would do. "They were . . . good cakes."

"Do you remember what I said to you? That night?"

Plotting and talking felt impossible. It could've been the heat of the town, or all she'd been through. A concoction of too many stimuli. She wasn't close enough to jam these jugs down the woman's throat yet. If they shattered, they would just burn them both on their exteriors, and Shesheshen wasn't as armored. Why did she have to plot murder and talk at the same time?

She was too wrapped up in what she was supposed to say. She came out of the daze of possible words in time to notice both of the Baroness's hands clutching other stones from the wall. Before she knew why, they whirled around, one smashing her in the ribs, and the other her skull.

Her eyes dislodged inside her head, spinning for a glimpse of light, and vision left her. She swung the wine jugs at Baroness Wulfyre, but midway through, both of her arms were impaled by steel and driven backward so hard her ligaments snapped. Bracing her feet did nothing, as she was tackled and tossed against some hard surface, then another. The third hard surface she hit was probably the floor.

She dug the fingers of a hand into the dirt, willing her bones to jut out and make a claw for her to fight with. Immediately her hand was stamped flat under a heavy boot, all her tissues bursting. One of her jugs broke, too, splashing that horrid burning sensation across her arm. Crying and growling didn't help, but she couldn't stop herself.

Above her, the Baroness's voice taunted. "Epigram has known my little secret for years. She thought it was priceless comedy. Wouldn't shut up about it if she thought we were clear of eavesdroppers. But you wouldn't know that. You're not family."

Shesheshen tried to answer, "You. Made me."

That boot ground its heel onto the broken bones in her hand, crushing them together. "You selfish little shit. You're a vessel for eggs. For my legacy."

Now Shesheshen's eyes found their sockets, although they ached when she tried to hold them there. Her vision was milky, like a membrane of lace was laid over her pupils.

Baroness Wulfyre unbuckled her gauntlet. It splashed in a puddle of that wine, and exposed her hand. The flesh there warped rapidly, four long claws of carved bone. It was like she'd cut them out of a dragon and held them inside herself for occasions just like these. They curled around her thick thumb. She licked each one, lubricating them for the penetration to come.

"This time, I'm going to find your egg sac. You can be a good girl and give it up, or we're going on an adventure."

Only one word would come to Shesheshen. She had to try it.

"Homily! Homi—"

A heavy boot came down on her jaw. Most of her teeth broke, spilling across her tongue and gagging her attempt to cry for help. Baroness Wulfyre stood over her, leaning that boot onto her mouth to keep her silenced.

"You spent all those years as a predator. You could terrorize anyone. Anything. Those were gifts from me to you, as you grew up. Now you're asked to give one measly thing, and you try to assassinate me?"

The four tips of those claws pricked inside Shesheshen's abdomen, making her flail her legs. They sank deeper, piercing several of her bladders, so that juices mixed with blood. That blood spurted hot out from her belly and across the Baroness's palm.

"Blood. We know where blood leads, don't we?"

Shesheshen ripped one of her limbs from the steel that impaled it, splitting the flesh in half. She snapped it into a makeshift tendril, wrapping it around the base of those claws. It was weak, but she squeezed as best she could. She gripped at what felt like a wrist—and the wrist kept sinking downward.

Claws snipped and fished through her entrails until she convulsed, her egg sac sinking further into her chest. It sucked every drop of Shesheshen's juices to turn into more blood. She couldn't concentrate enough to form a limb that could fight these invading claws. Meager tentacles swarmed up, each trying to sucker themselves onto those claws. Nothing slowed their advance.

"What the blazes?"

The boot shifted off of Shesheshen's head in time for her to hear the wet slapping of flesh on flesh. Claws tore out of the Baroness's body, whipping up in search of something. Shesheshen rolled onto her side, trying to see out of either of her blurry eyes.

The offspring was out, leaping onto the Baroness's shoulders and latching onto her armor with several limbs. It had two broader membranes, like ribbed bat wings, spreading as it tried to wrap around her head. All of its flesh was gray and straining for purchase.

Shesheshen wanted to beg the offspring not to fight. The damage to her body was too great for her to get up and help in time. She clutched at one of the Baroness's ankles and was kicked away, slumping over the spare jar of rosemary wine. For a moment, she tried to use that vessel of poison as an artificial limb to stand on.

The Baroness staggered across the room until she slammed into the wall head first. The offspring was crushed between her armor and the stones, and next she brought her claws up to rip at its limbs. They came apart like wings off a roast chicken.

She asked, "Where are your eggs?"

She tossed the offspring onto the ground, letting it spasm limply. She leaned over and picked up a cracked bottle of rosemary wine. A dribble of the stuff spattered on the offspring's flank, and it squealed like hot iron tossed into a trough.

Snorting, the Baroness raised the bottle, readying to tip it over and dump all the contents on the shriveled creature.

"Stop," Shesheshen said, trying to get herself upright. She clutched onto the jug beneath her, like it was a prosthetic leg. "Stop. You can have mine."

That bottle was transparent enough to show the poisonous wine licking up the neck, near the mouth. It was a twitch away from drenching her offspring.

The Baroness looked at her. "You'll give me what?"

She said, "My heart."

Baroness Wulfyre sloshed the bottle, letting another dribble cut a bubbling path across the offspring's skin. The sound it made would make metal weep.

Shesheshen stilled her voice as best she could, and said, "My eggs. The egg sac. All of it."

"I will have those one way or another."

She wanted to argue, a rare case when she desired to create more words. Now she did not have the leisure of words.

Instead she grunted, trying to rise up and face her creator. The Baroness that was the Baroness. Her limbs were feeble, and she needed her strength. The only solid part of her was the jug underneath her, that she'd wanted as an artificial limb. It threatened to crack under all her weight. Its poison would spill everywhere. It'd be the death of her.

She relied on the jug another way. Resting the bottom of her sternum against the mouth of the jug, she pushed downward as hard as she could. Her skin peeled open, the cuts those claws had left expanding into a dripping gape. While Baroness Wulfyre saw her shuddering and fighting with herself like she wanted to stand, Shesheshen swallowed the jug with her wound.

Her insides bulged, tissues complaining of the mild burn from all the rosemary residue on the jug. The mouth of the jug was the worst. It lodged beneath her rib cage, jamming up against the tender egg sac. The egg sac tried vainly to suck more blood into itself to circulate, coming so close to sucking on the jug.

Through her broken teeth, Shesheshen said, "Leave Homily alone. Be Epigram. She was more like you."

The Baroness scoffed. "You don't know anything about me. What I'm capable of."

"Promise. Homily. Is free."

Did that sound pathetic enough? Shesheshen thought she heard derisive laughter, but it was hard to focus. Her entire being filled up with the ache of rosemary rot beginning to set in. She clenched the jug upward until the egg sac had to sip from it. Oh, how it howled through her nerve endings.

Baroness Wulfyre couldn't help herself. With her mostly human face, she licked her lips. "I can smell them. Give them to me."

Too thirsty to do anything else, the egg sac sucked rosemary poison up from the jar. She braced for it to pump that stuff into her, but the sac's membranes went rigid on contact. It drank deeply of the poison and could not spit it out. Many of its fleshy walls went nearly crystalline from the poison.

Shesheshen was grateful for all the agony she'd suffered in recent days, for it prepared her to not give up now. She peeled her flesh further open, pulling her rib bones apart to expose the egg sac. It spurted hot gore, carving fragrant grooves across the dirt floor, all the flavors of blood obscuring the reek of rosemary. The egg sac tried to attack with all its spines and bone spurs, making little punctures all throughout her chest cavity. It was so thirsty for more fluids to circulate that it had to drain the jug. It shriveled and writhed, and agony made Shesheshen collapse to her knees.

It was too delicious a display for Baroness Wulfyre. She descended on Shesheshen, armored hands and new mouths tearing the egg sac right out of her body. It was a mercy that Shesheshen was too pain-addled to see her swallow it.

All she needed were the sounds. Those elongating teeth snagging the thinnest bits of the sac's membrane, and the wet popping of the Baroness crushing eggs between her molars. All that rosemary made patches of the flesh thicken up in pained response.

The Baroness's breathing hitched. She rolled her head back on her neck, eyes wide like she would vomit. Shesheshen scrabbled up her body with every limb that would listen to her, and wrapped herself around her creator's head. Shesheshen turned any tissue not dead into more musculature, until she was like one of those jungle snakes that pulverized its prey.

She ejected the rosemary poison jug from her body and poured the last of it into the Baroness's eyes. She only craved one object. In wrapping up the Baroness's head, Shesheshen swallowed up the Baroness's prized necklace with those two steel fangs. They pulled into Shesheshen's body, and she molded her face around them. In place of broken teeth, she had these steel fangs. And with the memory of the mother that never existed, she snapped these jaws down, biting the Baroness's mouth closed.

Foam rushed up between the Baroness's teeth, scalding Shesheshen's hide. The rosemary wine was doing its work, having burned through all of Shesheshen's offered blood, and now working on her creator.

Those claws raked at Shesheshen's back, trying to split her in half. But if she split in half, then two of her would hold on, until she died, or this creator did. Curses and moans died together inside Baroness Wulfyre's mouth, as Shesheshen refused to let it open and voice them.

Baroness Wulfyre fell against the wall and slid to one armored knee, grasping at her own armor. The heavy plates stood fast against her groping. All that armor protected her in battle, and hid her shapeshifting form from civilization. Now, it kept her from finding a way to vent all that poison she'd swallowed. A claw tore through one leather strap out of three on a single part of the armor, and then Shesheshen wrapped herself around that limb too. She let it tremble with her.

Her hold lasted for a while, against the worst of the thrashing. Eventually some of the burning poison spurted down the armored sleeve. The Baroness was trying to shed her own hand and turn her arm into a sluice. Shesheshen wrapped herself in tighter coils, a pinching brace to prevent anything from getting out. It was gratifying to hold on like this.

Gratifying, and exhausting. Shesheshen's senses faded, sight and hearing going number than her limbs. She barely felt the Baroness thrashing her toward the edges of the stairs, or finally shaking her off, to the ground. There were too many wounds, and too little meat in her system. She couldn't stop her.

The Baroness Wulfyre staggered away from her, out into the streets of Underlook. Most of the Baroness's head was missing. Fluids drained out of her exposed arm like from a ditch at the peak of a rainstorm. A few bubbles of something that had once been flesh rose from the neckline of her armor. When she turned left, the largest of the bubbles popped.

From further out, strings twanged. Two arrows struck her breastplate and snapped before they could fall. Four more flew in at better angles, piercing her plates. One sank so deep it'd be easier to pull out the other side.

Someone's voice asked, "Is that . . . ?"

"It's not her! It's the wyrm!"

That second voice was familiar. Homily swung into view, feet planting on the street, both hands wrapped around the haft of a spear with a red mane beneath the blade. Her mother's spear. She drove it into the neckline of the armor.

"This thing killed my mother and uses her face as a disguise. Go back to the abyss! For Mother!"

A pair of guards slammed thick shields into the Baroness, smashing her to the ground while yelling that they'd avenge her. A third guard appeared with a hammer that could have pulverized bricks. They swung it and shattered her breastplate flat. More guards flocked to slash and hammer at the thing dressed as their Baroness.

A stream of gore ran from her body, out from her ruined arm. To the untrained eye, it might've looked like the blood of a dying creature. But there was life in it. Tissue. Will.

It was snaking away from her corpse. The last vestige of a thing that wanted to find a shadow to grow in.

From nowhere, a blade lit by flame plunged down and severed the strand. That blade belonged to Malik, the last living monster hunter in town, freed, still in his prison clothes. He burned every inch of the thing he caught.

From around Malik there flocked more people, few in armor, most in the ragged clothes of citizens from the east side. They wielded torches and pitchforks. They screamed of the righteousness of good gods, above and below, and the vengeance of lost relatives. They were a greater beast than any single ruler or wyrm. Civilization tore the monster limb from limb.

Still carrying her mother's spear, Homily was the first to come to the cellar door. She rested a hand against the entrance and looked down at the pile of pained organs that was Shesheshen.

Shesheshen wanted to greet her. Wanted to say something kind for her.

She managed a twitch of two nubs of fingers. Really, Homily should've been grateful that Shesheshen still had any hand left to wave.

With tears and worse streaming down her mouth, Homily rushed down the steps to gather her up. She bundled Shesheshen in a riding hood and cloak before anyone else came to check. The fabric was coarse and snug around her, holding her body together. When the offspring chirped, Homily gathered it up, too, and hid it in the folds of the cloak.

"Don't worry," Homily said. "We'll get you fed and strong. We'll get your offspring out of here."

There they huddled in the growing light of a bonfire, as the citizens of Underlook burned something other than effigies for once. Someone tinkered on the town piano, crafting the first songs about how the town had slain its wyrm.

Resting against the inviting fat of Homily's bicep, Shesheshen closed her bleary eyes. She could scarcely see anything now, beyond the orange of firelight. Better to rest that sense.

There was one question that she needed to work out. Even as a pile of organs and scrap, it prickled at her.

She asked, "Do love stories often end this way?"

Homily stroked her side from over the cloak. "Why do you think it's over?"

PART EIGHT

PROBLEMS OTHER THAN MONSTERS

CHAPTER FORTY-FOUR

Shesheshen did not know how to go on a date.

It was easier to regrow her severed limbs, but perhaps that was because she had experience regrowing lost parts of herself. Sinew threaded through muscle. Bones were simple to bully into place. Sharing parts of herself with someone else for mutual entertainment felt somewhere between untoward and impossible. Nobody could really enjoy spending time with each other like that.

Could she enjoy spending time with anyone like that?

No. Never in the rest of her life span.

Could she enjoy spending time with one particular person like that?

She wanted that more than she wanted all the legs she'd ever lost.

Homily sat on the other side of the circular dining table from her, since apparently it was romantic to be inconveniently distanced from the person you loved. They ate up in the suite on the top floor of the Red Dragon Inn, since it afforded the best privacy in town. The suite was theirs for as long as they liked. But soon they would return to Homily's ancestral estate—and Shesheshen's current lair—so that in the shadow of the Baroness's demise, a Wulfyre's influence would still be felt in the isthmus. Homily would dissolve that influence, slowly, in time.

So today everything had to be just right. Using the guise of Epigram Wulfyre, Shesheshen made sure the local cookery got them a fancy spread of foods that humans enjoyed digesting. There were sausages stuffed with sweet Engmarese scallions and various meats. Fresh egg cakes steamed under a veil of napkins, beside porcelain platters of pastas and blueberry brioche. She procured every kind of wine that did not have rosemary in it.

For the main course, they were supposed to enjoy sheep's brains that had been boiled inside sheep's intestines.

This was fine dining. She did not understand how. These were things

Shesheshen would never have done to her own prey, and she was a monster so horrible the town was still celebrating having slain her.

Homily put a hand over her smile. "I don't know how we'll eat all of it."

Shesheshen was still not great at the talking part of communication, but Homily sounded less like she was complaining and more like she was daring them to devour it all.

Shesheshen tried to speak in kind. "Surely we will overcome," she said, and handed the basket of egg cakes to the love of her life.

For her part, Shesheshen focused on the savory foods. Locals put breadcrumbs in their sausages and meatballs, presumably to keep anyone with a functional sense of taste from stealing them. There was blood in the gravy, though, and ample fat. Those were things she could digest smoothly. She almost filled a wine glass with the gravy.

Then she thought about it. Who would judge her if she did?

"Would you?" she asked, holding out her glass to Homily.

Homily fought through a giggle fit as she poured the gravy for her. It hit the spot.

The offspring's tubular mouth poked out through Shesheshen's robe, patiently waiting for morsels of food that Shesheshen allotted to it. Most of its body was halfway inside Shesheshen herself, embedded in a pocket of flesh she'd carved out of her abdomen. Technically it was a wound she had elected not to fully heal. If its next bite of food did not come quickly enough, it squirmed and gave her a good ache. It was a bit like having an infection as a lunch guest.

She did not mind. From what she knew of civilization, all children were parasites. You were supposed to grow to like that about them.

As she finished picking the breadcrumbs out of half a meatball and depositing it into the offspring's mouth, Homily said, "It's strange, isn't it?"

Self-conscious, Shesheshen picked up her two forks again and tried to capture some of her pasta. Two forks were not enough forks for this. The spaghetti was versatile in its resistance. "Slightly strange. It's like an evasive bread."

"Not that."

"Is it the offspring? Should I not have brought it?"

Part of her tensed up, preparing to suck the offspring entirely inside her body and hide it from sight. Although that was not a good idea. She should not risk re-digesting her young like that.

Homily took a long drag off her wine. She set the glass down with a sharp clink. "It's got nothing to do with that. It's this. This is the first glass of red wine I've had."

"In your life?"

Despite having no wine left in her mouth, Homily swallowed again. "Since we killed Mother."

"Should you have a different beverage? Laurent says one of these wines has bubbles in it."

"That was the first sausage I've eaten since we killed Mother. That is the first napkin I've dirtied since we killed Mother. This is the first meal I've really sat down to since I drove a spear into her body, and released a monster hunter from prison to help me, and turned everyone against her."

Sitting away from her love was impractical. Shesheshen dragged her chair around the obnoxious circle of the table, all the way until her knee touched Homily's thigh. "Is it liberating?"

Homily blotted her napkin against her forehead. "It feels liberating like falling off a cliff feels liberating from the ground."

"Remember. I am the one who fell off a cliff."

There was a little smile there, gone before Homily lowered her napkin. But it had been there.

Homily said, "I'm still learning how to feel after that."

"I worry," Shesheshen said, "that if you feel too much guilt, eventually it will become you. Dwelling will be the thing you think you are meant to do."

"Can I stop myself? I don't see how to not think about her. About the whole family. For the rest of my life."

"You would not have a rest of your life if we hadn't done something. Your mother would have the rest of your life instead. You deserve it more."

Homily took one of those drinks of wine that was an excuse to not say anything. That was a custom that Shesheshen could see through. Shesheshen could be patient.

Eventually Homily said, "Thank you, for being part of the rest of my life. I don't know how to be. Not yet. But I'd like to be, with you."

Shesheshen raised a hand in offer, and Homily consented. Shesheshen petted the back of her hand, the same way she usually did now to soothe the offspring. "Does it make you nervous? Thinking you have to perform yourself for me?"

Homily went still in her chair. "How did you know?"

"Because I am nervous being myself for you. At least you have performed being a person before. You have experience."

"I guess this isn't easy for either of us. It feels terribly nice to do it, though, doesn't it?"

Shesheshen tried a smile. "You think you are self-conscious. I am used to eating alone. I have no idea how civilized people eat with their mouths closed. Is it a performance art?"

"What do you mean?" Homily asked, swirling a fork through some pasta dripping in chunky clam sauce. She shoved it into her mouth and chewed it with loud, wet noises, her lips refusing to seal around it.

Shesheshen reached for some forks to try to illustrate her problem. She got halfway through the closed-mouth function when understanding struck her.

She was being made fun of. And made fun of in a nice way, for once.

So she took a sausage in her bare hand, and with the offspring staring enviously at it, bit it hard enough that the rest of that animal's remains probably felt the pain. She chewed vigorously, shapeshifting her lips to further retract. Juices squirted from her gums and between her teeth, spattering on her robe and against Homily's cheek.

Homily slowed for a moment, strands of pasta dangling from her mouth. Then she grabbed the open wine bottle.

It escalated into a war. By the end, their clothes were thoroughly ruined, and Shesheshen started learning something useful. She started learning what it was like to laugh.

CHAPTER FORTY-FIVE

"I'm sorry!"

Homily flew up in bed as though someone in her dreams had thrown her. The left side of her face struck the headboard, the entire bed frame rocking and threatening to snap under her force. She would've fallen off the mattress and to the floor if Shesheshen hadn't caught her.

Darkness still draped the suite, the solitary reading lantern long since extinguished. Shesheshen had to root through the splaying quilts to wrestle for Homily's body. She wound her arms into long, smooth tendrils, with occasional elbows that Homily could grasp onto if she wanted to hold her in turn. Her limbs could not grow long enough to stop the woman's thrashing, though.

"I'm sorry! It should have been me!"

Her eyes were open, and still Homily screamed at the figments of her dreams. She bucked out of Shesheshen's grasp, both of her hands tearing at her scarf. Underneath it, she was so flushed from emotion that the white scars stood out, ivory on pink. She clawed at her own neck, tearing through the scarf and into herself, as though trying to peel the old wounds open.

Shesheshen gathered Homily's wrists, hugging them to her chest. It was the best way she could think to keep her from hurting herself worse.

Homily said, "It should have been me. It should have been. It's my fault."

There was no use joining the argument that existed only in sleep. Shesheshen was not a figment of anyone's dreams and could not fight dreams on fair terms. What she could do was offer her body to Homily, to rest against her until she calmed to the realization that neither of them was alone.

Gradually Homily sank into the offered softness of Shesheshen's body, starting with her chin resting against her shoulder. Her cheek flattened against her side. Her breathing percolated with hiccups from the fit.

"Shesheshen?"

"Yes."

"I . . . I killed my sister."

Homily worked her hands without trying to free her wrists. She looked curiously at her fingers, likely at what had coated them in dreams that was now gone. She curled the fingers to her palm, around an invisible object.

She said, "I never should have left home. I let her become what she did by leaving her, and then I killed her. I slit my own sister's throat."

Her hand trembled, not with a hiccup or a thrash this time. It was the tension of someone deciding which way to twist an unseen knife.

And the look on her face, as she imagined what to do with that knife? If there had been one single knife in their suite, Shesheshen would have hunted it down and snapped it. She never wanted to see a knife again. Neither a real one nor an imaginary one. Not after seeing the look on Homily's face.

Shesheshen said, "No."

Homily said, "I shouldn't have hurt her."

"She shouldn't have abused you until you ran from home. Your family shouldn't have built a household out of your pain."

The fingers around the imaginary object loosened, and let it drop into the land of sleep. Homily reached down and, finding Shesheshen's waist, slithered her arm around her. That warmly fatty arm held onto her for dear life.

Homily said, "It doesn't take away what I did."

"You did it for me. Am I to blame, for motivating you?"

Homily's eyelashes tickled Shesheshen's shoulder as she blinked into the moon-washed dark. She said, "I didn't mean it like that. I love you. I'm sorry that I woke you."

"I do not really sleep. I hibernate once a year."

"You don't ever dream?"

"Monsters prefer lurking."

There was a wet feeling against Shesheshen's shoulder. It could have been Homily yawning, or a kiss. Either made her blood rush the same way.

Homily said, "I wish I was as comfortable with myself as you are."

"I am uncomfortable around people all the time."

"Around me?"

"It is a risk. A struggle. I am not good at words. I want to be good to you, like you want to be good to me."

Homily held her fingers over the scars on her neck. She heaved out a full-bodied sigh that would have sent advancing storms sputtering back out to sea. "What if I'm always going to be like this?"

"You won't. You're going to get better. We're going to get better."

"What if the panic doesn't go away? What if no number of happy days together buries it?"

This many important words made Shesheshen's mind ache. How was she supposed to lift that much explanation? It would be easier to carry a house overhead.

She tried. "When I was young, I spent weeks at a time never leaving the ruins of the keep. I never spoke to another living soul, and feasted on vermin. When winters came, I found I had to slumber underwater, no matter how much I wanted to do something else."

Homily asked, "You got used to those things?"

"I became those things. I still am those things. But I became more than those things, too. So will you."

CHAPTER FORTY-SIX

One didn't build a body out of a single kidney. You took several kidneys, and yards of intestines, and at least one pancreas. Getting a body to walk took so many organs and rigging and support.

Slaying grief would be no simpler. It could not be solved by a single action. It required a life of choices and events. They had to form an organism.

How was that done?

It was done by hunting as a pack of three together, and sometimes having Homily be the one who chased the buck into the trap, and sometimes having her be the one who cut off the buck's escape. It was done by creating new memories with knives, memories of labor and of feeding her loved ones. Homily had to refuse to hide the bitter feelings that sometimes came up when she held a knife.

It was done by going out on picnics along the north seaboard of the isthmus. It was done by lying on top of each other to pool warmth on the gravel beach, with their feet kicked up and bare. Reeds swayed in the air and tickled the pads of their feet. Sometimes Homily tickled Shesheshen with those reeds. Her instinct was to deaden the nerves so it wouldn't bother her; later, she learned to keep the ticklish spots, and instead engage in tickle war games. The demonic noises Homily called laughter were sounds she couldn't live without.

It was done by asking Homily how to treat a bear's wounds, and helping her gather the ingredients for the poultice. Blueberry was hesitant to let Homily near her at first, and grunted at the sting of medicine over where the skewers had bitten her hide. By the end, Blueberry let the human ride on her back, and Homily got the hell stung out of her when the two stole a beehive for the honey. She showed off her sting-marked arms with pride for days.

It was done by sitting under the great spruce in the bomb hole in her lair's ceiling, honing how much shade they needed while still giving Homily enough light to read. Shesheshen offered her lap, and Homily plopped her head down in it, to read to her. Homily read to her of the legends of the L'État Bon countrysides and their many strongmen, and the stories of the cunning and sisterhood of Al-Jawi courtesans, and the blood-soaked sagas of Engmar's founders as they slew that region's ancient monsters. Shesheshen had a habit of ruining the Engmarese tall tales, as any plot the Engmars set to capture a monster struck her as something she would've seen coming. Sometimes Homily offered to write down how Shesheshen said things should've gone, correcting civilization's lies about monsters.

Homily said, "At worst, you could sell your stories somewhere that hates Engmar."

Shesheshen tickled her mercilessly for that one. She grew whole arms dedicated to revenge.

One morning Homily was reading about legends of wyrms and asked if Shesheshen ever hibernated on land.

"I can only hibernate in water. I think."

"Are you amphibious?"

"Do you mean if I can swim?"

"No. But can you swim?"

"Yes. Can't you?"

"No."

So they went swimming, utterly naked in the bracing waters of the sea. Clothing made cold water worse. Shesheshen kept at least two tentacles wrapped around Homily's biceps as she learned how to paddle, and how to kick. Any fish in the region surely thought they were a pair of inept predators.

On the shore stood the offspring, occasionally pawing at the water as though testing if it had become a solid yet. It kept amusing Homily. She laughed anytime she got her stride while swimming, and then always got water in her mouth. Her pale skin got terribly burnt, and painted with even more freckles.

That night, Homily had another of her screaming fits. She tore out of sleep with her hands up to ward off blows from no one. They talked through what of the guilt and grief they could. They built their defenses, so next they would be ready to fight its sieges.

Shesheshen attended to her every night, lurking to help her fight whatever haunted her.

There was no nightmare the next night.

Five nights later, Homily had her next screaming fit. Shesheshen held the woman, and soothed her, and they talked long of aching things. Somewhere inside Shesheshen's flank, the offspring tore at her. The pain was distracting. At some point she did something wrong with her face.

Homily looked concerned and sat up. "I'm sorry. I'm not trying to be ungrateful. How can I make it up to you?"

"You do not need to do anything for me."

"Did you eat today? Laurent will bring fresh food in the morning."

Laurent was their prime contact. Now that Homily Wulfyre was residing in her ancestral estate again, everyone was forbidden from approaching it without permission. The only way to gain an audience was through Laurent, and he only visited once per week. He knew enough to play his role, and whatever he suspected, he knew enough not to ask.

Right now, seeing another human felt overwhelming. Everything was harder than it should have been. How was she supposed to dull Homily's constant urge to give? What outlet would suffice?

Out of the night, the offspring launched itself around Shesheshen's right side. Two tendrils slapped the back of Homily's outstretched hand, although it had too little body mass to do real harm. Then its side opened up, and a dull butter knife jutted out like it had popped metallic acne.

Shesheshen grasped for the creature, ready to crush it into a ball and sit on it.

Homily grasped, too, taking the butter knife from its grip with a grace like it was helping her set the table. She dropped the knife behind herself, then returned her hands to the offspring. Tendrils sprang from around its mouth, whipping at her. She caught them and sifted her fingers through like she was braiding a friend's hair.

She asked it, "What's the matter?"

Shesheshen said, “It is upset because I will not eat it. It wants to become part of the whole again.”

Shesheshen tried to take the creature from her. It gave teapot hisses from openings on its flank and climbed along Homily’s arm, trying to bite her with its toothless mouth. That earned a meek smile from the woman.

Homily said, “Continuing to live is daunting, in its own way.”

“No,” Shesheshen said. “Do not let it hurt you. Do not try to prove you are generous by letting yourself be hurt.”

Homily stiffened some at that, while keeping the creature in her grasp. She held it up in both arms, lifting it off the ground. Its tendrils were unruly and asymmetrical, more like stringy clumps of fiber someone had pulled out of a gourd. Those wet tendrils flailed about, trying to find the floor.

Homily said, “Thank you, Shesheshen. Thank you for reminding me.”

Next, she squeezed the offspring around its middle with those powerful hands of hers. Many of its tendrils released her and retreated inside its body.

Looking down into the offspring’s mouth, Homily said, “You can cry. You can ask to be held. But you cannot hurt me just because you’re hurting. All right?”

There was no sign that the creature understood a word of the lesson. After a moment, it gave a perturbed whistle out of its flank, and wriggled to be returned to the floor.

As Homily put it down, she asked, “What is its name, anyway?”

Shesheshen rolled onto the floor and stuck her legs up. Perhaps sitting that way would make this make sense. “I do not know. It likes talking less than I do.”

“Really? Because I had a few ideas.”

They were wretched ideas. And Homily’s worst idea for a name was her favorite.

“You are not calling it that.”

Homily bumped against Shesheshen’s side. “Why not? It’s cute.”

“You will regret it.”

"I'm not going to regret a name."

The next day, they explored the corridors of her lair, or the ancestral Wulfyre homestead, together. It could be both ancestral home and present lair. Whatever name they called it by, its lower chambers dripped from the laden water table. Recent rains had nearly flooded the isthmus.

Perhaps it was those rains that had driven the offspring wild. It had disappeared, skipping two consecutive meals. All it liked to do was try to burrow into Shesheshen's flesh, bother Homily, and eat. It disconcerted them that it would miss an opportunity for all three activities.

Homily carried with her an uncooked leg of mutton, which she held aloft like a lit torch. The idea was its savory odor would attract the offspring the way the sight of light would another creature. Shesheshen was unsure how much of a sense of smell the offspring had, but agreed the bait seemed appetizing—so appetizing that she devoured the rest of the lamb herself.

"I thought I heard something this way," Homily said, opening a door to a musty servants' quarters. There were no skeletons in this one. The most life available was a decades-old wheel of goat's cheese, which over time had filled the air with festive spores. Homily pinched her nose shut against the odor and said, "And I don't see why I'd regret a name."

Shesheshen followed her inside, squinting at the wooden ceiling. The boards up there were laid out haphazardly. There could've been a crawl space up there.

Shesheshen said, "The name is too close. It'll remind you of your siblings every time you say it."

"I don't want to forget them. I want to be reminded, and I want us to raise your offspring to be better. We can do this."

"This thing is not a replacement for an abusive sibling."

"I know that," Homily said, putting down the lamb chunk and pulling a stool across the floor, until it was under a break in the ceiling boards. "Would you give me a boost?"

"We can give it another name."

"I think it likes this one." Homily took the leg of lamb and wobbled her way up onto the stool. She stuck her arms out like a weather vane, spinning to find balance. When she steadied herself without needing Shesheshen to catch her, she beamed with pride. "I know what I'm doing."

Then the offspring sprang out of the ceiling, launching itself at Homily's face. It was a snarl of pulpy tendrils and sucking orifices. It twined with all the locks of her hair, latching on to smother. The woman spilled off of the stool and into Shesheshen's arms.

Homily batted at the offspring's unruly limbs, yelling, "Epilogue! Epilogue, let go of my hair!"

Shesheshen grabbed the offspring by the loose flesh at the rear of its flank and pulled. "We are not calling it Epilogue."

CHAPTER FORTY-SEVEN

Once Epilogue hid in the wardrobe, and when Homily was selecting the day's clothes, it launched itself at her chest. Sometimes it hid underneath her bed to nip at her ankles when she got up to use the chamber pot. One time its attack was particularly effective, making her spill the pot's contents across the floor.

According to Homily, the odor was untenable.

More untenable to Shesheshen were the assaults themselves, and that nightmares often followed. She had to do something.

So she disguised herself as a well-coiffed human man with a little pocket money. It took more effort than usual to build this body, and she couldn't tell why. She used it to stroll through Underlook's revitalized east side. Buildings were going up and families were cooking in the open long after dark. They did not fear their monster anymore. They hummed songs, the lyrics of which celebrated Shesheshen's assassination.

They had little need for their poisons any longer. An elderly couple of blacksmiths sold her two-thirds of a bottle of rosemary perfume. It had been an anniversary present, so that the lady of the household could go to market before dawn without fear of being slain. They tried to sell her their mint perfumes as well, as they explained mint was the Wyrm of Underlook's true weakness.

After supper, Shesheshen put the bottle between herself and Homily. The residue around the stopper and mouth of the bottle stung her flesh.

"This is a way to make yourself safe."

Homily sniffed the perfume once before forcing the stopper in as deeply as it could go. "No."

"We can't have Epilogue harming you again and again."

"It's not that bad."

"You tolerating harm is that bad."

Homily took the bottle as though she was going to push it at Shesheshen, then instead placed it to the side, where it was near neither of them. "I will not poison this child."

"If you do not put down boundaries, your family will haunt any house we live in."

"If I push away Epilogue, then I push away a part of you. I'm not afraid of something wild. We need to learn to live together."

It had been months and Shesheshen had made strides in talking. At some point it had gone from *talking for Homily* to simply *talking to Homily*. It could become her nature eventually to discuss things.

Yet tonight, having a disagreement wore on her quickly. Her blood churned thickly in her, feeling as sluggish as her thoughts. It was almost as hard to put sentences together as it had been to build the body she'd used to go shopping.

Homily leaned across the table, hand out in a silent request to touch her. "Are you all right? Do you need to eat more?"

"I worry about you giving us too much."

"I'm fine."

"I worry about you taking too much harm. About old habits."

"So we'll find a way to make new habits with Epilogue. People have disciplined children for ages without having to wear poison."

Shesheshen scratched the table with her claws, frustrated at how hard it was to get her mind to lean into the words. "It harms you because it wants to be inside me. It is resentful. It wants to dissolve."

"And you won't let it die. I know. I love that about you. Now come here, and let me check you. Are you that color on purpose?"

Shesheshen looked at her gray fingers. She had not noticed her color fading until then.

Fortunately she was able to redirect Homily's attention to plotting. They bought the sternest wool in the isthmus and knitted a dense sleeve to encase Epilogue. The creature was swaddled, bulging against any weak seam. On her first stroll carrying it in its sleeve, it tore its way out to attack Homily again.

Twice more Homily sewed sleeves to attempt to contain it. On the last time it went beyond tearing free, going so far as to ingest most of the sleeve. It then vomited the remains of the ruined yarn onto Homily's bed. It excreted with vindictive intelligence, for it tucked the yarn vomit in under the blankets.

As Homily changed the sheets, she said, "I can't tell if it's more like a pet or a child."

Shesheshen chased Epilogue around her lair to chastise it. They climbed up through the bomb hole in her foyer's ceiling, scaling along the spruce's dangling roots. It definitely took her longer to climb up through there than it used to. Some of her limbs ached from the effort.

Halfway up, the sunshine lit on the succulent crimson and tangerine hues of the tree's leaves. They weren't green anymore. As Epilogue shimmied up into the branches, a dry leaf fell, fluttering down to land on Shesheshen's shoulder.

Then she knew why she was having troubles.

Autumn had sneaked up on them.

And she knew the season waiting after that.

Every activity started to become a labor. Homily stood before her, holding open a useless tome.

Shesheshen said, "I do not have use for books. Speaking is hard enough. Reading would be unbearable. I might die."

"Try it. Give yourself time."

"I do not think monsters can learn to read."

"If you can suck out someone's throat and use it to speak the same as they do, then you can learn to read something they wrote down. Reading feels complicated when you haven't done it. You'll learn. It's normal to be intimidated."

"I'm not intimidated by books. I would crush them in a fight."

Homily guffawed until she had to rest against Shesheshen's shoulder. "That's the spirit. Here. What does this letter look like to you?"

Shesheshen did not look at the page where Homily pointed. She kept her head cocked at the ceiling, to listen for subtle cues. Something was scuffling up there. She had never found a crawl space in this region of the lair, but Epilogue had found many she hadn't known about. Being pounced on from above had gotten old.

Homily said, "See how it's round? That's an 'O.' Your lips make the same shape when you say the letter. 'O.' See?"

"No. They do not look like that."

"Try it."

"No."

"Did you feel how your mouth moved when you said no? At the end, it was a circle."

Shesheshen did not notice that. Despite all the places her eyes had been, she had never looked at her own mouth that way. How did Homily know her mouth looked like letters? Perhaps Homily liked to read her books in a mirror.

No further sounds came overhead. If Epilogue was lurking up there, it was not about to attack. Perhaps it was listening. Perhaps it was studying them, and modeling their behavior. It would adapt its hunting patterns sooner or later.

If that was the case, Shesheshen had to give it something else to do other than hunt.

Homily plucked the page and wobbled it for attention. When Shesheshen looked, she tapped one of the scribbled lines of text. So many ink stains swirls and swoops and sharp lines. It was like being asked to read a row of wild grass. It went in all directions. It had no meaning.

Homily said, "This letter here is an 'O.' Can you see other Os on the page?"

A quarter of the page was covered in the insipid circles. Some of them were small, and others were bigger. Sometimes an "O" had a line next to it, or running through part of it. This "O" concept had to be a trick of some kind. Human language didn't use one sound that often. She'd heard humans talk more than she liked. They made an exasperating array of noises.

Homily asked, "Can you point to one? Any circle like that."

There was an onslaught of letters on the page. She resented them in their number. Her fingers coiled, and she wanted to tear the page out.

She knew why she was so on edge. It was the fatigue. It was the coming chill, and the separation that would bring.

"Homily. I do not want to read right now."

"It's an interesting book," Homily said, flipping the pages for another section. "Generations ago, the Wulfyres studied all kinds of life. They kept their family in the isthmus so they could have better access to taxonomies from different continents. I had no idea. Mother never spoke about it. They thought by better understanding other people and species, we could break the curses of the prior ages."

Shesheshen tried to follow Homily's line of enthusiasm. She truly tried. But by the time curses came up, she lost the point and coiled her fingers again. Her claws tore through inner tissue, wanting to slide out.

This was definitely the irritation of winter.

Homily went on. "I wonder if Mother created the idea of us being cursed because she knew about the old superstitions. From the reading, one in ten curses are real. Some are tricky to disprove. The power of false curses is in what they make us think they do. What we're convinced is inevitable."

"Homily. Stop."

Now Homily slid from one smile to one neutral expression. It wasn't a frown. It was the blankness of her going into deep thought. That deep thinking was about Shesheshen.

Homily asked, "Did I go too far? I meant to debunk what the public said about you. We don't have to do reading practice today."

"No," she said, too brisk and cold. Her tone made Homily flinch, and she hated herself for that instant. She forced herself to speak more calmly. "Homily. I have a curse-like thing."

"What do you mean?"

"Every year, I slow. Like a river drying up. It is not sleep. I need to hibernate."

"Oh." Homily nodded like she was thinking. "That was what you were doing when my brother invaded this lair, wasn't it?"

"Yes."

"I assumed you'd have to do it again eventually. There's nothing to be ashamed of with that."

"I am going to have to do it soon. The winter does it to me."

"Then we'll make this place safe for you."

Homily didn't understand. There was no string of words that got her to. It all annoyed Shesheshen, like an arthritis in her thoughts. Painful decay lining between her intentions. Her ears pulsed and she studied the ceiling again.

A faint scratching sound emanated through the wood, something either bone or metal. Epilogue was above. Waiting.

Shesheshen turned to Homily, so the woman could see all the shapes her mouth made. "We need to make this place safe for you. I do not know what will happen. When you are alone with it."

CHAPTER FORTY-EIGHT

It still came sooner than she expected.

They were in the middle of an expedition, searching for the berry bushes of folklore. According to some old dead Wulfyre's journal, idol berries grew in thorny patches along the north shore. In all of Homily's travels, she had only heard of idol berries growing in the Al-Jawi Empire. If they were native to the isthmus, it would be quite interesting to botanists.

Shesheshen did not grasp what a botanist was. It was some kind of intellectual herbivore. She was in the middle of asking Homily to define the word again when she collapsed.

Her head hit the ground first, and her teeth shifted in her gums. She dug both hands into the mossy earth and pushed upward, and still wasn't able to get up.

This was unfair. Two days ago she'd been sitting down and holding hands with Homily when her arm had fallen off. It swung loose and flopped right into the woman's lap. How was she more tired now than the day an arm fell off?

The earth wasn't even that cool to the touch. There were still some green leaves on the trees, amid all the reds and oranges. No snow had fallen anywhere. It was not winter. She should've had more time.

"Shesheshen!"

Homily was on her immediately, with Blueberry trotting shortly behind. The woman and the bear held her between them, hoisting her upright. Shesheshen tried to stand on her own, but her legs wobbled, like all the meat she'd attached to her bones was spoiling. A kneecap popped loose and she screamed into Blueberry's fur.

"Let's get you home," Homily said, stroking her back. "It's time, isn't it? For you to hibernate?"

"It's early. I think it's too early."

"By the calendar, winter is close."

Shesheshen glared up at the clear sky. "Not by the weather. I should have more time."

Homily asked, "Are you sure?"

No, she wasn't sure. All her life, she'd simply slinked off to the hot spring when she felt like it. When nature commanded her to retreat into the hot spring, she did so. She'd never obeyed a calendar or a bedtime. She'd never had to, because she hadn't been accountable to anyone else. Time was the sort of thing you had to care about when you belonged to more than yourself.

As a pathetic homunculus of three species, they waddled home together. Shesheshen spent much of the return trip slumped across Blueberry's back, the old bear walking slower than usual to accommodate her. Blueberry would have to slumber soon, too.

"She will take care of you," Shesheshen explained. "She will hibernate in the lair. If something happens, run to her. Disturb her. Bears are ferocious when stirred from hibernation."

"It's fine. Nothing's going to happen."

"If Epilogue tries to hurt you again."

"It won't."

"Do not let it."

"Shesheshen. It's going to be fine."

Homily somehow managed to carry one side of her and simultaneously rub Shesheshen's back. She did so much with just two arms. What a spectacular creature she was.

They were inside her lair. She was so tired she'd missed crossing the threshold and turning down this hallway. Homily's feet clopped along the very place where Shesheshen had once murdered her brother. It had been in self-defense. For reasons she didn't understand, she felt compelled to explain that whole battle. To apologize for surviving.

"I was hibernating. I woke prematurely. That day."

"This won't be like that time. We have Blueberry, and the town knows not to send people here without our request. You're not going to be disturbed."

"I ate his hand. I think I ate his hand first."

"Are you hungry? Do you gorge before you hibernate? I can fetch you something."

"No."

"You can change your mind."

"No. Stop."

They stopped inside the humid chamber. The air around them was white, with the water vapor that tasted on her tongue like nonconsensual rest. It was the feeling that humans must've complained of, that sleepiness that draped over them when their day was over and their work was unfinished.

They were deep in the lair, in the room that Shesheshen used to sleep in only once a year. The brackish pool waited in front of her.

Homily asked, "What do you need me to stop?"

Shesheshen said, "Be concerned for yourself. You are going to be alone. With the offspring."

"Epilogue will be fine. It will need to hibernate too, eventually. For all I know, it slipped to the bottom of this same pool this morning."

"No."

Epilogue was not in the pool. This morning the creature had been sucking the nails out of doorways. For weeks it had been collecting metal objects, like candlesticks and forks. It was growing, too. Since giving up its pursuit of burrowing back inside Shesheshen's body, it had regained much of its original body mass. At last sight, it had been a quarter the size of Blueberry herself. More than large enough to do disastrous things to Homily with a mouth full of metal teeth.

Bracing her limbs on the stone lip of the pool, Shesheshen gathered her regrets. She tried to mash them into persuasive sentences. She should've done more in the summer. She'd done her best to keep Homily and Epilogue separated, and to divert Epilogue into hunting rodents as an outlet for its violent urges.

She looked into the hot spring and the future it held, the helplessness that would come with it. Looking into the waters, she knew she hadn't done enough.

Homily said, "After you wake, maybe we can go on a trip. Have you ever thought about hibernating in other locales?"

"I do not know."

Her limbs ached until they dissolved under her weight. The mere act of keeping her eyes open and moistened was unbearable. Her vision blurred into swirls of dimness.

It was over. Their time was over.

She had to say something. There had to be parting words that would communicate how much she cared for Homily, how much she meant, and that she would miss her.

"Watch yourself" was too ineffective.

"Care for yourself" was not enough.

"Goodbye" felt too final.

"I love you," said Homily, backing out through the door with a hand over her heart.

They were the right words. They wouldn't have been if Shesheshen had said them, and they were right, all the same and instantly, because Homily had said them. Anything she said was the right thing.

Shesheshen dripped down into the water, until it was caustic on her skin. It soaked her clothing, and it permeated through her orifices. She became a part of the pool. Then she sank lower, limbs tearing into the muck at the bottom. Mud encased sore joints. It drowned out all the noises of the surface world.

It was a relief she hadn't known in several seasons. The memories came on her as heavy as the waters. Being snuggled in the reassuring intestines of her childhood nest. The peril of her siblings, and their hungers, and being chased through darkness. The flavors of biting them, in self-defense, and later for other reasons. All the things she had missed in so many other years.

Now missing things was part of her memories, corrupting a time meant for nostalgia. She relived waiting for Homily in the town hall on the night of a fitful supper with her mother, and the woman seizing up in her tent the night Blueberry was used as bait. There were so many ways to be separate. She was at the bottom of the hot spring, apart from Homily, trapped in memories of the other ways they were separated.

It was many weeks of memories before she remembered that, upon parting from her and Homily saying, "I love you," Shesheshen had not said those right words back to her.

It was a long winter, down in the depths.

CHAPTER FORTY-NINE

A few times in her life, intruders had interrupted her hibernation and forced her to defend herself. Last year she had woken prematurely to deal with the home invasion that changed her life. That had been so late in winter that she had stayed awake. Whereas in those other times, traditionally after dealing with an intruder, she could return to the warm underground waters to complete her rest.

Those other times had been a singular rousing from hibernation. They were onerous lapses, but they were dealt with.

This time her housemates made so much noise, with their snoring and smashing of tables and whatnot, that Shesheshen could not fall into the regenerative spell of hibernation. She existed in a limbo of exhaustion, with no sense of how much time had passed between each rousing. Was it an hour? Was it two weeks? Was it seconds between the sounds of blows in the same fight, and she couldn't tell in her delirium?

Once she roused out of the memory of the warm, reassuring intestines of her childhood nest, with their loving taste on her tongue. The next time she roused out of the memory of being held in Homily's meaty arms, wrapped so tight she could split in two like a worm, feeling like she had never been more whole.

Never did she get to truly delve into the old feelings, into those echoes of her adolescence. Instead, there were fragments of herself, of the struggle against her siblings, of the anxiety over what carnage Epilogue was perpetrating right now, of defending herself using jagged fragments of pelvic bone, and of stealing her creator's steel fangs and biting her creator's own mouth shut with them.

She couldn't separate one feeling from another decades later. Time ceased to be a flowing river of events. It was a pulverized, rotten carcass, every organ melting into the next. Her lifetime was carrion.

There was one solid part of her life. It was an anchor of limestone bricks, the lip of the pool that served as boundary between her hibernation and Homily's danger. Each time when she roused, she gripped the bricks with more tendrils, gradually hauling herself from the warmth of the water and into the chill of the present.

Shaking, she drew herself up into the stinging cold air. She had a scalp and a back. She had a hand. Soon she had several hands, each clawing at different bricks to hoist herself out of the dripping past. Her fingertips snagged the spaces between stones as she searched for any bones she'd left behind. Homily needed her.

Oh, she needed Homily to still be alive. To have survived long enough.

The thick, unyielding links of a chain greeted her palm. It was one of her classic artificial backbones. She sucked the chain inside herself, every last link, as a guide to build a torso. Then she rolled to the left side of the chamber in search of the sheep bones she'd set aside. They had sturdy ribs, and their legs were good starters. She had to reconstruct herself quickly.

She strained to listen for anything.

"Shesheshen? You're up?"

Homily's voice came from the doorway, as intimate and real as all the memories had been from her time in hibernation.

As Shesheshen's eyes developed, she saw the whole woman standing there. All of the parts of her were there. She was alive, and smiling in a way that showed off her crooked back teeth.

Homily had one hand on the doorway, and the other outstretched. Her hands were different colors. The hand on the doorway was her typical beige, with the additional colors of her sleeve, a knit shirt the white of a baby's teeth. She'd likely knitted it herself while she'd waited for Shesheshen. She was fine.

The other arm was a different color. Deep crimson dripped from the sleeve of her outstretched arm, running all the way to her hand. Her knuckles were obscured under the viscous blood that poured off her limb. It pattered like raindrops across the stone floor.

Behind Homily, gray fleshy limbs stretched out from beyond the doorway. A shadow fell across one side of her face as Epilogue emerged, its bulky coils writhing toward her.

Shesheshen tried to scream for her to run. It was no use. Her mouth had not formed yet.

Epilogue formed a mouth out of those coils, the flesh weaving together into a smooth tunnel. It wrapped around Homily's arm, sliding all the way up to her shoulder. Homily was jerked into the hall by its grip.

Shesheshen flung herself at the doorway, and her legs caved. The bones weren't aligned, and not enough tissue connected them. Her femurs tore halfway through her epidermis and she crashed to Homily's feet. Still she reached, trying to get in between them.

"It's all right," Homily said, smiling. She really was smiling. "It's a game we play."

With a torrid slurp, Epilogue drew its mouth away from Homily's arm. Every inch of the arm it revealed was intact. Her sleeve was no longer gory, cleaned down to the fibers. Not a drop of blood remained. There was no wound to explain all her bleeding.

Homily said, "I promise you, I'm not hurt. It's leftover gore from animals we cooked." She rolled up her sleeve to show her healthy, pudgy limb. "It's a game Epilogue and I play around mealtime. And Epilogue? Epilogue, look who's here."

She gestured into the room with both arms, equally clean and inexplicably unharmed. Whistles blew behind her, like organic tea kettles going off. Epilogue lumbered into the doorway, whistling and pushing Homily aside, revealing a body of so many gray rolls of flesh. The flesh undulated as though tasting and smelling Shesheshen from feet away.

Then Epilogue burst into the chamber, body squeezing as thin as Homily's arm. It was like an endless serpent, wrapping around and around and around Shesheshen's body. No matter the shape of the limb she sprouted, Epilogue trapped it in affectionate bondage.

It was not killing her. Nor was it burrowing inside her.

Homily trotted up and planted her wide backside on the edge of the pool, running a hand along Epilogue's flesh. The creature responded by forming two tentacles that wrapped around her fingers and squeezed her.

"You have a lot to catch up on. Epilogue will keep you up all night showing you her writing."

"My offspring . . . writes?"

"She does. And she won't stop drawing. I think she'll be a cartographer."

Shesheshen couldn't even comprehend that her offspring was a *she*. The creature had sprouted a gender while she'd been hibernating? Nobody was injured? They weren't fighting to the death?

Shesheshen was silent a moment, trying to figure out what to say, and how much of her throat was working. As she worked soft passages in her body, Epilogue relaxed as though giving her the space to breathe. The offspring itself—herself—kept her vocalizations to soft whistles.

Epilogue kept holding Homily's hand. That was a sight. That was a start. Shesheshen tried to focus on that detail.

"You are not hurt?"

Homily ran her thumb over the back of the creature's tentacle. "She got quite wrathful after you disappeared to hibernate. Things got hairy." Homily laughed like that hadn't been as life-threatening as it must have. "Some of her crankiness was from oncoming fatigue. She'd never hibernated before. She thought she was dying."

Epilogue rose from Shesheshen's body, bunting part of her bulk into Homily's side. Homily caressed the lump of oozing flesh.

Shesheshen said, "I don't remember her climbing into the pool with me. I would remember that. Wouldn't I remember that?"

"We wanted to give you space. Instead I heated a large kettle of water for her, by increments, to ease her into relaxing. It was like tending to a disgruntled stew. She only hibernated for a few weeks. I've been documenting it all. Did you hibernate for shorter durations when you were young?"

Shesheshen pursed some part of herself. "I do not know."

"It will be interesting to watch how she changes as she grows. But she was still quite wrathful when she woke up from her hibernation. Just being kind to her wasn't enough."

Epilogue wrapped a length of her flesh around Shesheshen's tentacle and Homily's knee, as though binding them together with herself.

This still made no sense. This safety. It wasn't something she was prepared for. Shesheshen had to know.

She asked, "You didn't hurt yourself? When you were alone? You didn't let her hurt you?"

Torchlight flickered in the moisture in Homily's eyes. She slouched down, nearly sinking into the waters with Shesheshen. "Every day was a brutal mystery, which we got through together. We learned about each other. The trick was realizing we both wanted the same thing. The thing that was worth going through all this for. That's what brought us together."

Shesheshen fidgeted with the chain inside her body, unable to get it straight. It was like she'd forgotten how to build herself, because she was too struck with wonder that both Homily and Epilogue were alive. She stared at them both, unable to blink, and Homily lifted her up in those powerful arms, into the waiting world.

Shesheshen asked, "What was it? What did you both want so badly?"

Homily answered, "You."

ACKNOWLEDGMENTS

Upon finishing this book readers may be surprised the first acknowledgment is for my mother. My mother not only gave me life, but kept me alive, taking me to hundreds of doctor visits in pursuit of answers in the face of terrifying health problems. She also always encouraged me to read, from giving me comic books as a kid when I struggled with literacy, to scooping up armloads of Stephen King and Michael Crichton from the local library when I was bedridden and needed stories to survive. Thank you for the examples you set, Mom.

Thank you to my literary agent Hannah Bowman, who believed in my weirdness long before we actually signed with each other. Hannah helped shepherd this project as she was bringing a new baby Bowman into the world. Shesheshen would be wowed by you. Thanks as well to Lauren Bajek, who helped give me advice on numerous nervous days during Hannah's maternity leave. I'll write you two a book with more snakes in it someday.

Thank you to Katie Hoffman, my editor at DAW Books, who grasped the queerness flowing through the heart of this book better than I ever imagined an editor would. From our first conversation, I hoped I'd get to work with you. Thank you for helping Shesheshen escape.

Many brilliant people read this book at various stages and helped shape it. Thank you to Vivian Shaw, Marissa Lingen, J.R. Dawson, Merc Fenn Wolfmoor, Alex Haist, Vanessa McKittrick, and Beverly Fox for all of your thoughts on Shesheshen's journey.

Vanessa and Bev are also part of my vagabond found family, alongside Nicholas Sabin, Nathanael Sylva, Cass Williams, Shelly Fleming, Key Dyson, and Max Cantor—doing those weekly calls and wacko movie tournaments with you folks made the first year of the pandemic (and the first year of working on this book) far less lonely.

Leigh Wallace hasn't actually read this book yet, but Leigh, when you basically cried at my description of Shesheshen growing a "heart" as she fell in love? After that, I was never going to change it. Thank you for being my inspiration bully.

Fascination with stories has kept me alive through many of the worst periods of my life, and I owe a debt to the collective world of storytellers that I will never be able to repay. That is the chiefest reason I write. I found permission to be myself on the page thanks to authors who showed sympathy and depth in non-human characters. Thank you to writers like Martha Wells, Vina Jie-Min Prasad, Jim Starlin, Gail Simone, John Gardner, and Madeline Miller whose work helped me imagine a space for myself. In addition to trailblazing authors, I have only slightly less serious gratitude to the plentiful monsters and villains I grew up rooting for: Medusa, Skeletor, Majin Buu, the vampire Eli, Jason Voorhees, Sadako Yamamura, Godzilla, and Captain Hook (a man who was so ridiculously defined by his disability that it became his name, but who also made that disability a weapon).

Additional thanks must go to the magazine editors who gave my work chances along this long and winding career. In 2009 Karen Smith picked my first short story out of slush for Flash Fiction Online. In 2016 Elsa Sjunneson and Brian White invited me to write my first guest editorial about being a disabled Horror fan for Fireside Magazine. In 2019 David Steffen at Diabolical Plots took a chance on my short story, "Open House on Haunted Hill," and if that story didn't blow up like it did, nobody might be holding this book in their hands today. This is a big and fraught industry. Nobody succeeds alone. It's better together.

AUTHOR'S NOTE

This book began during jury duty. One frigid morning, I sat among hundreds in a gray room for a jury selection pool. Our only stimulation was hearing a condescending prosecutor and an even more condescending lawyer as they probed us one by one over how sympathetic we'd be to a rich guy's emotional distress over minor property damage.

I brought a secret with me that day. On my phone, I had Tamsyn Muir's *Gideon the Ninth*. Waiting in my tiny wooden seat, I read, and its voice kept me warm and alive. Everything I'd been writing lately was restrained in one way or another, whereas this book wasn't. The voice was uninhibited, with every joke and literary trick thrown in to push it further. It was liberating to read. I'm pretty sure I was the only person in the selection pool who laughed that day.

I drove home wondering about great voices in fiction, such as Vladimir Nabokov's *Pale Fire*, Aravind Adiga's *White Tiger*, and Patrick Suskind's *Perfume*. Could I let myself cut loose like that? Write a voice so unapologetic, no matter how weird, funny, and intimate it got?

As a neurodivergent person, I've learned to hide myself. They call it "masking"—the process of presenting your personality like everybody else's. Even in our stories, we're conditioned to use traditional character psychology. To restrain our unusual thoughts or ways of looking at the world. If we write anything like our minds, we're unrealistic.

Dear reader, I tried. I made a monster out of it.

When I first wrote Shesheshen climbing out of her lair and looking for help, I never expected the audience she would find. I was excited by the freedom of writing someone closer to myself, and worried that nobody would want this story. This was the mistake so many teachers had educated me to avoid making.

There is no expression of gratitude great enough for all the readers who greeted my monster when she emerged. People who enjoyed her, or even saw themselves in her. I write this to you roughly nine months after the initial publication of *Someone You Can Build A Nest In*. On this rainy night, I'm still surprised by how many people my monster's voice has touched.

Thank you for all the exuberant messages on social media. Thank you for sharing the quotes that made you laugh, and the ones that made you weep. For the incredible and unhinged fan art, which I keep in a folder in my room. For every happy couple who has told me, "I'm the Homily, and she's the Shesheshen!"

While reflecting on writing this book, I think of the books that affected me so deeply, they felt like permission to speak up. John Gardner's *Grendel*. Martha Wells's *Murderbot*. Even (may he rest in peace) Akira Toriyama's *Dragon Ball*. You never forget the things that gave you permission to be yourself.

Thank you for being yourselves, with me.

—John Wiswell

DISCUSSION QUESTIONS

1. If you were Shesheshen, what or who would you build your body out of? Why?
2. Shesheshen isn't the hero we might expect from a fantasy novel. Who are some of your favorite antiheros in literature, in movies, in TV? How does Shesheshen compare to them?
3. Do you personally identify with Shesheshen or Homily? If so, which one, and how?
4. What do you think this book is trying to say about "monsters" and the concept of "monstrosity"?
5. How do you think Shesheshen and Homily would have related to each other if they'd met in a different way, if Homily hadn't nursed Shesheshen back to health? Do you think they would have developed the same dynamic?
6. If you could've given any advice to Shesheshen during the novel, what would it have been and at which point?
7. Did you have a favorite line or passage from the novel?
8. Did any moments make you laugh?
9. What moment was the most surprising for you?
10. If you were to cast actors to play Shesheshen (with a lot of CGI help, of course) and Homily in a movie, who would you cast?

READ ON FOR AN EXCLUSIVE

BONUS EPILOGUE

BONUS CHAPTER ONE

The three of them ate a supper together around an old table that Homily polished to look new. Homily and Epilogue wore the same kind of knitted wool skirts, dyed black, with plenty of room to hide things underneath. Most of the time Epilogue made herself sit with two legs and humanoid buttocks, although her upper torso kept devolving into a mass of boneless arms that snatched egg cakes and hunks of mutton. A couple times she slowed in her feeding, in order to lean over and rub a head-like appendage on Shesheshen's shoulder.

Shesheshen stroked the child's tendrils in response. This kind of affection was new to her. Especially from this source.

Homily explained, "When she used to burrow inside you, it was because she loved you. She just didn't know other ways of expressing it."

"Wishing oblivion on oneself is not love."

Homily gave her a look she wasn't prepared for. "Wanting to still be a part of your parents can be."

Shesheshen thought of Homily's mother. Of the woman who'd given birth to her, long dead and replaced with a manipulator. She thought of her own hibernation memories of being inside her childhood nest.

"No. Yes. That is fair."

Epilogue was not attacking her, nor was she trying to kill off Homily. The small creature had changed so much while Shesheshen had been in her daze. She had missed the entire détente between the two of them. Missed all their growth. Missed the moments that had turned her offspring into this. No number of words or sentences could answer it for her. Was she still unconscious? Was this something she'd made up?

Homily said, "The two of us wanted to ask you something. We've both been thinking about it for quite some time."

Epilogue intruded again, holding out a thick tentacle that ended in a mouth with nails for teeth. Those teeth gripped a leg of mutton. Epilogue shook it at her, leaving Shesheshen guessing about intent.

"Thank you?" she said, taking the meat. It was delicious. At the first bite Shesheshen took, Epilogue wiggled in her chair with what had to be raw satisfaction.

Shesheshen asked, "Is the question whether I like meat on bones?"

Epilogue's wiggling slowed. Homily reached over and patted the child on a pair of tendrils. "She has been so excited to see you again. Ze only hibernated for three weeks, in the very dead of winter. I suspect ze will wind up hibernating longer as ze ages. It'll be fascinating to see how ze grows. As the time passed, she's drawn map after map of the isthmus. She's curious."

Homily said that like Shesheshen should come to a conclusion. She didn't know what it was, though, and that weighed on her. Both her offspring and her love were waiting for her to say something.

"Is the question if I would look at Epilogue's maps?"

Her question was scarcely out of her before Epilogue erupted out of her chair and scampered wetly off to another room. Cloth and paper rustled like she was packing up the entire house to vacate immediately. Shesheshen didn't mean to make her run. She could come to the maps. She started to rise.

Homily gestured for her to stay. "It's about seeing new places. I love to travel, and see new things. This home is special. Epilogue knows it, too. But we wondered if, after you'd had time to wake from hibernation, you would come with us."

Shesheshen could think of many places to go. The town of Underlook. The ravine where she had met Homily. The woods where they hunted. This was a problem she could fix.

"Where do you want to go?"

"Away from the isthmus. Away from here."

She found her appendages gripping onto the table, like she might levitate up and away from it at any moment. "Away?"

BONUS CHAPTER TWO

She hatched in this lair. Had fought to survive every winter and summer and assassination attempt here. Underlook was a horrible town, but it was a town she knew how to navigate. How did someone just go *away* from the place that defined them? Like asking the ink on Epilogue's maps to go away from the paper. Like asking a word on a page to find another home. You couldn't do that.

Could she do that?

"New meals to share," Homily said as she helped Shesheshen step into scratchy wool trousers. They had a new guise for her, an old man whose face was mostly hidden behind a beard. "Every cook is different. New people to meet. New songs to learn to sing."

She didn't know how to sing. How did she tell Homily that they'd go all the way to some new country without her knowing how to sing when they got there?

With her bearded guise, she went out, but not away. She patrolled the grounds around the lair, to make sure it was safe. To make sure this place where her family lived was safe. Epilogue came tearing out after her, in the guise of a dog, allowing her to keep her snout close to the ground and smell things to pursue. She loved swallowing a skunk before it could spray. Her sense of smell was keen. Shesheshen was better at hearing, although all she heard was that no threats were out there.

Still Shesheshen insisted on patrolling, inside and outside, five times per day. Walking along inclines she'd never noticed, that Epilogue had marked in squiggly topographies. Epilogue patrolled with her every time, eager to run ahead, prancing in circles around her, her dog head bobbing freely.

At a meal, Homily asked, "Did you see anything concerning?"

Shesheshen nearly sucked the teeth out of her own jaw. "Not yet."

She kept at it. Kept this place safe from an unknown threat. There were no monster hunters on the horizon; no monstrous relatives; no angered gods here to deliver a destiny. A few times deer strayed into their dominion. The deer had few ill intentions.

Homily cooked with Shesheshen, and read to her from fables of Sour Island, about great journeys and friendships between animals that, as Shesheshen kept pointing out, could not become friends. Sometimes Shesheshen consented to look at the pages of these absurd stories. She was recognizing more letters now. Most 'O's were explicit, and she was better at catching the two species of the letter 'P.' In time, she would learn enough letters to write the names of places on Epilogue's maps.

At some point, the patrols didn't have to be quite so frequent. They trickled down, especially when Shesheshen had more chores, or wanted to learn more letters, which took more hours of daylight. There were only so many daylight hours.

Finally she caught sight of an unwanted man. A figure trekking alone, off the highway and towards her domain. The rings in his hair glittered under happy sunshine. It wasn't a great menace with an army behind it. It was Laurent, sweaty and nervous.

Shesheshen was so unsure of what to do that Homily was the one who went out and met him. He'd delivered a parcel that required their attention.

It was sheet of tacky paper. Laurent had come all this way to deliver a single letter. Both Shesheshen and Epilogue stared at the letter as Homily read from it.

Shesheshen asked, "What's so important if it could be on one piece of paper?"

Abruptly, Homily barked a laugh so heavy that it shook Shesheshen's wig. She actually blotted a tear from her left eye with the paper.

"Oh, that's good. That's very good."

Shesheshen asked, "What did the paper do to you?"

"It's a request from a neighboring town. They are begging the Wulfyres to come visit them. The need is quite urgent."

Upon saying it was urgent, Homily dissolved into giggling. She held up the page to read the whole thing again. Shesheshen pushed in to try to read it herself. The words fought her eyes, and won.

"Why is it funny? Do we not like the people who have an urgent need? Is their demise our pleasure?"

"No, it's not that. That town has always been sweet when I've visited them. Homily said, putting a meaty around Shesheshen's side and squeezing her in a loose hug. "But according to this letter, they need us to slay a monster."

BONUS CHAPTER THREE

It was only going to be for a week. If they made good time on the road, it would be less than five days before they were home again, under the hole in the ceiling and the familiar tree.

Shesheshen asked, "What are they called?"

"It's on the very east edge of the isthmus. It's called Grassotuck. It's not that long if we stick to the highway. Have you really never been there?"

"The only time I rode anywhere was off a cliff."

"This will be less of an adventure than that."

"You say that like we're not hunting something."

Homily kept showing her the letter of correspondence, not that it helped. It was written in some abominable language called cursive.

Few of the words were intelligible to her. Apparently one of these words meant 'vampire.'

They packed up research materials and various scent lures in a covered wagon. It was much sturdier than the cart Homily had used to ride in. Homily sat on the driver's bench in two layers of skirts, and Shesheshen sat beside her, in the guise of a human man with more beard than face. She'd come to like beards; she could hide so many facial alterations behind one.

In the covered wagon slept their family dog, an enormous creature with skin so rumpled one could've thought it was a costume. Whenever they stopped the wagon, it hopped out and tried to root rodents out of the earth so aggressively that its skin came loose. Shesheshen had to fix this very real dog's fur hide exterior.

They got far enough away that the tree atop their lair went out of sight. They crossed the shallowest patch of the river and ravine, and then that was out of sight too. Shesheshen kept waiting for herself to begin to fade, like she was unnaturally attached to the plot of land. The sun would see her too far away, and she would melt and drain off into the ocean.

Except she was not cursed. She was no vampire.

She was merely a traveler, experiencing anxiety. It was nice to know what that emotion was.

Grassotuck was not the wonder she'd expected. It was like if the town of Underlook was playing a prank on her. It was made up of alls and houses, and stone and brown wood structures, the same materials and stores and bickering humans, merely in different arrangements. Different human faces aged in the same ways. There were more tall buildings, and more of them were painted black. That was not so novel that Shesheshen couldn't see herself thinking she was home, if she was tired enough.

Homily asked, "What were you expecting? We didn't go to the moon."

"Are we going to the moon next?"

The citizens of Grassotuck looked at them funny for how Homily laughed at that.

The mayor received them with a battery of sheriffs, and introduced them to the victim's three aunts. They were all so concerned, and so grateful that a Wulfyre would come to banish their monster. Those aunts kept clasping Homily's hands and asking her to repeat prayers with them.

Their victim was a young boy, not near puberty yet. His name was Marion. He scarcely filled half of his cot, and he struggled to sit up on it. His complexion was ashen, akin to the whiteness of some greases. His aunts explained that the vampire that plagued him lurked on the south side of town.

Marion had enough strength to pet Homily and Shesheshen's dog, who sniffed at him and offered a cuddle or two. It was a good distraction as they examined him. He had no bite marks. He had one sign on his flesh, a religious mark drawn there by his aunts, to ward off the return of the vampire.

Shesheshen touched him with hidden tongues in her palms. His skin tasted of toxins and flawed organs. It was more like a sickness than a curse.

Shesheshen asked, "May I see the vampire's house?"

All went breathless at that request. The mayor needed a company of six sheriffs to go near the building. It was stout, its foundations partially sunken into the soft earth. It was condemned, with the windows boarded up. It didn't sound like anyone was inside.

"You remain here," Shesheshen told civilization. "I shall investigate."

She knocked, and there was no answer. She and Epilogue let themselves in, moving slowly so that if anything called this a lair, it could appear and meet them. Inside it smelled of raccoon droppings, and human urine, tainted with alcohol. They were not pleasant odors to reward all the work Shesheshen had put into building a functional olfactory passage.

Epilogue tracked those smells to the north-facing wall, which had the most privacy. That wall faced no other homes or businesses; it pointed at the town limits. Drunken humans likely relieved themselves behind this house. Drunken humans who were not afraid of vampires.

There were no dead raccoons on the premises, either. Shesheshen heard plenty of live ones, tucked away in the cellar. She didn't bother them for long. A brief encounter proved they were not vampiric raccoons.

After a couple hours of kneeling, and re-shaping her ears to listen for different kinds of sound, Shesheshen returned to the mayor and the sheriffs. They were stunned that she had survived.

She said to the mayor, "Sir, I have explored your house."

The mayor said, "It's not my house. It belongs to no living soul."

"It belongs to no vampires, either. Nothing of notable size resides there."

"You've dealt with vampires before?"

Shesheshen liked how her beard hid her expression. She said, "Please show me Marion's food supply. Does his family have a kitchen?"

The family did not. Homily was already at the community building, where several families pooled their resources. She had suspicions, too.

After a couple of days of subtle observation, it was clear Marion wasn't eating more than a few mouthfuls each meal time. When radishes were forced on him, within the hour he had coughing fits and his complexion worsened.

When Shesheshen held his hand, she could taste the allergic reactions on his skin. It seemed many kinds of food made his body act like there was a war afoot. She would fare no better if someone tried to raise her on a diet of rosemary.

Feeding him would be tricky. Fortunately with the Wulfyre family's resources, the boy's aunts could get a denser kind of bread made from different sources, and increase the fish in his diet.

Miraculously, in a few days Marion's color returned, and he wanted to kick a ball around with the older children. To help reintroduce him to the neighbors, Shesheshen's very real dog went with him, and kids could only pet the dog if they asked the boy first. He was soon popular. Once he was engrossed in the ball game, that dog came running back to Shesheshen's side.

No vampires appeared, not even the night that Shesheshen and Homily and their dog spent in their house. The place would make a fine lair. It would make a finer new community kitchen. The Wulfyre family would fund it.

On their way out of town, Shesheshen and Homily left strict instructions to feed Marion correctly. They would return to make sure.

One of his aunts followed them to the town limits, walking alongside their wagon. She asked, "You're sure it wasn't a vampire?"

Sitting up on the driver's bench, Shesheshen folded her two hands in her lap. She said, "Madame, sometimes there is no monster."